Challenge
Accepted

AMANDA ABRAM

For everyone who supported this book on Wattpad and FictionPress.

I can't thank you all enough.

Prologue

LOGAN

I stared down at the test lying on the desk in front of me and rolled my eyes so hard I think I might have strained something.

This. Is. So. Stupid.

I was taking this test for one reason and one reason only: my girlfriend was making me. Okay, maybe the term "girlfriend" was a little strong. We weren't exclusive or anything. *She* wanted to be, but she knew how I felt about stuff like that. I liked girls. A lot. I just didn't want to be in long-term relationships with them. At eighteen years old, why should I? I'd have plenty of time later in life to settle down and choose a woman to spend eternity with. Like maybe when I was in my late thirties or forties.

I knew exactly what Grace was doing in making me take this test. She was convinced whatever algorithm those nerds in Computer Club were using to run our answers against was going to reveal that she and I were perfect for one another. And she thought if it was proven to me that we were meant to be together, then I would want to take our relationship to the next level. You know, like I'd give her my class ring and take her to senior prom next year, and other dumb stuff boyfriends did in serious relationships.

But Grace didn't know me well at all. If she did, she would've known I didn't care what some computer had to say about who should or shouldn't be together. She would've known I had no interest in becoming her—or any girl's—steady boyfriend. Just the term "steady boyfriend" made me want to dry heave.

What she *did* know about me, however, was how easily I could be bribed into doing something if she threatened to take away certain physical activities. Which was how I ended up in my last study hall of the school year, sitting at a desk with a number 2 pencil in hand, filling out thirty tiny, little circles that represented absolutely nothing.

The whole thing was nothing more than a simple fund-raiser, where all the proceeds would go to next year's Project Graduation. The Emerson High Computer Club came up with the idea, and one of its members developed the algorithm. The concept was simple: pay twenty dollars, answer thirty relationship-themed questions taken directly from one of those annoying chick magazines girls like to read, and then sit back and wait for the computer software to run against all the tests and determine who your soulmate was. Or, at the very least, who you were most likely to hook up with over the summer.

After filling out all my personal information at the top, I glanced at the first question on the piece of paper and instantly groaned.

What is your idea of a perfect first date?

That was easy. Making out in the backseat of my car. Unfortunately—but not surprisingly—that wasn't an option, so I'd have to choose another one. Reading down the list, none of them sounded appealing to me. *Dinner and a Movie? A Romantic Picnic in the Park? Bowling? A Party? Bungee Jumping?*

Oh my God, this quiz was dumb. The questions were dumb. The intent of it was dumb. All the people who were taking it seriously were dumb. And yes, I was even including

Grace in that group of people.

Hey, I never claimed to be with her for her intelligence.

I guess, out of everything to choose from, *A Party* was the best one. It was most definitely the one Grace would choose, because she was a party girl. I, on the other hand, was not a big fan of parties, although I'd been to my fair share of them over the years and enjoyed most of them.

Preparing the tip of my pencil to fill in the circle next to *A Party*, I stopped for a second to think about what I was doing. I was about to choose the same answer Grace would. Which meant, if I did that on all the questions, the algorithm would pair us up. The exact opposite result of what I was going for.

And that's when a brilliant idea hit me. If I went through this entire quiz and intentionally chose the opposite of what I knew Grace would pick, then we *wouldn't* get paired up. And if we didn't get paired up, maybe she would start to question if we were good together. Maybe she'd get paired up with another guy she decided she liked more than me, and she'd dump me, and I'd no longer have to worry about her pressuring me to be a better boyfriend—or a boyfriend at all.

Inspired by my sudden stroke of genius, I sat up in my chair, hunched over my desk, and started furiously filling out circles next to each question. My method was quite simple: read each question and answer them all the way a total loser would. Sure, this would no doubt get me paired up with some plain Jane geek girl, but I would make sure to let her down easy. It would all be worth it to see the look of disbelief on Grace's face.

Five minutes later, I was done. With a smirk, I slouched back in my chair and clasped my hands behind my head. *Logan Reynolds,* I said to myself, mentally patting myself on the back, *you're one clever son of a bitch.*

Chapter 1

EMMA

"You are such a loser."

I glared over the top of my sunglasses at my so-called best friend, Chloe Marks. "Gee, thanks, Chloe. I needed that ego boost."

"What?" she said, all innocent-like. She didn't even look up from her magazine. "I'm telling you like it is. Tomorrow, Sophia and I are getting on a plane to go to Orlando for the summer—*sans parents*—and you've chosen to stay here to, what, organize your book collection?"

She said it like that wasn't an important thing to do. When you have as many books as I do—in the hundreds—you've got to organize them. Currently, they were simply in alphabetical order by author. But all year, I'd been meaning to switch it up. I wanted them to be organized into different genres first, and then alphabetized. I just hadn't decided yet whether I wanted them in order by author name, or title…

"Oh my God." Chloe moaned as she made a face at me. "You're fantasizing about organizing your book collection right now, aren't you?"

"No," I mumbled, taking a sip of my iced tea.

Truth was, while organizing my book collection was high on my Summer To-Do list, the real reason for not joining my friends on their Florida adventure was…well…I was kind of hoping to fall in love.

While both Chloe and Sophia were aware of the fact I took the Computer Club's Summer Fling Compatibility Test, neither one was aware of how seriously I was taking it. When you've gone nearly eighteen years of your life with no boyfriend, and you've never even been asked out by anyone, you'll take it seriously too. Neither Chloe nor Sophia could possibly understand. Despite being just as nerdy as I was, neither girl ever had a shortage of male suitors. Sophia, for instance, started dating in the eighth grade and she hadn't gone more than two weeks at a time without a boyfriend since.

Just a quick reminder: I'd gone nearly *eighteen years*.

I wasn't even sure why that was. I didn't think I was hideous or anything. Sure, I wore glasses half the time. Or most of the time, since I only needed them for reading and I was almost always reading. And sure, I was kind of tall and lanky—a look high school boys apparently weren't clamoring for. And yeah, whenever I hung out at the library, I'd get asked by people where to find certain books because they thought I worked there. And, okay, I didn't wear makeup, mainly because I had no idea how to put it on. So, I guess I could see why there hadn't been a line of guys waiting to take me out, but still.

This was why I was excited to take the compatibility test. It would essentially set me up on a date I didn't have to wait to be asked out for. And whoever I got paired up with would obviously be looking for the same things I was, since the whole point of it was to match up like-minded people.

But there was no way I could admit to my friends that the test was the reason I was foregoing a trip of a lifetime. They wouldn't understand. I wasn't even sure *I* understood.

Chloe half-smiled and shook her head as she set down her magazine and stretched out on the chaise lounge. "Man, I'm going to miss lounging by a pool all summer in the sweltering heat."

She was being sarcastic, of course, because she was going to be in Florida all summer, where there was a pool every ten feet, and the heat was always sweltering. She was teasing me, but I was okay with that. I'd made my decision and I stood by it. I'd take sweet, summer romance any day over whatever kind of antics those two girls were going to get themselves into while away from parental supervision.

"Knock, knock," came a sultry voice from a few feet away. I glanced up to see that our other friend, Sophia Ramirez, had joined us. In her hand, she carried a pile of envelopes.

"Mail's here," she said, dropping the pile onto my stomach before giving both me and Chloe air kisses.

My heart started racing in my chest. I'd been eagerly awaiting the mail every day this week because the results from my test were supposed to arrive no later than Thursday.

Quickly, I sifted through each envelope. Cable bill, electric bill, and a credit card offer for my parents. A birthday card for me from my Aunt Jo, even though my birthday wasn't for another three weeks (she always screwed that up). And finally, on the bottom of the pile, another envelope addressed to me, with the return address of nothing but *Emerson High Computer Club*. I couldn't help it; I squealed with excitement as I tossed all other mail onto the ground and ripped into the envelope with reckless abandon.

"Is that what I think it is?" Chloe asked, but she already knew the answer.

I nodded as I pulled out the piece of paper with shaky hands. In less than a few seconds, I would be finding out who my soulmate was. I didn't even care who it was. If the computer paired me up with him, it was because it viewed us as having a lot in common. He probably loved reading as much as I did.

Maybe even more! And he probably liked going to museums, stargazing, spending quiet evenings at home, cuddling…

I didn't realize I was staring dreamily off into the distance until Sophia waved a hand in front of my face and said, "Well? Are you going to read the letter, or what?"

Blinking, I brought myself back down to Earth and held the piece of paper in front of my face. Taking a deep breath, I carefully unfolded it and braced myself for whatever I was about to read.

Instantly, I let out a *whoosh* of air as I read the words printed on it.

Dear Emma Dawson,

Congratulations! We here at the Emerson High Computer Club have found your match! Are you ready to spend the summer getting to know your soulmate?

We have arranged a time and place for the two of you to meet. Please see below for details.

Sincerely,
The Members of the Emerson High Computer Club

"Well?" Chloe asked, sounding as excited as I'd felt a few short moments before. "Who is it? Who's the lucky guy?"

My shoulders slumped forward in disappointment. "I don't know yet. All this tells me is where to meet him."

Sophia grabbed the letter from my hands and read it herself. "Hmm, interesting. This is a cute idea. You're going on a mystery date!"

Chloe got up and took the letter from Sophia. "*You and your soulmate will meet on Friday, June 22nd, at the Dream Bean coffee shop at 7:00 p.m.,*" she read aloud. "*Included in this envelope is a card with a number on it. Your perfect match will be carrying the same card. Have some coffee, some good conversation, and plan your summer together. All results are final. No refunds. Thank you for your participation.*"

With a grunt, I grabbed the letter back from Chloe. "It's only Wednesday. I have to wait two more days?"

"Good things come to those who wait," Chloe pointed out in a singsong voice.

"Aw, we're not going to be here to see our girl off on her first date," Sophia said to Chloe with a pout.

Chloe gasped. "Who's going to do your hair? Your makeup? We can at least help you pick out your outfit before we leave, but—"

"Hey there, ladies."

Chloe was interrupted by the sound of a male voice behind her—an annoying male voice—and I looked up to see Logan Reynolds, my next-door neighbor and bane of my existence, poking his head over the fence that separated our houses.

Quickly, I stuffed the letter into the back pocket of my jean shorts before he had a chance to see it. I couldn't risk him finding out I'd taken that test because he would never let me live it down.

Logan Reynolds and I had lived next door to each other our entire lives. His father and my father grew up together as best friends. They were so close they went to law school together, became lawyers together, and eventually opened their own firm. They got married around the same time and their wives got pregnant with me and Logan only a couple months apart. As soon as Logan and I became old enough to start walking and talking, our parents tried to force a friendship between the two of us. Maybe when we were four we got along, but as soon as we started elementary school, it was all downhill from there.

I hated Logan, and he hated me. It was a beautiful thing.

"I thought I heard a couple of sexy voices over here. And Emma's." Logan glanced smugly over at me, clearly satisfied with his burn.

Ha-ha. With a roll of my eyes, I said, "Logan, don't you have a girlfriend to go torment with your presence?"

He placed both hands on the top of the fence and began to hoist himself up. "Thanks. I would love to join you guys."

While I began to seethe, Chloe and Sophia both giggled as they watched Logan effortlessly jump the fence and land gracefully on the grass before us.

"You're trespassing," I informed him, but he ignored me. Technically, he wasn't trespassing. My parents told him long ago that he was welcome over at our house anytime—day or night, rain or shine. Luckily, he'd never taken them up on the offer.

Until now.

"What are you girls gossiping about over here?"

Chloe opened her mouth to respond—most likely with the truth, so I shot her a warning glance. "Um," she said, taking the hint, "we were talking about the Florida trip Sophia and I are leaving for tomorrow."

"Oh, that's right," Logan said as he made his way over to us. "It's too bad. I'm going to miss having some scenery to look at around here this summer."

Chloe, in her blue and white striped bikini, and Sophia, in her short jean shorts and bright yellow bikini top, both blushed furiously at his comment, and I had to force a wave of bile back down my throat.

"Well, you'll still have Emma," Sophia chirped.

Logan snorted and turned his gaze to me. I was wearing nothing close to a bikini, or any other type of swimwear, even though it was about 95 degrees out. Instead, I donned a pair of shorts much more modest than Sophia's, and a vintage *Reading Rainbow* t-shirt that was loose enough to hide my underwhelming figure underneath. I looked like a frump in comparison to my friends, and Logan's reaction indicated that fact wasn't lost on him.

But, surprisingly, he refrained from making any snide comments. Instead, he said, "Well, I thought I would drop in to tell you two to have a good trip. I'm heading over to Matt's. We're going to the beach for the afternoon."

At the mention of Logan's best friend, Matt Fisher, my heart skipped a beat.

I shouldn't have been, but I was in love with Matt. I had been for years. He was your typical high school jock—tall and muscular with pretty-boy good looks. Dark blond hair that sometimes grew long enough to start falling into his eyes right before he'd get it cut. He'd lived across the street from me since about the fourth grade, and while he'd acknowledged me before with eye contact and waves when we both happened to be out in our front yards, we'd never had an actual conversation.

My unrequited crush on Matt was a majority of the reason why I wanted to take the compatibility test in the first place. I wasn't stupid; I realized Matt and I would never be a thing. He went for the popular, cheerleader type and that wasn't me. So, figuring it was about time I got over him, I took the test in hopes of finding somebody else to be in love with.

"Would you two care to join us?" Logan asked Chloe and Sophia, before turning to me and saying, "I'd invite you too, Dawson, but I know you want to get started on organizing your book collection."

Chloe stifled a giggle as my blood began to boil in my veins. The jerk had been eavesdropping on our conversation…which meant it was entirely possible he'd heard us talking about the compatibility test as well…

"That's okay," I said, my voice somehow calm and collected. "I have no desire to see you without a shirt on, anyway."

Admittedly, that was a lie. While I may have hated Logan Reynolds with every ounce of my being, I was still a teenage girl with occasional raging hormones, and the guy was hot. I'd seen both him and Matt shirtless before, most recently while playing basketball in Matt's driveway, and it was hardly the worst thing I'd ever seen.

But I couldn't let him know that.

Logan grinned. "Liar. Do you even own a bathing suit, anyway? Do you even know how to swim?"

It had been less than one minute since Logan jumped the fence between our houses, and I'd already had my fill of him for one day. "Screw you," I said. I bent down and grabbed my book off the lounge chair and began my march toward the sliding glass door to let myself into the house.

"Did I hit a nerve?" he called after me. He knew he had.

No, I didn't own a bathing suit because, no, I didn't know how to swim. I was familiar with the basics of it and all, I'd just never gotten good at it. Plus, my fear of the water didn't help matters. Logan was well-aware of this because he and I used to spend summers together growing up. Because our fathers were so close, we used to take family vacations together every summer to Mr. Reynolds' cabin on the lake and he got to see firsthand how much of a sissy I'd always been around bodies of water.

So, I ignored him. It was the only effective way to eventually get him to leave.

As soon I was inside the house, I sighed and dropped my book and the letter onto the kitchen table.

"Don't let him get to you," Sophia said behind me. She and Chloe had followed me—meaning Logan presumably had left the premises.

"I won't." I turned around to face them. "I have more important things to focus on right now."

Chloe nodded and grabbed the letter from the table. "Right. Like who Number 7 is!"

Number 7. The potential love of my life was associated with a lucky number, at least. That was a good sign, right?

"Are you sure you don't want to come with us on our trip?" Sophia asked. "What if Number 7 is a dud? Think of all the hot guys we're going to be surrounded by in Orlando every day. I'm sure you'd be able to find one to have a summer fling with while we're down there."

That was the thing. I didn't just want some summer fling, despite the fact I took a "summer fling" compatibility test. If I fell for somebody down in Florida, we'd have to part ways at the end of summer and never see each other again. That wasn't exactly what I was looking for. Besides, my reasoning behind foregoing the trip went a bit deeper than that.

I was kind of terrified of flying.

I was afraid of most things in life: water, flying, a variety of bugs, heights, public speaking, clowns, growing old and becoming a cat lady, snakes, etc. I was basically every psychologist's fantasy patient, but I was hoping to never end up in therapy. There wasn't enough money in the world to pay for all the sessions I'd need.

"I don't think this guy is going to be a dud," I said. "He is theoretically everything I've been looking for. That's the point of this test, right?"

"Yeah," said Chloe, "but just because this guy might be everything you're looking for, that doesn't mean he's the right guy for you. Sometimes, opposites attract."

I gave her a dismissive wave of my hand. I didn't do opposites. Matt would be the most opposite I'd ever go for, but since he was out of my league, it didn't matter anyway.

"I'm staying here. I'm meeting Number 7, we're going to fall madly in love and have a summer together that could easily be made into a romantic teen movie, and it's going to be wonderful." I smiled dreamily at my friends, who were looking at me like I'd gone crazy.

I gave up a dream vacation for the possibility of a dream romance. It was definitely crazy, I'd give them that, but it's what I needed to do.

"Well, suit yourself." Sophia threw her arm around Chloe's shoulders. "Chloe and I will be thinking of you as we're sipping virgin margaritas and ogling sexy, sweaty, shirtless boys on the beach."

"At least you'll have sexy, sweaty, shirtless Logan to ogle all summer," Chloe said, wiggling her eyebrows.

"Eww, gross." I playfully smacked her on the arm.

Both she and Sophia were laughing.

"Oh, c'mon, Em," Sophia said. "You can't honestly stand there and say Logan Reynolds isn't *hot*."

"Actually, I can. And I did."

The girls exchanged a glance and shook their heads. "Okay," said Chloe, "you're obviously insane—"

"Or in denial," Sophia chimed in.

"Yes, or in denial. Either way, if you can't admit Logan is hot, then we are bringing you to the emergency room right now because you are obviously going blind."

I wasn't going blind. I also wasn't denying I thought Logan was hot—because he *was*. In addition to looking good shirtless, he had bright, sparkling hazel eyes, an infuriatingly charming smile, and wavy brown hair most girls would kill to run their hands through. But, as the old saying goes, beauty is only skin deep. Underneath, Logan was as ugly as they came.

This conversation had already outworn its welcome, so I changed it back to what was most important at the moment.

"Who cares about Logan? He's irrelevant. All I care about is Number 7 and meeting him on Friday, and I can't believe you guys aren't going to be here to help me get ready for my date."

"Well," Chloe said, glancing down at her watch, "Sophia and I still have some time left before we need to get home to finish packing. Why don't we go shopping for a cute outfit for you to wear on Friday, and then we'll give you a few, quick make-up and hair pointers?"

It was a nice gesture, but I wasn't exactly a do-it-yourselfer. These girls could spend an entire year teaching me the basics of mascara application or hair styling and I would probably end up even more clueless about it all in the end.

But I shrugged and agreed to go shopping with them. After all, starting tomorrow, I was on my own for the entire summer.

At least I'd have Number 7 to keep me company.

Chapter 2

EMMA

I examined my reflection in the full-length mirror on the back of my closet door and thought to myself, *not bad*.

I was wearing a light blue sundress the girls had picked out for me at the mall the other day and a pair of white wedges that added a couple inches onto my height, which at 5'8" I didn't need. Hopefully Number 7 was tall.

"Omigosh, you look beautiful," Chloe gushed from the screen of my laptop. She and Sophia had insisted we video chat before my date, so they could give me last-minute tips, tricks, and advice.

"Thank you," I said, turning around to face them.

Chloe and Sophia were both on the screen, huddled together on a bed in what I was assuming was Chloe's Aunt Jessica's guest bedroom. The two girls were staying with her for the entire summer, but they didn't mind. Jessica was in her mid-twenties and incredibly cool, so it was basically the same as not having any adult supervision at all.

Even though they hadn't even been gone two full days yet, I couldn't help but note that Chloe's skin was already three shades darker. She was so lucky she tanned easily. Sophia was naturally tanned all the time, but still got that sun-kissed glow after spending the day outdoors. I, on the other hand, could spend four minutes in the sun without UV protection and end up looking like a boiled lobster.

"Are you going to kiss him at the end of your date to-night?" Sophia asked, staring at me intently.

My breath hitched in my throat at her question. To be honest, I hadn't given any thought to the possibility there might be kissing tonight. After all, it wasn't like this was a real date. It was more of a *pre*-date, or whatever.

I shook my head. "Guys, this isn't an official date. We're just going to get to know each other."

Chloe snickered and said, "What better way to get to know each other than by sticking your tongues down each other's throats?"

I rolled my eyes as both girls broke out into a fit of giggles. My friends could be so immature sometimes.

"I'm going to close my laptop if you two don't start behaving," I warned them.

"Sorry," they said in unison, but I could tell they weren't sorry at all.

I glanced over at my alarm clock next to my bed. "I should probably get going. I want to get there a little early. Get a good table."

"All the tables at Dream Bean are the same," Chloe said, but I ignored her.

"You two have fun. Don't do anything I wouldn't do."

"You wouldn't do *anything*," Sophia pointed out.

I shut my laptop before they could say anything else.

I heard a soft knock on my bedroom door and turned to see my mother standing in the doorway, looking at me with wide, teary eyes.

"My precious baby, getting ready for her first date," she gushed. Seriously, she was about to cry.

"It's not a—" I started to say, but I didn't feel like going through the whole explanation again about how this wasn't a date, so I didn't. Instead, I gave her a quick spin and asked, "How do I look?"

"Like the most beautiful girl in the world." Mom entered my room and made her way over to me. She'd been almost as excited for this "date" as I'd been, and I knew why.

My parents met and fell in love in high school. They started out as casual friends their freshman year, moved onto best friends their sophomore year, and then started dating their junior year. By senior year, they were officially high school sweethearts. On the night they graduated, my dad proposed to my mom and she said yes. They were only eighteen, so they took it slow. They decided to wait until after college to get married, figuring if they could make it through a long-distance relationship, they could make it through anything. One week after they graduated from college, they got married. Four years later, after my dad graduated law school, they had me. And now, fast-forward eighteen years, my parents were even more in love with each other than they were back then. At least, that's what they claimed.

This was what Mom wanted for me. She wanted me to meet someone in high school and have a lifelong epic love story like her and my dad. But I was going to be entering my senior year in the fall and so far, there were no prospects. Nobody but Number 7, who could turn out to be, as Sophia put it, "a dud".

"Do you think your mystery man could be Matt?" Mom asked. She'd always been privy to my crush on him.

I gasped. "*Mom!*" I hissed through clenched teeth, afraid Matt would be able to hear her from all the way across the street, even with my bedroom windows closed.

"What? It's a valid question."

"It's not," I said with a shake of my head. "I'm almost one

hundred percent sure Matt didn't even take this test. He doesn't have to. He could have any girl he wants." I paused and smoothed out the front of my dress. "Besides, I'm in the process of getting over him anyway."

I could tell she didn't believe me, but she let it go.

"So then, who do you think it could be?" she asked, as though she actually knew who went to my school and would recognize whatever name I threw out.

"I have no idea," I said with a shrug. I hadn't given much thought to who it could be. There were quite a few boys at my school who liked to read, who were kind of shy and reserved like I was, who I'm sure deep down also yearned for some good old-fashioned romance (although they would never admit to it). It could be any one of them. Or none of them. I just knew it wouldn't be Matt.

Even though he currently, as far as I knew, did not have a girlfriend, there were always potential ones eagerly waiting in the wings. Cheerleaders, mostly. So, unless he took the test for no other reason than to help fund Project Graduation, I could consider the chances of Matt being Number 7 as being slim at best.

"Well, whoever he is, he's a lucky boy." Mom took a step closer to me and sized me up from head to toe. "Did you put this makeup on all by yourself?"

Geez, I suddenly felt like a little kid who had just used the potty for the first time without help. That's how proud my mother sounded.

"Yes, I did," I mumbled, turning around to look in the mirror. I tried looking at myself the way a teenage boy would, and I instantly began to wonder why it was I'd never been asked out.

I was certainly no supermodel, but I was also no troll either.

I guess you could say I was "girl-next-door" pretty—which usually translated into "average-looking"—but I was okay with that. Chloe and Sophia were both considered to be traditionally beautiful, and while that landed them tons of boyfriends, most of those boyfriends were only interested in them for one thing and one thing only.

And right now, that thing was not what I was looking for, so my played-down physical appearance helped to at least keep the horndogs away.

Unfortunately, it kept the rest away as well.

"Well, you did a great job." Mom pulled me in for a quick hug.

"Oh, there you two are." The sound of my dad's voice from the doorway broke us apart. He had appeared out of nowhere, holding a camera.

"Hi, Pumpkin," he said to me with a grin and a wink. "I thought I could maybe get a few shots of you before you go out on your big date?"

I groaned. My parents could somehow manage to embarrass me even when there was nobody else around to witness it. My dad wanted to take pictures of me because this was my first "date" ever. It would no doubt get posted on all his social media accounts under the *"Emma's Firsts"* category (yes, that was an actual thing), along with old scanned photographs of me taking my first steps, me enjoying my first Christmas, me riding a bike for the first time, and even—horrifically enough—me taking my first bath. Don't get me wrong, I loved how much my dad doted on me (it's what happens when you're an only child), but sometimes it bordered on stifling.

"No, Dad," I began to protest as the flash of his camera hit my retinas.

Dad checked out the image on the camera's screen and

grinned. "Oh, this is a good one. You look so annoyed."

I rolled my eyes. "Because I am. Do you guys think maybe I could finish getting ready in peace?"

Mom strolled over to Dad and placed a hand on his arm. "Jake, let's leave Emma alone."

He held up his camera once more. "Not until she gives me one good shot. C'mon sweetie, one little smile? Pretty please?"

It was often hard to turn down my father's requests. He'd mastered the art of the puppy dog eyes, which I'd always thought was something that only worked for little kids. But no. When Dad widened those big, brown orbs, tilted his head to the side and pushed out his bottom lip just the slightest, you were done. You'd do whatever he asked. I'm sure it helped him in the courtroom. I wouldn't be surprised if he'd won a few cases with that look.

So, I gave the man what he wanted: a small, genuine smile for the camera.

"Great," he said cheerfully. "I'm going to go Instagram this." He started to leave my bedroom but then turned back around and added, "Oh, and Emma, be back by eleven. And if you decide you want a second date with this boy, we'll have to meet him first, okay?"

"Yeah, yeah." I motioned to the door as a hint for both my parents to leave.

"Okay, sweetie," Mom said after my dad was gone. "If you need any more help getting ready—"

"I don't," I said as politely as possible. "But thank you."

It was embarrassing how excited my parents were for this. The sad thing was, they should have already experienced this first-date excitement years ago, when I was fourteen or fifteen, not when I was nearly eighteen. It made me feel like a child.

After my room became parents-free, I took one more

glimpse of myself in the mirror.

Hopefully Number 7 liked what he saw.

Chapter 3

LOGAN

"Got a hot date tonight?"

I glanced over at my stepmother as I entered the kitchen. Rachel was sitting at the table feeding my baby sister, Abby. Or, should I say, *attempting* to feed her. There was currently more baby food on the table, the floor, and Abby's face than had made it into her mouth. But it was mashed peas, so who could blame her?

"Something like that," I muttered, walking past them to the refrigerator. I figured I was going to need a snack before my date, since it was going to be at a lame coffee shop where all they sold was puff pastries and lattes. I'd never understood the appeal of either.

"You don't usually dress up for dates with Grace," Rachel said, brushing a strand of hair out of her eyes, leaving a smudge of green goo behind on her forehead. She was referring to the fact I'd thrown on a freshly ironed button-up shirt, a pair of jeans with no designer holes in them, and I'd tamed my sometimes-unruly hair by putting a little gel in it. Yes. For me, that was dressing up.

I grabbed a pint of mint chocolate chip ice cream out of the freezer and a spoon from the silverware drawer. "Yeah, well, the date's not with Grace."

Rachel's eyebrows shot up in surprise. "You two broke up?"

I shoved a heaping spoonful of ice cream into my mouth before answering. "Not exactly."

She frowned. "Logan, you're not cheating on her, are you?"

"Not exactly." I swallowed the ice cream and realized I wasn't hungry after all, so I put it back in the freezer.

Here's what went down when both Grace and I received our test results on the same day and opened our envelopes together while sitting side by side on my living room couch: she blew a frigging gasket.

When Grace saw that our numbers didn't match—I was a 7 and she was a 13—her face got so red with anger that I actually feared for my life. Of course, she automatically assumed there was something wrong with the code. Or that somebody in the Computer Club was out to get her and intentionally paired us up with different people to spite her. Or that they simply put the wrong number in the wrong envelope.

I had a hard time keeping a straight face through her tantrum, which must have lasted a good half an hour.

Should I have felt bad about what I did? Maybe. But did I? Not really. After her meltdown on the couch, I considered telling her the truth and trying to play it off as a harmless prank, but I wisely decided against it. Grace wouldn't have found it funny. Grace didn't find many things to be funny, ever.

"So, you're going on a date, but not with your girlfriend?"

"*Sometimes*-girlfriend," I corrected her.

Rachel shook her head at me before turning her attention back to Abby.

My stepmother was hot. Well, at least she was before giving birth to my little sister six months ago. Don't get me wrong, she still had a smokin' body (she'd lost the baby weight in no time), but ever since Abby came along, Rachel always appeared tired and disheveled. Like right now, for instance, her dark brown hair was piled high on her head in a messy bun and looked like it hadn't been washed in a couple of days. She had bags under her eyes from lack of sleep and her oversized, light gray t-shirt was stained with baby food, baby spit-up, and baby who-knows-what-else.

I wasn't always a big fan of Rachel. She was nice enough. She was young—only twenty-eight—and because of that, she even bordered on cool sometimes. And she seemed to really love my dad, and vice versa.

But she wasn't my mom. And she never would be.

She never tried to be, though. If anything, she tried to be my friend instead. My annoying friend who attempted to impart unsolicited advice on me at every opportunity she had.

I could feel some of that coming on right now, so I figured I needed to make a quick exit.

"I'm gonna head out," I said. "Tell Dad I'll be back by curfew?"

"Sure," she agreed disapprovingly. For some reason, Rachel liked Grace—probably because she reminded her of herself when she was a teenager—and I could tell if anything ever went down between me and Grace, Rachel would be taking her side over mine for sure.

I walked over to the table and gave Abby a light kiss on the top of her peach-fuzzed head. "Be good, Kiddo," I told her, even though she couldn't understand words yet.

I said goodbye to Rachel and headed out the door. It was already after seven o'clock and the coffee shop was a few minutes away. In classic Logan fashion, I was going to be late.

Part of me wondered why I was even bothering to go. I wasn't going to, at first. But then, the thought of Mystery Girl Number 7 sitting alone at a table all night, not realizing her prince would never come, just seemed…mean. So, soon after

Grace left my house in a tizzy the other night (after claiming she was going to go meet her own mystery date), I decided the least I could do was meet this girl in person and let her down gently.

I was kind of a nice guy like that.

When I pulled up to the curb in front of the coffee shop, I was nearly thirty minutes late. After I turned off the engine, I sat there for a moment, debating on whether I should go in. Dream Bean was a pretentious coffee shop located downtown that had been serving hipsters and poetry nerds since it opened a couple years ago. I'd never set foot inside the place and I had no idea why the Computer Club chose that location for the meet-and-greet. Normally, I wouldn't be caught dead there, yet here I was, about to enter its doors for the first time, to go break the heart of some poor, unsuspecting girl.

And half an hour late, no less.

Taking a deep breath, I exited the car and began my trek over to the door. Before I got there, I stopped to look through the large windows in the front of the building. I saw a lot of kids I recognized from school, most likely all there to meet their summer soulmates. Most of them seemed happy with their results—all except for one girl, the only one there who was sitting alone.

Most likely Mystery Girl Number 7.

I couldn't see who it was at first. She was sitting so I could see her from the side, but her wavy, dark blonde hair was hiding her face. She was wearing a form-fitting light blue sundress, showcasing a modest rack and a set of long, lean legs—the kind of legs most guys wouldn't mind having wrapped around them. She looked like she could be tall, which was a plus. I liked tall girls, although I'd never dated one. Grace was only five-foot-three with heels on. Without heels, I was about a foot taller than she was. Most guys liked petite girls—I was no exception—but there was something about a tall girl that was just...sexy.

Hmm. Maybe this wasn't going to be as bad as I thought. I had yet to see her face, but if she was pretty enough, I could probably forget the fact she was apparently lame as hell, judging from her answers on that stupid test.

As I started mentally running through the list of blonde girls at school who were thin and tall, Mystery Girl ran a hand through her hair, brushing it away from her face and finally revealing her identity.

And I was hit with a feeling of dread as soon as I realized who she was.

Emma Dawson. Literally the last girl in the world I would want to be matched up with. This should have come as no surprise to me, though. I answered all the questions on that test like a total loser would and Emma was the biggest loser I knew. What did I expect?

Emma and I went way back, unfortunately. She was the girl next door, but not the kind you fell in love with. More like the kind you wanted to strangle because she was so annoying. She thought she was better and smarter than everyone else. She barely talked to anyone but her two best friends, but when she did, it was usually to correct grammar or to voice her opinion on something. My father adored her, because he and her father were besties, and he'd always tried to get me to be friends with her. But it was never going to happen.

Never. Never. *Never.*

For a moment, I stood there and observed her. She glanced down at her phone, took a sip of her drink, and glanced at her phone again. Now that I could just barely see her face, I could also see her disappointment. She knew she was waiting for somebody who wasn't going to show.

And she was right, because there was no way I was going in there now.

I didn't know for sure she was Mystery Girl Number 7, but I wasn't going to stick around to find out. I knew how she would react to me being her "match", and it would not go well. She'd probably yell and scream and throw a fit, and when she got angry, her voice was like nails on a chalkboard to me. This was not how I wanted to spend my Friday night. Not at all.

So, before she could turn her head and see me gawking at her, I quickly spun around and rushed back over to my car. I couldn't get away from that coffee shop fast enough— especially after having basically checked out the girl I hated with a passion. This was a bad idea. What the hell was I thinking?

Emma Dawson was about to get stood up and I wasn't going to lie—that put a smile on my face.

Chapter 4

EMMA

I was being stood up. It didn't take a genius to figure that out. All it took was a time-telling device and the absence of a boy holding a card with the number 7 on it.

Well, wasn't this ducky?

Glancing down one last time at my phone, I sighed. It was almost eight o'clock and Number 7 was a no-show. During the last hour, I'd watched several guys from school walk through the coffee shop's door. I'd heard that bell above it ding so many times it'd become almost Pavlovian. Every time a boy would walk in, my heart would begin to race, thinking he was the one, but every time, he'd go to another table to meet with another girl. I saw couples meet, greet, and leave together, only to be replaced by another couple. Meanwhile, I'd been sitting here all alone, trying not to look like I was bothered by the fact my match decided he didn't care to meet me.

But it did bother me. A girl wasn't supposed to get stood up on her first date.

I was about to push my chair back to get up from my table when the young barista who'd sold me my iced tea earlier appeared suddenly at my side, wearing a look of pity on her face.

"Hey," she said softly. The pity on her face had spread to her vocal chords. "I'm sorry to have to do this, but—"

"You want me to leave," I finished for her. I wasn't stupid. I'd bought one iced tea and had been hogging a table for nearly an hour, while more and more people had piled in. I was basically loitering at that point and I was surprised it had taken this long to get booted out.

I could tell the barista, whose nametag read Amelia, felt uncomfortable having to ask me to leave, and I couldn't help but feel as sorry for her as she probably did for me.

"Here, I'll tell you what." Amelia removed the pen she'd had stuck behind her ear and grabbed the napkin that had been sitting under my glass of iced tea. She handed me the pen. "Write down your contact info and the number on your card, and if your match shows up looking for you, I'll give this to him, so he can find you."

It wasn't a bad idea, but I knew it was pointless. He wasn't going to show up looking for me. This had turned out to be a total bust. But to humor the girl and make her feel less bad about kicking me out, I jotted down all the information she'd requested and handed it to her.

"Thanks," I said with a polite smile, before getting up to make my exit.

How humiliating. I got kicked out because my "soulmate" couldn't be bothered to come meet me. Nobody else seemed to have that problem, judging from the fact every table in there was occupied by two people. Nobody else had been stood up. Just me.

I should have known this would happen.

I made it all the way home before I started to break down. I tried convincing myself that this was for the best—that I probably wouldn't have been interested in this guy anyway—but it didn't help to soothe the pang that had taken up residence squarely in the center of my chest.

With a deep breath, I entered the house quietly, hoping maybe my parents wouldn't hear me come in. I didn't want to explain to them why I was back so soon. I kind of wanted to go upstairs to my room and call Chloe and Sophia before crying myself to sleep.

But as soon as I shut the front door my parents rushed out of the living room to greet me.

"Sweetie!" my mother said in surprise. Her hair was disheveled, and her shirt was crooked. My dad's hair was a little messed up too and both their faces were flushed pink. I suddenly wanted to barf.

I'd interrupted my parents' make-out session.

Groaning inwardly, I greeted them with a mumbled, "Hey," and made a beeline for the staircase.

"Wait, not so fast," Mom said, grabbing the back of my dress to stop me mid-stride. "Why are you home so early? What happened?"

I didn't want to discuss this with them, but I knew if I didn't, they would harass me for the rest of the night until I did. "He didn't show," I said, my shoulders slumping forward.

Mom's face fell while Dad's face went into over-protective father mode.

"What do you mean, he didn't show?" Dad asked between clenched teeth. This was why I didn't want to talk about it. Dad was going to be angry that a boy stood me up and Mom was going to probably sympathy-cry for me.

"He didn't show," I repeated with a casual shrug. I wanted to brush it off in front of my parents to make them think I didn't care. If they thought I didn't care, then they wouldn't worry about me and they'd let me go up to my room so they could continue where they left off on the couch…as much as the thought disgusted me.

"Oh, honey." Mom pulled me into a warm hug and stroked my hair. She was acting like I was five years old and just fell off my bike and got a boo-boo.

"It's fine," I said, struggling to remove myself from her embrace. "I probably wouldn't have liked him anyway."

"I'm going to find out who this punk is and I'm going to make him regret standing up my baby girl." Dad's hands began to form fists at his sides and I had to refrain from laughing. My father, while tall and muscular from the few days a week he went to the gym, was all bark, no bite. He would never hurt a fly, let alone some "punk" teenage boy who let his daughter down. I had no doubt in my mind that he *wanted* to hurt him, I just knew he wouldn't.

"Dad, seriously, it's not a big deal. I'm already over it." I sounded so sincere, I almost convinced myself.

He exchanged a glance with my mother and I could tell neither one believed me. But my parents were smart. They knew it was best to let me deal with this on my own.

"Okay," Dad said, softening a bit. "You want to go get some ice cream or something?"

Going out on a Friday night with my parents to get ice cream, after being stood up on a blind date? No way. That would only add to my humiliation.

"Thanks, but I'm just gonna go upstairs and read a book. Maybe call Chloe and Sophia and see what they're up to down in Florida."

"Okay," Dad said with a nod. "But if you change your mind, let us know."

I gave him as much of a smile as I could muster. "I will."

Once my parents finally let me go, I ran up to my room, shut the door, and let out a sob.

This was not going as planned. I was supposed to still be out on my date, getting to know Number 7, and starting to plot out our entire summer together. What went wrong? Did he not get the letter in the mail? Did they give him the wrong time? Did he forget? Did he get into an accident on the way to meet me? Or, worst of all, did he see me sitting in the coffee shop from afar and was totally repulsed?

I had to talk to Chloe and Sophia, and I hated that I couldn't tell them to come over to comfort me. When I thought I was going to be potentially spending my summer with a boyfriend (or, at the very least, a boy who was a friend), I wasn't as bothered by the fact that my best friends would be hundreds of miles away. But now, it was the worst thing ever.

Taking my phone out of my purse, I dialed Chloe's number. Surprisingly, she picked up right away.

"Hey, Em!" she exclaimed. "How was your date? Oh, wait, let me go grab Sophia so you can tell us both!"

I opened my mouth to tell her not to bother, but she went silent for a moment while she went to find Sophia. Half a minute later, she returned.

"Okay, Sophia's here and you're on speaker," she said. "Don't worry, we went somewhere private so no one else can hear our conversation. So? Who's Number 7? Tell us *everything.*"

That's exactly what I did. I told them how I had no idea who Number 7 was because I never got to meet him. Because he apparently didn't want to meet me. When I was done with the story twenty seconds later, I was met with total silence on the other end.

"Guys?" I said, wondering if maybe we'd gotten disconnected.

"Emma, we're so sorry," Sophia finally said. The pity in her voice sounded just like the barista's earlier. "What a jerk!"

"Well, hey," Chloe said, "we don't know what his reason was for not showing up. He could have had a family emergency or something."

"Family emergency my *butt*," Sophia said. "The dude intentionally stood up our girl and he needs to pay."

"Sheesh, you sound like my dad," I said, playing with the hem of my dress. "Guys, it doesn't matter if it was intentional, or if he had a family emergency. I don't even know who *he* is."

"The Computer Club does," Sophia said. "You could ask one of those guys. Maybe bribe one of them to tell you."

"Why does our school even have a Computer Club, anyway?" Chloe asked. "It's just an excuse for geeks to sit around after school playing retro video games with their teacher, who's still living in the nineties. I mean, that computer they used to get the test results is probably some piece of junk from the eighties and not all that accurate. So maybe you dodged a bullet, Em. Maybe you wouldn't have liked who they paired you up with anyway."

"Chloe's right," Sophia agreed. "Besides, when you think about it, do you want a romance based purely on an algorithm? We've seen the romance novels you have on your bookshelf, Em. You want the real thing. You want the natural progression of falling in love. You want it to be organic, not forced by some dumb computer. Maybe Number 7 not showing up tonight was a blessing in disguise. Now you won't be tethered to some idiot all summer, which will be good in the event you meet the *real* love of your life."

Suddenly, I really missed my friends. They knew exactly what to say to make me feel better in any situation.

"It's not too late to come to Florida," Chloe said. "You could fly down this weekend and we can spend the next month and half finding you a boyfriend. Emma, there are *so many* cute guys down here, you have no idea."

"She's not lying," Sophia assured me.

It was a nice thought. Had it not been for my paralyzing fear of flying, I might have taken them up on it. My parents had been supportive of the idea of me joining the girls on their vacation, and even though a last-minute ticket would be pricey, I had no doubt in my mind Dad would pay for it without hesitation.

"Thanks, but no thanks. You're forgetting one thing: I still need to organize my book collection."

I could almost *hear* them rolling their eyes.

"Okay," Chloe said. "Well, think about it anyway, will you?"

"Will do." I wouldn't.

After telling me to keep my chin up, the girls let me go to get back to their activities. As soon as I hung up with them, I heard a soft knock on my door.

"Emma, sweetie?" My mom opened my door just enough to poke her head in. "Are you okay?"

I set my phone down on my nightstand and rested my hands on my lap. Staring down at them, I whispered, "Not really."

Mom let herself into my room and came over to join me on the bed, throwing an arm around my shoulders and pulling me close. "I'm so sorry, Emma."

"It's fine," I said, trying to sound nonchalant, but the break in my voice gave away the lie. With a shaky sigh, I rested my head on her shoulder.

"You know you don't need a boyfriend, right?"

"I know that. I just…I want to know what it's like. I want to know how it feels to have a boy look at me the way Dad looks at you. I want what you guys had—what you *still* have."

Mom blushed slightly and smiled. "Honey, your Dad and I are a special case. Not everyone finds the person they're going to spend the rest of their lives with when they're in high school."

"Yeah, but I can't even find the person I'm going to spend the day with. Is that too much to ask for?"

She chuckled as she tucked a loose strand of hair behind my ear. "Someday your prince will come. It may happen when you least expect it, and it may happen with *whom* you least expect. But it *will* happen, I promise."

My mom, like Chloe and Sophia, always knew the right thing to say. And even though on the inside I was inconsolable, her words of encouragement allowed me to at least mask my pain on the outside.

"Thanks, Mom." I sat up straight, stretched my arms out and faked a yawn. "I'm tired. I think I'll do a little reading and then go to sleep."

Mom removed herself from my bed. "Okay. But if you want to talk, you know where I am."

I smiled and nodded as she let herself out of my room. As soon as she was gone, my smile vanished. Reaching into my purse, I took out the card with the number 7 on it and threw it in the trashcan next to my computer desk.

For the rest of the night, a part of me still held onto the hope that I'd get a call from Amelia from Dream Bean, letting me know that my mystery date had arrived late, and was crushed to discover I'd left.

But my phone never rang, and my dream of having a romantic summer with my soulmate was officially dead.

Chapter 5

LOGAN

I woke up the next morning to the sound of my phone vibrating on my nightstand. Still half-asleep, I reached over and grabbed it. The screen was lit up with a picture of Grace smiling sweetly at me, but I knew that was false advertising. I knew if I answered it, she wouldn't have anything good to say. Maybe she was calling to apologize for the way she acted the other night. Maybe she was calling to tell me she had fallen in love with her mystery man.

Either way, it was too early in the day to converse with Grace. With one swipe of my thumb, the call was ignored.

When I saw what time it was, I groaned. It was already eleven o'clock. If I wasn't careful, I was going to sleep my entire summer vacation away. With a yawn, I forced myself out of the bed and headed to the bathroom for a quick wake-me-up shower.

The smell of bacon hit my nostrils as soon as I exited the bathroom and I smiled. Rachel must have heard me get up and figured she would cook me some breakfast. She often did that for me on the weekends and it was much-appreciated. I followed the scent down the stairs and into the kitchen, where Rachel stood at the stove, holding Abby in one hand, and a spatula in the other.

"Good morning," I said cheerfully. The shower had done its job and woken me up and I was now ready to conquer the day—right after I got my bacon on, that is.

"Morning," Rachel responded. Her voice sounded tense, like something was bothering her.

I wasn't going to pry, though. On the off-chance it had something to do with my Dad, I didn't want to get in the middle of their relationship troubles.

Instead, I walked over to her and removed Abby from her arms so that she could focus solely on making my breakfast.

Abby giggled as I placed her on my hip and bounced her up and down a few times. I was ashamed to admit I hated Abby when she first arrived. I'd spent seventeen years as an only child and although during those years I occasionally yearned for a sibling—especially a brother—I was always spoiled by all the attention an only child gets, so I was ultimately content.

But then my mom died seven years ago. My dad met and fell in love with Rachel five years later, they got married, and did what a lot of married couples do: they had a baby. At first, I was resentful of Abby because I knew she was going to become the main focus of the household. Then, I was resentful of her because she had a mother and I didn't. It was stupid, I know, because it wasn't like it was her fault. But she was an easy target for me to blame all my anger on, so I did. However, after a few months, the kid started to grow on me. I still wasn't her number-one fan, mostly because she was gross, but I didn't hate her anymore. How could I? Her cheeks were so chubby. Like, seriously—pinchably chubby.

Taking a seat at the kitchen table, I set Abby onto my lap and turned on my phone. I had one voicemail and a bunch of missed texts from Grace. Apparently, she had something important to say to me. I was about to listen to the voicemail when Rachel set a plate of bacon, eggs, and toast onto the table in front of me…and placed a card down next to it. A card with the number 7 on it.

"What's that?" she asked me, taking Abby back so I could eat.

As I glanced at it, I couldn't help but feel a small, tiny bit of guilt form in the pit of my stomach. I vaguely remembered removing it from my pocket when I got home last night and dropping it onto the kitchen counter. "That? Oh, that's something from school. A fundraiser thing."

"Huh," she said, in a way that indicated she already knew exactly what it was.

I shifted uncomfortably in my chair as I shoveled a forkful of scrambled eggs into my mouth.

"You know, I was out taking Abby for a stroll earlier and I ran into Olivia Dawson."

I swallowed hard. Emma's mom. Why would Rachel be telling me about running into Emma's mom? "Oh yeah?" I said, taking a sip of orange juice.

"Yeah," she said, taking a seat across from me. "She and I got to talking and she mentioned that Emma was supposed to go on a blind date last night. Some fundraiser thing from school, apparently. But the guy never showed. He stood her up."

I could feel her eyes boring into me, like she was waiting for some sort of reaction. One that I wasn't going to give her. "Huh. You don't say?"

"Oh, I do say," she said. I could tell from the tone of her voice that she was unhappy with me and I wished I could swipe to ignore her like I just had with Grace. "See, she happened to mention something about a number. The number 7. And as soon as she said it, I remembered seeing this card laying on the counter this morning and I thought…there's no way Logan was supposed to be Emma's date, right? Because if that were the case, that would mean *he* stood her up. And you wouldn't do that, would you, Logan?"

More bacon and eggs suddenly found their way into my mouth, preventing me from answering. I took my time chewing, buying myself some time to think of a way to respond to this. But I wouldn't have to respond. Rachel knew. She wasn't an idiot.

"How did you two even get matched up to begin with? You guys couldn't be any more different."

The guilt on my face must have given away the fact there was more to the story than I was letting on.

"Logan, what did you do?" she asked, her voice laced with accusation.

With a nonchalant shrug, I replied, "I may have lied on the test."

"Lied?" she echoed. "Why? Why would you do that?"

So, I explained to her why, leaving no detail out. There was no use in hiding it. She would have broken me down and forced it out of me eventually.

When I was done, she sighed. "Seriously, Logan, that's messed up."

"It's not that bad," I assured her, pushing the eggs around my plate with my fork.

"Not that bad? You let that poor girl sit alone in that coffee shop all night, waiting for someone that didn't even exist."

I snorted. "Emma is anything but a 'poor girl'. She got what she deserved."

Rachel's jaw dropped, and her face reddened slightly in what I could only assume was anger. "Logan, I don't know what your issue is with Emma, but she is quite possibly the sweetest girl I've ever met. You shouldn't have stood her up. That was a lousy thing to do."

I pushed my breakfast plate away. I suddenly wasn't hungry anymore. "Look, Rachel, Emma and I don't get along, okay? We never have, and we never will. Me standing her up was the best thing I could have done for her. Trust me—I'm sure she'd rather get stood up by some unknown guy than to think for one second that she and I have anything in common."

Rachel shook her head, not buying it. "I can't even begin to tell you how disappointed I am in you, Logan. But I can tell you this: you're going to make it up to her."

My eyebrows shot up in surprise. Was Rachel about to threaten me? "Oh yeah?" I said, my voice laced with challenge. "Or else what?"

A contemplative look passed over her face, as if she was trying to think of what the "or else" would be. I saw the precise moment the light bulb lit above her head.

"Well," she said, a devious grin forming on her face. "You know how your father and I are taking Abby to New York for a week in July, to meet my family?"

"Yeah," I replied slowly, not liking where this was going. "How could I forget? You guys are letting me stay here alone that week."

"Well, I was thinking, maybe you should come too. My family would love to meet you. And it would be nice for all four of us to spend a week together—you know, do some family bonding." She paused, studying me. "All it would take is for me to suggest it to your father. I'm sure he would think it's a great idea. I could also maybe plant a seed of doubt in his mind about leaving you home alone. It's too bad, though, because I know the same week we're going to be gone, the Dawsons and the Fishers are going on that couples retreat together for the weekend, leaving pretty much the entire street to just you kids. That would have been the perfect opportunity to throw some kick-ass parties, huh?"

It was official. My stepmother was of the evil variety. She knew I'd been looking forward to their week in New York ever since they planned it five months ago. She knew I was aware that the only two other currently occupied houses on our street—Emma's and Matt's—would be parents-free that same week, and that I was planning on throwing, as she put it, "some kick-ass parties".

And she knew exactly how to take that all away from me.

I narrowed my eyes at her. "You wouldn't."

"Oh, I would."

Sitting back in my chair, I crossed my arms tightly over my chest. "And how do you suppose I 'make it up to her'?"

Rachel shrugged. "That's for you to figure out, not me. But you'd better make it good or I'm having a talk with your father tonight. And I can guarantee he will not be pleased to find out you stood up Jake Dawson's daughter. That alone will encourage him to make you come with us to New York. It will be your punishment."

There was no doubt in my mind that she was right. My dad thought Emma was the greatest. And while both he and Mr. Dawson had both spent years trying to get the two of us to bond with each other and become friends, my dad was way worse about it than Mr. Dawson. I think my dad was so adamant about it because he thought Emma would be a good influence on me. Especially after we entered high school and I started hanging out with all the cool kids and getting myself into trouble, and Emma...well, Emma stayed her old boring, goody two-shoes self.

If Dad knew what I'd done last night, he'd probably kick me out of the house.

I ran a hand through my hair. "I have to do this today?"

"Yep." Rachel stole a piece of untouched bacon from my plate before getting up from the table. "And you know what they say: there's no time like the present. The sooner you get this over with, the sooner you can stop worrying about having to go to New York with us." She paused for a moment before adding, "By the way, Abby appears to be prone to carsickness. I figured I would throw that out there, since you'll be riding in the backseat with her for six hours or so."

Boy, Rachel sure knew how to play dirty. I glanced over at Abby in her highchair and cringed. I'd seen that kid projectile vomit before and it wasn't pretty. There was no way I was going to spend six *seconds* in the backseat of a moving car with her, let alone six *hours*. Pushing my chair back, I stood and said, "Fine. I'll go talk to her."

"Splendid." Rachel smiled, and I could tell she was mentally patting herself on the back for a job well done.

Grabbing the card off the table, I headed out of the house and started in the direction of Emma's. I had no idea what I was going to say to her or how I was going to "make it up to her". I was going to have to wing it and come up with something on the fly.

I couldn't remember the last time I'd knocked on her front door. I wasn't sure I'd *ever* knocked on her front door. I'd never made it a habit to visit her, and when I did, I would just jump the fence between our two yards because I knew how much it irritated her. I chose not to take that route today, because she was already going to be plenty irritated enough after she heard what I had to tell her.

The door opened only a few seconds after my knock. Upon seeing that I was the knocker, Mrs. Dawson's eyebrows shot up in surprise and confusion. "Logan," she said. "What a pleasant surprise. What brings you by?"

I shifted my weight from one foot to the other. "Is Emma here?"

Her look of surprise and confusion intensified at my query. "Uh…yeah, she is. She's out back by the pool…" She studied me, as if trying to figure out what my deal was. I'm sure it was shocking enough for her to see a boy knock on her door to see her daughter, but for that boy to be me? I had to be blowing her mind right now. "You can head around back."

With a smile and short nod, I said, "Thanks, Mrs. Dawson."

"You're welcome, Logan."

I could feel her eyes on me as I crossed the front yard to head out back. As I began my journey, I started rationalizing in my head how maybe it wouldn't be so bad to go to New York with Dad, Rachel and Abby after all. Rachel mentioned having a younger sister around my age, and if she was half as hot as Rachel was, that might be incentive enough right there to go. And even if she wasn't hot, she was probably a lot nicer than Emma.

By the time I'd convinced myself that Abby's continuous vomiting in the back seat of a hot car for six hours was preferable to having to deal with the girl next door, I was already out back, and she'd already seen me.

"What are you doing here?" she asked with a glare, her voice full of venom.

She was sitting by the pool, book in hand, glasses on face, her long legs—the ones I'd inadvertently checked out the night before—stretched out before her on the lounge chair. Surprisingly, her jean shorts were shorter than usual, and she was wearing a tight camo tank-top in lieu of one of her usual oversized t-shirts with some sort of nerd logo on it. Maybe me standing her up somehow made her question her fashion sense?

That was doubtful. This was probably a fluke.

Clearing my throat, I said, "Hello to you, too."

Setting her book down on the ground, she sat up, folding her arms across her chest, and repeated, "What are you doing here?"

She was making this hard. "I was wondering if we could talk?"

Emma removed her glasses from her face and slid them up to rest on the top her head. She wanted to make sure I could see her glare loud and clear, with no obstructions. Mission accomplished. But what I could also see was the slight puffiness around her eyes, like she'd spent a greater part of the night before crying.

"Talk? What could you possibly want to talk to me about?"

There was no reason to prolong this, so I cut right to the chase. Pulling the card out of my pocket, I walked over to her and dropped it into her lap.

She stared down at it for a moment, as if trying to decipher what it was. When she picked it up and saw the number printed on it, her jaw dropped. "Where did you get this?"

"I got it in the mail," I replied.

"No." She shook her head. "*I* got this in the mail."

"We *both* got it in the mail," I said slowly, hoping it would help the realization sink in.

I could see the precise moment when it did. Her normally pale face turned about three different shades of red as she jumped up from the lounge chair.

"You're Number 7," she said numbly, staring at the card in disbelief. "No. That's impossible. You and I have nothing in common." She slid her judgmental gaze up and down the entire length of my body. "*Nothing.*"

"Yeah, believe me, I know," I grumbled, becoming increasingly frustrated at the bitchy tone in her voice.

"So then how did this happen?" she asked, placing her hands on her hips.

It was truth time. I wasn't sure I was prepared for this; she looked like she was about ready to murder somebody. Most likely me. "I lied on the test."

She stared at me, slack-jawed. "You what?" she asked, her voice barely above a whisper.

"I lied. On the test," I repeated, suddenly realizing what a horrible idea that was.

"You lied?" I could tell she was trying to control her anger. "Why would you lie on a compatibility test?"

I knew no answer I gave her would be an acceptable one, so I opted for the truth. With a defeated sigh, I said, "I didn't want to get matched up with Grace."

Emma closed her eyes as her hands slowly formed into fists at her sides. When she reopened her eyes and they landed on me, I was glad looks couldn't kill. Through clenched teeth, she asked, "Why would you not want to get matched up with your *girlfriend*?"

"*Sometimes*-girlfriend," I corrected her weakly, but that only earned me another death glare from her. "Look, Grace made me take that stupid test because she thinks we're soulmates. I didn't want to get matched up with her because...well, because I'm not as serious about our relationship as she is, and I didn't want her getting the wrong idea that we're, like, meant for each other or something."

Emma chuckled at that, but it was a crazy chuckle. Like she was about to go postal on me. "If you're not serious about Grace, why don't you break up with her?"

My eyes widened at her suggestion. "Are you serious?

Grace would kill me if I broke up with her. Quite literally. I'd have to make our breakup look like it was *her* idea, otherwise she'd make my life a living hell."

Finally, it appeared to make sense to her. With a slow nod, she said, "So, let me get this straight. You lied on that test to get your *sometimes*-girlfriend to question your relationship, and in turn, you also screwed *me* out of the chance of finding my match *and* left me sitting alone in a coffee shop all night, unknowingly waiting for no one?"

"Uh, yeah, I guess," I said. When she put it that way, it did sound kind of douchey. But before I could stop myself, I added with a grin, "Bonus."

You would have thought I'd slapped her across the face. Angry tears sprang to her eyes as she threw the card at my chest. "Get out," she hissed, turning around to head back toward to the pool.

I chose not to address the fact we were outside, therefore, "get out" was not really the appropriate phrase to use.

"Look, Emma, I'm sorry, okay? I didn't know the computer would match *us* up. And I didn't show up last night because when I figured out you were my match, I knew it would just make you angry anyway. I wasn't in the mood for a public blow-out at a coffee shop."

Emma stood still, her back facing me. "Some people took that test seriously, you know," she said, her voice thick. When she turned back around, I could see she was on the verge of crying and I wanted out of this backyard, pronto. "But I wouldn't expect you to understand why. Now, please leave."

I would have loved nothing more than to follow through with her request, but I knew Rachel would be waiting for me back at home, expecting specific details on how I fixed this mess. Problem was, I still had no idea how I was going to do that.

But then a brilliant idea hit me. The simplest solution of all. I had no idea why I hadn't thought of it immediately.

Making my way over to her, I reached into my back pocket. "Here, let me make this up to you."

I pulled out my wallet, opened it and rifled through the bills inside. When I found a twenty, I grabbed it and held it out to her.

She blinked down at it, looking completely dumbfounded. "What's that?"

"Twenty bucks. To pay you back for the test."

I guess maybe I expected her to look grateful at my offer, but instead, she looked insulted. Yanking the bill out of my hand, she crumpled it up and threw it into the pool.

"Hey!" I protested. "That was a perfectly good twenty!"

"Then go jump in and get it. I don't want your money, Logan. I want you to leave."

I wasn't about to jump into her pool to retrieve it. She'd come to her senses eventually and realize it was a nice gesture. Maybe later, she'd even call to thank me.

Yeah, right.

"Fine." I put my wallet away and began to back up. "But don't say I didn't try."

"GO!" she bellowed, thrusting out her finger in the direction she wanted me to leave.

On my way back over to my house, I started to worry. That hadn't gone well. At all. And I only had the rest of the day to make things right with Emma before Rachel had a talk with my dad.

"Well?" Rachel called out as soon as she heard me step through the front door. I rounded the corner to see she was sitting on the living room floor playing with Abby. "How did it go?"

"Lousy," I said, plopping down on the couch and covering my face with my hands.

"What happened?"

"I explained everything to her. I apologized. I offered her a twenty-dollar refund for the test and she threw it in the pool."

Rachel gaped at me. "Are you kidding me? You robbed Emma of the chance of having a summer romance, then you stood her up, and you actually thought twenty dollars could possibly make up for all that?"

"What?" I said defensively. "You think I should have given her a fifty instead?"

She shook her head and laughed. "You're lucky that twenty-dollar bill was all she threw in the pool. I would have thrown *you* in right behind it." She glanced down at Abby, meeting her eye-to-eye, and said to her, "Abigail Reynolds, don't ever get yourself mixed up with boys, okay? They're not that bright, and they certainly aren't worth all the trouble they cause."

I rolled my eyes. "Look, money was my only option. Emma hates my guts—she hated them before I went over there, and now she hates them even more. I offered her an apology, she didn't accept it. I offered her money, she didn't take it. She wants nothing to do with me, so I can't offer her anything else. What do you expect me to do?"

Rachel picked herself and Abby up off the floor. "The same thing I expected earlier. I expect you to make it up to her." She walked past me toward the kitchen, calling out over her shoulder, "You have until the end of the day to come up with something. Otherwise, you might as well start packing."

My shoulders slumped forward in defeat. That wasn't an empty threat. I had less than twelve hours to come up with something and I'd have to make it good.

Chapter 6

EMMA

As I stormed up to my bedroom, taking two stairs at a time, the only thought that kept running through my head was, *I want to kill Logan Reynolds.*

Granted, this thought was nothing new, as I wanted to kill Logan Reynolds on a regular basis. Like every time he spoke, or every time he breathed. But this time was different. This time I wanted to make his death intimate. I wanted to see the life drain out of his cold, hazel eyes as I slowly but steadily tightened my hands around his neck. I wanted him to beg for mercy, only to have me laugh in his face and tell him, *"Sorry, I have no mercy left to give."* I wanted to be the last thing he saw before embarking on his journey of pitch black, eternal nothingness, and I wanted him to know that I was the one sending him packing.

It was bad enough he lied on that test. It was even worse that he didn't show up for our "date". But to try to hand me a twenty-dollar bill, as if that somehow made up for it all? The boy was an idiot. A heartless, arrogant moron. A douchebag of epic proportions.

And, not to mention, a spineless coward. Who goes to such great lengths to get their "sometimes-girlfriend" to break up with them? And doing it at the expense of somebody else, no less?

When I got to my room, I slammed the door behind me,

and let out a cry of frustration.

Immediately, I dialed Chloe.

"Hola, chica!" answered a voice that was not Chloe's, but Sophia's. In the background, I could hear loud music and laughing.

I couldn't help but feel a brief stab of jealousy in my gut. My two best friends were hundreds of miles away, having the time of their lives without me, while I was now stuck here all summer, pining after the romance that could have been but never would be.

"Hey, Soph," I said, throwing myself onto my bed. "Why are you answering Chloe's phone?"

She paused for a moment and giggled. "Oh gosh, this is Chloe's phone, isn't it? We must have switched again. Hey, Chloe!" Her voice was now muffled. "We switched phones again! Em's calling you!"

"So, what's up?" she said back into the phone.

"I found out who Number 7 was."

Sophia gasped and whispered, "She found out who Number 7 was!"

"Omigod, who was it?" I could hear Chloe ask in the background.

I scowled up at the ceiling. "Logan," I said through clenched teeth.

There was a long pause before Sophia said, "Logan who?"

"What do you mean, Logan who? Logan Reynolds."

"What?!" the two girls exclaimed in unison.

"How is that possible?" Chloe said. "You two are the least compatible people we've ever met."

I took a deep breath and told them the story about how Logan lied on the test and why. When I was done, they both sounded furious.

"What a jerk!" Sophia said. "That's low, even for Logan."

"Emma," Chloe chimed in, "you *need* to come down here. You've got nothing holding you back now."

"Not true," I said. "Remember? My book collection?"

"Screw your book collection, girl!" Sophia said. "Chloe's right! Get your butt down to Florida! We miss you. And besides, we met a group of three guys that are totally cute, and we've hung out with them a couple times. Chloe and I each have one picked out for ourselves, and the third boy, Max, would be perfect for you! He's sweet, kind of shy, a bit of a nerd, but in a hot way—"

"Let me stop you right there," I interjected. "Guys, I'm not coming down to Florida. I'd love to spend the summer with you two. I'd maybe even love to meet this Max guy. But it's not going to happen."

"Why not?" the girls asked in unison.

Because I'm terrified I'll die in a fiery plane crash. "Because I've got other things to do."

"Besides organizing your book collection, what other things do you have to do?" Chloe asked.

There was no good answer to that question, so I said, "Oh, my mom's calling to me. I've got to let you go. Talk to you later?"

"But—" both girls started to say, but I hung up before they could say any more.

I heard a soft knock on my door before it opened slightly. I sat up to see my mom poking her head in.

"Hey, sweetie. What was that all about? What did Logan want?"

"Nothing," I mumbled. I didn't feel like telling the story again, so I didn't.

"It didn't seem like nothing."

"He just came over to harass me, as usual," I said.

Mom furrowed her brow. "Harass you about what?"

"Nothing, okay?" I snapped, feeling immediately bad about it. "Sorry, Mom, he put me in a bad mood and I don't feel like talking about it right now."

She studied me before saying, "Okay. I won't pry." She paused for a moment. "Your dad and I are leaving in a bit to go see some old friends. You can come with us if you'd like."

"No thanks. I've got some things I wanted to do today." *Like murder Logan.*

"The library?" Mom guessed with a smile. She knew me so well.

I returned her smile with a nod. "Yes, the library."

"Well, have fun. We'll be back before dinner. Call us if you need anything."

I opened my mouth to tell her I would, but I was interrupted by my dad, who had suddenly appeared behind her.

"Hey, I found this twenty-dollar bill in the pool," he said, holding it up for us to see. He looked right at me. "Know anything about this?"

"Oh, yeah. I think that's mine." I walked over and grabbed it from him. "I was using it for a bookmark and the wind must have blown it away when I wasn't looking."

Dad rolled his eyes and shook his head. "Sweetie, you shouldn't be using money as a bookmark. If you need a new bookmark, I'll buy you one."

"Or, *she* can buy herself a new one with that twenty-dollar bill," Mom quipped, and Dad nodded in agreement.

"Okay, well you two enjoy yourselves," I said, ushering them out of my room once again. It seemed like I was having to do that on a daily basis now.

Once they were gone, I looked down at the soggy, chlorine-scented bill in my hand. It was dirty money. It was *Logan's* money. But it was still money nonetheless and it would buy me a few new bookmarks. Or at least a couple books at the used bookstore downtown. All I had to do was throw it in the dryer for a little while and it would be as good as new.

And after it was dry, I was going shopping.

Chapter 7

LOGAN

It only took me an hour to come up with a solution to my problem. A brilliant solution that would satisfy Rachel's requirements and maybe even make Emma hate me a little bit less:

I was going to find her a boyfriend. Somebody to have a summer fling with. It wasn't going to be easy, because I had no idea who this poor soul was going to be yet. I didn't know too many guys who were looking to hook up with boring, plain, bossy girls who spent their nights with their noses stuck in a book. But I would hire somebody if I had to. Anything that would get me out of that "family bonding" trip to New York with Little Miss Pukes-A-Lot.

The hardest part was going to be getting Emma to listen to my proposal—let alone agree to it. I was pretty sure I was the last person in the world she wanted to see right now, but I was on a tight schedule. I had to get this over with today or it was all over. Every plan I'd already made for the week Dad and Rachel were going away would have to be scratched, and I wasn't going to let that happen.

Not because of Emma Dawson.

My timing was perfect when I left the house to go see her. She had just exited her own house and was heading for her car. Quickly, I called out her name as I jogged over to her.

She glared at me as I approached. "Go away, Logan."

"Wait," I said, standing between her and the car to prevent her from getting in. "I want to talk to you about something."

"The two of us talking never ends well. You should know that by now."

"I do know that. But I wanted to apologize. For earlier. I was an insensitive prick and I'm sorry."

My apology seemed to throw her off-guard. She almost looked less irritated for a moment. She also seemed to be considering how to respond.

"Thanks," she said finally, but her voice was tight and unsure.

"And I want to make it up to you," I added.

She snorted. "What, do you have a fifty you want to give me or something?"

I perked up. "Would that do it?"

She looked up at me with a smirk. "No, that wouldn't do it. Logan, what you did was lousy. You've ruined my summer. No amount of money is going to make up for that."

"I know, I know. That's why I came up with a plan on how to *un*-ruin your summer."

I could tell that intrigued her. Folding her arms over her chest, she said, "Oh yeah? And what exactly is this plan of yours?"

"Well," I said, leaning against the side of the car. "I screwed you out of a summer romance, so I'm going to *give* you a summer romance."

A look of nausea washed briefly over her face as I realized what she must have been thinking. "Oh, God," I said, scrunching up my face. "I didn't mean with me."

The look of nausea was quickly replaced with one of relief. "Good. You scared me there for a second."

I refrained from making a snide comment about how she

could only be so lucky to have a summer romance with somebody like me, but I didn't want to get any further on her bad side than I already was.

"So, then what *did* you mean?"

I pushed myself off the car. "I mean, I'm going to help you get a boyfriend. Is there anyone you're interested in right now?"

The instantaneous blush on her cheeks indicated there was. Interesting. What nerd had managed to take Emma's attention away from a book long enough for her to develop a crush on him?

"No," she denied, but if her face hadn't given away her lie, her voice would have.

"Oh, come on. There had to have been at least one guy that you were secretly hoping would walk into Dream Bean holding a card with the number 7 on it."

There was. I could see it in her eyes. Shaking her head, she said, "Even if there was, there is no way I would tell you who it is. You can't be trusted. You—"

She was about to go on, but the next words out of her mouth were halted by the sound of a voice behind us.

"Hey, Logan!"

I turned to see my best friend, Matt Fisher, crossing the street and jogging toward us. Matt, in all his star quarterback glory. If he could wear his letterman jacket all summer long without passing out from heat exhaustion, he would. That's how much of a jock he was. He and I were opposites when it came to sports, in that he played them, and I didn't. But I didn't need to—at least, not to attract girls. And wasn't that the main reason why most guys in high school wanted to play sports?

"Hey, man," I said as he stopped in front of me and gave

me a fist-bump greeting. "What's up?"

"Not much," he said. He looked over at Emma and gave her a nod. "Hey, Emma."

Emma's mouth opened slightly, like she was going to maybe say hello back, but all that came out was a squeak.

She was so awkward, it was painful.

Matt didn't appear to notice. Turning back to me, he said, "I'm heading to the beach to meet the guys. I figured you could ride with me."

"Yeah," I said. I gestured over to Emma. "I just have to talk to Emma about something first. Give me a few minutes?"

"Sure," Matt said with a smile. He glanced at her and added, "You can come too if you'd like."

At that, Emma's face turned a shade of bright pink that I don't think had ever been witnessed on human skin before. What was her deal? Why was she blushing like a—

"Th-thanks," Emma stuttered, her voice barely audible. She stared down at the ground as she spoke.

He chuckled slightly, told me to meet him at his car when I was ready, and jogged back across the street.

When he was out of earshot, I gaped at Emma and said, "Oh my God."

Her face was already starting to revert to its normal color of pale white. "What?"

I couldn't help it—I laughed. Like, *really* laughed. To the point where I was practically doubled over.

"What's so funny?" she asked, and I knew immediately I had to calm down. She was angry, and I hadn't yet made amends with her. I would have to tread lightly here.

But my brain ignored that fact, and before I could stop myself, I said, "You have a total lady-boner for Matt!"

There was that otherworldly pink color again. Only this

time, it was brought on by rage, not lust. "A lady *what?*" When it dawned on her what I'd said, her face crumpled in disgust and she punched me in the arm. "You're disgusting, Logan. I do not have a *lady-boner* for Matt."

"No, you totally do," I said, finally calming down. Once the laughter had subsided, I chewed on my lower lip, deep in thought. *How the heck am I going to make this work?*

"Okay, um…" I started, rubbing the back of my neck with my hand. "This is a bigger challenge than I was expecting. I figured you probably had the hots for one of the band geeks or a chess club nerd—you know, somebody who's in your league. But…" My voice trailed off as I glanced over at Matt's house. "I think I'm up for the challenge."

"Challenge?" Emma echoed as she narrowed her eyes at me. "What are you talking about?"

"Emma Dawson," I said with a devious grin. "I'm going to get Matt Fisher to fall in love with you."

Her jaw dropped in shock. "You're going to *what?*"

I took a step closer to her. "You want a summer romance? I'm going to give you one with Matt, since he's the boy you think about every night while you drift off to sleep. It won't be easy, mind you. I mean, we're definitely going to have to make some improvements." I lowered my gaze down the length of her body and back up again. "A *lot* of improvements. Starting with your appearance."

"What's wrong with my appearance?" she asked defensively, tightening her arms across her chest.

I didn't have time to tell her all the things that were wrong with the way she looked; Matt was waiting for me. So instead, I said, "Don't worry, I have a plan for that as well. What do you say we meet tomorrow, at noon?"

I knew if I gave her time to respond, she would deny me. If

I walked away before she had time to protest, then she would spend the rest of the day thinking about it, until it finally started to sound like a good idea. So, I began to walk backward down her driveway. "By the end of the summer, you're going to be *thanking* me for lying on that test."

She looked like she was going to say something, but she didn't. I'd left her speechless.

I turned around and crossed the street toward Matt's house. I had no idea how I was going to pull this off. Sure, I could pay Matt to ask her out and pretend to be into her, but then I ran the risk of the truth coming out. And if the truth came out and Rachel caught wind of it, my life would be officially over until I left for college. She had a *lot* of influence over my dad.

No. I was going to have to find a way to do this for real. I was going to have to somehow get Matt—the good-looking, popular jock—to fall for Emma—the plain Jane bookworm—on his own, and before Dad and Rachel left for their trip in a couple weeks.

I had my work cut out for me, but it would be worth it in the end.

Chapter 8

EMMA

As I left my house at exactly twelve o'clock the next afternoon, I seriously began to question my sanity.

I hadn't told anybody—not Chloe, not Sophia, not Mom or Dad—about Logan's offer to set me up with Matt, because in all honesty, I had no idea what to think of it. Was he for real? If I knew only one thing in life, it was that Logan Reynolds could not be, under any circumstances, trusted. So why was I even contemplating taking him up on his offer?

Because I was still hopelessly in love with Matt, that's why.

Logan was right. As I sat there all alone at Dream Bean the other night, I was hoping Matt would walk in with the matching number 7 card. I knew it wasn't going to happen, but that didn't stop me from fantasizing about it.

There was no way a guy like Matt could ever fall for a girl like me—no matter how much Logan was able to "improve me". He was far from a miracle worker, and that was exactly what I was going to need if I wanted to attract Matt's attention.

But there I was, twelve o'clock on the dot, walking down the front walkway to meet Logan, who was already there and leaning against the side of my car. I had to admit I was impressed with his punctuality. He was usually late for everything.

"Good afternoon, sunshine," he said with a cocky grin. He glanced at me over the top of his shades. "Are you ready to head out?"

"Not so fast," I said, stopping a few feet away from him. "I don't even know what we're doing."

"Well, first we're going to go grab something to eat. Are you hungry?"

The slight grumbling in my stomach told me that I was. But there was no way I was going to go "grab something to eat" with him. Logan and I had never, in our entire lives, gone anywhere together, just the two of us. I could only imagine how disastrous such an event would be. We needed somebody there to play referee; somebody to stop us if our arguments got too heated.

I could tell he was sensing my hesitation, so he added, "It's on me."

That changed my tune. Wherever he took me, I'd order the most expensive thing on the menu that I could find.

"Fine. Whatever."

"Great." His cocky grin morphed into a more sincere one. "We'll go over everything while we eat."

Everything? That worried me. What, exactly, was I getting myself into?

"I'll drive," he said, pushing himself off my car and heading over in the direction of his driveway.

"No, we can drive separately," I said. There was no way I was getting into a car with him. I'd seen the way he drove. I wanted to at least live long enough to see if I had any sort of chance at all with Matt.

"Nonsense." He turned back around, came over to me, and grabbed my arm. "We'll go together."

"Hey," I protested, trying to remove my arm from his grasp. But my attempt was futile. The guy spent way too much time in the gym and I spent way too *little* for it to be an even match. So, I let him lead me over to his car. There was no use in fighting it.

Logan always got what Logan wanted.

I briefly contemplated yelling out, "Kidnap!" but the only people around to hear it would be my mom, and maybe one of the Fishers across the street, and none of them would believe I was actually being abducted.

The one thing—and I mean *only* thing—I liked about Logan was his car. A bright yellow Mustang with two black stripes running up the hood. It was safe to say that Mr. Reynolds spoiled Logan every chance he got, hence the car. From what I'd heard, it was a gift for applying—not getting *accepted into*, just *applying*—to Harvard. Apparently, Mr. Reynolds was so overjoyed by the knowledge his son wanted to follow in his footsteps that he took him out to the car dealer as soon as the application was sent.

"So, where are we going?" I asked as soon as we were in the car.

"Rodeo Roy's," he replied as the Mustang roared to life.

I groaned. I'd only been to Rodeo Roy's once in my life, and I'd hoped it would be the first and last time I ate there. The food wasn't bad, just standard steakhouse fare, but the atmosphere was annoying. For some reason, a lot of people who ate there felt the need to start acting like cowboys and cowgirls as soon as they stepped through the door, and they would spend their entire meals hooting and hollering—especially if their favorite country song started blasting over the speakers—and acting like a bunch of jackasses.

So, I wasn't surprised that Logan wanted to go there because he was the biggest jackass of them all.

"Do you have something against Rodeo Roy's?" Logan asked as he pulled out of the driveway. "You're not a vegetarian, are you?"

"No, I'm not." His question really drove home the fact that he knew nothing about me.

"Good, because they've got the best steaks there."

I glanced out the window and smirked. They had *expensive* steaks there, and he'd said the meal was on him.

"So," he said as we neared the end of our street. "What's new with you?"

I held up a hand. "Let me stop you right there, Logan. We don't need to engage in small talk, okay? In fact, I would prefer it if we didn't. It's too…weird."

He nodded in agreement. "No small talk. Got it. How about big talk? What made you decide to go along with this?"

"First of all," I said, "I don't even know what *'this'* is, so I don't even know if I'm going along with it yet. Second of all, why don't we wait until we're at the restaurant to talk?" *While the music is too loud for me to hear you.*

"Okay…" He drew out the word, and I could tell he was getting irritated. A tiny part of me felt bad for being so cold with him, but then the large part of me remembered why I was in his car in the first place: because he lied on that test.

So, we rode in complete silence the rest of the way to the restaurant, the car's engine providing the only soundtrack to our awkward ride.

When we arrived at Rodeo Roy's, the parking lot was so packed that we literally got the last available parking space. Groups of people were hanging around outside, holding onto those round pagers that light up when your table is ready.

"Uh-oh," I said with fake disappointment. "Looks like there'll be too long of a wait. Maybe we should go somewhere else."

"Don't have to," he said with a lopsided grin. "I called ahead and reserved us a table. They're ready for us."

He'd made reservations at Rodeo Roy's? Classy.

"Awesome," I mumbled under my breath.

We exited the car and made our way through the crowd of people standing near the door. When we stepped inside, we were immediately greeted by the hostess—a tanned brunette who was wearing cowboy boots, a cowboy hat, short jean shorts and a white blouse that had been buttoned halfway down to expose her ample cleavage, and tied into a knot at her waist to expose her bare midriff.

It didn't take a genius to figure out why Logan wanted to eat there. Judging from the recognition on the young woman's face, he was a frequent patron.

"Logan!" she exclaimed. She flashed him a charming smile, which faltered slightly as her gaze flickered over to me. She sized me up briefly—long enough to make me feel incredibly insecure about myself—and then turned back to Logan. "Your table is all ready, if you'd like to follow me."

Oh, I had no doubt he wanted to follow her. I could tell by the way he stared at her butt the whole way to our table. I rolled my eyes and shook my head as she motioned to our booth.

She set our menus down in front of us as we sat down. "Your server will be right with you," she said, winking at Logan.

"Thanks, Brandy," he said with a bit of a drawl. Why wasn't I surprised that he knew her name?

I groaned inwardly as I watched him watch her walk away.

"Come here often?" I opened my menu and started looking for the highest price tag I could find.

"I've been here a few times," he replied, looking at his own menu.

"I'm sure you have," I said as a carbon copy of the hostess

made an appearance at our table.

"Hey, y'all! Welcome to Rodeo Roy's!" the waitress said, placing a couple sets of napkin-wrapped silverware in front of us. She was wearing the same outfit as our hostess, but didn't fill it out quite as well. She also looked older, like in her late-twenties instead of early-twenties. "My name is Brittany and I'll be your server today. Can I start you off with something to drink?"

"Yeah, I'll take a Coke," Logan replied.

I glanced over the beverages section. I couldn't do much damage there without ordering alcohol, but there was a pricey strawberry lemonade that came with actual chunks of strawberries in it. "This strawberry lemonade, does that come with free refills?"

"I'm afraid not," she said with a sympathetic pout.

I pretended to mull it over for a moment before shrugging and saying, "That's okay. I'll just order another one if needed."

"Okie dokie!" Brittany said cheerfully. "I'll go grab those for you and give you two a couple minutes to look over the menu!"

Logan and I didn't talk while we looked over our menus. By the time Brittany came back with our drinks, we were ready to order.

"What can I get for y'all?" she asked, holding up her tiny notepad.

Logan nodded over to me. "Ladies first."

I turned my head to glance up at Brittany. "I'll have the Royal Rodeo Cheeseburger." It was hardly the most expensive thing on the menu—in fact, it was one of the cheaper entrée options—but after contemplating the thirty-dollar steak and lobster combo, I realized I was craving a burger. I'd have to financially screw over Logan another time.

"That sounds good," Logan said. "I'll have the same thing." He grabbed my menu, combined it with his, and handed them both to Brittany.

"Sure, I'll put that right in for you!" she said before strutting away.

Once she was gone, Logan leaned back and took a sip of his Coke. "Okay, down to business."

This was going to be good. Leaning back myself, I said, "Yeah, about this 'business'. What exactly are you proposing here?"

"Exactly what I said to you yesterday: I'm going to get Matt to fall in love with you."

"And how do you plan to do that?"

His finger traced the rim of his glass as he contemplated his answer. "I've been giving it a lot of thought since yesterday and I've come up with a few ideas."

"Like what?"

"Like, for starters, we have *got* to do something about your wardrobe."

I glanced down at myself. I was wearing a pair of flare jeans and a gray t-shirt that said, "BOOK NERD", where every straight vertical line of each letter was the spine of a book. I thought it was clever. "What's wrong with my wardrobe?"

"Honestly, *nothing*…if you weren't trying to attract the attention of Matt Fisher. Which, by the way, is confusing to me. What about him makes you so hot and bothered? It can't just be his good looks because *I'm* good-looking too and you *hate* me."

I couldn't stop myself from blushing. I didn't want to talk about why I liked Matt so much, especially with Logan. Partly because I had no idea why I liked him. Yeah, he was extremely good-looking, but I didn't know the guy. We'd lived across the street from each other for years and we'd never had a conversation with each other about anything. I didn't even know if he was nice, or funny, or smart. I didn't know what his hobbies were, or if he even had any. He could have been a serial killer for all I knew, but it never mattered. I always had a crush on him and I'd never thought to ask myself *why*.

As if sensing he wasn't going to get an answer out of me, Logan moved on. "Anyway, that doesn't matter. What does matter is that I know exactly what kind of girl Matt Fisher likes, and no offense, that girl isn't you. At least, not the way you are right now."

I took full offense to that. "What do you mean, the way I am right now?"

Logan gave a slight shrug. "You know how you are, Emma. Do I need to spell it out for you? You don't dress up, you don't wear makeup, you don't ever do anything with your hair. And that's just the outside. Let's talk about your personality."

I glared over at him. "What's wrong with my personality?"

He chuckled softly. "Where do I begin? You're too shy and quiet. Too reserved. You give off the impression that you hate everybody."

"I do, mostly," I grumbled.

"See? That kind of attitude is a turn-off to guys. Especially guys like Matt. Matt likes carefree, bubbly girls who want to have fun. Girls who aren't afraid of their own shadow."

"I'm not afraid of my own—"

"You need to loosen up a little," he continued, interrupting my interjection. "But have no fear, that's where I come in. I'm going to teach you how to get a life."

"Hey," I said defensively. "I have a life!"

"Oh really? You let your two best friends go to Florida for the summer without you, while you stayed home to organize your book collection."

I sighed. Yet another person who didn't understand the importance of organizing a book collection. Still, maybe the jerk had a point.

"So, what you're basically telling me is that to get a guy like Matt to fall for a girl like me, I'm going to have to change everything about myself?"

Logan nodded. "Exactly."

"Then I'm out," I said simply, throwing my hands up in defeat. "I like Matt, but not enough to change who I am. I'm not bubbly or carefree, and I can't pretend to be. I don't like to wear makeup or revealing clothing, and yeah, sometimes, maybe I am afraid of my own shadow, but only in certain light when I'm home alone, and only for like one split second because I scare myself into thinking that somebody's broken into the house and it's *their* shadow. Perfectly normal."

Logan stared at me in awe for a moment before breaking out into a smile. "Wow, Emma, that's messed up. The whole shadow thing was just a figure of speech."

I could feel my face burning bright red.

"Look," he said, leaning forward, "You want to know what I think?"

"Not really."

"Well too bad, I'm going to tell you anyway. I think, deep down inside you, there's a wild and crazy girl waiting to spread her wings and fly. I think you've spent your whole life so wrapped up in the lives of all the characters in the books on your shelf that you forgot to have a life of your own. And I think, if you tried having some fun once in a while, you might find you enjoy it."

It was my turn to stare at him in awe. He thought he knew me so well, did he? He didn't know me at all. And I was about to tell him that when Brittany returned to our table with our food.

"Two Royal Rodeo Cheeseburgers," she said, setting down the plates in front of us. "Can I get you guys anything else?"

Yes. A doggy bag so I could take my food and get as far away as possible from the guy sitting across from me.

"No, thanks, I think we're all set," Logan replied with a flirtatious smile. Brittany returned in kind before walking away.

"You should be more like Brittany," Logan said, before taking a gigantic bite of his burger.

I briefly fantasized about him choking on it.

Ignoring his comment, I took a bite of my own burger. For a few short moments, we ate in blissful silence (save for the obnoxiously loud country music playing over the speakers) before Logan spoke again.

"So, what do you say? Are you in?"

I shook my head as I stuffed a fry into my mouth. "Nope. No deal."

"Oh, come on. Give me a week. If you're not starting to see some results, then you can give up."

I eyed him suspiciously. "Why are you so interested in helping me with this?"

"Because," he said. "Even though it wasn't intentional, I feel bad about ruining your summer, and I want to make it up to you. That's all."

There was more to the story, I could tell. But this was the lie Logan had decided to go with, so he was going to stick to it, no matter how hard I tried to pry the truth out of him.

But he did ruin my summer—intentionally or not—and he deserved to have to put in a little hard work to make things right. And trying to get Matt Fisher to fall for me? That was going to be a lot of hard work.

"Okay, fine," I said with a sigh.

Logan's face lit up and the corners of his mouth turned upward into a genuine smile. "Great. We'll start right away. After we're done eating, we're going to the mall."

Ugh, the mall? I took another bite of my burger. I was already regretting this decision.

Chapter 9

LOGAN

She did it. Emma agreed to go along with my plan. It was a miracle.

It was also a miracle that we'd made it through an entire meal together, *alone*, without killing each other. Now we'd have to make it through our shopping trip without killing each other, which was probably going to be difficult as soon as I began pointing out the type of clothes Emma would have to start wearing to attract Matt's attention.

It was safe to say she was not going to like it.

We entered a boutique I'd unfortunately been in many times in the last year. It was Grace's favorite store, and she often liked to drag me in there and make me stand around waiting for her while she tried on fifty different outfits, only to leave empty-handed most of the time. That was a typical Saturday afternoon for us.

As soon as Emma and I walked in, the girls behind the front registers stopped whatever conversation they were having and made a beeline for us. Or, more accurately, for me.

"Hello, welcome to Ashley's Boutique!" The two girls spoke at the exact same time, a fact neither apparently liked very much, judging from the glares they shot at each other.

The brunette girl quickly stood in front of the redhead and smiled brightly up at me. "Please let me know if there is anything I can help you with."

"Or me," the redhead chimed in, nudging the other girl out of the way.

"Thanks," I said, holding back a snort. We were in a clothing store for women, yet these girls were speaking directly to me instead of Emma. What could they possibly help *me* with?

Emma smirked and shook her head as we walked away. "Seriously?"

"What?" I asked.

"Is there anywhere we can go where girls don't throw themselves at you?"

I thought about it for a moment. "A gay bar, maybe?" I paused for a moment before adding, "But then it would be guys throwing themselves at me."

She laughed, but I detected no humor in her reaction. "Unbelievable."

I sighed as I mistakenly asked, "What?" again.

Emma ran her hand down the length of a floral sundress on the rack in front of her. It was a similar style to the blue one she'd worn the other night. "Nothing," she muttered. She cleared her throat and said, "So what are we looking for here, exactly?"

"Clothes," I replied, glad that she wanted to change the subject. "Low-cut, form-fitting. Something that will showcase your...*assets*."

Emma blushed and I think she knew exactly what I was referring to. If there was one thing that could be said about Emma—and one thing that would work to her advantage with the whole Matt thing—it was that the girl had a decent body. Granted, it was hard to see it beneath all the layers of loose-fitting clothing she liked to wear on any given day, but I knew it was there. That sundress she'd worn the other night had proven it.

But that was why we were shopping for a new wardrobe. Matt was more of a boob guy, and Emma had more going on around the back, but I could work with that. Matt was still a hot-blooded male and at the end of the day he would take what he could get.

"Okay, then…start picking stuff out," she said.

"Huh?"

"I don't know what kind of clothes Matt likes to see on girls. You claim you do, so go start picking stuff out for me to try on."

"Um…" I glanced at our surroundings. Ashley's Boutique was a small store, but it was filled with so many racks of clothing it was hard to even walk around. I guess I hadn't thought this part of the plan through.

"Well?" Emma said, hands on hips, tapping her foot against the tiled floor.

She was getting impatient, so I had to act fast. Luckily, thanks to Grace, I knew the layout of the place like the back of my hand. I knew where all the good stuff was, so I started going over to every rack and pointing to what I knew Matt would like. Emma picked out her size for each one and within three minutes she was holding onto an armful of clothing to try on.

"See? That wasn't so terrible, was it?"

Emma glanced down at my choices. "Actually, I—"

"Hold that thought," I interrupted. I waved to the brunette who'd greeted us when we walked in. "She'd like to try these on," I said, motioning to Emma.

"Absolutely," the brunette said with a big smile, once again directed at me, not Emma. She grabbed the set of keys she had dangling from the lanyard around her neck. "Follow me."

We followed her to the back of the store where the dressing rooms were. "How many items do you have?"

Emma glanced down at the pile of clothes in her arm and counted. "Six."

The girl went and grabbed a tag with the number 6 on it, unlocked one of the dressing room doors, and hung the tag on the doorknob. "There you go!" she said to Emma. She turned to me with a wink before walking off, purposely swaying her hips from side to side in hopes that I was looking.

I was.

Emma groaned behind me. "Can we just get this over with, please?"

I returned my attention to her. "Yes. Get in there and start trying things on. But I want you to show me everything as you go, so I can help you decide what to get. Just because it looks good on the rack, that doesn't mean it's going to look good on you."

Honestly, I didn't mean that to come out sounding as much of an insult as it did, but Emma took it the wrong way. With a huff, she stepped inside the dressing room and slammed the door shut.

"I'll be waiting right here," I informed her, but I was met with total silence.

I stood there for a moment and glanced around the store. One good thing that could be said about Emma was that she wasn't into this scene. She seemed like the type of girl who would go to the nearest department store, blindly grab clothes off the rack, and bring them to the nearest register without even trying them on. That would explain why her outfits sometimes looked mismatched and why a lot of her shirts were too big for her. The girl obviously didn't care about how she looked.

I was about to turn back around to face the dressing rooms when I caught something—or, rather, some*one*—out of the corner of my eye that instantly filled me with fear and dread.

Grace. She had just walked in with a few of her friends.

Muttering a few swears under my breath, I turned so that she wouldn't be able to see my face. This was bad. I couldn't let Grace see me at her favorite clothing store—and with another girl no less. Especially after I'd been avoiding her calls and texts for the last couple of days. This would no doubt end badly for me.

"Um, Emma," I said quietly through the dressing room door. "Are you almost done?"

"Are you rushing me?" Emma asked, sounding irritated.

Yes, I was rushing her. Because this was a small store, and there was nowhere for me to hide from Grace. I needed to disappear, and fast. I had maybe a few seconds before her gaze fell upon me and all hell broke loose.

"Emma, open up," I said, my voice low. "Please. It's an emergency."

"A what?" She opened the door. She was wearing the floral sundress she'd been admiring earlier.

As soon as the door was open, I grabbed her shoulders and gently nudged her into the back of the tiny dressing room and shut the door behind us.

She gasped. "Logan! What the hell are you doing?"

"*Shh,*" I hissed, placing a finger against her lips to indicate I wanted her to shut up. She quickly—and quite angrily—swatted it away.

"You can't be in here!" she whispered frantically. "*Why* are you in here?"

"Grace is out there," I whispered back.

Emma's face twisted into an expression full of annoyance. "You're hiding from your girlfriend? Why would you be hiding from your girlfriend?" She paused. "Sorry—*sometimes-*

girlfriend."

I smirked. She was finally learning. "Because," I said, "we got into a big fight the other night and I've been sort of ignoring all her calls and texts since then. I don't even know if she's my girlfriend right now, but what I do know is that if she sees me here without her—and with another girl—I'm a dead man. And trust me, you won't want to deal with her wrath either."

Emma bit her bottom lip as she glanced in the direction of the dressing room door. She knew I was right. While she and Grace had probably never spoken one word to each other, I was sure she was aware of Grace's reputation.

"Please, let me hang out in here for a little while?" The request was ludicrous, but I had no other option.

She seemed to be considering it, although I could tell she wanted to murder me. So, to get her to agree, I decided to sweeten the deal.

"If you let me stay in here until Grace leaves, we'll call it a day on the clothes shopping after we leave here, and I'll take you to the bookstore next door and let you spend as much time there as you'd like. What do you say?"

Her face lit up at the suggestion and I couldn't help but smile. Apparently, the way to Emma's heart was through her reading glasses.

"Okay, fine," she said finally. "But how long are we going to have stay in here?"

"It could be a while," I admitted. "This is her favorite store."

Emma face-palmed. "I'm not sure even a trip to the bookstore is worth putting up with you in a small enclosed space for an undisclosed amount of time."

"Boy, you sure know how to flatter a guy," I said dryly, taking a seat on the bench in front of the mirror. "Feel free to keep trying stuff on."

Her jaw dropped slightly. "No way am I undressing in front of *you*."

"Don't worry, Emma, I have no desire to see any of your bits and pieces. I'll close my eyes and turn around." I stopped for a moment as I took in her appearance. The dress she'd already tried on looked good on her. Like, *really* good. It was much shorter than the blue one she'd worn the other night, with the hem coming down to only mid-thigh, and the fabric clung to her every curve, revealing a respectable hourglass figure I didn't know she had.

Paired with the right hair style and some makeup, this dress could most certainly grab Matt's attention.

"You need to buy that dress," I said matter-of-factly.

"Yeah?" She looked at herself in the mirror. "You think so?"

I nodded. "I *know* so. Matt would love this."

She smiled as she turned slightly to see as much as she could from the back. "It's actually kind of cute."

"See? This isn't so bad, is it? I know what I'm doing."

She shook her head. "*I'm* the one who picked this dress out, not you."

"But I approved it, so I should be able to at least take half-credit for it."

Emma rolled her eyes. "Sure. Whatever. Now get up and turn around so I can try on something else."

I was surprised she was going along with this so willingly, and that she trusted me to stay turned around while she undressed. Truth be told, while I wasn't actively seeking out a glimpse of her 'bits and pieces', I also wouldn't turn down the opportunity if it was presented to me. She was, after all, a girl, and I was, after all, a guy. And it wasn't like she was grotesque or anything.

She just wasn't my type.

Standing up from the bench, I turned around to face the wall. I could hear the rustling of clothing behind me as she removed the dress, and I had to make sure to think about something else—anything else—to prevent me from thinking impure thoughts. Impure thoughts like how, if I were in this situation with any other girl besides Emma right now, things would be going a little bit differently—such as, she'd be taking off the dress, but she wouldn't be putting anything else back on for a while.

Luckily, Emma was a fast dresser. In less than thirty seconds, she said, "Okay, you can turn around."

The next outfit she'd chosen to try on was a white halter top that left an inch or two of her abdomen exposed above the pair of *very* short jean shorts I'd picked out. Once again, I hated to admit she looked good. Like her dress the other night, the shorts really showcased those long legs…

"Well? What do you think?" She spun around for me.

"Um," I said, clearing my throat. Those shorts looked even better from the back. And with that realization, I suddenly wanted out of that dressing room.

"Looks fine," I said, running a hand through my hair. "Hey, could you peek out and see if Grace is still out there? I'm getting kind of claustrophobic in here."

She gave me a funny look before saying, "Gladly." She cracked open the door and peered out. "Looks like you're in luck. Grace has left the building."

"Thank God," I breathed. "I'm gonna go wait for you outside the store. I think you can handle it from here. Get the dress, get that outfit, get whatever else you think looks good."

"Okay…" Emma tilted her head to one side and glanced at

me curiously. "I'll meet you out there in a few minutes?"

"Yeah, sure, okay." I glanced out the crack in the door myself to make sure the coast was clear before exiting. "Bye."

She opened her mouth to probably say goodbye back, but as soon as I was out of the dressing room, I bolted for the exit before I could hear her.

Well, at least I could say I learned something from our little adventure: Emma looked damn good in normal teenage girl clothes. And if *I* could think that, *Matt* could, too.

Maybe this wasn't going to be as hard as I thought.

Chapter 10

EMMA

I grabbed a random book off the shelf and brought it to my nose, breathing in its glorious scent. The jerk leaning against the shelf beside me stared at me like I'd sprouted a third eye.

"Did you just *smell* that book?"

I placed the hardcover novel back on the shelf. Yes. I sniff books. It's a weird quirk of mine. I don't even realize I'm doing it half the time—which is how I happened to do it in front of Logan, who undoubtedly was about to give me a hard time for it.

"Yeah, so what?"

He smiled and shook his head. "You are such a weirdo."

I turned to face him. "Am I? Tell me, do you like the smell of gasoline? Burning rubber?"

Logan rolled his eyes. He knew where I was going with this.

"Of course, you do," I answered for him. "Because you love cars. Well, I love books, so I love the smell of paper and ink. Nothing weird about it."

He dragged a hand down his face before taking his phone out of his pocket and checking the time. "Good God, woman, we've been in this bookstore for nearly an hour now."

"Hey, you told me we could stay here for as long as I'd like."

"Within reason."

"You didn't disclose that part."

"I didn't think I had to. It was implied."

I glanced down at my own phone to look at the time. He was right, we'd been there for almost an hour. I could've stayed there for another hour or two, but I didn't want to spend any more time with Logan than I had to, so I figured now would be a good time to call it a day.

"Okay, we can leave," I said in defeat.

His gaze flickered to my empty hands. "You're not getting anything?"

"Nah," I said with a shrug. "Nothing spoke to me."

"You probably mean that literally, don't you?" Logan smirked and leaned in close. Staring me straight in the eyes, he said in a soft, mock-concerned voice, "Do your books talk to you, Emma?"

I reached out to shove him away, but he was too quick; he grabbed both my wrists before my hands could make contact with his shoulders and backed away on his own.

"Play nice," he warned with a lazy smile.

I scowled as I broke my wrists free from his grasp. "Remind me again why I decided to go along with this idea of yours?"

"Because you're in love with *Matt*," he replied in a singsong voice.

"Shut *up*!" I hissed, punching him in the arm and instantly regretting it. Dude had some serious muscles going on in the triceps area, and I'm sure I hurt myself way more than I hurt him.

Logan laughed. "Don't worry, nobody heard. Look around, Emma. Nobody from school is here. It's summer vacation— they're at the beach, they're having pool parties. You're the only loser choosing to spend a beautiful Sunday afternoon inside a bookstore instead of spending it outside with friends, enjoying the nice fresh air…getting a little color, which you could desperately benefit from."

I threw him a glare as we began making our way toward the exit. "You mean I could desperately benefit from a bout of skin cancer?"

He gave me an incredulous look. "Are you kidding me? Emma, you've got some serious issues."

"I never said I didn't," I mumbled as we left the store.

Logan led me over to a bench outside the bookstore and took a seat. He motioned for me to join him.

"So," he said, "I've come up with a list of things for us to do."

"A list?" I said curiously. "Of things for *us* to do? What are you talking about?"

"I'm talking about the fact that if you want to have any chance with Matt at all, we're going to have to get you out of this shell you've been hiding in for nearly eighteen years now." He turned on his phone and tapped the screen. "And doing that is going to require that you step out of your comfort zone and do some things you don't normally do. Starting tonight."

I blinked at him. "What's tonight?"

"We're going to a party."

I blinked again. "*We?*"

"Yeah. *We.*"

"We're going to a *party?*"

Logan sighed like he was already tired of this exchange. "Yes. *We* are going to a *party.*"

I shook my head adamantly. "No. No way. I'm not going to a party. Especially not with you."

Logan pinched the bridge of his nose and I reveled in the thought I might be giving him a headache. "Emma, do you want to get Matt to fall for you, or what? He likes parties. He likes girls who like parties. He's going to be there tonight. This is kind of a no-brainer."

He was right, of course, but I hated parties. Detested them. They were just an excuse for kids to get loud and drunk and grope each other. I shuddered at the thought of having to attend one.

"What else is on your list?" I inquired, leaning closer to him to try and see the screen on his phone.

He was quick to jerk it away. "Sorry, you're going to have to wait. You'll find out each one right before we do it. That way, you won't have time to overthink things and back out."

"But you're giving me plenty of time to back out of going to the party, if it's not until tonight," I pointed out.

He thought about it for a moment. "True. But you're not going to back out."

I raised an eyebrow. "Oh yeah? And what makes you so sure?"

He gave me a lopsided grin. "The fact I'm not going to let you back out. You bought a couple of hot outfits I know for sure will grab Matt's attention. And I also know, deep down, you're curious. You've never been to a high school party before, have you?"

The answer to that question was obvious, so I didn't even bother to respond.

"I figured. So, here's what we're going to do. You're going to put on those shorts and that white top you bought earlier, I'm going to knock on your door tonight at seven o'clock sharp, and you're going to answer it. We're going to get into my car, and we're going to that party. End of discussion."

I opened my mouth to protest, but he didn't want to hear it. "End. Of. Discussion," he repeated, with a little more emphasis this time. He stood from the bench and motioned for me to follow.

Our little afternoon excursion was over, and it was now time to prepare for our evening one.

I was going to a party. With Logan Reynolds.

I must have been more desperate than I thought.

***

"I'm sorry, you're going *where* with *whom*?" Chloe asked me through the screen of my laptop. She, Sophia and I were once again video chatting while I got ready for the party.

She'd heard me just fine, but I repeated myself anyway. "I'm going to a *party* with *Logan.*"

I was inside my closet, changing into the clothes I'd bought earlier, so I didn't get to see the girls' faces when I told them the news. Instead, I got to listen to the stunned silence that made me briefly wonder if our connection had been cut off.

"You guys still there?" I called out as I pulled the white halter top over my head, completing the outfit.

"Yeah," Sophia answered. "We're just…not sure we heard you correctly. Either time."

I stepped out of the closet and into the view of the laptop. As soon as Sophia and Chloe saw me, they both gasped.

"Holy bananas, Em," Chloe said. "What are you wearing?"

Glancing down at myself subconsciously, I said, "What's wrong with what I'm wearing?"

"Are you planning on Logan getting you *pregnant* at this party?" Sophia joked, a mischievous grin forming on her face.

My jaw dropped at her question, as the thought of ever doing anything with Logan that could lead to me getting pregnant suddenly made me want to hurl.

"What the hell is wrong with you, Soph?"

Chloe giggled. "It's a fair question, Em. You look hella hot in that outfit. If those shorts were any shorter, they could pass for denim panties."

I saw Sophia cringe. "Chloe, you know how I feel about that word."

Chloe turned to Sophia and said directly into her ear, "Panties. Panties. Panties. Panti—"

Sophia placed a hand over Chloe's face and shoved her out of view of the webcam. "Seriously, Em, what's up with that outfit, anyway? And how did you end up getting invited to go to a party with Logan?"

I hadn't told the girls yet about Logan's offer to help me get a boyfriend—specifically Matt—and I still wasn't sure I wanted to. "It's kind of a long story," I said, pulling my hair back into a loose ponytail and tying it with an elastic. "I'll fill you guys in later, I promise. Logan's going to be here any minute."

"No," Chloe said. "Emma, you can't leave us in suspense like this!"

"Sorry, guys! Got to go! Love you!" I blew them a kiss and disconnected before they could say another word.

I glanced at the alarm clock next to my bed. I had about five minutes before Logan claimed he would be there to pick me up, which meant I probably had closer to twenty to finish getting ready. I figured I would use that time to attempt to put on some makeup.

I wasn't going to do what Chloe and Sophia referred to as "the works", which included concealers, toners, foundations and blushes (to be honest, I didn't pay a whole lot of attention to that lesson), and instead decided to go with just eyeliner, eyeshadow and mascara—the "eye trifecta", as the girls often liked to call it.

In less than five minutes, I managed to apply the eyeliner, the shadow, and the mascara. I was pleasantly surprised at the outcome. The makeup made me look older, more mature. Maybe even borderline *sexy*. The smoky eyes look was the only one I knew how to do because that's the one Chloe and Sophia had taught me. But it was the only one I needed to know because it looked awesome.

As soon as I stepped out of the bathroom, I heard a knock at the front door. Pulling my phone out of my back pocket, I checked the time. He was only two minutes late.

Impressive.

"I'll get it!" I called out to my parents as I ran down the stairs and threw open the door.

As expected, Logan was standing on the other side, and also as expected, he looked good. Not that it was a surprise. Logan *always* looked good. I may have hated him, but even *I* couldn't dispute that fact. He was wearing a pair of faded light blue jeans and a black Pink Floyd graphic tee that clung nicely to the muscles in his chest and upper arms. His slightly wavy hair was a bit unruly, like he'd just run his hands through it a couple of times to intentionally mess it up.

It had probably taken him less than a minute to get ready, yet he looked like a walking Abercrombie & Fitch advertisement. Why did guys have it so easy?

His eyes widened when I opened the door. He let his gaze slowly travel down the length of my body, lingering on certain areas as he brought his eyes back up to meet with mine. "Whoa, Dawson. Not bad. It actually looks like you put some effort into this."

My own eyes narrowed into a glare. "Thanks. I'll take that as a compliment, since I'm sure that's the best you can do."

Logan gave me a smirk, but quickly morphed it into a sincere smile when he saw my dad walk up behind me.

"Mr. Dawson," he said brightly. Pleasantly. "Hello, sir, how are you?"

My dad shook his head. "Logan, how many times do we have to go over this? Start calling me Jake and *stop* calling me 'sir'. It makes me feel old." He shuddered.

"Sorry, Jake," Logan said with a grin. I couldn't believe how different he was around my parents than he was around me. It was safe to say Logan adored them as much as they adored him—the unfortunate downside to our dads having been engaged in a lifelong bromance.

I, however, was no different around Logan's dad, and even his stepmother, Rachel. Mr. Reynolds—or *Mark*, as he liked me to call him—had always been like a second father to me. And technically, I guess he sort of was, since he was listed as one of my godparents. It was too bad Logan and I didn't get along, or we'd all be one big, happy family.

"So," Dad said, glancing between me and Logan. "You're going to a party together, huh? I didn't realize you two were friends."

"We're not," Logan and I said at the same time.

We stared at each other, wide-eyed. "Jinx!" we also both said at the same time, after which we proceeded to glare at each other.

Dad chuckled softly. "Ah, you two and your jinxing. Brings back memories of when you were little. You guys used to end up in simultaneous jinxes all the time and it was always so nice to have that reprieve from your constant bickering."

Logan and I both turned to my dad with pleading eyes. It was childish, but apparently Logan and I still took jinxes very seriously. Dad was right. When Logan and I were kids, we used to somehow manage to jinx each other quite often and nobody would say our names for what seemed like forever. I guess now we knew they'd done that on purpose.

And while I loved the idea of never having to hear Logan speak again, I wanted to be able to talk again at some point. *If only I could telepathically ask my father to say* my *name and not* Logan's…

"*Emma, Logan,*" Dad said finally, a look of pure amusement on his face, "you are both unjinxed."

At our release, Logan and I both breathed a sigh of relief at the same time and exchanged a wary glance, as if wondering whether simultaneous sighing was a jinxable offense. With a simultaneous shrug, we silently concluded it was not.

"Logan's…helping me with something," I explained, hoping my father wouldn't press me for specific details.

"At a party?" Dad asked, looking confused. He glanced down at me with a slight frown as he seemed to suddenly take notice of my appearance. "Emma, sweetie, are you going to be warm enough?" This was Dad-speak that loosely translated into, *"I see what you're wearing is quite revealing, but I feel uncomfortable approaching the issue, so I'm going to find a subtle way of making you put more clothes on without coming out and asking you to."*

"Dad, it's still nearly eighty degrees out. I think I'll be fine." To make him feel better, though, I added, "But I'll go grab a hoodie, just in case."

"Great idea, honey," he said with a smile.

I quickly ran upstairs and grabbed the hoodie I knew he'd approve of the most: an over-sized navy-blue zip-up that came down past my shorts.

When I made it back to the foyer with the hoodie in hand, Dad and Logan were so busy laughing about something, neither one had noticed my return.

"What's so funny?" I asked.

Dad slapped Logan on the back and said, "Oh, nothing. You two have fun tonight."

I didn't like how chummy they were acting with each other, so I quickly ushered Logan out of the house, saying goodbye to my father as he closed the door behind us.

"It must pay to be a goody-goody," Logan said as he led me to his car. Surprisingly, he opened the door for me like a gentleman would.

"Why do you say that?" I asked, mentally slapping myself for not giving him crap for calling me a 'goody-goody'.

"Well, for one, your father is letting you leave the house looking like *that*." He motioned to my outfit. "And he's letting you go to a *party*. With a guy you're not even friends with."

"He trusts me."

"I know. He trusts you because he knows his precious little girl would never do anything wrong or inappropriate." He placed a hand on the top edge of the passenger door and leaned in close—too close for my comfort; his face was only a few inches from mine. "Well, tonight, we're going to break that trust."

A small smirk began to form on his face as I gaped at him. I did not like the sound of that. At all.

I knew I was making a huge mistake by going to this party with Logan, but I got in the car anyway. And I did so because…well, because I was tired of being thought of as a 'goody-goody'. I was tired of sitting home alone while my friends had the time of their lives in Florida.

Maybe Logan was right. I needed to start living a little.

Chapter 11

LOGAN

Parties. I wasn't a big fan of them. I knew Emma wasn't either, which was why I chose to bring her to one. I knew she would feel uncomfortable, awkward and out-of-place, and that's exactly how I wanted her to feel. Not only because I experienced great pleasure in watching her squirm, but also because I wanted to toughen her up a little bit.

As soon as we walked in, I saw her tense up and freeze in place, like a deer caught in headlights.

This was going to be fun.

I hadn't shown Emma the list on my phone earlier, because so far, the only thing on that list was this party. I figured I would wait and see how things went before bothering to come up with anything else. I had to know for sure that she was going to be able to step out of her comfort zone without having some sort of monumental panic attack or something.

Absent-mindedly, I reached out my hand and placed it on the small of her back. My sudden touch made her jump.

She turned to look at me and for a split second, I regretted bringing her. She looked almost…scared. Fragile. If we were friends, I would have wrapped my arms around her and pulled her close and whispered into her hair that everything was going to be okay.

But we weren't. So, I didn't.

"Hey," I said, leaning in closer so she could hear me over

the music. "There's no need to freak out, alright? This is just a party with a bunch of kids you go to school with. No big deal."

She gave me a look that clearly said, *"Yeah, right."*

"So, what's the plan?" she asked, glancing nervously around.

"The plan," I replied, "is we stay here for a little while. I bring you around to a few people—specifically Matt and his friends—and then we can leave."

Her eyes widened. "Matt? You're going to bring me to Matt?"

"Yes, I'm going to bring you to Matt. Why *wouldn't* I bring you to Matt? He's the reason we're here."

"But I'm not ready for that," she said softly.

I threw her a curious look. "You're not ready for what? To talk to him? I hate to tell you, Emma, but when you start dating him, you're going to have to talk to him."

Emma narrowed her eyes at me. "*When* I start dating him? That's a little presumptuous, don't you think?"

"Not at all. I know what I'm doing."

She shook her head in disagreement as we began to make our way through the crowd. I grabbed her hand so I wouldn't lose track of her and she immediately yanked it away. Okay, apparently, she didn't like to be touched. That would be another thing we'd have to work on.

I was scanning the living room looking for Matt when a hand clamped down on my shoulder.

"Dude!"

I recognized the voice as belonging to the party's host, Justin Daniels. Justin was one of the most popular guys at our school. Football player. Class President. Last year's Prom King. And he was also a womanizer. A player. A giant tool. He and I weren't close, we just ran in the same circles, and had some of the same friends. I never made it a habit to hang out with him, because for the most part, he sucked.

"Hey, man," I said. "Nice party." That's how our conversations usually went: three or four words each and we were done.

"Thanks," he said with a grin. His gaze flickered over to Emma and something changed in his expression. And whatever it was, I didn't like it.

Instinctively, I moved to block her from his view, but he gave me a playful shove, moving me out of the way.

"Emma Dawson, is that you?"

"Yeah," she answered in a voice so small, it could barely be heard over the music.

"Wow." He blatantly began to check her out, his eyes lowering to her chest and staying there for a moment before taking in the rest of her. I was surprised he didn't ask her to turn around for him, so he could check out her ass too. "Damn, girl, you look *good*."

Her face grew pink at his compliment. "Thank you."

Justin briefly returned his attention to me. "Heads up, bro. Your girl is making her way over here and she looks *pissed*."

I groaned. *'My girl'* was Grace. I knew she would be at the party—she was at all the parties—but I guess I hadn't given any thought to the fact I'd have to face her. Or maybe I knew I'd have to face her, but I felt it was safer to do so in a crowded area. Where there were plenty of witnesses.

"Logan," I heard her voice call out behind me. I closed my eyes and breathed in slowly, holding my breath until I began to see stars.

After counting to five, I turned around and found myself face-to-face with my sometimes-girlfriend.

She looked *hot*. Hotter than usual. Maybe it was the fact I hadn't seen or talked to her in a few days. Or maybe it was the fact she knew I would be at this party and she wanted to make sure to look her best so she could seduce me into being "on-again" with her. Either way, her appearance instantly made me forget the reason I was there in the first place.

"Hey, Grace," I said casually. I couldn't let on that I was aware she was angry. It was best to pretend like I hadn't done anything wrong. Otherwise, she would smell my fear and use it against me.

She stopped about a foot away and put her hands on her hips. She glared up at me and said, "Logan, where the hell have you been? Why haven't you been answering any of my calls or texts?"

She was incredibly sexy when she was angry. "I've been busy."

"Busy?" she echoed. She flipped her hair over her shoulder—something she often did right before she attacked. "Doing what?" Her gaze flickered over my shoulder. "And what are *you* doing here?"

It took me a second to realize she was talking to Emma. I'd almost forgotten she was still there, standing silently behind me, probably wanting to crawl into a hole somewhere.

Emma's eyes widened and opened her mouth as if to respond, but Grace didn't give her the opportunity.

Returning her full attention to me, Grace said, "Did you come here with *her*?" She thrust an accusatory finger in Emma's direction.

Justin, who was also still standing there, draped an arm around Emma's shoulders and said, "We'll leave you two alone to *talk*."

Emma shot me a look of panic over her shoulder as Justin began to lead her away. I sort of shrugged, not knowing what to do. I had to stay and talk to Grace. If I'd tried to follow

Emma and Justin, she probably would've literally tried stabbing me in the back.

"Well?" Grace said, now folding her arms across her chest. "Explain yourself."

I sighed. "Look, Grace, I'm sorry I haven't been answering your calls or responding to your texts. To be honest, after the fight we had the other day, I wasn't sure what the status of our relationship was, and I wanted to make sure you had a few days to cool down before we talked."

Grace softened slightly, but I could tell she still wasn't happy with me. "I would have thought you'd like to know how the date with my match went."

Here was where I had to put my acting abilities to the test. I had to act like I cared how her date went, or who the date was with. "How did it go?"

"Horrible!" She threw her hands up in exasperation. "My match was Owen Lockwood!" She grimaced.

"What's wrong with Owen?"

"He's a jerk!" she exclaimed, scrunching up her face in disgust. She could have done a lot worse than Owen, who was another one of the most popular guys in our class, especially with the girls.

"I'm a jerk, too," I pointed out.

"Yes, but you're *my* jerk." She pouted slightly. "So, who was *your* match?"

I stiffened, not knowing how to answer that. But I didn't have to. As soon as she asked, my gaze instinctively flew over to Emma, who was now standing all alone in the crowd, looking miserable as she glanced around the room, probably in search of a familiar, friendly face. She was unlikely to find one.

"No. No way." Grace shook her head vigorously back and forth. "Emma Dawson was *not* your match."

"Actually," I said, "she was."

Grace's jaw dropped. "That's impossible! How did you get matched up with *her*? You two have *nothing* in common!"

"Apparently, we do."

She looked horrified at the possibility. "So, what, are you dating her now or something?"

I almost wanted to say *yes*. I almost wanted to make her think that Emma and I were dating. After all, wasn't that the whole point of lying on that test? To make Grace think that she and I weren't compatible? To make her think that maybe my taste in women had changed so she would give up on me?

But I couldn't do it. I couldn't tell her the truth either, so I instead opted to go with, "No, I'm not dating her. I'm helping her out with something." I figured I might as well go along with what Emma had told her dad earlier. At least then our stories would be straight.

"What could you possibly be helping her out with?" Grace asked, undoubtedly confused by all of this.

"It's a long story," I said, hoping she would drop it.

Luckily, she did. With a sly grin, she placed the tip of her forefinger on the center of my chest and batted her eyelashes up at me. "Well, then, if you're not with her, what do you say we take this conversation to an empty bedroom upstairs? I put one on reserve with Justin earlier, in case you showed up."

Before I could respond, Grace lifted herself up on the tips of her toes and pressed her lips against mine in a soft kiss before whispering into my ear, "But we don't have to talk, if you don't want to."

I could feel her lips forming into a smile and I swallowed hard in an attempt to tamp down the sudden feeling of desire that washed over me. With a low groan, I carefully pried her off me.

"As nice as that sounds, I should go check on Emma," I said.

I knew right away that was the wrong thing to say. The smile vanished from her face and was replaced by a scowl. Her eyes narrowed and her face reddened—most likely from anger, but also most likely from the embarrassment of me turning her down. I'd never done that before.

Grace pushed me away and stepped back, her hands forming into fists at her sides. "Are you seriously choosing that nerd over me?" Her voice was dangerously low.

"She shouldn't be alone," I said. "She's never been to a party before and I don't exactly trust any of the guys here."

"And since when do you care, huh? You *hate* Emma. How many times have you whined and complained about her to me? And now, suddenly you're bringing her to parties and worrying about guys hitting on her?"

She had a valid point. But even though Emma and I weren't friends, I'd brought her to the party, so I was responsible for her. I promised her father I'd bring her back unscathed.

"Logan," Grace said, softening her tone just the slightest. "Forget about Emma. She'll be fine." She took hold of my hand and pulled me toward her. "I want to show you how much I've missed you this last week." She lifted herself up again and ran the tip of her tongue lightly against my bottom lip before taking it gently between her teeth.

She knew that was a weakness of mine. She was evil.

Placing a hand at the back of her head, weaving my fingers through her beach-waved hair, I pulled her face closer to mine and kissed her—hard, fast, deep, and she returned in kind.

I guess I'd kind of missed her this last week as well.

But I couldn't forget why I was there. Leaving Emma alone at her first high school party, with guys like Justin on the prowl, wasn't fair to her. And I couldn't risk it traumatizing her to the point where she no longer wanted anything to do with my plan.

So, I used every bit of willpower in my body to remove myself from Grace. "I'm sorry."

Her face twisted into a look of pure disgust as she placed her hands on my chest and attempted to give me a shove. "Go to hell, Logan. We're through—for good this time."

I'd heard those words so many times in the last year, but something about the way she said it now made me think she was serious this time.

"Grace," I said weakly, reaching out to her.

"Don't," she spat, swatting my hand away. "You were right, Logan. You *are* a jerk." She glanced over my shoulder and added, "Oh, and you might want to go rescue your new *girlfriend*. Looks like Justin's trying to get her drunk."

I whipped my head around in time to see Justin returning to Emma's side and handing her a red plastic cup. "Oh, I don't think so," I muttered to myself. As I began to move, taking long strides through the crowd in hopes of making it over to Emma in time, I heard Grace yell out after me.

"Screw you, Logan!"

A small group of kids standing nearby heard her and turned to glance curiously at me. This wasn't the first time my relationship with Grace had created a spectacle at a party, so they were all used to it. They turned back to their own conversation as if nothing had happened.

I made it over to Emma just as the rim of the cup met her lips. "I'll take that," I said, grabbing it out of her hands before she had a chance to take a sip.

Justin scowled at me. "Whoa, what the hell, Logan?"

"Emma's not interested in getting drunk, Justin."

"It's just Coke," Emma said, all innocent and naive-like.

I snorted. "Just Coke my *ass*." Justin could have put anything in that drink, and if the stories I'd heard about him at past parties were true, he probably had.

"Emma," I said, grabbing her arm. "We're leaving."

She stared at me in confusion. "What? Already? Why?"

I ignored her questions as I began to lead her away. Away from the creep standing in front of us. Away from this stupid party. What was I thinking, bringing her there?

As soon as we were outside, I dumped out the drink and tossed the cup into the bushes.

"What was that all about?" Emma asked as we made our way to my car. "Justin was just being nice."

I stopped dead in my tracks. "What, are you into Justin now or something?" I was suddenly more annoyed with her than usual.

"Of course not." She frowned. "Are you okay?"

I raked a hand through my hair. "I'm fine. Grace dumped me and I'm not in a great mood."

"Oh." She bit her bottom lip. "I'm sorry. What happened?"

I didn't feel like getting into the specifics, especially not with the girl who technically was the reason for the break-up. "She got upset about something, and then I didn't do or say the right thing, so she dumped me."

Emma remained silent for a moment, deep in thought before saying, "Why don't you go back in there and try talking to her? Apologize for whatever you didn't say or do? She's crazy about you. I'm sure she'll take you back."

Except, I didn't want her to take me back. Grace and I had been playing this game with each other for a year now, and I was tired of it. She was fun and hot, but girls like her were a dime a dozen.

"Nah," I said as I began walking again. "I'm done. I don't need that kind of drama in my life, you know?" I glanced down at her with a sympathetic smile. "Sorry I didn't get a chance to bring you over to Matt."

Emma shrugged. "No worries. I have no idea what I would have said to him, anyway." She gave me a sheepish grin. "I don't know if you've noticed, but I can't seem to formulate words when I'm around him. At least not ones I can get to come out of my mouth properly."

I chuckled as we approached my car. "I've noticed. But don't worry, that's what I'm here for—to be your own personal Cyrano de Bergerac."

Emma laughed. "I don't think I could trust you to be my Cyrano."

"Why not?" I playfully nudged her.

"Because you'd probably have me say something stupid or embarrassing."

"I would never," I said innocently, but we both knew I was lying.

"Hey, you want to go grab a quick bite to eat?" I asked her. "Then maybe we can head over to my house and we can flesh out this plan of mine a little more? Obviously, I could use a little help, considering how much of a bust tonight turned out to be."

She seemed surprised at my suggestion. "Um, sure," she said, after what appeared to be careful deliberation.

I opened the passenger door for her and she climbed into the car. When I turned to make my away around to the other side, I could see Grace standing in the doorway, staring out at us with fierce disapproval.

A brief feeling of dread washed over me as I got in the car beside Emma. Something told me I'd made a huge mistake with Grace…and she was no doubt going to make me pay for it.

Chapter 12

EMMA

It was only a little after eight-thirty when Logan pulled his Mustang into his driveway. In the span of an hour and a half, we went to a party, Logan got dumped, I was flirted with by one of the most popular guys at school, we left the party, we stopped at a fast food restaurant and quickly and silently ate a couple cheeseburgers, and then we drove home. We were nothing if not efficient.

I hadn't been inside Logan's house for years. The last time I was there, it was for his eleventh birthday party. That was the last one my parents forced me to attend, and the last one his parents had forced him to invite me to. Needless to say, it was weird stepping inside. It was like I was a little kid again.

"Emma Dawson!"

As soon as we shut the door behind us, Logan's father stepped out of the living room to greet us.

"Hey, Mark," I said with a smile and a wave.

"I thought you guys were going to a party?" He glanced curiously at Logan.

"We went," Logan said. "It was lame. We decided to leave."

"Is that Logan and Emma?" came a voice from the kitchen. A few seconds later, Logan's stepmother, Rachel, emerged carrying a salad bowl. "Oh hey, you two. We were getting ready to have some dinner. Would you like to join us? There's more than enough food."

"No, thanks," Logan replied politely. "We grabbed something on the way home. We're gonna go upstairs. We've got some stuff to work on."

Mark looked confused. "Stuff?"

"Yeah. School stuff."

"But school's out for the summer."

"I realize that, Dad. This is a...summer project. For extra credit."

"Oh." Mark didn't look like he bought that, but he let it go. "Okay then. Have fun, I guess?"

Rachel returned to the kitchen and set down the salad just as a wailing cry came from upstairs. Her shoulders sagged slightly. "Abby does this every time. It's like she knows when we're getting ready to do something and she starts crying on purpose." She started heading for the stairs. "She's going to be a fun teenager, I can already tell."

Surprisingly, Logan placed a hand on her arm to stop her. "Go ahead and eat. I'll go check on Abby."

Rachel's face morphed into an expression of gratitude. "Really? You don't mind?"

"Not at all," Logan replied.

"Thank you," Rachel breathed. She smiled at me and said, "It's nice to see you, Emma," before heading back to the kitchen with Mark.

"That was nice of you," I said as we started up the stairs.

"I'm not always a jerk, you know."

To me, he was, but I decided not to say that out loud.

Abby's nursery was located at the end of the hallway, right next to Mark and Rachel's bedroom, and it was the cutest room I'd ever seen. Three of the walls had been painted pale pink, while painted on the other wall was a breathtaking mural of a forest. On the wall above her crib, her name was spelled out in large, bright pink, sequined letters, and it was surrounded by framed prints of Disney princesses. Little stuffed animals—bunnies, kittens, puppies, lambs, monkeys, owls, you name it—were scattered throughout the room, even though she wasn't old enough yet to appreciate them.

"I know," Logan said, taking note of my expression of awe. "Disgusting, huh? It's like Tinkerbell projectile vomited all over the room."

"Not at all. This room is amazing."

"Not as amazing as the baby who sleeps in it," he said, reaching into Abby's crib and picking her up.

The instant she was in his arms, the crying stopped. It was like he'd found a switch somewhere on her back and flipped it, that's how sudden the transformation was.

"Wow," I said, thoroughly impressed. "You're really good with her."

"Thanks," he said, bouncing her slightly on his hip. She rested her little head against his chest as she fought to keep her eyes open. "But I can't take credit for that. It's science."

I blinked in confusion. "Science?"

"Yeah. Science. They've done studies and have found babies react exceptionally well to beautiful people. Something having to do with them finding aesthetic features to be calming."

I groaned and rolled my eyes. "Seriously?"

He flashed me a cocky grin. "Here, we'll test it out." He held Abby out to me and without thinking about what he was doing, I took her from him.

She seemed as comfortable with me as she did with him and Logan frowned.

"Huh," he said. "I guess that study was bunk. She seems fine with you, too."

I made a face at him and gave Abby back. "Ha-ha, very funny," I said at his insult attempt.

He laughed softly as he placed Abby back in her crib. "It looks like the little princess just wanted some attention. She's already asleep again." He turned and motioned toward the door. "Shall we?"

I followed him out of the nursery and we headed across the hall. Logan's bedroom was far less showy than Abby's nursery. There was a lot of dark gray and black. Minimal. And surprisingly neat, too.

"So, this is Logan Reynolds's infamous bedroom, eh?" I said, stepping inside.

"*Infamous?*" He scoffed. "I think you meant *famous.*"

"No, I meant *infamous,*" I said with a smirk. "So, what are we doing here, anyway?"

Logan went over to his computer desk and searched through a pile of books. When he found the one he was looking for, he grabbed it and walked over to the end of his bed and sat down.

Giving the empty spot next to him a pat, he said, "Here, join me."

I hesitated for a moment. Sitting on a bed with Logan? Not really something I wanted to do. Ever.

"Oh my God, Emma, don't worry. I'm not going to try to seduce you or anything. You're not my type." He shook his head in disbelief.

With a scowl, I sat down beside him and glanced curiously at the book in his hands: it was our yearbook.

"Why did you grab the yearbook?"

"Because I want you to sign it," he joked with a sly grin. "But seriously, I thought it might be a good idea if we went through it and looked at all the girls Matt has ever dated."

My heart deflated inside my chest. There was a good chance that could take all night. Matt had dated a lot of girls in that book. "Why? So you can drive the point home that he's way out of my league and that I should try for somebody a little more attainable?"

"Not exactly. I've been best friends with Matt forever, and I know why he dated each one of these girls. I figured maybe this would give you some ideas of what you may need to change about yourself, so we can add *you* to this list."

Well, wasn't *that* romantic? More and more this whole idea of Logan's was sounding worse and worse. Still, I hated to admit I was kind of curious to know what attracted Matt to all those girls. And maybe, just maybe, I could learn something valuable.

"Fine," I said with a sigh. "Who's the first girl?"

Logan seemed pleased at my willingness to proceed. Opening the book, he flipped to the juniors first. "Okay, in alphabetical order, starting with our class: first up is Kristy Andrews." He pointed to a picture of a perky girl with long, straight brown hair and perfect teeth. "Matt dated Kristy our Freshman year. He liked her for the simple fact her boobs grew two cup sizes over the summer before we entered high school." He moved onto the next page. "Next up is Samantha Bridges. He dated her a few months after he broke up with Kristy. He liked her because she smoked. Of course, he thinks smoking is gross now, but when he was fourteen, he thought smoking looked cool, therefore he thought Samantha was cool."

He turned the page. "Alison Dodge. He liked her because she had red hair and freckles and that made her unique. Melissa Grimes, she was peppy and always so positive about *everything*. It was annoying to me, but Matt ate it up. I think all that positivity just made him feel good. Jenny Livingston, he liked her because she was good at…" His voice trailed off as his lips formed into a slight smirk. "Well, I'll let you use your imagination on that one."

A feeling of unease washed over me as Logan continued to point out girl after girl. I knew Matt had dated a lot of girls, but I'd never actually counted. By the time Logan was done with our class alone, the count was at twenty. Before he could go onto the upper or lower classmen, I grabbed the book from him and closed it.

"Hey, we were just getting started," Logan protested. I knew he could tell I was greatly disturbed by Matt's eclectic taste in girls, and I also knew how much he was enjoying my misery.

None of the girls Logan pointed out were shy nerds or geeks, like me. Maybe that should have given me hope—like maybe I could be his first in that category—but it didn't. Suddenly, I wanted nothing to do with any of this anymore.

Tossing the yearbook onto the bed behind me, I stood and said, "I'm going home."

I moved to leave but Logan's hand shot out and grabbed mine, stopping me.

"Wait," he said. "Don't leave. I wasn't trying to discourage you, you know."

He almost sounded sincere. "Well, you did anyway. I get it, okay? I'm not Matt's type and you'd be wasting your time trying to turn me into a girl who is. All I learned from this is apparently to get Matt to notice me, I need to grow bigger boobs, start smoking, dye my hair, pretend everything is wonderful, and become a pro at certain physical activities I've never done before, because I've never even *kissed* anyone." When I realized my embarrassing admission, I cringed, waiting for Logan to make some smartass comment.

But surprisingly, he didn't. Instead, he looked like he felt sorry for me. Like he pitied me. That was even worse.

"Go ahead, make fun of me. You know you want to."

"I wasn't going to make fun of you," he said, his voice sincere. He let go of my hand, got up, went back over to his computer desk, and grabbed a notebook. "So, what? You've never kissed anyone. That's easy enough to fix."

I snorted. "How so?"

He took a step forward so that we were only a few inches apart. He lowered his gaze to my lips. "I could kiss you right here, right now, and then you wouldn't be able to say you've never kiss anyone anymore."

At his words, my mouth went dry as my heart leapt up into my throat. His sudden proximity, mixed with the spicy scent of what I assumed was his aftershave, made me lightheaded. I would have pushed him away if I hadn't completely frozen in place.

"But I won't," he continued, backing away. "I'm guessing you're saving that kiss for somebody special, but Emma, a word of advice? Maybe try to get that first kiss out of the way before you get with Matt."

I swallowed hard as my pulse began to slow to a normal speed. "Why is that?"

He returned to his bed, sat down and opened the notebook. "Because Matt has kissed *a lot* of girls, and he'll be able to tell right away how inexperienced you are. And believe me when I tell you, Matt has no interest in being anybody's first anymore—and that goes for *everything*."

It didn't take a genius to figure out what he was referring to. Feeling deflated, I plopped down into his computer chair, rested my elbows on my knees, and cradled my face in my hands.

"Hey," Logan said. "Don't worry. We'll figure out the kissing thing later, alright? Right now, we've got other things to discuss."

"Like what?"

"Like what we're going to do this summer."

I removed my face from my hands and eyed him warily. "Logan, why are you so interested in helping me with all this? It's summer vacation. You should be spending all your time with your friends, not me. You hate me, remember?"

Logan stared down at the notebook in his hands. "Hate's an awfully strong word, Emma."

"But it fits, doesn't it?"

He thought about it for a moment. "Okay, so we've never exactly been friends. And I've always thought you were a know-it-all goody-two-shoes with an irritating voice—" He stopped for a second when I threw him a glare. "But maybe it's time we grow up and be adults. Aren't you tired of hating me for no reason?"

I threw my head back and laughed. "Are you kidding me, Logan? I have all the reasons in the world to hate you. For starters, I hate you for calling me a know-it-all goody-two-shoes with an irritating voice. And I hate you for lying on that compatibility test and ruining my chances of having a genuine summer romance with somebody I wouldn't have to change myself for."

"I know. That's why we're doing this. I'm trying to make that up to you."

"By telling me my wardrobe sucks and my personality sucks and I need to change everything about myself to get a guy to like me? Geez, thanks, Logan. How can I ever repay you?"

Logan held out his hands in surrender. "Okay, let's stop for a moment, alright? Emma, I never said you had to change everything about yourself to get a guy to like you. I said you'd have to do that to get *Matt* to like you. I'll help you get whatever guy you want. We can go sit outside the library tomorrow and snag you a boyfriend within an hour, if that's what you'd prefer."

He leaned forward and held my gaze. "But Emma, this isn't just about getting Matt to like you. This is about getting yourself to loosen up and live a little. This is about not having to rely on lame compatibility tests to find a boyfriend for you." He paused for a moment, as if deciding whether he should continue. Finally, he said, "Can I be perfectly honest with you?"

I wasn't sure I wanted him to be, but I nodded anyway.

"There's nothing wrong with how you look," he said. "You're tall, you're literally girl-next-door pretty, and you've got a nice figure that you unfortunately hide underneath unnecessary layers of clothing. Honestly, you're kind of hot—like sexy librarian hot."

I could feel my face starting to burn at his words. I had no idea that I could be considered anywhere near "hot", especially to somebody like Logan Reynolds.

"And when you blush like that, it's one of the most adorable things I've ever seen."

I shifted uncomfortably in my chair. What was going on here? Logan was being uncharacteristically nice to me and I wasn't sure how to handle it. And he wasn't just being nice, he was also bordering on *flirtatious.*

He must've sensed my discomfort, because he was quick to add, "Don't worry, Dawson, I'm not coming on to you. That's where the compliments end. The reason you've never had a boyfriend has nothing to do with how you look, but everything to do with how you act. I've known you my whole life, so I know you don't put yourself out there because you're shy and reserved. But to guys who don't know you, they see that and mistake it for you being a stuck-up snob who thinks she's better than everyone else. Pair that with the fact you've always got your nose stuck in a book and guys want nothing to do with you. They think you're uptight and boring. A stick-in-the-mud. That's what we need to work on. You need to start having fun and stop being so damn scared of everything."

I opened my mouth to defend myself, but he didn't give me the opportunity. He held up the notebook in one hand a pen in the other. "This is where I come in. I'm going to teach you how to get a life."

"I have a life," I grumbled, staring down at my hands.

"But not an interesting, exciting one." He clicked the end of his pen and started scribbling something on the paper. "Tell me, are you still afraid of heights? Afraid of the water? Large crowds?"

"Did this just turn into a therapy session?"

"Answer the questions, Emma."

I leaned back in the chair and sighed. "Yes. To all three."

He jotted down some more stuff. "You still don't know how to swim, correct?"

I stared up at the ceiling and gritted my teeth. "I know how to swim. I just don't know how to swim *well.*"

"Okay, we'll definitely be changing that," he muttered.

"What? Why?"

"Because Matt's throwing a pool party next week, and you're going."

"No, I'm not," I said, returning my gaze to him.

"Yes, you are."

"I wasn't invited."

"*I'm* inviting you."

"And I'm turning you down."

"Emma," he said, setting the notebook down beside him. "When Matt is your boyfriend, you're going to have to attend his pool parties. And you'll have to do so in the skimpiest bikini you can find. You might as well start now."

The word "bikini" instantly triggered a minor anxiety attack. I didn't do bikinis. I didn't do tankinis. Or one-pieces. Or any form of swimwear in general. I felt so exposed in bathing suits, which made me feel uncomfortable, and which was probably one reason why I never properly learned how to swim. There was no way I was going to go out and buy a bikini and wear it in front of Matt, let alone half the students in our class.

"I can go bikini shopping with you, if you'd like." He flashed me a lopsided grin.

"I wouldn't like," I said with a roll of my eyes. "So, what have you been writing over there?"

He closed the notebook. "Just some ideas. Hey, what are you doing tomorrow?"

I was planning on starting my book-organizing project, but I wasn't about to admit that to him. "Nothing. Why?"

"Because," he said, "we're going to hang out."

"Hang out? And do what?"

"That's for me to know and you to find out. Remember? I have a list."

I didn't like the fact he had this "list" and wouldn't let me see it. It wasn't fair that I didn't even get a say in what was on it. Still, I found myself saying, "What time?"

Logan grinned. "How about noon again?"

Another afternoon hanging out with Logan? What was I getting myself into? I was about to blindly follow a guy I'd spent my entire life loathing, and now I was not only putting all my trust in him, but I was also going to be spending my summer vacation doing things I didn't want to be doing.

Unless...

"Noon sounds fine," I said, my lips curling into a devious smile as an idea began to form in my head. "But I have a proposal."

Logan arched an eyebrow. "A proposal?"

"Yes. Why don't we make things interesting? If I'm going to be stuck doing all these things on your list that I'm not comfortable doing, it's only fair that you do the same."

He stared at me blankly. "I don't follow. This isn't about me."

"Sure, it is. You lied on that compatibility test because you didn't want Grace to think you two had anything in common. She may have dumped you, but you and I both know she's going to change her mind and want you back. Is that what you want?"

"Well, no, but—"

"So, here's what I propose: you get me to do things that will turn me into somebody Matt will like, and I'll get you to do things that will turn you into somebody Grace *won't* like."

"Things?" he echoed. "Like what type of things?"

I grinned. "That's for me to know and you to find out."

Logan chuckled. "Hey, that's my line." He paused for a moment, looking lost in thought. "I don't know, Emma..."

I leaned forward in my chair. "What's wrong? Not up for the challenge? Don't think you could handle it?"

That instantly changed his tune. "Oh, I can handle whatever you have to throw at me, Dawson. I just don't want to spend my summer vacation alphabetizing books."

"That's fine," I said, casually crossing my arms over my chest. "Maybe we should call this whole thing off then."

A look of panic flashed across his face so quickly, I had to wonder if I was just imagining it. "Okay. You win. We'll do it your way."

"Excellent!" I jumped up from the chair and headed toward the door. "*I'll* pick *you* up at noon tomorrow." I flashed him a wicked grin over my shoulder before leaving the room.

I was going home to make my own list.

This was going to be fun.

Chapter 13

LOGAN

What had I gotten myself into?

I pondered this the next day while getting ready for another afternoon with Emma. She was picking me up at noon to take me somewhere boring and dumb—I was sure of it.

I had no idea why I'd agreed to go along with *her* version of *my* plan. How had this happened? I knew how. I was desperate. Desperate to get this whole thing over with so Rachel would give me the thumbs-up and tell me I didn't have to go on the family trip to New York. She was thrilled when I told her what I was doing—attempting to get Emma together with her dream boyfriend—but she informed me that to get out of the trip, I'd have to actually land the deal. I'd have to get those two crazy kids together for at least one date.

Easier said than done.

I was going to give it an honest try, but if we got closer to the date of the trip and I'd still failed to make it happen, I wasn't against resorting to paying Matt to take Emma out. Even if Rachel found out, it wouldn't be until after she got home from New York, at which point, there was no punishment I couldn't live with.

A little before noon, I exited the shower and returned to my room to get dressed. I had slept in later than I'd wanted to, and now Emma would have to wait for me. I had no doubt she'd be there at twelve o'clock on the dot.

Sure enough, my alarm clock read twelve as I heard a soft knock on my bedroom door, as I was about to put my shirt on. Deciding that could wait, I walked over to the door and opened it to see Emma standing on the other side.

As soon as she saw me, her gaze immediately fell to my bare chest and her cheeks turned pink. I swear, that girl blushed so much, she must've had a medical condition. It wasn't normal.

She opened her mouth to speak, but no words came out. And on top of not being able to talk, she also couldn't seem to tear her eyes away from my abs.

"Hey, Emma," I drawled, placing a hand on the door frame next to her and leaning slightly forward. I figured I might as well have a little fun with this.

She cleared her throat and finally moved her eyes upward to meet with mine. "You're not ready yet?"

"Nah, sorry. I overslept." I stepped aside and motioned for her to come in.

"That's okay," she said, entering the room. "Looks like you're almost ready, anyway." Her eyes flickered briefly to my chest again.

I was loving this. Obviously, Emma didn't have a whole lot of experience being around shirtless guys, and it was making her uncomfortable. And if there was one thing in life I enjoyed doing, it was making Emma Dawson uncomfortable. And for that reason, I prolonged putting on my shirt, opting instead to put on my belt next. In slow motion.

"So, where are we going, anyway?" I asked.

Emma averted her gaze to the wall beside her. "I'm not telling you."

"You're going to have to tell me. Otherwise, how am I going to know where to drive us?"

She returned to her eyes to mine. "You're not driving us anywhere. I'm driving."

I snorted. "I don't think so, Dawson. I'm not going anywhere in that clunker of yours."

Her "clunker" was a 2010 Corolla that was in good enough shape. I just enjoyed giving her a hard time about it because it wasn't my Mustang. She knew that, so she didn't let it faze her.

"Besides," I continued, "I'm not sure I trust your driving."

That, however, offended her. "There is nothing wrong with my driving!"

"I didn't say there is. I said I don't trust it."

She scowled at me. "Fine. Whatever. You can drive." She stopped and lowered her gaze to my chest. "Are you planning on putting on a shirt at some point today?"

I glanced down at myself and smirked. "What's wrong? Is my naked torso making you feel things? Things you've never felt before?" I placed a hand gently on her shoulder and stared deeply into her eyes. "It's okay, Emma, those feelings are perfectly norm—"

She interrupted me with a punch to the arm—one that I hated to admit kind of stung.

Rubbing the spot where her fist had made contact, I backed away. Obviously, the girl wasn't in the mood for joking around. Not that she ever was. I went over to the bed, grabbed my shirt and quickly threw it on.

"There," I said, "is that better?"

Emma smiled. "Yes. Much better."

I shook my head. I didn't understand her. Most girls would have asked that I please never put on a shirt again, but not this one. She wanted nothing to do with my pecs or my abs. She could not have been less impressed.

What a weirdo.

Less than a minute later, we headed down the stairs, said goodbye to Rachel, and left the house. As we made our way over to the Mustang, I said, "You don't have to tell me where we're going, just tell me when I need to turn. Deal?"

"No need," she said. "Head downtown and park in the parking garage. We'll walk to our destination from there."

Hmm. Downtown. That was a clue, but it wasn't much to go on. Downtown had a little bit of everything.

We got inside the car and as soon as I turned it on, Emma's hand flew to the radio dial.

"Um, what are you doing?" I asked her.

"If you insist on driving, then I insist on choosing the music."

I groaned. Great. Like I wanted to drive my Mustang around blaring sappy love ballads with chimes and harps and high-pitched singers who could break wine classes with their voices.

But surprisingly, Emma tuned it to the nearest classic rock station, which was currently playing a Rolling Stones song. Imagine my surprise when she started softly singing along with it.

I glanced sideways at her as I pulled out of the driveway. "You like classic rock?"

She looked at me like she thought I was an idiot for even asking. "Uh, *yeah*. Who doesn't?"

I didn't even miss a beat. "Grace doesn't." Grace liked boy band crap. She loved it when they sang about how beautiful and amazing she was and how she never needed to change because she was perfect.

"That's her problem, not mine."

I chuckled as I pulled to a stop at the end of our street. "Well, I've got to say, I'm impressed with your taste in music. Your singing voice, however, could use some work."

She rolled her eyes at my insult, but didn't verbally respond to it. Probably because she knew it was bogus. Her singing voice wasn't half-bad. In fact, it was pretty good, considering her talking voice usually made me want to puncture my eardrums with Q-tips.

"I've grown up on this music," she said. "My dad's obsessed. Zeppelin, Floyd, Stones, you name it."

"Yeah, my dad's obsessed, too," I said. "I guess that makes sense, considering they're best friends. Maybe their love of classic rock was what forged their friendship." I glanced over at her with a fake expression of hope. "Maybe it will forge a friendship between us as well."

She chortled at the suggestion. "It's going to take a lot more than a shared love of classic rock for us to ever be friends, Logan."

I placed a hand over my heart. "That's hurtful, Dawson."

"It is what it is," she said, a small smile playing at her lips.

We didn't talk for the rest of the trip, which was how I liked it. Since Emma and I weren't friends, and had nothing in common but liking the same music, there wasn't anything for us to talk about. Neither one of us felt the need to engage in forced small-talk.

I guess that was another thing we had in common.

Once we arrived downtown, I headed straight for the parking garage and parked the car, as requested.

"So, where are we going?" I asked as we made our way to the elevator.

Emma pressed the button for the ground level. "Somewhere close by. You'll know when we get there."

I hated how mysterious she was being, but to be fair, I was being no different. Still, I couldn't help but fear for my life, considering she was probably taking me somewhere to do something that would bore me to death.

And I had every right to have that fear, because after less than two minutes of walking, she stopped in front of a large, brick building that I recognized immediately as—

"The art museum?" My shoulders slumped forward in disappointment. "Please tell me we're not going in."

"Oh, we're going in," Emma said in a bubbly voice I almost didn't recognize. She was genuinely excited about this.

I groaned as I reluctantly followed her through the entrance doors. The last time I'd been to the art museum, it was for a field trip my sophomore year. I hated it then, too, even though I'd managed to get Melanie Appleton to sneak off with me to make out behind some weird phallic-shaped sculpture.

"Emma!" the middle-aged woman behind the counter exclaimed as soon as we entered the lobby.

"Mary!" Emma exclaimed back, and I had to refrain from snorting. Apparently, Emma was a frequent visitor. Why wasn't I surprised?

"Where are your friends?" Mary asked as we approached her.

"They're in Florida, remember?"

"Ah, yes. That's right." Mary smiled and nodded, averting her gaze to me. Raising her eyebrows slightly, she said, "And who is *this* friend of yours?"

"This is Logan," Emma replied. "But he's not my friend."

Mary's smile widened. "Oh, sorry. Boyfriend?"

Emma burst into laughter so loud it echoed throughout the lobby.

Geez, I knew the idea of me being Emma's boyfriend was humorous, but I didn't know it was practically *rolling-on-the-floor-laughing* humorous.

After her laughter subsided, Emma wiped tears from her

eyes and said, "Logan's an *acquaintance*. We're working on a project together."

Mary pursed her lips. "Okay, if you say so."

Emma's mirth quickly dissipated, and I could tell that she was done talking about what kind of relationship she and I had or didn't have. Taking her wallet out of her pocket, she pulled out some money and held it out for Mary to take.

"Nonsense, honey," Mary said, pushing Emma's hand away. "Admission's free today."

Emma narrowed her eyes at the woman. "For just us, or everybody?"

Mary gave a wink and said, "You two enjoy."

"Thank you, Mary," Emma said politely, returning the money to her wallet. She glanced up at me. "Are you ready for this?"

No, I wasn't, but I followed her anyway.

"Why did you bring me here?" I asked her quietly, not knowing if I should keep my voice down at art museums, or if that was only libraries.

"Because," she replied with a smirk. "I know whatever you're going to have me do today will be something I hate, so I figured I would have *you* do something *you* hate. It's only fair."

She had no idea how right she was about hating what I had planned for her. There was a good chance she was even going to kill me after it was over. So, I'd be a good sport about the art museum. It was the least I could do.

We entered a room lined wall-to-wall with modern art paintings. I didn't know a lot about art, but I could tell the difference between modern art and old school art. Modern art, for the most part, made no sense to me. A lot of it was stuff I felt I could do myself if I had a canvas, a paintbrush and half a brain. Old school art, however—Michelangelo, Monet, Van

Gogh, Renoir—I had a bit more respect for. Those guys knew what they were doing.

"So, you come here often, huh?" I said, scanning my eyes across a large painting of different colored squares. Like I said, I could do that myself.

"Yeah." Emma stared at the same painting but looked more impressed than I felt. "Chloe's going to art school when we graduate, so we come here all the time, mostly for her, but Sophia and I enjoy it as well. They sometimes have different exhibits to check out."

"Hmm," I said, trying to act interested. "Where are the Magritte paintings?"

Emma blinked up at me. "The what-now?"

"Magritte paintings," I repeated. "You know, René Magritte? The surrealist painter?"

"I know exactly who Magritte is. I just didn't realize *you* knew who Magritte was."

I took great enjoyment at how impressed she sounded. "Hey, I paid attention in art class. He was the only artist Mrs. Marsh covered that was worth paying attention to. The man was a genius. His art makes you think. I like that."

"Well that's unfortunate," she mumbled.

"What is?"

"That's something else we have in common. I love Magritte."

That *was* unfortunate. If Emma and I kept discovering things we had in common, we might start to consider becoming friends. And *that* would be the most unfortunate thing of all.

With a dismissive wave of my hand, I said, "Let's forget we even had this conversation. Why don't we keep moving?"

She seemed pleased at that suggestion, so that's what we

did. After stopping at every painting in the room, we headed into another one containing a bunch of sculptures, including that phallic-shaped one I'd made out behind. I couldn't help but smirk at the memory as we walked past it.

I glanced down at my watch after every room we walked through, expecting it to tell me that hours had passed between each one, but it was only ever just a few minutes. Emma knew what she was doing by bringing me here.

It was pure torture.

I didn't want to give her the satisfaction of knowing that, though, so I pretended to be interested in every painting she pointed out, and even pointed some out myself to really sell the bit.

"When you and Grace get back together, you should bring her here," Emma said as we walked through the last exhibit. "She'll hate it."

I scoffed. "Grace and I are never getting back together."

"Sure, you're not," she said, a small smile playing at her lips. She didn't believe me.

I wasn't sure I believed me either.

"Okay," she continued. "I think you've been tortured enough for one day. I suppose we can move onto whatever you have planned for me now."

She sounded nervous, and rightfully so. If she only knew what I had planned for her, she would have never left that museum.

With a sly smile, I turned to her. "Alright then. Let's go."

***

We arrived at our destination less than thirty minutes later. As soon as I pulled into a parking space, Emma glanced over at me curiously.

"An amusement park?"

"Not just any amusement park," I said as we exited the car. "This is Funland Park."

"I know this is Funland Park," Emma said. "But, what are we doing here?"

"We're going to have fun, like the name suggests."

Emma smirked and shook her head. "So, this was your big plan for the day? To bring me to an amusement park to have 'fun' because you don't think I'm capable of having fun?"

"I think you're capable of having fun, I just think you choose *not* to."

We walked up to the ticket window and I flashed a toothy smile to the woman behind the plexiglass. "Hello, there. Two adult bracelets, please." I dropped some bills onto the counter and pushed them toward her.

"Sure thing," the woman said politely. She rang us up and asked for our wrists to snap the blue bracelets onto. Once our transaction was over, we proceeded through the turnstile and entered the park.

"Are you hungry?" I asked Emma. "We could go get some fried dough or something."

She didn't respond. Instead, she was too busy staring up at all the rides surrounding us. In the distance was the Thunderbolt rollercoaster, the tallest in the state. A short distance from that was The Belly Drop, one of those rides that goes straight up, stops at the top, and then suddenly plunges a couple hundred feet toward the earth. But we weren't there for either of those rides. Not yet, anyway.

We were there for the Ferris wheel.

My plan was quite simple. See, I knew a guy. My cousin, Beck, to be exact. Beck was in college, and a couple weeks ago, he'd landed a summer job at Funland Park, where on any given day he would alternate between operating rides and running game booths. This afternoon, he just so happened to be operating rides. More specifically, he was operating the Ferris wheel. All it took was one phone call to him the previous night and the promise of a twenty-dollar bill for him to go along with my request.

Finally, Emma turned to look at me and answered my question. "No, thanks, I'm not hungry. I'm more curious as to what you've got planned for me here." She paused for a second. "You're not taking me on the Thunderbolt, are you? Or The Belly Drop?"

I laughed and threw an arm around her shoulders as I began to lead her deeper into the park. "No way. I would never do that to you. What we're going to do is something a lot lamer."

She looked relieved at the prospect, but that look dissipated the closer we got to the wheel. As she started to figure out where I was taking her.

"No," she said, stopping dead in her tracks when we were only a few feet away from the sparse line of people waiting to get on the ride.

"Yes," I said, taking her arm and attempting to pull her forward. But she pulled in the opposite direction, leaving us standing exactly where we were. She wasn't that strong, and I could have forced the issue, but instead I stopped tugging and said, "C'mon, Emma, please? I endured the torture of the art museum. You can endure the torture of a Ferris wheel—which most people don't even consider to be torture, by the way."

Emma yanked her arm out of my grasp. "Logan, you know

I'm afraid of heights."

"Yes, I do know that. That's why we're doing this. When was the last time you went on a Ferris wheel? Maybe it won't be as bad this time."

Emma nervously bit her lower lip. "I've never been on a Ferris wheel," she admitted in a small, ashamed voice.

I blinked at her. "Are you serious?" I grabbed her hand and began to pull her again. She must have let her guard down because she stumbled forward slightly as she attempted to keep up with me for the remaining distance. "We're getting on this ride."

"Logan," she protested. She tried to slip her hand from my grasp, but I held on tighter this time. "Why? Why are you making me do this?"

"Don't you want to be with Matt?"

She threw me a confused glance. "What does going on a Ferris wheel have to do with me wanting to be with Matt?"

"Matt loves Ferris wheels," I lied. Well, it wasn't a total lie. Matt liked Ferris wheels, but it wasn't a deal-breaker or anything. But Emma didn't have to know that. "And he loves girls who are willing to face their fears." That wasn't necessarily true, either.

The line started moving forward and I looked at Emma expectantly. "What do you say? Are you going to be a big girl today and face your fear?"

Her big, wide eyes went from me, to the wheel, to the line in front of us. Taking a deep breath, she said, "Okay. Fine. I'll go on this stupid thing."

Victory. With a grin, I glanced over at Beck and caught his eye. I gave him a nod to let him know the plan was still on and we were good to go.

"Hey, isn't that your cousin?" Emma asked, following my

line of vision.

"Yep, that's Beck," I said, waving at him.

When Emma wasn't looking, I reached into my back pocket and pulled out the twenty-dollar bill I'd stashed in there earlier for easy access. As we approached Beck, I held the folded-up bill in the palm of my hand so Emma couldn't see it. Once we were first in line, I shook Beck's hand and inconspicuously transferred the money to him, while making it look like we were conducting a secret cousin handshake.

"Hey, man," Beck said, flashing us both a grin. "How's it going?"

"Good," I replied as I felt the money slip from my hand. "How've you been?"

"Living the dream." Beck chuckled as he moved his gaze to Emma. "Hey, Emma. Long time, no see. You guys here on a date?"

I narrowed my eyes into a glare. He knew damn well Emma and I weren't there on a date, as I had explained the whole situation to him in detail the other night over the phone. He was just doing this to be an ass.

"Nah, man," I replied. "Just friends."

"Cool, cool."

The next car stopped at the bottom and Beck motioned for us to get in. Knowing Emma wasn't going to do it on her own without any help, I tightened my grip on her hand and pulled her forward. I got in first and she followed, taking a seat next to me.

Beck winked as he lowered the bar over us. "Enjoy, you two."

"Thanks," I said. I glanced sideways at Emma and for a second I contemplated calling the whole thing off. She stared straight ahead, looking paler than normal. Her hands gripped the bar so tightly, her knuckles had turned white. She was genuinely scared.

I opened my mouth to say something. Maybe to tell Beck we wanted to get off the ride, but before I could, we started to move slowly backward. It was too late to turn back now.

I heard the sharp intake of breath next to me and I looked over to see how Emma was holding up.

"Hey," I said to her. "How are you doing?"

She didn't respond, just closed her eyes tightly as we continued to move. As we moved closer to the top, she started breathing in short spurts, inhaling deeply but never truly breathing out.

She was hyperventilating.

"Emma," I said, placing my hand gently over hers. "Are you okay?"

With her eyes still closed, she shook her head forcefully back and forth.

Shit. I'd made a huge mistake. I had completely underestimated her fear of heights. I figured it was mild, at best. I had no idea she would freak out this much. Which made me *really* regret what was about to happen next.

That twenty I'd slipped Beck was for him to stop us at the top for two minutes.

When the wheel came to a stop as promised a few seconds later, Emma cringed. "What's going on?" she panted, her eyes still tightly closed.

"It's okay," I assured her. "Beck stopped the ride. I asked him to."

Her jaw dropped. "Why would you do that, Logan?" she screeched. Her breath was still coming in short bursts.

Because I'm a jerk, I silently answered. "Because I wanted you to face your fear. I wanted you to see that sometimes heights aren't so bad."

But this was a failed experiment. The girl was more terrified than anyone I'd ever seen in my life, and I was the one who'd caused it. I felt lower than low. No wonder she hated me.

"Hey," I said softly, placing my hand on the side of her face. "Open your eyes, Emma."

"No," she said stubbornly, shaking her head again.

"Emma, please. Look at me." I gently turned her face toward me. "You're okay. Just open your eyes."

Surprisingly, her eyes fluttered open at my request; her gaze immediately landing on mine. I expected to see anger there. Fury. But there was only fear, and I hated myself for being the one to have put it there.

"Just breathe," I instructed. "Take a deep breath in through your nose and let it slowly out of your mouth."

She did as she was told, as a tear escaped her eye and traveled slowly down her cheek.

I promptly brushed it away with my thumb.

We held each other's gaze as she continued to breathe in and out. When I finally felt she had calmed down enough, I said, "Okay, now look around."

She closed her eyes again, but only briefly this time. "No," she whispered.

I gently rubbed the back of her neck. "Trust me."

She had no reason to, but she did. Prying her eyes back open and tearing them away from mine, she turned her head and looked at our surroundings. She inhaled sharply again, but this time I could tell it was for a different reason.

"Oh my God," she breathed.

I grinned. "Pretty awesome, huh?"

She stared in awe at the view surrounding us. "Wow."

"Look over there." I pointed past her. "The ocean. You can

see the curvature of the earth. How freaking amazing is that? And if you look over to the other side, you can see the mountains."

Emma turned her head to where I was pointing now, her eyes wide with wonder.

"You can't get these views from the ground," I said. "Look at all you've been missing out on this whole time."

She returned her gaze to mine. Her eyes were welled up with tears, but this time it wasn't from fear. She opened her mouth to say something, but we started moving. Gripping the bar again, she turned back to stare straight ahead as we started going down.

Without thinking, I put my arm around her shoulders and pulled her closer to me. "Are you going to be okay to go around a couple more times? Otherwise, I can have Beck stop the ride when we get to the bottom."

"No, I think I'll be okay," she said softly, pressing herself into me.

I swallowed hard as we rounded the bottom. Beck caught my eye, grinned and gave me the thumbs-up. I smiled weakly at him as we started going around again.

Despite the fact Emma had calmed down, I still couldn't help but feel like a dick. I had traumatized her—to the point where she was nuzzled up against me and not making any snide comments or pushing me away. I'd ruined her.

Suddenly, this whole idea of mine didn't seem so great anymore.

Chapter 14

EMMA

Words could not even begin to describe how badly I wanted to murder Logan.

What the hell was he thinking? He not only put me on a Ferris wheel, knowing full-well about my fear of heights—but then had his stoner cousin stop it at the top just to torture me even more. I mean, yeah, I got on the Ferris wheel willingly—it wasn't like he forced me at gunpoint or anything—but I only did it because I knew if I hadn't, he never would have let me live it down. And that was just as much a threat as a gun would have been.

As soon as we exited the ride and were out of the way of the other people piling out of the gate, I turned to him and gave him a shove. He must not have been expecting it because he stumbled backward a step or two.

"Hey," he grumbled. "What was that for?"

I gaped at him. "Are you serious? You know I'm afraid of heights!"

He held out his hands in front of him to ward off another attack. "In my defense, I didn't know you were *that* afraid of heights."

"Yeah, right. You just wanted to laugh at my reaction and make fun of me."

Logan tilted his head to the side. "But did I?"

I crossed my arms over my chest. "N-no," I stammered. He

had a point. He *hadn't* laughed or made fun of me. In fact, he'd been almost…sweet. Trying to comfort me. Calming me down. Holding me close…

But that was just as infuriating because now I was confused. Logan Reynolds was not known for being nice. Well, not known for being nice to *me*. So, something was up. He was playing some sort of game. A game I had no interest in playing.

With a huff, I turned and began to stalk off as fast as I could away from the jerk.

"Wait, Emma!" he called out. It took him no time to catch up, and within seconds, he was falling into stride beside me. "Emma, stop."

He took a step in front of me, causing me to crash into his chest. Reaching out, he placed his hands on my shoulders to steady me and lowered his head so we were eye-to-eye.

"Emma, I'm sorry," he said, his voice sincere. "I didn't know how bad that was going to be for you, and I regret it. I'm a stupid jerk. But, you have to admit, it *was* pretty cool. That view up there was beautiful."

He was right. It *was* beautiful. And after I managed to stop freaking out for a second, I got to enjoy it. Deep down, I knew Logan had good intentions. I knew it wasn't a malicious attempt to traumatize me. But still. I couldn't forgive him that easily.

"What can I do to make it up to you?" he asked, letting go of me. "You want some cotton candy? Want me to play some ring toss and win you an oversized stuffed animal? Talk to me, Dawson."

My lips betrayed me as they began to curl into a smile. "Those games are all rigged. I doubt you could win me anything."

"Oh yeah?" he said, eyebrows raised. "Is that a challenge?"

"No, it's not. I'm mad at you and I'd kind of just like to go home now."

"Emma, you're *always* mad at me," he pointed out. "You should be used to it by now." He started backing up. "I'm going to win you a stuffed animal."

"No, you're not," I said, placing my hands on my hips and standing my ground.

"Yes, I am. And there's nothing you can do about it, because I'm your ride, and I've got the keys. You're stuck here."

"I have a phone, I can call a taxi."

He stopped. "That's an empty threat. The taxis around here are sketchy at best. You're afraid of everything, and I assume that includes getting rides in junky cars from strangers that—for all you know—could be serial killers."

I furrowed my brow. He was right.

With a sigh, I threw my hands up in defeat. "Fine, whatever. *Try* to win me a stuffed animal."

Logan clasped his hands together and grinned before turning on his heel and heading in the direction of the carnival games.

I took my time following him and when I made it to the ring toss booth, he was handing a dollar bill to the college kid behind the counter.

"My friend here doesn't think I can win her a stuffed animal," Logan said to the guy while motioning to me.

"I'm not his friend," I informed the kid, who looked like he couldn't have cared less about what either one of us had to say.

He stared at me blankly for a moment before turning to Logan and saying in a lifeless voice, "Okay. Well, good luck, I guess."

Logan held up one of the rings and winked at me. "I'll bet you I'll be able to get one of these six rings around one of those bottles."

I laughed. "I'll take that bet. What do I get if I win?"

"If you win, you get the satisfaction of rubbing it in my face that I suck at something. If I win, I get your forgiveness for the whole Ferris wheel thing. You'll also get a stuffed animal, so you'll win either way."

"Sounds fair," I said with a smirk.

He tossed the first ring and it bounced off the top of one of the bottles, and fell to the ground.

"I'm just rusty," he mumbled as held out the next one. "Haven't done this since I was, like, ten or so."

"Mmhmm. Likely story," I teased. This was fun. I was so used to seeing Logan excel at everything and it was annoying. But apparently, tossing rings onto bottle tops wasn't one of his many strengths.

He tossed the second ring and missed again. And again. And then again, three more times.

Grinning from ear-to-ear, I clapped my hands joyously at his misfortune. "I win!"

Logan scowled first at me, then at the kid behind the counter, and then finally at the rows of bottles in front of him. Reaching into his pocket, he pulled out another dollar. "I'm going to try again."

"That wasn't the deal."

"Well, we didn't shake on it, so…" He shrugged and exchanged his money for more rings.

I rolled my eyes as I felt my phone vibrate in my back pocket. The picture on the screen indicated it was either Chloe, or Sophia calling from Chloe's phone. I thought about letting it go to voicemail so that I could continue to enjoy witnessing Logan's monumental ring toss failure without interruption. However, I didn't want to lose out on the opportunity to speak with the girls, since I was missing them terribly.

I swiped to answer. "Hello?"

"Hey, girl!" Chloe's voice chirped through the phone.

"Hey, Chloe, what's up?"

"Not much. Sophia and I just wanted to check in on our favorite bookworm. How's the book organization project coming along?"

I was about to answer when I heard Logan swearing at the bottles and I looked over to see he had gone through his second set of rings with no success. I giggled and declared, "I win again!"

He glared at me as Chloe said on the other end of the line, "Huh? You win *what* again?"

"Oh, sorry, I was talking to Logan."

As usual, I was met with silence. "Emma, where are you?"

"I'm at Funland Park with Logan," I replied. "I'm currently watching him suck at the ring toss game." I gave him a toothy grin and a wave.

He flipped me off as he started his third round.

"Emma…" Chloe's voice trailed off, like she was trying to figure out how to say her next words. "Are you and Logan *dating*?"

I snorted. "Gross, Chloe. No, we're not dating."

Logan's head whipped over in my direction. "Hey, please inform Chloe that I'm just as disgusted by that prospect as you are."

"Logan wanted me to inform you that he *wishes* we were dating," I said to Chloe. "In fact, he's trying desperately right now to win me a stuffed animal because he thinks that's going to win my heart."

Logan shook his head as he concentrated on his next throw. "You suck, Dawson."

"Hey, I'm not the one who can't get a simple ring over the top of a bottle."

He stepped back and held out a ring. "Here. You think it's so easy, why don't you give it a try?"

"Emma, are you still there?" I heard Chloe say.

"Yeah, I'm still here," I replied, taking the ring from Logan and tossing it aimlessly over the counter.

It landed right over the top of one of the bottles.

Logan's jaw dropped. So did mine. My hand flew up to cover my mouth as I started laughing. "Oh my God, that was so easy!"

I could tell Logan was having a hard time deciding whether to be impressed or pissed. I think he went with a little of both.

"Hey, Chloe, can I call you back later? I have something I literally need to rub in Logan's face right now."

"Um…sure?" Chloe said.

"Cool. Love you guys! Talk to you later!" I put the phone back into my pocket and turned to the kid behind the counter. "I get to pick out a stuffed animal, right?"

He nodded unenthusiastically. "You can pick one from that section over there." He pointed to the far corner of the booth.

"Hmm." I tapped my upper lip with my index finger. "I'll take the fuchsia monkey." I glanced over at Logan. "I love fuchsia monkeys."

Logan sneered in response as the monkey was handed to me. I gave it a good squeeze before thrusting it in his direction. "Here, I want you to have this."

He shoved it away from his face. "I don't want your stupid monkey."

I pouted. "What's wrong? Are you upset that I won on the first attempt without even trying, when you couldn't do it in thirteen tries?"

Logan tossed the remaining rings in one big heap over the counter and sighed. "We're done here."

I smiled as we walked away from the booth and clung tightly to my monkey. I was glad Logan didn't take it. I kind of wanted to keep it for myself.

"Okay, even though I didn't win that for you, do you forgive me now?"

I pretended to think about it for a minute. Truth was, there was really nothing to forgive. Yeah, I was mad at him for that little stunt, but something told me that he really didn't do it to be a jerk. I think he was truly trying to help me.

"Yeah, sure. Why not?"

Logan's face lit up. "Excellent. Okay, now for our next adventure—"

I stopped walking. "No more adventures today, Logan. I don't think I could handle it."

"Relax," he said as we began moving again. "I'm not talking about today. I'm talking about Thursday."

I glanced at him curiously. "What's Thursday?"

"Another party. *BUT*, this one is way different than the last. It's at Justin's parents' camp on the lake. There's not going to be a whole lot of people there, so it'll be more…intimate. Matt's going to be there, of course, and this time I'm making sure you get a chance to talk to him. This is sort of an all-day event, so we can go late in the afternoon and stay for however long you'd like. I'll leave it up to you."

The thought of attending another party made me feel queasy. The last one didn't go so well, although we were only there for a few minutes. That fact was the only decent part of the whole night. Still, something about this one sounded like it would be more tolerable. Maybe even enjoyable, if I could spend some time talking to Matt.

"Yeah, okay," I found myself saying.

He blinked at me in surprise. "Cool. It's a date." He paused for a moment and crinkled his nose. "Well, not an *actual* date. That would be terrible."

I threw my head back and laughed. "Yet another thing we can agree on."

We exchanged smiles, and for a split second, it almost felt like we were friends—like actual friends who were just hanging out and enjoying each other's company.

It was weird.

He must have thought so too, because he cleared his throat and said, "So, what do you have planned for me next?"

That was a good question. I hadn't yet made a list of things for us to do that were super lame and boring. Although, even if I had, I wouldn't have told him.

"All I can tell you is that it's going to be a doozy," I said.

"A *doozy*?" He raised his eyebrows. "Did the stress from riding the Ferris wheel age you about sixty years or something? Who under seventy years old still uses the word 'doozy' these days?"

"*I* do, thank you very much." I playfully bumped his shoulder with mine and instantly regretted it. That was a little too flirtatious for my liking. Moving a couple steps sideways to put more space between us, I said, "Can we go home now? I've had enough of you for one day."

"Ouch, Dawson. Tell me how you *really* feel."

I chuckled as we began to head in the direction of the parking lot. "Can you honestly say you feel any different about me?"

A small smile played at his lips. "Nah, I've reached my daily Emma quota too, I suppose."

We walked the rest of the way to the car in silence, and less than half an hour later, Logan was pulling into his driveway.

"I'll see you on Thursday?" he said, turning in his seat to face me. When I nodded, he added, "Just think, you get to spend the next couple of days without me. How cool is that?"

I wiped an imaginary happy tear from my eye and said, "I couldn't have asked for anything better."

Logan rolled his eyes and we exited the vehicle.

Lifting my fuchsia monkey's hand, I moved it back and forth in a waving motion. "Bye, Logan."

He just smiled, shook his head, and gave me his own wave before turning and heading inside his house.

I glanced down at my watch. Both of my parents were still at work, so I had the house all to myself. I wasn't a huge fan of being home alone, but it wasn't so bad in the middle of the afternoon…especially considering Logan was right next door. Not that he would ever come to my rescue if somebody broke into my house and tried to kidnap me.

He'd probably assist them.

As soon as I walked through the front door, I pulled out my phone and dialed Chloe's number.

She answered halfway through the first ring. "Okay, Em, you've got some serious explaining to do."

"I'm doing well, thanks, and you?"

"Cut the crap, girl!" Chloe exclaimed. "You're dating Logan!"

I removed the phone from my ear so that I could glare through it at Chloe. "I am not. You take that back."

"Give me the phone," I heard Sophia's muffled voice say in the background. A second later, it came through loud and clear. "Emma, Chloe's accusation is legit. It *really* does sound like you and Logan are dating."

"I don't care how it *sounds*. We're *not*."

"No?" Sophia said. "Then what *are* you doing? Besides shopping together, going out for lunch together, going to parties together, going to art museums together, going to amusement parks together. For crying out loud, Emma, you and Logan have done more date-like activities in the last two days than I have done during the entirety of all my relationships combined."

I had broken down the night before and told the girls all about what Logan and I were doing, and I was seriously regretting it at the moment. I had to admit, to an outsider, I could see how that would all look like dating. Still, Chloe and Sophia knew how much I'd always hated Logan, and how much he'd always hated me. They also knew how much I liked Matt, and how I was doing all of this to get him to like me.

"Guys, will you stop it? Please? Logan and I are not dating."

"It would be okay if you were, you know," Chloe said, and I could tell I was on speaker now. "Soph and I would support it one hundred percent. Logan is a total hottie and we've always thought there might be some underlying sexual tension there between you two—"

"Oh my God, I'm hanging up now!"

The girls giggled. "Sorry, Em," Sophia said. "We'll stop teasing you. In all seriousness, we really hope this all works out the way you want. You know how much we support the idea of an Emma and Matt relationship."

It was true. The two of them had been shipping me and Matt for years now.

Intent on changing the subject, I went on to ask them how their vacation was going and if they'd met any new boys since the last time we spoke. We talked for close to twenty minutes before we ended the conversation and hung up.

Glancing down at my stuffed monkey, I said, "Hey, you want to go help me organize my book collection?"

It didn't answer, just stared up at me lifelessly. I ran my hand over the soft fake fur on its head and smiled. It had felt so good showing up Logan at the ring toss game. Amazingly enough, he'd been a decent sport about it, although I'm sure it ate him up inside.

As I walked upstairs to my room, I tried desperately to forget the conversation I'd just had with the girls. I didn't like their assumption that something could be going on between me and Logan. Hopefully, the party on Thursday would change all that. Maybe I'd get to talk to Matt this time.

And I had the next two days to plot out exactly what I would say to him.

Chapter 15

LOGAN

My two-and-a-half-day break from Emma was awesome and it really gave me the opportunity to start fleshing out my plan. By the time Thursday came, I figured it was time to kick things into high gear.

It was time to get the Emma and Matt ball rolling.

My plan for Thursday was simple, but hopefully effective: Emma and I were going to hitch a ride with Matt to the party. When it came time for us to leave, I would conveniently find a reason to get a ride home with somebody else, forcing Matt to take Emma home alone. Maybe nothing would come of it—and probably nothing would—but it would at least get them socializing. It would at least put Emma on Matt's radar.

Emma was unaware of my transportation plans, and when I arrived on her doorstep that afternoon and told her we'd be riding with Matt, she immediately perked up.

"Really?" she said with a smile. "That's a great idea."

Hmm. Not what I was expecting. I thought she would hate the idea of being stuck in a car with him, having to maybe even spark up a conversation with him. But maybe all this hanging out we'd been doing was starting to help. Maybe she was starting to come out of her shell.

"Of course, it is," I said. "I told you, I know what I'm doing." I glanced over my shoulder at Matt's house and noticed an unfamiliar car was parked next to his in his driveway. Turning back to Emma, I said, "Are you ready?"

She nodded and shut the door behind her.

As we made our way across the street, Matt exited his house, followed closely by a girl I didn't recognize. My heart instantly sank. I had no idea who she was, but she was tall, brunette, beautiful, and scantily clad in a pair of short jean shorts, a bright pink bikini top and a white button-up that was left unbuttoned, but tied at the waist. She looked like she could be a waitress at Rodeo Roy's.

And she was apparently Matt's date to the party.

I snuck a glance over at Emma, who looked utterly destroyed. I couldn't help but feel bad for her. She knew there was no way she could compete for Matt's affections with somebody like this girl. And I also couldn't help but feel bad for myself. The trip to New York was starting to look more and more like a reality for me.

When Matt saw us, he grinned and waved. "Hey, guys!" He and Smokin' Hot Barbie bounced down the front steps to greet us.

"Logan, you remember my cousin, Riley, don't you?" He motioned to the girl beside him.

I could hear Emma breathe a sigh of relief next to me at the revelation that Riley was Matt's cousin, not his new girlfriend.

My jaw dropped. "Riley Cavanaugh? No way. That can't be you."

Riley Cavanaugh was my first kiss. We were at Matt's twelfth birthday party and a group of us had decided to play 7 Minutes in Heaven. I got paired up with Riley, who at the time was a skinny tomboy with frizzy hair and a retainer, and for seven glorious minutes, we awkwardly made out in a broom closet. I thought I was in love with her for the rest of the day, but after she went back home to New Hampshire that night, I forgot all about her.

Until now.

She was no longer a tomboy. She'd filled out quite nicely, and from the looks of it, she'd learned how to tame her hair, which now fell in loose waves down her back.

"Logan!" she exclaimed, throwing herself at me and pulling me into a tight embrace.

Unfortunately, it only lasted for a few seconds before she removed herself from me.

"It's so good to see you!" she gushed.

"Yeah, uh, it's good to see you, too," I said, suddenly feeling like a shy, awkward twelve-year-old again.

Emma raised an eyebrow at me and looked like she was trying desperately not to smirk at my reaction. I threw her a subtle glare.

"I'm Emma," she said, holding her hand out to Riley.

Riley, who was maybe only an inch taller than Emma, looked down at her curiously and shook her hand. "Oh right, the girl next door. I remember seeing you around whenever I'd come to visit. Usually, you were being chased by Logan, screaming at the top of your lungs at him."

"That sounds about right," I said, throwing Emma a lopsided grin. She didn't seem as amused as I was.

"Riley and her parents are up here visiting for the summer," Matt explained. "She was bored, so I suggested she come with us to the party tonight."

"Sounds good to me," I said a little too eagerly. I could tell Emma picked up on it, but no one else appeared to.

We all headed over to Matt's Jeep. Since nobody had called shotgun yet, a light bulb flipped on above my head.

"Hey, Emma, why don't you sit up in the front?" I suggested. When everyone turned to look at me, I said to Matt, "Emma gets carsick riding in the backseat. And unless you want her blowing chunks all over the place, it would probably be best if she stayed in the front."

Matt grimaced slightly at the thought. Riley snorted. Emma narrowed her eyes into a death glare. I subtly shrugged at her, as if to say, *"Be cool, I'm doing this for you."*

I had no idea if Emma was prone to carsickness, but it didn't really matter. I had to find an excuse to get her to sit next to Matt. It would take us close to twenty minutes to get to the party and that was twenty minutes they could spend making small talk.

However, that's not what happened.

Instead, Riley talked most of the way. Some of the time she was speaking to me, asking me what I had been up to all these years, but she kept including Matt in the conversation and thus successfully talk-blocking Emma.

Oh well. I'd make sure they'd have plenty of time to talk at the party.

It was nearly six-thirty when we arrived at the camp and only a few people had shown up already. Justin was tending to the grill and a group of his friends had already started a game of beer pong on the deck. There were a few others wandering about, but all in all, it was a low-key event so far. I could tell from the look on Emma's face that she appreciated that.

I was glancing around, trying to think of an excuse to get Emma and Matt alone, when Matt spoke up.

"Hey, Riley," he said, grabbing her arm. "Since you're going to be up here all summer, I might as well introduce you to everyone. You'll probably be seeing a lot of them."

He gave me a nod that said he'd catch me later, and they walked off toward Justin.

Okay, well there went *that* opportunity. I turned to Emma.

"You want to take a walk or something?"

She blinked at me in surprise. "A walk?"

"Yeah. I can show you the lake."

"I've seen the lake before."

I rolled my eyes. "I know that. But would you rather go check out the lake, where there appears to be nobody hanging around, or would you rather stay here and participate in a rousing game of beer pong with a bunch of jocks?"

She glanced over my shoulder at the group of already-drunk football players on the deck. "The lake it is."

I figured as much. As we started down the long, stone path leading to the dock, Emma ran a hand through her hair and said, "So Riley turned into quite a looker, huh?"

I raised an eyebrow, amused. "A looker?"

"Yeah. I remember seeing her come up from time to time to visit with Matt. She used to look so…different."

I nodded in agreement. "She has definitely filled out, that's for sure."

Emma chuckled softly. "I'm just glad she's Matt's cousin. For a split second there, I didn't recognize her. I thought she might be his new girlfriend or something."

She could have easily been. If you took away the blood relation between the two, she probably would've been. She fit Matt's type to a T.

"Well, the good news is that she's not," I said as we approached the water. "But she's exactly the type of girl he's looking for. Carefree. Fun. Hot. Has no problem walking around in a bikini. Which reminds me, when are we going bikini shopping? This weekend is fast-approaching, and you *have* to come to Matt's pool party."

Emma shook her head. "I already told you, Logan, I'm not going."

"Oh, come on. It will be fun."

"There is no part of a pool party that would be fun for me," she said. "I can't even swim and I'm afraid of the water so…nope. I'm not going."

We stopped walking once we reached the lake. Grabbing her hand, I began to lead her down the dock.

"Logan, what are you doing?"

"We're going to take an up-close look at the water."

She tried desperately to remove her hand from mine, but it only made me tighten my grip. When we arrived at the very end of the dock, I placed my hands on her shoulders and gently moved her so that she was now at the very edge, staring down at the water.

"Logan," she said nervously, "this is a little *too* up-close."

"Emma, it's just water," I said, removing my hands from her. "It's harmless. It's not very deep here. Nor is it very deep in Matt's pool. You're not going to drown. There will be plenty of people around to save you if you go under. I promise." I paused for a moment before leaning in and whispering in her ear, "*I'll* save you."

She jumped slightly at that and whipped around to face me. As she did so, her heel slipped off the edge of the dock and she stumbled backward with a gasp. My quick reflexes kicked in and I reached out to grab her; there was no way I was about to let her fall into the lake. Hooking one arm around her back, I stopped her from falling. Hooking my other arm around her waist, I pulled her in close. So close her chest was now pressed firmly against mine. So close I could feel the pounding of her heart against her ribcage.

Relief washed over her face as she realized I'd done what I'd just claimed I would: I saved her.

I had to admit, I was a bit relieved myself. I didn't know

how deep her fear of the water actually went, and I didn't want to be the reason I found out firsthand.

Despite the fact she was safe and sound and both feet were now firmly planted on the dock, something was preventing me from letting her go. Maybe it was because I suddenly noticed how good she smelled—like apples. Fresh, crisp apples. Probably her shampoo.

Or maybe it was because I noticed how substantial she felt in my arms. She was thin, but she wasn't *Grace*-thin. She wasn't a size negative zero. She had some meat on her bones, and in all the right places.

Maybe it was because I noticed how perfectly her body molded into my embrace.

Maybe it was because I noticed how soft her hands were as they clung to both of my arms, holding onto me for dear life.

But worst of all, maybe it was because I noticed what holding her close was doing to me. It was making my head fuzzy, my breathing shallow. And when our eyes locked, my pulse began to race, matching hers beat for beat.

Fortunately, the moment was fleeting—ending when a deep voice behind me yelled, "Incoming!" before I felt two hands on my back, shoving me forward...sending both me and Emma flailing into the lake.

She managed to get out a yelp before we landed in the water, sinking below the surface on impact.

The water wasn't all that deep, which was a good thing considering Emma couldn't swim. It took her only a second to resurface after me, but she did so while coughing and sputtering.

I glared up in the direction of the dock to see one of Matt's football teammates, Jackson Rowe, laughing and pointing at us.

"What the hell, dude?" I shouted at him. "What did you do

that for?"

"Sorry, bro," Jackson said, clutching his stomach from laughing so hard. "I just saw you two standing there like you were about to make out and I couldn't help myself."

My mouth clamped shut at his words. Emma and I were *not* about to make out. Why would he even say that?

"Not cool," I grumbled and turned my attention to Emma, whose coughing had subsided. "Are you okay?"

I expected her to either just nod and maybe join me in chastising Jackson for his actions, or to be freaking the hell out at the fact she was in the water. But instead, she scowled at me and yelled, "What the hell is wrong with you, Logan?"

My jaw dropped. "What's wrong with *me*? Jackson's the one who pushed us in!"

"He wouldn't have been able to if you hadn't forced me to the edge of the dock in the first place," she said, wading past me in a huff. "You're such a jerk."

Oh, here we go again. "That's just great, Emma. Blame the victim, why don't you?"

She ignored me as she climbed the ladder up to the dock.

Jackson noticed right away how nicely her wet, white t-shirt was now clinging to her and let out a low whistle as he leered at her. "Nice bra, Dawson."

He wasn't kidding. From what I could tell through the now-see-through material, it *was* a nice bra. Pink and lacy, and not at all what I pictured her choice of bras to be.

Not that I'd ever given it any thought.

She looked confused for a second before glancing down at herself and seeing what he was referring to. Instantly turning a dark shade of red, she promptly crossed her arms over her chest and began to stalk off in the direction of the camp.

"Emma!" I called after her, quickly pulling myself out of

the lake. I gave Jackson a good shove as soon as I stepped onto the dock.

"You're a real prick," I muttered before taking off after Emma. He just threw his head back and laughed in response.

"Emma, wait!" I broke into a jog to catch up to her. "Are you okay? I'm really sorry about that."

"Yeah, well, you should be." She stopped and threw her hands in the air. "Now we're going to have to spend the rest of the night in soaking wet clothes. Plus, I think I inhaled some lake water up my nose, and I've probably contracted a brain-eating amoeba."

"If it makes you feel any better, I've probably contracted one, too."

"At least it will be a quicker death for you since there's less there for it to eat away at," she snapped, but followed it up with a small smile.

"Funny," I said with a fake laugh. "Taking a shot at my intelligence when you know darn well that my grades are just as good as yours, if not better. You know what? You deserve to suffer the rest of the night in wet clothes."

She just shook her head and hugged her arms tighter across her chest. Her bra was still visible through her shirt, and I could tell it was making her feel incredibly insecure. So, being the gentleman I was, I decided to help her out. Lifting my shirt up and over my head, I took it off and held it out to her.

"Here, take this."

She stared blankly at the shirt and said, "What am I supposed to do with that? It's just as wet as my own clothes."

I twisted the material to squeeze out as much of the water as possible. "Yes, but it will at least cover you up so the entire party won't be able to see that you shop at Victoria's Secret for your unmentionables. Although, that might not be a bad thing because it would actually make you seem somewhat cool…"

Emma rolled her eyes. "Put your shirt back on."

Once the shirt was off, I wasn't planning on putting it back on. At least, not while it was still wet. I was about to suggest we go ask Justin if there was a dryer inside the camp that we could throw our clothes into when Matt and Riley suddenly appeared by my side.

"Aw, these two already went for a swim without us," Riley said to Matt with a pout. Her gaze flickered to my chest and her pout turned into a smile. "Nice muscles, Logan. You didn't have those the last time I saw you."

My gaze flickered to *her* chest for a split second and I couldn't help but think, *and* you *didn't have* those *the last time I saw* you. Judging from the small smirk that played at her lips, she knew exactly what I was thinking.

Her bikini top could barely handle what she had going on underneath it.

At the sound of Emma clearing her throat, I looked over to see her standing there looking uncomfortable and miserable. Her mascara had started running, creating dark circles under her eyes, and her hair was all wet and matted. She was a stark contrast to Riley, whose everything was all perfectly in place, and it was obvious Emma was aware of that.

I felt bad for her. Especially since her crush was standing right in front of her, taking in her disheveled appearance with a faint look of amusement on his face.

Removing her white shirt and unbuttoning her shorts, Riley looked at me and said, "Is the water warm? I feel like going for a swim."

Before I could answer, she lowered her shorts and stepped out of them. My mouth hung open when I took in the full view of her in a bikini. I didn't even care that she noticed the fact I was blatantly checking her out.

"Would you like to go with me?" she asked, batting her eyelashes at me and running a finger across my stomach. "Since you're already wet and everything."

"Um…" Swallowing hard, my eyes flickered over to Emma, who was busy studying the bark of the tree next to her. I looked at Matt and a brilliant idea hit me.

"I'd love to," I said to Riley before turning to my best friend. "Hey, Matt, why don't you take Emma back to the camp and show her where the dryer is, so she can dry her clothes?"

The perfect opportunity for them to be alone.

"Uh, okay," Matt said, shoving his hands into the pockets of his shorts. He turned to Emma. "Shall we?"

Emma and I exchanged a glance and I gave her a small smile, which she didn't return. Surprisingly, she looked less than thrilled at my suggestion. She was probably scared of having to spend alone time with the guy she could barely speak two coherent words to. Too bad. She'd thank me later.

They took off together and Riley grabbed my hand and started leading me back toward the dock.

"So," she said as we walked, "Matt told me that you and your girlfriend recently broke up. Sorry to hear that."

With a dismissive wave of my hand, I said, "It's no big deal. We weren't really serious or anything."

She nodded. "And Emma? What's going on between the two of you?"

I glanced sideways at her. "Nothing's going on between us. Why would you even ask that?"

"I don't know," she said with a shrug. "Back there it just seemed like she wasn't too happy that you agreed to go swimming with me. Like she was jealous or something."

I couldn't help but laugh at that. "You're delusional. Emma doesn't care what I do, or who I do it with. In fact, she's madly in love with Matt. That's why I asked him to take her back to the camp—to get them alone together." I felt bad about outing Emma's crush to Riley, but I had to. I could not let her think for one second that there was—or ever could be—something going on between me and Emma.

That was just ridiculous.

"Oh," she said, sounding relieved. "Cool." She glanced down at the ground. "I just got out of a relationship, myself. My boyfriend of two years dumped me right after school let out."

"No way." I cocked an eyebrow at her. "There's no way a guy dumped *you*. What kind of idiot would do such a thing?"

She chuckled and placed her hand on my forearm. "You're too sweet, Logan. You know, I thought I was going to be miserable being up here this summer, just spending my time thinking about who my ex is hooking up with back home. But now I think I'm going to like being here." She grinned and let her clothes drop to the ground.

"Meet you in there?" she said with a wink, motioning her head toward the lake. Without waiting for me to answer, she turned and ran down the length of the dock and dove into the water.

I took a deep breath and let it out slowly, raking a hand through my hair. I was pretty sure Matt's cousin was just flirting with me.

And I was pretty sure I was okay with that.

Chapter 16

EMMA

I glanced down at my phone and sighed as I realized I'd already been at Justin's party for nearly two hours. Two hours of my life I was never getting back.

As requested by Logan, Matt had escorted me to Justin's bathroom, where I was able to quickly dry my clothes, blow-dry my hair and wash off the mascara that had smudged around my eyes, making me look like a distraught raccoon. And despite the fact I think Logan had wanted to give me and Matt some time alone together, as soon as he showed me where the bathroom was, he took off to find his friends.

So much for that.

After I got myself looking presentable again, I took off in search of Logan, but he was nowhere to be found. Neither was Matt or Riley, and for one panicky moment I wondered if they might have left without me. And to make sure they hadn't, I went and verified that Matt's Jeep was still parked where it was earlier. Sure enough, it was still there.

I searched aimlessly for no more than five minutes before I decided to head down to the dock, away from the crowd that had grown exponentially since we'd first arrived. Since I didn't know anyone there except for the three people I came with (the same three people who were MIA), I had no interest in standing around by myself in the middle of the crowd, looking like a total loser.

So that's how I ended up sitting alone at the end of the dock, my feet dangling in the water, checking the time every thirty seconds to see if the night was over yet.

It wasn't.

I was lucky my phone was even working, after taking that tumble into the lake. My dad had gotten me a waterproof case for Christmas, due to the fact I'd had a history of dropping my phones into puddles. If I had to be hanging out alone at this party without my phone, I probably would have hitched a ride home by now.

I tried texting both Chloe and Sophia to see what they were up to, but neither had responded. I tried playing some Bookworm, but I couldn't concentrate enough to find anything other than simple three-letter words. That wasn't like me, I usually excelled at that game. I could tell something was nagging at my subconscious. Like, for instance, where the heck was Logan? He dragged me to this stupid party and then abandoned me. He got me pushed into a lake, but not before we had a weird moment that I couldn't stop replaying in my head, no matter how hard I tried.

When he saved me from falling off the edge of the dock by wrapping his arms around me and pulling me against him, my mind had gone completely numb. It was the second time in one week he'd held me close, and it was the second time I hadn't hated it. And I hated myself for not hating it. Because I hated *him*, and his touch should have repulsed me.

But it didn't.

I told myself it was normal. I may have hated Logan, but he was tall, good-looking and smelled good. I would have had the same reaction had it been *any* guy fitting that description who had enveloped me in his warm, solid embrace. Logan wasn't special.

At least, to me he wasn't. To Riley, that was apparently a different story. The girl could not have been any more transparent, stripping down in front of him and inviting him—and only him—to go for a swim. And he was no better himself, quickly getting rid of me and Matt so he could have his own alone time with Riley.

I was about to text Chloe again when somebody spoke behind me.

"Emma Dawson." I recognized the voice right away as belonging to the party host himself.

I glanced over my shoulder to see Justin unsteadily making his way toward me, a red plastic cup in his hand.

"Hey, Justin," I said unenthusiastically.

He took a seat next to me, so close that his shoulder was touching mine. "What's a girl like you doing, sitting all alone out here in the dark? Haven't you ever seen any of the *Friday the 13th* movies? Pretty, innocent girls and lakes don't mix. It's not safe."

I couldn't help but chuckle at that. "Well, it's neither Friday *nor* the 13th, it's not completely dark out yet, and I'd hardly say I'm alone. There are people everywhere." I motioned to the groups of kids standing only a few yards away.

"Fair enough," he said, taking a drink of whatever was in the cup. "So, you keep showing up at my parties. I'd start to think maybe you had a thing for me if you didn't keep showing up with Reynolds." He grinned and added, "What's up with that, anyway? Is it true you're the one that broke up him and Grace?"

I gaped at him. "Is that what people are saying?"

He nodded with a low chuckle. "Oh, yeah. At least, that's what Grace is telling everyone."

Great. That's just what I needed—to have the most popular

girl at our school telling all her friends that I was the reason she and her boyfriend broke up. And even worse, it would lead people to believe that Logan and I were *together*. I shuddered at the thought.

"So? Are you?"

I glanced sideways at him. "Am I what?"

"The reason Logan and Grace broke up? Are you and Logan a thing? Or, am I free to hit on you right now?"

My jaw dropped. What was happening? This was the second time Justin had flirted with me at a party. Granted, he was wasted both times. Like right now, he reeked of beer like he'd showered in it, washed his clothes with it, and gargled with it.

"Um…" I said as he shifted his position so he was facing me.

He reached out his free hand and tucked a strand of hair behind my ear. "You're really pretty, Emma," he said softly.

My breath caught in my throat. I'd waited my whole life to have a guy look me straight in the eye and tell me he thought I was pretty, and even though Justin was sloshed and probably not even aware of what he was doing, it still made my heart skip a beat. Drunk or not, Justin was hot and popular, and was definitely hitting on me. And as his gaze slowly lowered to my mouth, I started to panic.

Was he thinking of kissing me?

Suddenly, I was bombarded with all sorts of conflicting emotions. Yes, I wanted to be kissed—*finally*—but did I want to be kissed by a guy I had no romantic feelings for? First kisses were supposed to be special, and there was nothing special about this scenario. I barely knew Justin, I didn't particularly like him, and he wasn't going to remember he'd even kissed me in the first place.

As soon as that last thought entered my head, I remembered something Logan had said to me when I'd confessed to him that I'd never been kissed. He'd told me that I would want to get the first one out of the way before I got together with Matt, so he wouldn't know how inexperienced I was.

And this was the perfect opportunity. If Justin was as drunk as he smelled, he wouldn't remember any of this in the morning. I'd be able to use him as practice. Sure, I'd be forfeiting that special first-kiss high you get with someone you're in love with, but it would be worth it if I at least learned something from it. Matt would—*hopefully*—be my first *real* kiss. This would just be a practice run.

I was excited by the prospect as Justin leaned in close. My instinct was to pull back, but I forced myself to lean in as well. The quicker I got this started, the quicker it would end.

Justin's lips were almost touching mine, and my eyes were in the process of closing when a voice behind us spoke out, causing us to both to back away from each other.

"Yo, Justin. Your beer pong boys are getting out of control. You might want to go put them in check."

I turned around to see Matt standing only a few feet away from us, eyeing us suspiciously.

Justin groaned and hoisted himself up. "This always happens," he grunted as he stumbled off, not even saying another word to me.

I guess I'd dodged a bullet.

Embarrassed by the fact my crush had just caught me almost kissing another guy, I rested my elbows on my knees and planted my face in my hands.

"Sorry about that," Matt said, taking a seat beside me.

I blinked over at him in surprise. "Sorry about what?"

"I lied about the beer pong thing," he said sheepishly. "They're actually playing a friendly, peaceful game right now. I just thought maybe you could use some interception. That is, unless you *wanted* him to kiss you, in which case, I apologize for interrupting."

"No," I said, a little too quickly. "You don't need to apologize. I'm glad you interrupted. I guess I just…got caught up in the moment."

Matt smiled, and my heart melted. "Justin's a good guy. He is. But sometimes at parties, especially when he's had a few drinks, he can get kind of…handsy. Some girls are into it. I figured you probably weren't."

"You figured correctly," I said, returning his smile. "Thank you."

"No problem." He stared out at the lake. "So, what are you doing hanging out down here all alone?"

I shrugged. "I tried to find Logan, but he seems to have gone missing. Along with Riley."

"Ah, yes," Matt said with a smirk. "Knowing those two, they probably ducked into one of the bedrooms for some *catching up*, if you know what I mean."

I swallowed hard as I felt a sudden wave of bile enter my esophagus.

"Are you alright?" Matt asked. "You look a little sick."

I took a deep breath and let it out slowly. "Yeah, I'm fine. I just feel a little queasy. I haven't eaten in a few hours, and I'm not sure I trust Justin's grilling skills enough to partake in any of the food here."

"Smart girl," Matt said with a laugh. "Well, I'm feeling kind of hungry myself, and I'm kind of over this party. What do you say we find Logan and Riley and go grab something to eat somewhere?"

I knew there was no significance to his offer to go get food, especially since he wanted to include Logan and Riley, but a small, silly part of me wanted to pretend like he was asking me out on a date.

Pushing aside that thought, I snorted and said, "I would hate to interrupt whatever those two are doing right now." Mostly because I had no interest in *witnessing* whatever they were doing, whether it be making out or something far worse.

Just the idea of it made me even queasier.

"Let me deal with that," Matt said, standing up. He held out his hand for me to take. "I'm good at interrupting things."

I stared at his hand for a moment before slipping mine into his grasp. I'd never had any sort of contact with Matt before, so this was kind of a big thing for me. I'd lost count of how many times in the last few years I'd dreamed of holding his hand in mine, and now it was about to become a reality. Granted, it was only for the purpose of him helping me up, but I would take it.

"There you guys are," a female voice said as soon as I stood.

Apparently, Logan and Riley had finished "catching up" and were now standing next to the dock watching us.

Logan's gaze flickered down to where I was still holding Matt's hand. With a cocked eyebrow, he gave me a quizzical look.

"Are we interrupting something?" he asked.

I quickly let go of Matt's hand as Matt said, "Nah. Emma and I were just about to look for you guys to ask if you'd like to leave and maybe go get something to eat?"

"I'm in." Riley grinned and hooked her arm around Logan's. "It'll be like a double date."

Apparently for the two of them it would be a date, judging from how close they were standing, and the fact Riley had practically draped herself over Logan.

Matt gave an awkward chuckle. "Uh, yeah, I guess."

Logan, who'd had yet to remove his gaze from mine, said, "So, what were you two doing down here all alone?"

I opened my mouth to tell him we were doing nothing, but Matt spoke before I had the chance.

"I was just saving her from Justin," he said with a lopsided grin and slapped me on the back. "He was in the process of putting the moves on Emma here and they were about to go into make-out mode before I intervened. I'm kind of a hero."

Mouth agape, Logan's gaze flickered over to Matt briefly before returning to mine. "You were going to kiss Justin?"

"Ooh, nice," Riley said approvingly. "Justin's a hottie."

Logan scowled at her. "Justin's a giant douche."

Riley shrugged. "Who cares? He's still hot. And I'll bet he's a great kisser." She winked over at me.

I wanted to die. I was hoping the near-kiss with Justin would stay a secret between me and Matt.

"Are we all ready to leave?" Matt asked, and I was thankful for the change in subject.

Riley smiled and nodded. Logan just kind of grumbled something. Matt made his way up the dock and he and Riley began to walk back toward the camp.

"We'll meet you at the car," Logan called to them over his shoulder before glancing back at me. He made no attempt to begin following them.

"What?" I said, suddenly feeling like I was under scrutiny.

"Really, Emma? *Justin?* What were you thinking?"

Something in the sound of his voice put me on edge—like he was judging me for almost kissing Justin or something.

"Hey, you were the one who told me I should get my first kiss out of the way," I pointed out.

"Yeah, well I didn't mean you should do it with Justin," he

mumbled.

With an arched brow, I folded my arms over my chest. "No? Who would you expect me to get it out of the way with, then?"

"I don't know. Anyone *but* Justin. The guy's a dirt bag."

"Well, if you don't have any better suggestions, I'm just going to have to take what I can get," I said, walking past him.

He began to follow me. "I would kiss you myself before I'd let Justin get anywhere near you again."

Wait, what? I glanced sideways at him just as my foot caught on a twig and I stumbled forward.

"Are you okay?" he asked, placing a hand on my arm to help steady me.

I quickly brushed him off me. "I'm fine."

He looked at me, clearly amused. "Emma, don't worry, I'm not going to kiss you."

"I'm not worried," I muttered as I regained my balance.

"Oh, so you *want* me to kiss you?" He grinned, wiggling his eyebrows suggestively.

"Ew, gross, no," I said, giving him a playful shove.

"Then I guess you're just going to have to save your first one for Matt. Hopefully you don't end up embarrassing yourself."

I shot him a glare. "Stop trying to scare me, it's not going to work."

"Believe it or not, I'm not trying to scare you," he said. "You might be *really bad* at it, and you'll never know until it's too late."

I rolled my eyes and shook my head as we neared Matt's Jeep. Matt and Riley had already gotten in.

My hand was just reaching out to grab the passenger door handle when Logan leaned over and murmured into my ear,

"I'm serious, Emma. If you ever want to practice, I can show you a thing or two."

His words, along with the feel of his breath tickling my skin, sent an involuntary shiver down my spine. With a soft chuckle, he stepped back and let himself inside the vehicle, winking at me as he did so.

The jerk was trying to unnerve me, and it was working. He had no intention of helping me; he just wanted to see my reaction. Not that I would ever take him up on the offer, anyway. Even though I had no doubt that he *could* teach me a few things...

And he probably was a really good kisser...

I violently pushed the thoughts out of my head as I yanked open the passenger door and climbed in beside Matt.

"Is everything okay?" Matt asked, presumably because I'd slammed the door shut.

I glanced in the visor mirror to see Logan smirking at me from the backseat. Furiously, I flipped the visor up and turned to Matt with a smile. "Everything's fine."

Except everything wasn't. Visions of kissing Logan were now dancing through my head and they weren't making me feel as nauseated as they should have been. It was infuriating.

I was quickly starting to realize this whole plan of Logan's was a really bad idea.

Chapter 17

LOGAN

Boredom. That was my excuse the next day for walking over to Emma's house and knocking on her front door mid-afternoon. Matt was busy with family stuff and I didn't feel like going to the beach for the umpteenth time with all my other friends, so my only other options included either staying home and playing Peek-A-Boo with Abby, or harassing Emma.

Emma was the lucky winner.

And boy, did I love harassing that girl. I could tell I'd totally freaked her out the night before by offering to give her kissing lessons, after which she was notably more quiet and grumpy than usual for the rest of the night. She barely spoke a word while the four of us stopped for food, and then on the ride home. Neither Matt nor Riley seemed to notice, but I did.

I had no idea what possessed me to offer my services, even though it was an empty offer anyway. Well, it was *half*-empty. I *would* kiss her before I'd let Justin try it again. It made my blood boil to think about him putting the moves on her. Emma was sweet and innocent. Justin was slimy and as far from innocent as he could get. I'm not sure that guy had ever been innocent a day in his life. There was no way I was going to let that tool steal Emma's first kiss—and I wasn't about to let her just hand it to him either.

Which is why I'd decided not to take her to any more parties. Instead, I figured we could take a break from the activities

I had planned and see what she had in store for me. That was a lot safer.

She answered the front door a few seconds after I knocked, and I watched as her face fell with disappointment when she saw me standing on the other side.

"What do you want?" she asked firmly, placing a hand on her hip.

"Hello to you, too," I said brightly.

Her eyes narrowed slightly. "Seriously, what do you want, Logan? I don't remember making any plans to hang out today."

"We didn't. But Matt likes girls who are spontaneous, so I figured we could work on your spontaneity. Starting with me showing up unannounced at your door and demanding we hang out."

"I can't. I kind of already have plans."

Arching a brow, I teased, "What kind of plans? You got a hot date or something?"

"As a matter of fact, yes," she said, flipping her hair over her shoulder. "With Justin. We're going to the drive-in. I have no idea what movie we're going to see, but it doesn't really matter, since we'll probably just spend the entire time making out in his backseat."

My hands instantly clenched into fists at my sides. I was going to kill Justin. "Are you serious?"

She stared at me blankly for a moment before breaking out into a giggle. "No, I'm not serious. And I'm offended that you would think for one second I would actually go on a date with Justin."

I breathed a sigh of relief. "Why wouldn't I think that? You were willing to kiss him last night."

Emma rolled her eyes and stepped aside, opening the door

wider. Ignoring my comment, she said, "Would you like to come in?"

"I thought you'd never ask," I said with a grin as I stepped through the doorway.

It had been a long time since I'd been inside the Dawson home. From the looks of it, not much had changed since I was a little kid.

"This brings back a lot of memories, doesn't it?" she asked, closing the door behind us. "The last time you were here, I tried to push you down the stairs."

I chuckled. "Oh yeah, that's right. Thank God your mom has great reflexes and was able to stop you in time."

"Yeah, I suppose..." she said with a small smile as she headed over to the staircase. "I was just about to go up to my room before you knocked on the door. Care to join me?"

Emma Dawson was inviting me to her bedroom? Hell yeah, I wanted to join her. I hadn't been in her room since the day she tried to push me down the stairs, when we were eleven, but I remember it being very pink—like a cotton candy machine had blown up inside it. I wouldn't be surprised if it hadn't changed at all since the last time I saw it, and I was fully prepared to make fun of her for it.

However, I was sorely disappointed when she opened the door to her room to reveal no pink whatsoever. Instead, the walls had been repainted light blue. All her stuffed animals, dollhouses, and pinups of boy band members were gone and were now replaced with...well...books. Lots and lots of books. Every wall was lined with bookshelves full of them. No wonder she wanted to stay behind to organize them all. She'd be lucky if she had that project done by the time we graduated.

"Wow," I breathed, stepping into the room.

"Impressive, huh?" she said, beaming. She was clearly

proud of her collection.

"Definitely." I walked over to the bookshelf closest to me and ran a finger down the line of book spines in the middle. Some were old, some were new. Some were hardcover, others were paperback. "How were you able to afford all these?"

She shrugged. "Baby-sitting money, birthday money, Christmas money. I got some of them real cheap at yard sales. Some were given to me as gifts. Others were handed down to me from my mom and my grandmother. Bookworms kind of run in my family."

"Have you read all of them?"

She threw her head back and laughed. "No way. I haven't even read half. Sometimes I think I'm more into collecting them than reading them." She paused for a moment before saying, "You know, I was about to start my organization project when you knocked on the door."

I couldn't help but snort. "Really? That's what your 'plans' were this afternoon? Organizing your books?"

She frowned. "Well, you've kind of been distracting me since summer vacation began. This was the first opportunity I've had to start it." She paused for a moment, raising her eyebrows questioningly. "Would you like to help?"

I really didn't care to do anything that involved books and wasn't school-related, but I was bored and had nothing better to do, so I said, "Yeah, sure, why not?"

"Really?" A look of disbelief washed over her face. "Okay, well, the first thing we need to do is take all the books off the shelves and stack them on the floor. You can start with this shelf." She pointed to the one next to me.

Why had I agreed to this? If any of my friends found out I helped organize a book collection on a beautiful summer afternoon instead of going to the beach and checking out hot chicks in bikinis, I would instantly lose my popularity status.

Indefinitely.

Yet here I was, about to do it anyway. With a self-defeated sigh, my eyes danced around all the spines on the shelf. *Here goes nothing.* With both hands, I went to grab the first five or so books, but the very first one on the top shelf suddenly caught my attention: *Emma*, by Jane Austen.

Grabbing it, I took it down and spun back around, holding it up for Emma to see. "Let me guess. This is your favorite book?"

She glanced at it to see what it was and shook her head. "No, actually. That's my mom's favorite book. Hence, why my name is Emma."

"Really? Your dad let your mom choose your name based on the titular character of a chick-lit novel?"

"First of all, *Emma* is not 'chick-lit'. It's classic literature. Second of all, *Emma* is ultimately about two friends falling in love. My parents were two friends who fell in love and I was the product of that, so yeah, my dad was okay with naming me Emma." She walked over, grabbed the book, placed it back on the shelf and removed the one next to it and handed it to me. "I'm more of a *Pride and Prejudice* kind of girl."

I knew a little something about that book because I'd watched the most recent film adaptation a couple years ago when I was going through a Keira Knightley phase. "Isn't that the one about two people who don't like each other but end up falling in love anyway?"

"That's the one."

"So then, if you and I ever fell in love and had a kid, we'd have to name it either Elizabeth or Mr. Darcy?" I joked, but immediately regretted it.

I watched as the blood drained from her face, like she was

going to be sick at the thought of falling in love and having a kid with me. Admittedly, I wasn't doing much better myself. Why I'd even made the quip to begin with was beyond me. I just figured since *Pride and Prejudice* was her favorite book and it was about two people who didn't like each other—like she and I didn't like each other—the joke just made sense. Plus, I thought maybe she'd be impressed by the fact I knew the names of the two main characters.

Apparently not.

"Sorry, bad joke," I said, clearing my throat. For once, *I* was the one getting red in the face.

She eyed me suspiciously for a moment before her expression softened and she smiled. "It was kind of funny, actually. And good job with the names. The Keira Knightley movie?"

I returned her smile. "How did you know?"

"Lucky guess," she said with a laugh. She turned and walked over to her computer desk and grabbed a rolled-up piece of paper off the top of it.

"Okay," she said. She returned to my side and unrolled it. "Here are the plans I have for where I want everything to go. I've been debating for weeks how I want to organize my collection. Right now, everything is in alphabetical order by author. But it's time for a change, and I finally decided this morning that I still want them in alphabetical order by author name, but separated by paperback and hardcover, and then by genres. However, I also want the *genres* in alphabetical order. I took the liberty of mapping it all out. See?" She pointed to the piece of paper, but I couldn't bring myself to look at it.

I was too busy staring incredulously at her.

When she noticed my lack of reaction, she glanced at me and pushed her glasses up the bridge of her nose. "What?"

"Are you for real?"

She narrowed her eyes into a glare. "Yes, I'm for real. I've put a lot of thought into this. Don't make fun of it."

I chuckled. "I'm not making fun. As a matter of fact, now that I look at your blueprints here, I'm sort of impressed. But still, Emma…"

She studied me for a moment before removing her glasses and setting them down on the desk along with the piece of paper. Her shoulders slumped forward slightly. "I know. This isn't going to help me attract Matt."

That wasn't what I was going to say, but now that she mentioned it, she was right. If she had just shown all this to Matt, he would have stared at her cross-eyed for about ten seconds before turning right around and heading out the door without saying one word.

And he wouldn't have ever come back.

"No, it's not," I admitted. "But he doesn't have to know. It can be our little secret." I nudged her shoulder with mine and gave her a wink.

She smiled at that as we both got back to work.

I couldn't believe how eclectic that girl's taste in books was. While romance seemed to be the dominating genre by far, even *that* had variety—contemporary romance, classic romance, historical romance, romantic suspense, etc. But then on top of all those romance books, she had general fiction, classic literature, mystery, sci-fi, horror, autobiographical. She even had books from her childhood, like the entire Dr. Seuss collection.

She was obsessed.

And while it was incredibly nerdy, I also couldn't help but find it all to be somewhat…endearing.

We worked diligently for about fifteen minutes, with me stopping every few seconds to tease her about some of the covers of her historical romance novels. I mean, come on, did all guys really have six-pack abs back in the eighteenth century?

When we were finished, we stood side-by-side and assessed the damage. Her room now looked like a disaster zone, with books taking up a majority of the available floor space.

"Okay, now onto the fun part." Removing an elastic band from around her wrist, Emma pulled her hair back and tied it into a high ponytail. "The organizing." She flashed me a grin.

I winced. "Um, yeah, about that. I don't know enough about any of these books to know which ones belong to which genres. Besides," I glanced down at my watch, "I think there's somewhere I need to be right now."

She placed her hands on her hips and cocked her head. "Oh yeah? And where would that be?"

Think fast. "Uh…" Dammit, that wasn't fast enough. Usually, I was pretty good at thinking on the spot.

"That's what I thought," she said with a slight smirk. "Why don't we take a short break? Would you like some lemonade?"

I *was* feeling particularly parched, so I nodded and followed her out of the room and down the stairs.

"You know," she said as we entered the kitchen, "I have a confession to make."

"Is that so? What do you need to confess?"

She took the pitcher of lemonade out of the refrigerator and grabbed two glasses out of the cabinet next to it. She set them down and began to pour.

"On Wednesday, I had my mom take me shopping and I bought a bikini. You know, for Matt's pool party tomorrow."

My eyebrows shot up in surprise. "For real? Wait, you're planning on going?"

She shrugged as she returned the lemonade to the fridge. "If I'm still invited, yeah."

"Wow." I was impressed—both that she broke down and

bought a bikini, and that she was going to be attending the party with me. She'd been so adamant about *not* going. "Okay, well, I want to see this bikini you bought. Go put it on."

She froze mid-drink. "Huh?"

I rolled my eyes. "You heard me. Go try it on. I want to see it."

Her face did its usual thing of turning bright red. "Um, I don't think—I mean, I don't—"

"Emma, if you're planning on going tomorrow, I'll be seeing you in it anyway. Don't you want to know what I think of it before you show it to the rest of the world?"

"Not really," she mumbled. But she set her glass down on the center island and said, "I guess it wouldn't hurt to show you, though. I'll be right back."

I watched her leave the kitchen with an amused look on my face. I loved torturing her and right now I knew she was *very* tortured. It scared her—the thought of walking around in a bikini in front of anyone. I'm sure it also scared her to walk around in one in front of *me*, because she knew I would be her harshest critic.

But I'd be nice and keep most of the comments to myself. After all, I'd been the one pushing her all week to go to this party.

About a minute later, I could hear her descending the stairs. "Okay," she called out, "promise you won't make fun of me, alright?"

I smirked into my glass. "Sure, whatever you say."

I took a big gulp of my lemonade just as she entered the kitchen—all hesitant and shy-like—and the tart beverage took an immediate detour down my windpipe when I saw her, sending me into a fit of coughs and splutters.

"Are you okay?" she asked, her face morphing into a look

of concern. She started to walk toward me, but I held my hand out in front of me and took a step back to keep her away.

"I'm good," I managed to get out in a strained voice.

She waited a moment for my coughing to subside before she spun around and motioned to herself. "Well, what do you think? How do I look?"

How did she look? She looked frickin' hot. Like, *making-you-choke-on-your-lemonade-out-of-shock-of-how-hot-she-looks* hot.

The bikini itself was hot. Red and white checkered, like a picnic blanket. Both the top and the bottom had small ruffles that somehow made it look both innocent and naughty at the same time. But the girl wearing it…

I'd had my thoughts of what Emma would look like with less clothes on. It's not like I'd ever fantasized about it or anything, it was more of a curiosity thing. But no part of my imagination had done her any justice. In a bikini, her legs looked even longer. Her stomach was flat but soft—like a girl who ate right but had never done a sit-up in her life. Her chest was…more amply endowed than I'd given her credit for. And when she spun around to show me the back…

I began to cough again. Not because of the lemonade, but because I was now feeling incredibly uncomfortable in her presence.

"You look fine," I said, but it came out sounding more like a question than a statement. And when I watched as her face fell, I felt like a jerk.

Just tell her she looks amazing. Sexy, even. But I couldn't do that. This wasn't how our relationship worked. We didn't give compliments to one another. It would be too weird.

"Do I at least look okay enough to go to the party tomorrow?" she asked quietly, as if she was afraid of what my answer might be.

The answer was, of course, *hell yes*. In fact, she'd probably be the best-looking girl there, if only because she'd be the one girl the guys had never seen half-naked before. She'd be like a brand new, shiny object for them to examine, and that would be the problem. For instance, Justin would be there. He'd already hit on her twice while she'd been wearing more clothes; I could only imagine what kind of reaction he would have to seeing her like *this*.

It made me want to punch him in the face.

No. Suddenly, the whole pool party thing was a bad idea. Even if Justin were to pay no attention to her, plenty of other guys there would, and she wasn't ready for that yet. Sure, it would be the quickest way to get Matt's attention—and affection—but did she want it based purely on hormones and physical attraction? Doubtful.

She watched me in anticipation, waiting for my response. Clearing my throat, I said, "Actually, you know, I've been thinking. Maybe we shouldn't even go to that party. I'm over parties right now, and you've been so against the idea of going that I kind of assumed we weren't, anyway."

"Oh," she said in a disappointment-laced voice as she stared down at the floor.

"But hey, why don't we have our own pool party?"

Her head snapped up. "What do you mean 'our own pool party'?"

What *did* I mean, exactly? The suggestion had come out of nowhere and I think I just said it to try to make her look less miserable. Thinking fast, I said the first thing that popped into my head. "Um, well, I could ask my dad if he'd mind firing up the grill, and you and your parents could come over for a cookout. How long has it been since we've all gotten together?"

She stared at me blankly for a moment. "Are you saying you want to forego a pool party that all your friends are going to be at, to spend the day with me and our parents?"

"And a baby. Don't forget about Abby."

"What's wrong with you?"

I laughed. "Nothing's wrong with me. I just think it would be more fun than a stupid high school pool party. What do you say? You know you didn't want to go anyway."

What *was* wrong with me? Why would I want to spend a Saturday afternoon with two sets of parents, a baby and my dorky next-door-neighbor, when I could be spending it with my best friend, his insanely attractive cousin, and all my other friends? All just so that guys wouldn't have the opportunity to hit on Emma?

Since when did I become her protector?

And why?

"Yeah, okay," she finally replied. "That does sound way better. Have your parents call my parents and we'll set something up."

"Great," I said, averting my gaze away from her. Grabbing the glass of lemonade I'd abandoned, I guzzled the rest of it as quickly as I could, wiping my mouth with my arm after I was done.

"Great," I repeated, trying so hard not to look back at her as I made my way to the sliding glass door that led out to the deck. "I'll see you tomorrow then, I guess?"

"You're not going to help me anymore with my project?"

"Nah, I just remembered I agreed to look after Abby this afternoon, so Rachel can go get a mani-pedi."

That was a lie. And judging from the doubtful expression on Emma's face, she was aware of that.

"Okay. I'll see you tomorrow, then. Thanks for the help."

"No problem." I gave her a short wave before sliding open the door and bolting out of it.

I knew leaving her house as quickly as I did would tip her off to the fact something was off with me, but I didn't care. I couldn't take it one second longer standing in that kitchen with her in that bikini. It was threatening to put thoughts into my head that I simply didn't want to have there.

Bad thoughts. Impure thoughts.

Which was exactly why I didn't want her anywhere near that pool party tomorrow, because I wouldn't be the only one having those thoughts.

When I arrived home, Rachel and Abby were sitting on the couch watching *Sesame Street*, both looking like they needed a nap.

"Hey," I greeted them, leaning against the doorframe.

Rachel glanced up at me with a curious look. "What are you doing back so soon? You've only been gone like half an hour."

I shrugged. "Emma wanted me to help her organize her book collection. I wasn't really feeling it, so I just decided to come home."

Rachel smiled and shook her head. "I love that girl."

With a roll of my eyes, I said, "Hey, do you think Dad would be up for hosting a cookout tomorrow with the Dawsons?"

"Are you kidding?" she asked with wide eyes. "He'll probably cry real tears of joy if you suggest it. Of course, he would be up for that. What's the occasion?"

Keeping Emma away from horny douchebags. "Nothing. I just thought it would be nice for us all to get together. It's been a while."

"It has, and I agree. I'll talk to your father when he gets home."

"Cool, thanks." I started to head up to my bedroom, but then I remembered the lie I'd told Emma. Not only did I feel bad about lying to her, but I also wouldn't put it past her to investigate to see if Rachel had, in fact, gone for a mani-pedi. After all, I saw a few *Nancy Drew* books in her collection today and vaguely remembered her going through a detective phase when we were eight.

"Oh, hey," I said, poking my head back in the living room. "You look like you could take a little break for a while. If you'd like, I could watch Abby while you go out and do something fun. Like, I don't know, maybe get a mani-pedi or something."

The look that came over her face was priceless. It was a mixture of confusion, relief, gratitude and excitement all rolled into one expression. "And now *I'm* going to cry real tears of joy. Logan, that is so sweet. I would *love* that."

"Awesome," I said, relieved that she was going to take me up on the offer.

She got off the couch, walked over to me and pulled me into a hug. "What did I do to deserve such an amazing stepson?"

"You married my dad."

With a chuckle, she let go of me and ruffled my hair. "And you're a comedian, too." She glanced over her shoulder at Abby. "Abby, sweetie, mommy loves you, but I'm going to head out for a bit without you, okay?"

Abby pointed at the TV screen and giggled at something Elmo just did. She couldn't have cared less what mommy had to say.

"You're my hero, Logan." Rachel gave my shoulder a squeeze before scurrying off into the kitchen to grab her purse and keys.

"I'll be back in time to cook dinner," she said as she breezed past me and out the front door.

With a satisfied smile, I walked over to the couch and took a seat next to Abby. There. I had just successfully turned a lie into a truth.

But then my smile slowly morphed into a frown. Now, if I could only get the images of Emma in a bikini out of my head...

Chapter 18

EMMA

"This is nice. We should do this more often."

"Oh, definitely. I'm not sure why we haven't been doing it all along."

My eyes darted across the picnic table at my mom and Rachel as they exchanged pleasantries. When we arrived earlier, they both acted like they were best friends who hadn't seen each other in years, when I was pretty sure I saw them talking to each other from their driveways just the day before.

Bored of their conversation, I turned my attention briefly to my dad and Mark, who were over by the grill slapping each other on the back and talking excitedly about something I couldn't hear, but imagined was about sports.

Abby, who was sitting in Rachel's lap, was busy shoving brightly colored plastic keys into her mouth, and looking like she was having a way better time than I was.

As for Logan, he'd had yet to make an appearance, much to my irritation. He was the one who had planned this whole thing, and now he was late for it. If he was even going to show up at all. For all I knew, he might have still gone to Matt's pool party and was there right now, while I was stuck hanging out with two sets of parents and a baby. Maybe he was pranking me. I wouldn't put it past him.

Not that I was in any rush to see him after what happened yesterday. He had no idea how hard it was for me to put on that bikini and show it to him, and his reaction solidified why I didn't even want to buy one in the first place.

Apparently, I looked hideous in it.

That had to be the only explanation. First off, he told me I looked "fine", which was bad enough, but the *way* he said it indicated I looked anything *but* fine. As soon as I asked him if it was okay enough to wear to the pool party, he suddenly had no interest in going anymore. As if I looked so terrible in that bikini that he didn't want to be seen with me in it. Like it would embarrass him or something. Then he couldn't get out of my house fast enough and wouldn't even look at me on the way out.

He sure did know how to crush a girl's confidence.

Or, more accurately, *my* confidence. He'd had no trouble at all staring at *Riley* in a bikini the other night.

And for some reason, that put me a bad mood and had me hoping this *was* all a prank and that he *was* at Matt's party, so I wouldn't have to spend the afternoon with him.

Unfortunately, no more than three seconds later, Logan emerged from the sliding glass door and stepped onto the deck. His eyes immediately found me, and a weird look came over his face as he gave me a small wave.

Apparently, he was as happy to see me as I was him.

"Logan. Nice of you to join us." Rachel motioned for him to take a seat at the table next to me.

"Hey," he greeted me as he sat down on the bench. I immediately scooted a few inches away from him.

He looked offended but quickly shrugged it off. He smiled over at my mother. "Hello, Olivia. Thank you for coming."

I swear my mom melted a little. "Thank *you* for inviting us."

"It was my pleasure." He turned to me and poked me in the arm. "How are you, Emma?"

I had to refrain from scowling at his question. "I'm fine," I mumbled.

My mom cast me a curious glance before turning to Rachel and saying, "Is there anything I can help with in the kitchen?"

"As a matter of fact, there is." Rachel glanced at me and Logan as she removed herself and Abby from the bench. "Can I get either of you something to drink?"

"No, thank you," Logan and I replied at the same time.

A small smile played at my mother's lips. "What, no jinx?"

I rolled my eyes. "Mom, please. Jinxing is juvenile."

"Oh, pardon me, I didn't know." Mom rolled her own eyes before she and Rachel shared a chuckle and headed inside.

Logan glanced sideways at me with a smirk. "*Jinxing is juvenile*? We just jinxed last week. What's with the sudden maturation?"

"We all have to grow up sometime," I mumbled.

"Are you okay?" he asked, turning to me. "Because you seem like you're in a bad mood."

I opened my mouth to respond, but the sudden *ding* of his phone interrupted me.

Taking it out of his pocket, he swiped at the screen and chuckled at whatever he saw.

"Riley keeps texting me," he explained. "She claims we're missing one hell of a party over there right now."

His phone dinged again and this time, his eyebrows shot up as he let out a low whistle. "Whoa."

Curiosity got the best of me and I leaned over to see what was on the screen. I automatically wished I hadn't.

Riley had texted him a selfie of herself standing by the pool giving the camera a weird pouty, duck-face hybrid expression that looked simultaneously sad and sexy. The picture was taken from the ever-flattering perspective of her holding the phone high above her head, and as she looked seductively up at the camera, Logan could look down her bikini top at the plentiful cleavage displayed at the front and center of the screen.

"That's hot," he said with a smirk and I suddenly wanted to slap him upside the head. Hard.

That right there—*that* was the kind of reaction a girl wanted from a guy after modeling a bikini in front of him. Not the one he'd given me yesterday. He'd really hurt my feelings with his blatant distaste for seeing me in swimwear and now he was just rubbing salt in the wound by practically drooling on his cell phone at a stupid picture of Riley.

"Well, maybe you should go to the party instead, then," I snapped, sliding off the bench and heading towards the pool.

He wasted no time in following me. "Okay, so I was right. You *are* in a bad mood. What's up?"

I took a seat in one of the lounge chairs and folded my arms tightly over my chest, staring straight ahead at the pool water. I said nothing. What was there to say? That I was upset because he thought Riley looked amazing in a bikini but thought I looked ridiculous?

"Nothing's 'up'. I'm just saying if you'd rather be at the pool party, you should go to the pool party."

"Are you trying to get rid of me?"

"I'm *always* trying to get rid of you, Logan."

"Hey, not nice," he mumbled and put on a fake pout that mimicked Riley's. "Well, I don't want to go to the pool party, so you're stuck with me."

"Oh joy," I said, making sure to infuse as much sarcasm into those two words as I possibly could.

"Hey, kids!" my mom called over to us from the deck. "Come over here, we have something amazing to show you!" She then waved over to my dad and Mark at the grill to join them over at the picnic table as well.

Logan and I exchanged a curious glance and a shrug as we proceeded back to the table.

As we all took a seat, my mother stood at the head of the table, holding something behind her back. "You all will never guess what Rachel happened to stumble upon the other day that she couldn't wait to show me." She gave us only a few seconds to stare at her blankly before revealing the item she'd been hiding, holding it out straight in front of her for all of us to see. "Ta-da!"

It took me a second to realize what it was, and as soon as I did, I could feel all the color drain from my face. At first glance, it looked like a harmless but fiercely decorated three-ring binder. But upon closer inspection, it was easy to see it was a scrapbook.

And going even beyond that, it was a scrapbook that had the words *Logan & Emma* scrawled across the front in tall, glittery letters. On the backdrop of a large red heart. With other little hearts surrounding it.

It was a scrapbook devoted to me and Logan. What kind of special hell had I just been transported to?

Mark gasped before reaching out and grabbing the book from my mother. "Oh my God, I'd forgotten all about this!"

"All about what?" Logan asked, looking just as disturbed as I felt. "What is that?"

"This," Mark said, opening the book, "is a scrapbook your mother put together a long time ago, back when she thought you two would someday…you know…"

Logan and I both stared at him, mouths agape.

"Fall in love," he finished with a slight smirk.

I didn't know whether to laugh, cry or vomit. Sure, it was no secret that our parents had always hoped one day Logan and I would wake up and realize we had a burning passion for one another, but it was something that was never discussed. Our parents knew it was a sore subject. They knew how much Logan and I had grown to detest one another over time, and I thought they had accepted it.

But apparently, the hope was still alive. Or, if nothing else, it lived on for eternity in the form of a scrapbook.

The adults all gathered around the book and started pointing and cooing at what was inside.

My mom glanced over at me with a guilty smile. "I just figured since you two seem to be becoming friends, maybe you'd get a kick out of seeing this."

No. She was wrong. This was a nightmare. This was horrifying. I didn't want to see *any* of this.

Judging from the look on Logan's face, he felt no differently than I did.

"Oh, look at that." Rachel pointed to the very first picture in the book. "*Logan and Emma's First Introduction*," she read aloud.

Mark swiveled the book around, so Logan and I could see what she was referring to.

In the top center of the first page was a picture of my mom and Logan's mom, Heather, standing in the foyer. Heather was holding onto what I assumed was a baby Logan and my mom was next to her holding onto a baby me. Both young women were smiling broadly, and each held out their free hand in the form of the letter *c* and had connected them together to make it look like they were forming a heart.

"This was the day I brought you home from the hospital," my mom said fondly. "I came here first before bringing you to our house. I couldn't wait for you and Logan to meet."

I looked closely at the picture. Logan and I were both in

tears in our mothers' arms. Apparently, neither one of us was as excited about the introduction as they were.

Logan began flipping through the pages, one-by-one. *Logan and Emma's First Halloween* (I was a ladybug, he was a monkey). *Logan and Emma's First Visit with Santa* (the mall Santa held me in one arm and Logan in the other; the jolly old man was smiling, but Logan and I were once again crying). *Logan and Emma's First Easter. Logan and Emma's First 4th of July. Logan and Emma's First Day of Pre-School…*

Why had I been forced to share so many of my firsts with Logan?

"Um, what's *that?*" Logan asked, pointing to a photo a few pages in. From the looks of it, it wasn't one of our "firsts". We looked to be around four years old.

And we were dressed like a bride and groom.

"Mom," I squeaked, staring up at her in horror. "What is this?"

She glanced down at the photo and immediately shared an amused expression with my Dad and Mark before the three of them burst out laughing.

Logan and I, however, were not amused.

"Mom," I scolded her.

"I'm sorry," she said, wiping away a tear. "That picture was taken on Halloween. You two were four at the time. The office Heather worked at was throwing a family-friendly Halloween party, and they were giving away prizes for the best costumes. We really wanted to win, so we thought it would be funny if all our costumes were part of the same theme. Heather's idea was to dress the two of you as a bride and a groom and we'd all go dressed as the wedding party. So, she threw on the most hideous dress she could find—her Prom dress—and she was the bridesmaid. I was the flower girl—"

"I was the priest," Mark cut in.

"And I was the wedding singer," my dad added. "The one from the Adam Sandler movie."

Mom chuckled. "Everyone loved it."

Not me. I didn't love it. And I could tell from Logan's expression he wasn't particularly fond of the whole thing either.

I studied the picture for a moment and was taken aback by how close Logan and I looked. This time, we were smiling big, toothy grins at the camera instead of crying. We stood side-by-side, hand-in-hand, looking like the best of friends.

Or, I guess, husband and wife.

It was hard to believe there was ever a time in our lives where we got along and maybe even liked each other. But this photo was proof.

I wanted to rip it out of the scrapbook and burn it.

Beside me, Logan sighed. "Did you guys at least win?"

"Sadly, no," my mom replied somberly. "We came in third."

"What a shame." I reached over and shut the book and turned to my dad. "Don't you guys have some burgers to grill up? I'm hungry."

Dad raised his eyebrows. "Well, the princess has spoken, people. Back to work! We don't want her wasting away!"

I shot him a glare as he and Mark laughed, got up from the table, and went back over to the grill.

"We'll just leave the book out here, in case you guys want to keep looking at it," my mom said before she and Rachel took off for the kitchen.

Once everybody had dispersed, Logan and I sat in awkward silence for a moment, staring at the scrapbook.

Finally, Logan cleared his throat and said, "Well, you and I certainly have quite the history, huh? We used to be friends.

We even got *married*."

"I want a divorce."

He chuckled softly as he traced a finger along the edge of the scrapbook. I had to wonder if it was hard for him to look at it, knowing his mother had made it. It had been a few years since she'd passed away, after a long battle with cancer, and I knew he'd had a hard time dealing with her death. I'd even heard my parents talking soon after about him having to go to therapy to help him deal. I remember feeling so bad for him at the time, even though I hated him. I remember wanting to run over to his house and pull him into a big hug and tell him that everything was going to be alright. To hold him and console him like a friend would.

But we weren't friends. Not anymore.

"It's crazy to think we used to get along. That we used to be friends." He glanced sideways at me. "What do you think happened?"

I couldn't tell if he was being serious or not. He wasn't sure what had happened between us to turn us from friends to enemies? Did he have selective amnesia or something?

"You've got to be joking," I muttered shaking my head. "What happened is you became a jerk, always picking on me. Teasing me. Making fun of me. Humiliating me."

His eyes shot up to the sky as though he was trying to recall a time he was ever mean to me. When he took too long, I decided to help him out.

"For instance, do you remember in the fifth grade when I got my first pair of glasses and you not only started calling me Freaky Four Eyes, but you also got the rest of the school to start calling me that as well?"

It only took him a second to remember. With a grin, he said, "Oh, yeah. Right. But hey, in my defense, those frames were *way* too big for your face. You looked like a bug. It *was* freaky."

"Or, how about the time in eighth grade when you spelled out the word *BOOBS* in numbers on your calculator and then handed it to me, declaring—in front of our entire math class, mind you—that I should take it because those would be the only boobs I would ever have."

Logan broke out into a laugh. A good, hearty laugh that indicated he did not feel one drop of remorse. "I remember that. Classic. At least I was mostly wrong, though. I mean, you've got a little something going on there." He motioned to my chest.

My face burned with anger. "And the list goes on and on. You've been a jerk to me for seven solid years now, Logan, always making me feel like such a loser. And you're still doing it! Yesterday was a great example of that."

His face fell as a look of confusion replaced his look of amusement. "What are you talking about? What did I do yesterday?"

I bit my lower lip. I hadn't planned on throwing that out there, it just came out before I had a chance to stop it. "You know what I'm talking about," I grumbled, staring down at the wooden surface of the picnic table.

"No, I don't."

"Your reaction to the whole...bikini thing. You couldn't have acted more disgusted if you'd tried."

His jaw dropped. "Disgusted? Emma—"

"And whatever, I get it. I don't look like Riley. Or Grace, for that matter. But you could have at least mustered up *some* form of a compliment, other than just a lackluster 'fine'. Believe it or not, that took a lot of courage for me to show myself off to you like that, and you couldn't wait to leave so you wouldn't have to look at me anymore. Meanwhile, when Riley's walking around in a bikini or sending you selfies, you have a hard time keeping your eyes in their sockets—"

"Whoa, Emma, stop." Logan held out his hands in front of him defensively. "I didn't—"

"Burgers are ready!" Mark called out as he headed over to the table with a plate full of meat.

My mother and Rachel both returned to the deck at the exact same moment with trays of condiments and burger toppings.

"Emma, sweetie," Mom said as she set down her tray in front of me, "would you mind helping us with the rest?"

I glanced quickly over at Logan, who was staring at me with a serious look on his face that I couldn't quite decipher, before turning back to my mom.

"I would love to," I replied, thankful for the opportunity to get away from Logan before I could humiliate myself any further.

I moved to get up to follow my mom, but Logan grabbed my arm and pulled me toward him.

"We'll talk about this later," he said, his voice low so that nobody else could hear.

Something about the way he was looking at me when he said it made my stomach flip-flop. I chalked it up to hunger, but somewhere in the back of my mind, I knew it had to do with something else.

I just wasn't sure what that was.

Chapter 19

EMMA

I didn't talk to Logan for the rest of the afternoon, despite his attempts at getting me alone to do so. I made sure to spark up whatever conversations I could with Mark and Rachel, my own parents, and even Abby (even though she didn't talk back) and then encouraged Mom and Dad to leave soon after we were done eating.

I'm not even sure I said goodbye to him.

I knew I was being kind of a jerk, but I didn't know why, exactly. Why should I care what he thought about me, anyway? It wasn't Logan I was trying to impress, it was Matt.

With a sigh, I set my book down on my nightstand and stared up at the ceiling. It was close to midnight and I had made no attempt at trying to fall asleep. I wasn't very tired; I was too busy feeling annoyed. Still, I wanted to get up at a reasonable hour in the morning, so I leaned over to turn off the light when my phone buzzed next to my book.

Weird. Who would be texting me at this time of the night? Probably Chloe or Sophia, who I was sure stayed up as late as they could every night while not under their parents' supervision. Turning on the phone, I expected to see either of their names staring back at me, but instead, it was Logan's.

Logan: u awake?

My first thought was to not respond, but I knew that was pointless. His bedroom window faced mine, and obviously he was sending this text because he saw my light was on— therefore, he was assuming I was awake and he would send text after text for the rest of the night until I finally responded. Sure, I could just turn off my phone, but I hated to admit I was curious as to why he was contacting me so late. So, I texted him back.

Me: No.

It only took him a few seconds to respond.

Logan: nice try. I see a light on
Me: So?
Logan: so…we need 2 talk
Me: About what?
Logan: meet me outside
Me: Why would I do that? It's late.
Logan: matt would be so impressed if he knew u snuck out of the house
Logan: he likes rebellious girls

I rolled my eyes at that. Whenever Logan wanted to get me to do something nowadays, he would just throw out Matt's name and tell me he liked girls who did those sorts of things. Sadly, it seemed to work on me most of the time.

Me: Okay. Fine. Give me a couple minutes, I'll meet you outside.
Logan: great. I'll be waiting in ur driveway

Tossing my phone aside, I changed out of my sleepwear and threw on a pair of jean shorts, a dark gray graphic tee that read *Keep Calm and Read a Book*, and slipped into a pair of sneakers before exiting the bedroom. Slowly and quietly, I tiptoed down the hallway, making sure to take extra care as I passed my parents' bedroom. The noise of the stairs was going to be the biggest challenge, but luckily the creaking was mild, and I made it to the bottom with no problem. Grabbing my keys off the decorative table in the foyer, I headed out the door, locking it behind me.

Logan was already waiting for me as I exited the house. "I can't believe you actually did it," he said in a half-whisper as I approached him.

"Me neither," I half-whispered back. My gaze flickered down to his hands, where he was holding onto a flashlight and a blanket. "What's with the props?"

"We're going on an adventure," he replied, flashing me a grin.

I glanced at him skeptically. "An adventure? In the middle of the night?"

"Those are the best kind." He turned on the flashlight. "Walk with me?"

"Walk? To where?"

"You'll see," he said mysteriously as he began to walk down the street.

The sensible part of my brain tried to encourage me to turn right around and go back inside the house. But the foolish part of my brain—the part that won out—told me to follow him.

So, I did.

I fell into stride beside him and we remained silent for a few steps, listening to the sounds of crickets chirping and frogs croaking in the distance. I loved the sound of nature at night in the summer; it was one of the many reasons I loved living on our street. There were only five houses: mine, Logan's and Matt's, and two houses farther down belonging to seasonal families that hadn't made it up for the summer yet. It was a private, dead end street surrounded by woods, so there were a lot of nature sounds to be heard on a regular basis. Some of them were frightening, but for the most part, I found the other sounds to be therapeutic. Sometimes, I would just sit out on the deck at night, close my eyes and listen.

"I wasn't disgusted, you know," Logan said suddenly.

I turned my head and blinked at him. "What are you talking about?"

"You insinuated earlier that you thought I was disgusted at seeing you in a bikini, but I wasn't. I'm sorry if that was the impression you got."

"Oh," I said, biting my lower lip and staring down at the ground as we walked. I was hoping this conversation wouldn't be brought up again.

"The truth is, I thought you looked hot."

My breath hitched in my throat. Did Logan Reynolds just tell me he thought I looked hot? Was he feeling okay? I resisted the urge to reach over and feel his forehead to see if he was burning up.

But I was too distracted by the fact my own face was burning up. "Um…" was all I managed to get out.

Logan chuckled softly. "I've made you uncomfortable, haven't I?"

"No," I lied. I was just thankful for the fact it was pitch black out and he couldn't see me blushing.

"Right," he said, drawing out the word. "Look, Emma, I just didn't think it was a good idea for you to go that party. Your naiveté would have made you an easy target with all the guys there."

"My naiveté? What are you talking about?"

"See? You're even naive about what you're naive about." He stopped walking and motioned to his right. "We're here."

I wanted to press him further, but my confusion over why we'd stopped walking took over. "What do you mean, we're here? This is an empty lot of land for sale." I pointed to the FOR-SALE sign stuck into the ground in front of us.

The land was put up for sale a couple years ago and an out-of-state couple purchased it and had the space all cleared out in preparation of building their dream home there. But apparently something fell through and before they started building, they put the land back up for sale, leaving an empty lot at the end of a long, dirt driveway shaded by trees.

"I know. It's perfect," Logan said, stepping onto the end of the driveway.

"Wait, we can't be here," I said.

"Why not?"

"Because this is trespassing."

Logan rolled his eyes. "Oh, come on, Emma. Nobody is going to care. Nobody is even going to know we were here."

I folded my arms over my chest and kept my feet planted firmly to the ground. "It's still illegal."

"Even more reason to do it, then. Matt likes girls who break the law," he said with a smirk.

It was my turn to roll my eyes. "Seriously, Logan, I am not setting foot on this property."

"Okay, I can work around that."

I was wondering what he meant by that as he dropped the blanket onto the ground, stalked over to me, wrapped his arms tightly around my waist and lifted me off the ground.

"Logan!" I exclaimed in a whisper. "Put me down!" I attempted to push myself away from his chest and out of his grip, but to no avail. He held on tight as he carried me over the property line and after only a few steps, he slowly lowered me back to the ground.

"There," he said in a low voice. "You've set foot on the property. You have now broken the law and there's no undoing it, so you might as well make the best of it while we're here."

I would have been furious with him at that moment had I not realized he was still holding on to me, his hands now resting loosely on my hips, his chest still grazing mine, his face close enough that I could feel the slight tickle of his breath against my skin...

Swallowing hard, I pushed him away as forcefully as I could. He had some nerve, getting me to trespass and invading my personal space like that. Why did I keep willingly hanging out with him?

Retrieving the blanket from the ground, Logan pointed the flashlight at me and said, "I think you're going to like what we're about to do."

"Which is what, exactly?" I asked as we began to walk again.

He said nothing until we reached the end of the path and the lot opened up to about an acre of nothing but flat, grassy land.

He pointed at the sky. "We're going to stargaze."

I gaped at him. "We're going to *what* now?"

"Stargaze. It's where you gaze. At stars."

"Yes, I know what stargazing is, genius. I'm just surprised, that's all. What inspired this?"

Logan shrugged as he set down the flashlight and opened the blanket, laying it out on the ground. "I got the impression you were mad at me earlier, and I wanted to make it up to you by having us do something I figured you would enjoy. Do you enjoy looking at stars?"

"Of course, I do," I said with a nod.

"Well, so do I."

That had to be a lie. There was no way that Logan liked stargazing. That was way too boring and nerdy of an activity for him.

"Okay…" I said as he sat down on the ground and motioned for me to join him. Absent-mindedly, I obeyed him, taking a seat next to him on the blanket. "But why did we have to come *here* to stargaze instead of just doing it in one of our backyards?"

"What's the fun in that? This way, I got you to do a couple things you normally wouldn't do, like sneak out of the house and break the law. Besides," he said, "being here gives us privacy. We can talk without having to lower our voices, since there's nobody around to hear us."

I wasn't sure what there was to talk about, but I figured it wouldn't hurt to at least lie back and tune him out while I searched the night sky for shooting stars—one of my favorite pastimes when I was little.

As soon as I was on my back, he lay down next to me—so close our arms were just barely touching. A strange, unfamiliar feeling settled in the pit of my stomach. If I didn't know any better, I would have said it was nerves. But not the kind of nerves I got when I thought about flying, or the kind I'd gotten on the Ferris wheel the other day. No, these nerves felt different. They sort of fluttered in my stomach before traveling to my chest and quickening my heartbeat.

"You know, my mom and I used to do this all the time," he said suddenly.

I turned my head to look at him. He was staring up at the sky with a wistful expression on his face, most likely recalling fond memories from his childhood.

"She would bring me outside to look at the stars every opportunity she could get," he continued. "Sometimes, she'd even wake me up in the middle of the night if there was some sort of event like a meteor shower or a lunar eclipse. She loved this kind of stuff and wanted to make sure I did, too."

Arching a brow, I said, "And do you?"

He smiled. "I do, as a matter of fact. But don't tell anyone because they'll think I'm a nerd. Like you." His smile turned to a smirk when I poked his shoulder with my finger.

I sighed as my eyes traced invisible lines between some of the stars, designing my own constellation. "I miss your mom," I said softly. It was true. Heather Reynolds was breathtakingly beautiful, caring, funny, and sweet. In a lot of ways, she was always like a second mother to me, and my heart broke the day my parents told me she'd passed away.

I could only imagine how Logan felt.

"Me too," he said quietly, all visible signs of mirth gone from his face.

I could tell this was a topic Logan didn't want to delve too deeply into, so I refrained from saying anything more. Instead, I waited for him to speak again.

"So," he said finally, a minute or so later. "You still into Matt?"

His question caught me off guard. Was I still into Matt? Of course I was still into Matt. Why wouldn't I be?

"Um, yeah, I am," I said. I turned onto my side and propped myself up on my elbow. "And I'm starting to wonder when you're going to come through with what you promised."

He turned and positioned himself similarly to me, so we

were now facing each other. "Hey, these things take time. Good things come to those who wait."

"Yeah, well, I'm beginning to think it's never going to happen." I plucked a piece of grass out of the ground and flicked it in his direction. "I don't get the impression he'll ever be into me, no matter how much you try to change me."

"What are you talking about? I saw you guys holding hands at Justin's party the other night."

I snorted. "He was just helping me up from where I was sitting on the dock. You happened to arrive right after I stood up."

"Oh." He plucked his own piece of grass out of the ground and twirled it between his thumb and forefinger.

"What about Riley?" I found myself asking, lowering my gaze to the ground. "Are you two a thing?"

He let the blade of grass drop. "Me and Riley? Nah. I mean, I don't know. She's definitely my type, but we haven't talked about getting together or anything."

"Something tells me she'd like to."

Cocking an eyebrow, he said, "Oh yeah? What makes you think that?"

I tapped a finger on my chin as I pretended to think about it for a moment. "Hmm, let's see. She seems to enjoy stripping in front of you. And finding whatever reason to touch you. And texting you half-naked selfies. The girl wants you. Bad."

Logan grinned and raked a hand through his hair. "What can I say? I'm irresistible."

"That can't possibly be true. *I'm* able to resist you."

He scoffed. "I'm sure in the right situation, even *you'd* be unable to resist me, Dawson."

I shook my head adamantly. "Nope."

"Come on, the signs are all there. *You're* touching me all the time—"

"Yeah," I interjected, "to hit or punch you because you just said or did something stupid."

"And *you* couldn't wait to strip for me yesterday—" he continued like I hadn't even said anything.

"Because you practically begged me to," I pointed out.

We held each other's gaze for a moment before starting to laugh and collapsing onto our backs again.

"In all seriousness," I said as our laughter subsided, "Have we even made any progress where Matt's concerned? Has he said anything about me? Have you talked to him about me yet?"

"Uh…not yet."

"What are you waiting for? Am I that much of a lost cause that we need to take all summer to fix me first?"

He gave me a lopsided grin. "No, it's not that. It's just…I thought it would be better if this all happened organically, you know? I don't want to just tell him point blank that he should date you. I want him to come to that realization on his own. Trust me, you'll want that, too."

"Okay, but…" I clasped my hands together over my stomach and began twiddling my thumbs. "I haven't really had many interactions with him yet. How is he supposed to come to the realization he wants to date me if we never even see or talk to each other?"

He appeared to mull that over for a moment. "Good point. Okay, how about this? He's coming over to my house tomorrow to hang out. What if I suggest we do a group get-together sometime? Like you, me, Riley and Matt. We could all go mini golfing or something. It will give the two of you the chance to get to know each other a little better, and it will give you both an idea of what it would be like to date each other."

The corners of my mouth tipped downward into a frown. Why did Riley have to be included in this? I didn't really know her that well yet, and so far, she'd given me no reason not to like her, but I couldn't help but feel incredibly insecure around her. She was beautiful and perfect. But I just had to remind myself it didn't matter—she was Matt's cousin, therefore not my competition.

"That sounds great," I said. I felt a sudden kink in my neck and reached a hand up and started massaging the spot.

"You okay?" Logan asked.

"Yeah," I said. "My neck hurts a little, that's all. You forgot to bring pillows."

He chuckled. "Here," he said, stretching out his arm to the side. "You can rest on my arm."

I lifted my head and he slipped his arm underneath. I was immediately surprised by how soft he was. He was certainly no pillow, but I expected him to feel as hard as a rock, knowing how much the guy worked out. Maybe it was because he wasn't flexing, or maybe it was because anything was better than the ground.

Absent-mindedly, I moved closer to him and rested my head on his shoulder.

"Is that better?" he asked softly, turning his head slightly so his words vibrated against the top of my head.

I yawned as I nodded. "Much better, thank you."

If I hadn't been overcome with a sudden, overwhelming wave of sleepiness, I would have seriously questioned the position we were in right then. If anyone were to stumble upon us, they'd most likely mistake us for a couple having a romantic moment under the stars. But there was nothing romantic here. We were just two neighbors—barely even friends—gazing up at the stars together. For a few minutes, I think we talked about the constellations. We marveled at the possibility that some of the stars we were looking might have burned out long ago. We even took guesses as to which ones they might be. At one point we witnessed a shooting star blaze across the sky and we each made a silent wish.

Eventually, my eyelids grew heavy and I think I might have mumbled something about it being late and how we should get home.

It was the last thing I remembered before closing my eyes and drifting off to sleep in the warmth and comfort of Logan's embrace...

Chapter 20

LOGAN

I woke up the next morning to warm sunlight caressing my face, the sound of birds chirping in the distance, the pleasant scent of apples filling my nostrils, and the feeling of holding a girl in my arms.

Wait...*what?*

My eyes flew open to reveal a very confusing view above me—light blue sky, white fluffy clouds, muted golden sunlight—and I instantly began to panic.

Why was I waking up outdoors? And who was I holding in my arms?

It didn't take long for the memory of last night to come flooding back. I was stargazing with Emma. We were talking. She fell asleep. I didn't have the heart to wake her. And then apparently, *I* fell asleep.

And neither of us woke up until morning.

I lifted my head slightly to assess the situation. Her face was nuzzled against my neck, her arm draped across my abdomen, her hand resting on my waist, one of her legs tangled with mine. Meanwhile, my arm—numb from the flow of blood being cut off from her sleeping on it—was around the small of her back, my hand resting low on her hip.

Lifting my free arm carefully, I glanced at my watch. It was almost seven o'clock. We needed to get home. And fast.

"Emma," I said, softly nudging her.

"Hmm?" She stirred slightly. Her hand moved to my chest as she snuggled even closer.

I gulped as I stared up at the sky. This was the first time I'd ever woken up next to a girl and the first time I'd ever slept with one in the literal sense. I hated to admit it, considering who the girl was, but it was nice. The feel of her in my arms…warm…soft…

I didn't know what to do, especially considering that when she woke up, she was going to freak the hell out.

"Emma," I said a little louder, shaking her this time.

"What?" she mumbled, sounding annoyed. Her eyes fluttered open and her gaze caught mine. For a moment, we stared at one another. A small smile graced her lips as she brought her hand up and placed it along the side of my face. "Hey," she whispered.

"Hey," I found myself whispering back as my pulse suddenly quickened. This wasn't the reaction I'd been expecting.

But it was short-lived. It only took maybe three seconds before she realized something wasn't right. Maybe it was the fact we were outside. Or the fact she was lying on the ground next to *me*. Whatever it was, it hit her hard. Her smile instantly vanished as she gasped. She pushed herself away from me and stumbled backward.

"What the hell?" she squealed. She glanced at our surroundings with a look of pure confusion on her face as she struggled to stand.

"We must have fallen asleep," I explained as I sat up.

With shaky hands, Emma reached into the back pocket of her shorts as if looking for something but came up empty-handed. "Where's my phone?" she asked, patting her other pockets. "What time is it?"

"It's a little after seven," I replied. I stood as well, bunching up the blanket and grabbing the flashlight.

"*Shit*," she hissed, raking a hand through her slightly mussed-up hair.

My jaw dropped. "Whoa. Did Emma Dawson just swear?"

Emma shot me a glare. "I swear all the time, just usually when I'm talking about you."

Apparently, Emma was a grouch first thing in the morning.

"We're going to be in so much trouble," she moaned, now practically yanking her hair out of her head.

"Calm down," I said, walking over to her. "It's a Sunday morning. Our parents are probably still asleep and don't even know we're gone."

That was a lie. There was a good chance at least Rachel was awake, since Abby was an early riser and liked to cry loudly if nobody came to get her by the time the sun was up. I wasn't sure about Emma's parents, but it didn't really matter. Our cars were both in our respective driveways, so there'd be no reason for them to suspect we weren't asleep in our bedrooms.

We would just have to find a way to sneak in without anyone catching us…

"You're right. My parents usually sleep in on Sundays," she said, her voice surprisingly calm. "Either way, we'd better get home. *Now.*"

She broke into a run and I followed. Luckily, we weren't too far away, and it would only take us a minute or so to make it to our houses. I was feeling hopeful that everything was going to go smoothly, but as we approached my house, I saw Rachel step out the front door to retrieve the newspaper. And then she glanced over in our direction.

Thinking quickly, I chucked the blanket and flashlight into the bushes before she could notice them and grabbed Emma's arm, leaned in and said, "Just follow my lead."

As we approached my driveway, Rachel gave us a curious look. "Hey, you two. What are you guys doing out so early in the morning?" She sounded suspicious.

"We just went for a jog," I said; my breathlessness from our run lending credibility to my lie.

"Yeah," Emma said next to me between gasps of breath. "A jog. Just jogging."

"Oh, really?" Rachel blinked over in my direction. "Logan, you're never up at this hour of the morning—especially not to engage in physical activity. Are you feeling okay?"

"Never better." I grinned, giving her a thumbs-up. "Emma's trying to get me to start waking up earlier. She doesn't think I should sleep my summer vacation away."

Rachel smiled. "I agree." She glanced between us. "I was just about to start cooking up some breakfast. Emma, would you like to join us?"

"Oh, no thank you," Emma replied politely. "I'm going to go home and collapse on the couch. I'm not used to exercise."

Rachel chuckled. "Okay, then. See you later." She gave Emma a wave before disappearing back inside the house.

As soon as she was gone, Emma breathed a sigh of relief. "That was close."

"Yeah, no kidding," I muttered. "Hopefully your parents aren't up, but if they are, just feed them the same lie we gave Rachel."

"I will," she said with a nod. She started walking toward her house, but stopped two steps in and turned around. "Last night was nice, by the way."

I couldn't help but smile at that. "Yeah, it was. Talk to you later?"

"Sure," she said, smiling back. "Let me know what Matt thinks about your mini golf idea."

"Huh?" At first, I didn't know what she was talking about, but then I remembered I had thrown out the idea of having a possible pseudo double date with Matt and Riley at some point. "Oh, right. Yeah, I'll let you know."

"Great." She gave me a small wave before turning on her heel and walking briskly over to her driveway.

Rachel was waiting for me by the front door when I entered the house.

"So, how's your project coming along?" she asked, unfolding the newspaper.

"My project?"

"Yeah, you know, helping Emma find love? Made any progress yet?"

Why was she asking me this right now? With a shrug, I walked past her toward the kitchen. "A little bit."

"A little bit?" she echoed. "Logan, what are you waiting for? The clock is ticking. I would've thought you'd put a rush order on this, knowing you have such limited time before our New York trip."

"I'm working on it, alright?" I snapped, opening the refrigerator and taking out a pitcher of orange juice. "In fact, Matt's coming over this afternoon and I'm going to suggest that he and I take Emma and Riley mini golfing tonight."

Rachel made a face. "You're going to invite Riley along?"

I took a gulp of orange juice. "Yeah, why?"

"Oh, nothing," she sighed, grabbing a carton of eggs from the refrigerator. "Actually, I take that back. You know, as soon as I saw that girl step out of the car across the street, I knew you'd be all over that."

"*All over that?* Really, Rachel?"

She shrugged. "Look, I'm sure Riley's a great girl and all, but she seems a little too much like Grace. And I liked Grace, you know that, but she wasn't good for you, and I don't think Riley will be, either."

I downed the rest of my juice and walked over to the sink to rinse out the glass. "Okay, first of all, I've hardly spent any time with Riley since she arrived here. Second of all, even if she and I decide to hook up for the summer or whatever, she'll be heading back home before school starts, so it's not like we're going to embark on a relationship like Grace and I did. So, your concerns are invalid."

My phone vibrated in my pocket. Taking it out, I saw I'd received a text from Emma.

Emma: Parents still asleep! Crisis averted!

My phone buzzed again with another text, this time a photo of her standing in the doorway of her parents' bedroom with her parents asleep in their bed in the background. She was giving the thumbs-up with wide eyes and a goofy, open-mouthed grin.

I laughed as I started typing out a response.

Me: glad 2 know ur reputation with ur parents remains untarnished!

"What's so funny?" Rachel asked, cracking an egg into a bowl.

"Nothing. Just Emma," I replied, sticking the phone back in my pocket.

"Oh, I see," she said with raised eyebrows.

I narrowed my eyes at her. "What?"

"What?" She blinked at me innocently.

"Your voice had a *tone* to it."

"I have no idea what you're talking about," she said with a slight smirk. "Anyway, back to our discussion, don't jump into things with Riley, okay?"

"Yeah, yeah," I muttered. "Whatever. I'm going to go take a shower. Save me some eggs?"

Rachel nodded. "I'll even save you some bacon, too."

"You're the greatest stepmother ever." I gave her a quick peck on the top of her head before exiting the kitchen.

As I ascended the stairs, I took my phone back out to see if Emma had maybe texted me again and I'd just missed the notification.

She hadn't.

And as I headed for the bathroom, I decided not to question why I was suddenly filled with an intense feeling of disappointment.

***

The doorbell rang at exactly one o'clock and I knew it was going to be Matt. That dude was the most punctual person I'd ever met. It was annoying.

Sure enough, when I opened the door, he was standing on the front porch...with Riley at his side.

"Uh, hi," I said, my gaze flickering from Matt to Riley and then back to Matt.

"Hey," he said. "I know we were supposed to bro out this afternoon, but Riley was bored to tears—"

"Literally," she interjected, putting on a fake pout. "There's nothing to do up here. When I found out Matt was coming over to hang out with you, I invited myself to join him. I hope you don't mind." She tilted her head and batted her eyelashes at me.

It was an old trick, used by many girls in my lifetime, but it worked. Stepping aside, I motioned for them to come in. "I don't mind at all," I said, although Rachel's earlier advice suddenly popped into my head as Riley brushed past me.

I ignored the thought as I shut the door behind us.

"This might be boring for you, though," I warned her. "Matt and I were just going to play video games all day."

"I don't mind," she said with a shrug. "Watching you two play video games beats hanging out with my parents and my aunt and uncle."

"What about Jade?" I asked, even though I already knew the answer.

Jade was Matt's younger sister. She was thirteen going on three hundred. I say that because she often looked like a vampire. She'd been going through a goth phase for at least a year now, staying out of the sun so her skin would remain translucently pale, wearing dark red lipstick, black eyeliner and eyeshadow, and dressing in nothing but all black clothing. I'd seen her a few times since summer began, and even on the hottest days she'd been clad in a black t-shirt, a long black skirt and black combat boots.

In other words, not exactly the type of girl Riley probably liked to hang out with.

Riley responded with a giggle. "I love my little cousin, but at the same time she kind of frightens me."

"Try living with her full-time," Matt mumbled.

I chuckled as I led the way down to the finished basement—or as Dad liked to refer to it, the "Man Mansion".

It wasn't as big as the name would lead you to believe, but it did run the whole span of the first level of the house, so it was probably around fifteen hundred square feet of gaming consoles, leather armchairs, a foosball table, an air hockey table, a sixty-five-inch TV, a mini-fridge stocked with cans of beer, and many other dude-centric items that kept Rachel from ever spending time down there.

"I feel like I shouldn't be here," Riley said, glancing around.

"It's all good," I said with a dismissive wave as I plopped down onto the loveseat. I opened the drawer on the side table next to it and grabbed two PlayStation controllers and gave one to Matt. "Women are welcome. They just usually don't care to be here."

"Oh, good." She smiled and took a seat next to me. Like, *right* next to me, so that the entire sides of our bodies were touching.

I wanted to move away from her slightly, but I was already sitting up against the arm of the loveseat, so I had nowhere to go.

Well, this was going to be fun.

Matt glanced at us and smiled before dropping into the leather armchair he always sat in. In fact, he sat in it so much that my dad actually designated it as Matt's chair, and never sat in it himself.

"What do you want to play?" I asked Matt.

He shrugged. "I don't know. Football?"

I groaned inwardly. Matt always wanted to play football games and I always wanted to play shooters. Whenever we were at my house, since he was the guest, we'd play football. Whenever I went over to his house, we'd play something with either zombies or snipers.

I turned on the TV and the console. "Well, what do you know? The disc is already in there because we always play this when you come over."

Matt grinned. "What can I say? It helps me stay sharp with the real thing."

"No, it doesn't," I said, rolling my eyes. He said that every time.

A few minutes into playing, I could tell Riley was bored out of her mind. Girls typically didn't like to watch boys play video games unless they were gamers themselves. But even still, most could probably stomach the games I liked to play because sometimes they were like watching movies. The sports games, however, usually sent girls packing.

Which was probably why Riley had pulled out her phone and was busy texting or browsing a shopping app or whatever it was girls did on their phones when they were bored.

I was surprisingly beating the crap out of Matt when Riley suddenly shifted sideways and stretched out, draping her smooth, tanned, bare legs across my lap.

Normally, I would be all about that. I was a leg guy, so having a girl practically shove hers in my face was a welcome gesture. However, when I was in the middle of a game where I was trying to beat my best friend at something he should be winning, considering he played football in real life, it was more of an unwelcome distraction.

But I didn't say anything because, at the end of the day, Riley was a beautiful girl who was apparently into me. And she had a killer set of legs.

"So," I said, clearing my throat. I figured now would be a good time to throw out my double date idea, as promised. "Matt, I was just thinking the other day, it's been a while since we've had a friendly game of mini golf."

Matt snorted as he kept his eyes glued to the screen. "That's because you can never remain friendly when we play."

"What are you talking about?" I scoffed.

"You know exactly what I'm talking about, dude." Matt paused the game and turned to Riley. "This guy has a temper when it comes to competitive sports. Every time we play mini golf, I beat his ass and he throws a hissy fit."

"I do not throw a hissy fit," I grumbled, even though what he was saying wasn't all that far from the truth.

Riley laughed. "Is that so? I've got to see this."

"Perfect," I said, "because I was thinking the three of us could go play sometime. Maybe bring Emma along and we could play as pairs."

"Oh, yes!" Riley squealed. "That sounds awesome. I'm in!"

Matt looked skeptical. "I don't know…"

"I promise I'll be good," I said. "Scout's honor and whatnot."

He proceeded to think about it for a moment. "Okay, sure. Could be fun."

"Great. How about tonight? You guys have anything planned?"

Matt and Riley exchanged a questioning glance and shook their heads.

"No, tonight would be fine," Matt replied.

"Excellent." I set my controller down on the table next to the loveseat and moved to get up. Riley took the hint and removed herself from me.

"I'm going to go grab something to drink," I said. "Can I get you guys anything?"

"I'll take some water," Riley replied.

"You can grab me a Coke," Matt said as he snatched the latest copy of *Sports Illustrated* from the coffee table and began flipping through it.

I nodded. "Be right back."

As soon as I made it to the kitchen, I took out my phone

and texted Emma.

Me: if ur available 2night, mini golf with Matt and Riley is on

A few seconds later, she texted back.

Emma: Nice! Thanks for setting that up. You're the best!

I couldn't help but smile at her response. I really was the best. I was now fully putting into motion her romantic future with Matt. It was entirely possible that tonight would be the start of it all.

As I grabbed a couple cans of Coke and a bottle of water from the fridge, I felt my smile begin to fade. Something was suddenly nagging at me and I couldn't quite put my finger on it. But the feeling was short-lived, so I just ignored it as I headed back downstairs.

It was probably nothing.

Chapter 21

LOGAN

"You ladies are in for a real treat tonight."

I glared at my best friend as we neared the first hole of the mini golf course. "Watch it, Matt," I warned him.

Emma, who was standing beside him, gave him a curious look. "Why do you say that?"

"Because Logan here doesn't play well with others," Matt replied. "And when he starts to lose this game tonight, he's going to have a major meltdown."

I scowled as Emma began to laugh. She'd been doing a lot of that this evening, ever since she, Matt, Riley, and I got in the car to come here. Of course, she was only laughing at the stupid things Matt was saying, and I wanted to pull her aside and warn her to tone it down a little. She was being way too obvious that she was into him.

But Matt was eating it up. He was used to girls fawning over him and laughing at all his jokes, so this was nothing new to him. But *Emma* was new to him, so I could tell he was quite enjoying it.

"So, Logan's a sore loser?" Emma teased. "Why am I not surprised by this?"

"Hey," I said defensively, "I'll have you know that the one or two times I had a meltdown over a game of mini golf, it was because Matt cheated."

Matt put on his best innocent face. "I don't cheat at anything." He turned to Emma and added with a grin, "I don't need to."

She smiled at him and I rolled my eyes. I was quickly starting to wonder why I'd set this whole thing up to begin with.

"What do you say we play as teams?" Riley suggested behind me. "Emma and Matt versus me and Logan."

The most logical pairing, if I wanted to win, was me and Matt. Boys versus girls. But I wasn't here to win a game of mini golf. I was here to start the ball rolling—no pun intended—on Emma and Matt's relationship, so I nodded. "Sounds good."

"As usual, losers pay for ice cream later," Matt declared. Again, he turned to Emma. "It was so safe to assume Logan's going to lose, I didn't even bring my wallet." That was a lie. He'd taken out his wallet just minutes ago to pay for the game.

But again, Emma laughed. Actually, it was more like a giggle. I'm talking a *schoolgirl* giggle.

I bit my tongue to keep myself from saying anything I'd regret. That girl was going to owe me big-time for this.

"Okay, I'll go first," Riley said, placing her purple ball down on the ground. "Don't worry, Logan, mini golf skills run in my family."

Matt snorted. "You mean your *lack* of skills runs in your *other* side of the family." Leaning in close to Emma, he added, "These two are going to be no match for us. Start thinking about what you want for ice cream. Money is no object."

Another laugh from Emma. Another dirty look from me. Matt sure was good at pushing my buttons tonight. Maybe he was trying to impress Emma. Which should have excited me, because that meant my job as matchmaker would be a whole lot easier, but it didn't. It annoyed me.

Riley gracefully hit the ball with her putter, sending it down the long strip of green carpet. The first hole was just a simple straight shot with no obstacles, and while she didn't get it in on the first try, it stopped only about an inch away.

"Nice try, cuz, but you're supposed to get it in the hole, not next to it," Matt heckled, causing Riley to flip him off.

I shook my head as I set my ball down. "And you claim *I* don't play well with others," I muttered. I lined the ball up as best I could with the hole and hit it with the amount of force I figured it would need to make it down there. It stopped just shy of Riley's.

"Aw, man, that's too bad." Matt slapped me on the back. "I'll let Emma go first, and then I'll show you how it's done."

Now he was *really* starting to piss me off, but I said nothing as I stepped aside to let Emma play. She glanced at me with a small smile before taking her shot. She was by far the worst out of all of us; her ball made it nowhere near the hole.

With a sheepish smile, she said, "I'm rusty. I haven't played this in a while."

"It's okay," Matt said softly, placing a hand on her shoulder and giving a squeeze. "You did just fine."

Her cheeks turned dark pink—her signature shade—as she stared down at the ground, tucking a strand of hair nervously behind her ear.

My eyes narrowed at the scene. Riley and I had been very close to sinking our balls and Matt harassed us about it. Emma's ball landed nowhere in the vicinity and Matt was being all sweet and encouraging.

This whole night was starting to get on my nerves.

Matt took his turn next and sank the ball in one shot, then turned to me and Riley to gloat. "See? That's how you do it."

"*See? That's how you do it*," Riley mocked in a baby voice and stuck her tongue out at him as she proceeded to take her next shot.

Both she and I both sank our balls on the second try and it took Emma two more swings—which meant our teams were tied, but it was still very early in the game, and we still had seventeen more holes to get through.

It was going to be a long night.

"So, Emma," Matt said as we headed for hole number 2, which consisted of a small bridge over a stream. "What have you been up to so far this summer?"

I glanced at him curiously. Matt was making small talk? That wasn't like him.

"Um…" She examined the pink golf ball in her hand. I could tell she didn't know how to respond to that.

"She's been organizing her book collection," I offered, immediately wondering why I would tell him that.

Emma appeared to be wondering the same thing—and she wasn't pleased, if the narrowing of her eyes was any indication. The goal here was to *not* make her look like a loser in front of Matt.

Riley chuckled and stopped when she noticed nobody else was doing the same. "Oh, you were serious?"

"That's not *all* I've been doing," Emma mumbled, staring at the ground.

"Do you have a big book collection or something?" Matt asked.

Emma seemed taken aback at Matt's question, like she wasn't used to anyone expressing interest in her love of books.

"Yeah," she replied sheepishly. "A few hundred or so."

Matt's eyes went wide, but not in a judgmental sort of way. "Wow, that's impressive. I'm not much of a reader, but that's only because I don't really have time to read anything. Between school, football practice, and hanging out with friends, I don't have a lot of time to do much of anything."

Emma nodded like she understood. "Well, if you ever get some free time and would like a book to read, I'll let you borrow one of mine."

"Thanks," Matt said with a genuine smile.

"I'm not sure you'd really care for any of her books," I chimed in before I had a chance to stop myself. "Unless you like romance novels about shirtless dudes."

Matt snorted, while Emma looked like she was about to kill me.

"Emma, why don't you go first this time?" Riley suggested, suppressing a smirk.

"Sure, okay," she said through clenched teeth. She set her ball down and swung at it a little too forcefully. It went airborne, soaring over the bridge and bouncing off the ground before leaving the brick barrier and landing in the area belonging to hole number 3, narrowly missing a guy who was about to take a swing of his own.

We all had a good laugh at Emma's expense as her cheeks turned three different shades of red.

"Sorry," she called out to the guy, who just smiled and waved dismissively. She moved to go retrieve the ball, but Matt was way ahead of her. He jogged over and grabbed it, apologized to the guy himself, and jogged back.

"Looks like you need some lessons," Matt said with a grin, handing Emma her ball. "Maybe I can help. Here, stand like this."

He placed his hands on her shoulders and turned her sideways, and then stood behind her and moved his hands down to hers.

"Okay," he said into her ear, "Put your left hand up here, and your right one down here. Now, when you swing, you don't want to put too much force behind it or the ball's going to, you know, fly off and almost hit someone."

Emma's bad mood instantly turned around as she giggled.

With his hands still on hers, he gently guided the putter back and swung it to hit the ball. It rolled smoothly over the bridge and stayed in a perfectly straight line as it headed for the hole.

And sank right in.

"Yes! A hole in one!" Emma exclaimed as she and Matt high-fived.

I rolled my eyes. "Hardly. Are you forgetting your first shot? Your ball landed in somebody else's game."

"That one didn't count," Matt said, shaking his head.

"The hell it didn't."

"C'mon, dude, lighten up." He placed his own ball down and I bent over to scoop it up.

"Nope," I said. "If you're not going to count Emma's first swing, then we're going to count her 'hole in one' as *yours* since you're pretty much the one who sank it, and she can go again—without your help."

I could tell Matt was getting irritated with me, which was fine. The feeling was mutual. Throwing his hands up in surrender, he stepped aside and motioned for Emma to return to the spot she was in just a few moments ago.

"See what I mean?" he leaned in and muttered to her. "The meltdown is imminent."

My hand clenched around my putter so hard I could feel my knuckles turning white. Riley must have noticed because she stepped in front of me and placed her hands on my chest.

"Ignore him," she said. "He's just trying to throw you off your game."

My gaze flickered over Riley's shoulder to look at Matt, but it landed on Emma first. She was clearly not impressed with my attitude and the disappointment etched in her features reminded me why we were here in the first place.

I took a deep breath and let it out slowly to calm myself down. "Whatever. We'll count Emma's last swing as a hole in one and Matt can take his turn." I forced a smile onto my face. While I was seething on the inside, I wasn't going to give Matt the satisfaction of seeing it.

There would be no meltdown tonight.

We continued on for a few holes with no issues. Emma started getting better with her swings and between that, and the fact Matt kept sinking his ball on the first or second try, by hole 18, it was obvious which pairing was going to win.

But I kept my cool. I didn't freak out. It helped that my partner was hot, so I would just push away my irritation and instead focus on her butt every time she bent down to pick up her ball. And she was very touchy-feely tonight. Every time either one of us scored a one or a two, she would throw herself at me, squealing with joy, pushing herself right up against me.

Definitely a good distraction.

Emma, however, couldn't seem to hide *her* irritation. I had no idea what had gotten into her, but while she was perfectly cheery and chatty for most of the game, she started becoming quiet, reserved, and moody around hole 14.

After taking my shot at the last hole and Matt prepared to take his, I pulled her aside, out of earshot of the others.

"What's wrong?" I whispered.

Emma shrugged. "Nothing's wrong."

"Liar." I crossed my arms over my chest and studied her for a moment. "You should be over the moon right now. Matt seems to be digging you. I've never seen him have so many conversations with a girl before—and with a genuine smile on his face no less. I think he likes you."

For a brief moment, her eyes lit up with what I could only guess was a glimmer of hope before they clouded over again.

"He doesn't," she said with a frown. "He's just being nice. Because he's a nice guy. But you certainly haven't been helping, you know. What were you thinking, talking about my book collection like that? It was *your* idea to make me look cooler to him, and you turned right around and told him how much of a nerd I am. What's up with that?"

It was a good question. One I really didn't know the answer to. Luckily, Matt interrupted before I had to try and come up with a response.

"As expected, Emma and I beat the crap out of Logan and Riley," he said proudly, holding up the scorecard. He shifted his gaze to me. "Would you like to have your tantrum right now, or do you want to wait until after you buy me and Emma our ice cream?"

"I'm cool," I lied. "Good game, guys."

Matt narrowed his eyes. I could tell he was suspicious of my calm demeanor, but he let it slide.

Instead, he walked over to Emma, swooped her up into his arms and gave her a congratulatory hug.

She responded with her three hundredth giggle of the night.

"Isn't that cute?" Riley said behind me.

"What?" I asked, noting the sudden irritation in my voice but choosing to ignore it.

"Those two." She pointed over to Emma and Matt, who had broken apart but were now talking and laughing about something we couldn't hear. "I think they would make a cute couple."

Instinctually, I snorted. "Those two? They couldn't be any more different—" My mouth clamped shut. No, wait. It was a *good* thing Riley thought they'd make a cute couple. That was the whole point of all this. Why was I suddenly losing sight of what I was trying to accomplish here?

"You know what they say, opposites attract." With her forefinger, Riley traced a line down my arm. "Then again, sometimes it's nice to be on the same playing field. Don't you agree?" She smiled up at me seductively.

"Um, yeah, I suppose," I said, suddenly feeling uncomfortable. Riley was obviously referring to the two of us and I wasn't quite sure how I felt about that.

Did I find Riley attractive? Hell, yeah. Did I think she would be fun to hang out with? Sure—and probably fun between the sheets, too. But Rachel was right; she was too much like Grace. Been there, done that, not looking forward to doing it ever again. The last thing I needed was another girl trying to pressure me into being a reliable boyfriend. I just didn't have it in me.

Although, Riley was only up here for the summer, so it wasn't like she'd be looking for a long-term relationship. And we probably could have a good time together. Maybe after I got Emma and Matt together and some of my time freed up...

"Hey, Logan," Riley said, snapping her fingers in front of my face. "Are you okay?"

I blinked. "Yeah. Why do you ask?"

"Because you just zoned out and started frowning for no apparent reason."

Weird. I hadn't even noticed.

"Okay, losers, time for ice cream," Matt called over to us.

Gritting my teeth, I put on a fake smile and said, "Great. Lead the way."

Riley bounced over to Matt and Emma. I didn't know what she was so excited about; she was going to have to pay for half the ice cream bill.

The four of us returned our putters and headed toward the ice cream shack. Halfway there, Matt stopped walking and turned to the girls.

"Hey, why don't you two go pick out what you want? Logan and I will be right there."

Emma and Riley exchanged a curious glance before nodding and walking away.

I sent my own curious glance Matt's way. "What's up?"

Matt stuffed his hands into the pockets of his shorts and shrugged. "Are we cool? I'm sorry for ribbing you so much back there. It was all in good fun."

I could tell he was being sincere. I knew his harassment hadn't been malicious in any sort of way, but that didn't stop it from being annoying. Still, he was my best friend and I couldn't stay mad at him.

"Yeah, man, we're good." I smiled and slapped him on the back. I began to move forward again, but his next words stopped me dead in my tracks.

"So, um, what's up with you and Emma?"

I stared blankly down at the ground for a moment, letting his question swim around my head before turning back around. "What do you mean?"

"I mean, are you guys, like, dating?"

I burst out laughing. "No, we're not dating. Don't you think if we were, I would have made her *my* golfing partner tonight?"

Matt nodded like he thought that made some sense. "Okay. Well…do you *want* to date her?"

My laughter abruptly came to a halt. Swallowing hard, I said, "What kind of question is that?"

He thought about it for a moment. "A valid one."

I began to laugh again, but this time it sounded strained and inauthentic. "Well, I think it's a dumb question."

"One that you haven't answered yet." Matt's eyes searched my face. "Do you like her?"

"Dude," I said, taking a step back. "What's with the sudden interrogation?"

He sighed and ran a hand through his hair. "I'm just curious. I mean, you've practically spent all summer with her so far, and you're always bringing her along to things. You even skipped my party yesterday to hang out with her. It just seems like maybe you like her."

I guess I could see why he might think that. I *had* been hanging out with Emma a lot lately. But I couldn't tell him the real reason: that I was grooming her to be his love interest.

"Yeah, well, I don't," I said, biting the inside of my cheek.

Matt smiled. "Cool," was all he said before walking past me. "Let's go get some ice cream."

I watched him for a second before starting to follow him. Why was he suddenly so interested in what was going on between me and Emma? And why did he look so happy when I told him I didn't like her?

More importantly, why did that suddenly put me in a really bad mood?

Chapter 22

EMMA

For the first time in my life, I held an open book in my hands, but I couldn't concentrate on reading it. And not just because it was like a hundred degrees out by the pool, or because the book was boring.

I couldn't concentrate on it because I couldn't stop thinking about the previous night.

After mini golf, we all got ice cream and hung out for a while. Matt and Logan hit some balls in the batting cages, leaving me and Riley alone to sit in awkward silence as we watched them. I tried on a few occasions to spark up a conversation with her, but every time she would just nod, say, "Mmhmm," and pull out her phone to text someone.

At one point, I could tell she had texted Logan because as soon as she sent it, Logan paused, took his phone out of his pocket to read it, and then glanced over at her with a smirk on his face. She responded with a suggestive smile and a small wave. I just rolled my eyes as I tried not to think about what she might have texted him. She'd been throwing herself at him all night, constantly putting her hands all over him, and he seemed to really be enjoying it.

Whatever. It was none of my business.

What *was* my business was *Matt*. While it's not like I really got anywhere with him, he did talk to me a lot. And then there was the moment he helped me out with my golf swing…standing behind me, his hands on mine, speaking softly into my ear…

I bit my lip to prevent myself from smiling at the memory, but I couldn't help it. The whole thing made me so giddy I could squee.

Squee. I was not the type of girl who would squee over *anything.* I even hated the word itself because it wasn't a real word. But after last night, it was the *only* word I could think to use.

As I struggled to remove the goofy smile from my face, my phone rang on my lap. Assuming it was either Chloe or Sophia, since I hadn't talked to either one of them for a couple days, I didn't bother to look to see who it was before answering it.

"Hello?"

"Hey, book nerd," said a smooth, masculine voice into my ear. Even if I hadn't recognized the voice as Logan's, I still would have known it was him. I was currently wearing a tank top that said, *Book Nerd* on it, which meant chances were good he was spying on me from his bedroom window. Assuming he was, I glared up in that general direction.

"What's that look for?" he asked defensively, confirming my assumption.

"What do you want, Logan?" I asked, sighing heavily. I still hadn't fully forgiven him for last night, when he tried to make me look like a dork in front of Matt.

"I wanted to know if you were interested in hanging out," he replied. "It's the hottest day of the summer so far, and I thought maybe you'd like to come over and go for a swim."

Funny he should mention that. I'd put on my new bikini underneath my shorts and tank top on the off chance I wanted to take a dip in the pool. It was crazy hot out and it wasn't even noontime yet.

"If I want to go for a swim, I've got my own pool to swim

in."

"Yes, but you shouldn't swim alone," he said. "You should always swim with a buddy in case you almost drown—that way, there's somebody there to give you mouth-to-mouth if necessary."

I snorted. "Well, in that case, I'm *definitely* not coming over."

"But I give great mouth-to-mouth. I could provide you with testimonials, if you'd like."

"I'm good, thanks," I said, fanning myself with my book, due to the fact the air around me suddenly felt about ten degrees hotter.

"Okay, we don't have to go swimming. Come over anyway. I have a nice air-conditioned basement we can chill out in."

"My house is air-conditioned as well."

"Oh my God, Dawson," Logan said, "why do you have to be so difficult? Just get your butt over here, alright? I have some information regarding Matt that I think you might find interesting."

I sat up in my lounge chair and dropped my book onto the deck. "Oh yeah? Like what?"

"Like, I'll tell you when you get here," he said and hung up.

I narrowed my eyes at my phone. Was this a trick? A bait-and-switch? Like I'd get there and his "information" would be something dumb like, "Matt likes girls who hang out in basements on hot days"? That would be just like him. It wouldn't surprise me in the least.

Still, it could be something legit. And for that reason, I foolishly began my trek over Logan's house.

He was waiting for me at the front door when I arrived, wearing a cocky grin on his face.

"I knew you'd come," he said as I ascended the porch

steps. "It was the possibility of mouth-to-mouth with me that convinced you, wasn't it?"

I brushed past him into the house, where it instantly felt about thirty degrees cooler than it did outside. "So, what's this information you've got about Matt?" I asked, cutting right to the chase.

Logan shut the door behind us and put on his best hurt expression. "You know, I'm starting to feel like you're just using me to get closer to my best friend."

"Good call," I said with a smirk. "That's exactly what I'm doing."

Logan just shook his head and said, "Follow me to the basement."

When Logan said he had an air-conditioned basement, I was expecting to see something similar to the basement at my house: dark, dirt-scented and full of spiders. But it was nothing like that. It was bright, bug-free and fully-finished, with a large TV, ample seating, an air hockey table, and a mini-fridge. The place was like a man cave on steroids.

"Welcome to the Man Mansion. Have a seat." Logan motioned to the loveseat in front of me. "Can I get you anything to drink?"

I shook my head as I sat down. "No, thanks," I said as he took a seat next to me. "I just want you to tell me what information you have about Matt that I supposedly would be interested in."

"Boy, you have a one-track mind, don't you?" He grabbed two PlayStation controllers off the coffee table and handed me one. "You play video games?"

"I've dabbled," I said with a shrug. My dad owned a few video games and occasionally he and I would play racing games together.

Logan turned on both the TV and the console. "You should try out this game. It's mostly a button masher, so you don't have to be worried about not being an experienced gamer. I think you'll like it because you'll get to beat the crap out of me."

I smiled at that. "While that does sound enticing, I didn't come over here to play video games with you. I came over to talk about Matt."

"We'll get to that, I promise," Logan said as the game started up. He picked a character out of a list of male avatars and instructed me to do the same with the list of females. "I'll tell you what you want to know after you win a round."

I scowled at him. "That's not fair. I've never played this before."

"Just hit any combination of any of these buttons at any time. You'll do fine."

A few seconds later, the game started, and our two characters appeared on the screen. The women in these types of games could not be any more unrealistic. My character was bleached blonde, had huge boobs, a tiny waist, a bubble butt, large, muscular thighs and was dressed in hot pants, a crop top and knee-high combat boots. No woman in real life looked like this.

I did what Logan had instructed me to do, and that was just hit as many of the buttons as I could as quickly as I could. His character defeated mine within seconds and I turned to him with an angry pout.

"This is so unfair. You are obviously very experienced with this game. I don't stand a chance."

"Sorry," he said with a smirk. "I'll go easy on you next round."

"No," I said, shaking my head. "I don't want you to do

that, either. I can beat you fair and square."

He arched a brow. "You think so, do you?"

"Yep." I sat up straight and moved to the edge of the couch, holding the controller tightly in my hands. "Bring it on."

The next round began, and Logan once again started kicking my butt—no matter how many buttons I mashed or how quickly. At one point, my whole body got into the action, tilting from side to side while I moved the controller up, down, and all around, in hopes that it would somehow help me win.

It didn't.

When Logan's character ripped mine in half and her cartoon blood started spurting out all over the place, I dropped my controller onto the table, stood and crossed my arms over my chest.

"Okay, first of all, this game is disgusting," I said, wrinkling my nose at the gruesome image still displayed on the TV screen. "Second of all, it's a really stupid game with no point. Third of all, just tell me the important information you have about Matt."

Logan chuckled and tossed his own controller aside. "Okay, fine. I'll tell you, right after you admit this game is kind of fun."

I tapped my foot impatiently against the floor. "Yeah, okay, it's moderately entertaining. Happy now?"

"Very." He smiled and gave a pat on the empty cushion next to him. "Here, sit back down and I'll tell you."

I begrudgingly did as I was told and dropped back down onto the loveseat. I turned so I was facing him. "Well?"

His grin indicated that he seemed to enjoy leaving me hanging, which made me want to wring his neck.

"Logan, I swear, if you don't tell me what—"

"Matt asked about us," he blurted out.

I stopped and stared at him blankly. "Us?"

"Yes, us. Me and you."

I chewed on my lower lip, trying to figure out what he was saying. "What about us?"

Logan shrugged and picked his controller back up. "He asked if we were dating."

"Why would he ask that?"

"I'm not sure. He didn't say. But if I had to wager a guess, I'd say maybe he wanted to make sure we didn't have something going on before making a move on you."

My heart leapt into my throat. I studied him for a moment, looking for any indication he was lying. "You're making this up."

"I'm not," he said innocently.

"When did you guys have that conversation?"

"Last night, when he sent you and Riley off by yourselves to get ice cream. That's what he wanted to talk to me about."

"Huh." I sank into the back of the loveseat and started biting one of my fingernails. Whenever something made me nervous, I became a nail biter.

"I think it's safe to say you're now on Matt's radar." Logan shifted so he was facing me. "It's possible he's becoming interested in you, but he's not quite there yet. If he were, he likely would have just told me and then asked you out. But the interest is there. Now all you need to do is make sure you hold onto it."

"How do you suggest I do that?" I asked.

He thought about it for a moment. "Well… I think you need to try being flirtier with him. I mean, you were fine with him last night. You at least spoke actual words instead of just stammering a bunch of gibberish at him—which was a definite improvement, don't get me wrong. But you're going to have to step things up a notch when you're around him. You need to channel your inner Riley."

I pursed my lips at the mention of Riley and I spoke before thinking. "You mean I need to act desperate?"

He looked taken aback by that. "Actually, I meant you need to act *sexy*."

I couldn't help but laugh. "You really think the way Riley acts is sexy? The girl tries way too hard."

"And it works," he said with a nod.

My laughter came to an abrupt halt. "Yeah, it works on *you*. And only because you're easy."

It was his turn to laugh. "I am *not* easy."

"Yes, you are."

"No, I'm not. Riley's just that good." He got up from the couch and held out a hand for me to take. "Here, stand up."

With a sigh, I obeyed.

"Okay, let's do a little practice run." Logan's eyes sparkled as he spoke, like he thought this was the greatest idea ever. "Act like Riley and try to seduce me."

I gaped at him. "Come again?"

He chuckled softly. "I said, try to seduce me. Show me what you've got. I want to see if you're capable of doing this."

I didn't like this. I didn't know how to seduce someone, so I was likely going to make an idiot out of myself. But I guess that was kind of the point. If I sucked at it, Logan was there to help me. He'd give me tips and pointers, and he'd make sure the next time I saw Matt, I'd be ready.

"Okay." I took a step back, closed my eyes and breathed in deeply. *Just channel my inner Riley.* All I had to do was giggle and bat my eyelashes and touch his chest. Piece of cake.

Opening my eyes, I reached up and removed the elastic band holding my ponytail in place. I ran my hands through my hair to smooth it out, letting the natural waves cascade down my back.

I could do this.

Flipping an invisible switch, I shut off Emma and turned on Riley. Widening my eyes, I stared at Logan in awe.

"Oh, Logan, you are so good at hitting balls with putters," I said, adding a little giggle at the end for effect.

Logan, looking amused, said, "I told you to *channel* Riley, not flat-out plagiarize her."

But I ignored him. Since I had no idea how to seduce a guy, my only option was to basically copy everything I'd seen Riley do with Logan since she got here.

I took a step closer to him and placed a hand on his chest. "Wow, Logan, you feel so strong. You must work out." I lowered my hand, tracing a line with my forefinger between his pecs and his abs.

"I do," he said with a cocky grin. "Thank you for noticing."

"How could I not?" I bit my lip. Guys liked it when girls bit their lips, I knew that much.

"Take your shirt off," I instructed. I could tell instantly my demand surprised us both.

"Um, what?" His grin faltered slightly.

That was a good question. I think I had dialed into Riley's channel a little too much, but now it was hard to get out of it because…well…it was kind of fun.

"Take your shirt off," I repeated, more confidently this time. When he didn't immediately obey, I added, "If you show me yours, I'll show you mine."

His eyebrows shot up so fast he was lucky they didn't fly off his face. "What—"

Feeling bold, I put some space between us, grabbed the bottom of my tank top, and lifted it up over my head, revealing my bikini top underneath. As soon as it was off, I tossed it at him. He caught it without even looking; he was too busy keeping his eyes focused on mine.

"Want to go for a swim?" I asked in my best Riley voice.

Logan's face fell as soon as I start undoing the button of my shorts. Suddenly, all traces of amusement were gone from his face. Apparently, I was taking this further than he'd expected I would and he didn't know how to react.

His hands shot out and grabbed my wrists to stop me from removing my shorts. "Emma, this wasn't exactly what I meant."

"Why not?" I asked with a sultry pout. "This is what Riley did at Justin's party, and you were all about it. This is what guys like, right? Girls who are bold and aren't afraid to strip down in front of them?"

"Well, yeah, but—"

"You don't think this would work on Matt?"

"Yes, it would, but—"

"Then what's the problem?"

He opened his mouth to respond, but nothing came out. He was speechless.

Luckily for him, he didn't have to respond because we were suddenly interrupted by Rachel's voice at the top of the basement stairs.

"Logan, are you down there?"

He immediately let go of my wrists and took a giant step away from me. "Yeah," he called back in a strained voice, quickly raking a hand through his hair.

We heard her footsteps coming down the stairs before we saw her. "Good. I was wondering if maybe—"

She stopped when her gaze fell on us. Or, more specifically, me. I guess she wasn't expecting to see me standing there practically half-naked—and with Logan still holding onto my shirt.

He realized he still had it in his hands at the same moment I did and his face reddened as he tossed it onto the couch. Clearing his throat, he said, "You were wondering what?"

I could feel my own face beginning to burn as Rachel removed her gaze from me and moved it onto Logan. "Am I interrupting something?"

"No," Logan and I answered swiftly and in unison.

"We were just…getting ready to go for a swim," Logan lied.

Rachel blinked. "Oh. Well, that's a good idea." She didn't seem to believe us, but she also didn't seem to care.

"Anyway," she continued, "Logan, I have a favor to ask." She glanced between him and me. "Both of your fathers—and their beautiful wives—have been invited to a very important dinner tonight by a potential client, and I was wondering…would you be able to watch Abby for a few hours?"

"Um…" A look of guilt came over Logan's face. "I kind of have plans with Riley tonight."

I whipped my head in his direction so fast I felt a muscle pull in my neck. "What, like a date?"

He turned to look at me and shrugged. "Yeah, kind of. I don't know."

"And, what, a date with Riley is more important than looking after your baby sister?" I shook my head in disappointment.

"I didn't say that," Logan replied defensively.

"Well, I don't see you jumping at the opportunity to cancel your plans with Riley to take care of Abby."

"Because you haven't given me the opportunity yet," he said, the irritation in his voice becoming more prominent with each word he spoke.

Rachel, whose eyes had been bouncing back and forth between us as though she were watching a tennis match, held up a hand to stop us.

"Guys, it's okay. I'll just find somebody else—"

"I can do it," I blurted out before really thinking about it.

Rachel raised her eyebrows in surprise. "Seriously?"

"Yeah, why not? I don't have anything better to do tonight. I would love to watch her for you."

Rachel's face dissolved into a look of relief as she launched herself at me, pulling me into a tight embrace.

"Thank you," she breathed into my hair. When she released me, she was grinning from ear to ear. "This will be the first real night out I've had since Abby was born. I'm going to go pick out something to wear!"

She squealed and clapped her hands together as she turned and headed back up the stairs, leaving me and Logan alone in uncomfortable silence.

"You don't have to do that," Logan said quietly. "I can cancel my plans."

I brushed past him to grab my tank top. As I pulled it on, I said, "It's fine. I like babysitting, and Abby's amazing. It would be stupid for you to cancel your plans when I don't have any at all."

Logan nodded and glanced down at the floor.

I smoothed out my shirt and ran a hand through my hair. "Well, I should get going."

He returned his gaze to me. "Are you sure? We have some other things to go over."

I shook my head. "I'm going to go talk to Rachel and see when she wants me back here, and then I have a few errands to run."

"Oh, okay."

"So…I'll catch you later?" I said, heading toward the staircase. I suddenly felt like I couldn't get out of there fast enough.

"Yeah, sure."

"Cool." I took the first step and glanced back over at him before heading up. "Have fun on your date."

I couldn't help but note the sarcasm in my voice as I spoke. Part of me hoped he *wouldn't* have fun on his date...while the other part of me wondered why I even cared.

Chapter 23

EMMA

"You're all alone in Logan's house? Chica, what are you doing wasting time talking to us when you should be snooping around in his bedroom?"

I rolled my eyes at Sophia through the screen of my laptop. I'd been alone at the Reynolds house for nearly an hour now. When I arrived, Logan was already gone, and Mark and Rachel were out the door before I even made my way inside the house. Abby cried for the first fifteen minutes—most likely due to the fact it was the first time since she was born that she'd been separated from her mother—and then she quickly fell asleep afterward, making my job incredibly easy. After watching TV for about half an hour, I decided to make good use of the laptop I'd brought with me and set up a video chat with Chloe and Sophia. It had been way too long since I'd talked to them.

"I'm not alone. Abby's here."

"Abby's a baby, Emma," Chloe said. "Who's she going to tell? I'm with Sophia on this. You need to go ransack that boy's room and fill us in on everything you find."

"I'm not going to do that." I stretched my legs out in front of me on the couch and set the laptop on my lap. "I don't even care what's in his bedroom. Why do *you*?"

Chloe and Sophia exchanged a glance.

"Uh, because Logan is one of the hottest guys at our

school," Sophia replied, "and we want to know as much about him as possible."

"Yeah," Chloe agreed. "Like what color his bed sheets are, or how many condoms he keeps stashed in the drawer of his nightstand."

I gaped at her, appalled. "Chloe! That's disgusting!"

"What?" Chloe said, all innocent-like. "You know he must keep them somewhere. That boy most definitely gets it on."

Sophia nodded. "In fact, he's probably getting it on with Riley right now."

I glared at the two of them as they proceeded to giggle and make kissy noises at each other. I loved my best friends, but lately, every time we spoke on video chat, they ended up saying something that made me immediately want to close my laptop.

"Can we change the subject, please?"

They stopped giggling and exchanged another glance.

"Emma, does that bother you?" Chloe asked.

"Does what bother me?"

"The thought of Logan and Riley…you know…*doing it*."

"Of course not," I scoffed. "Why would that bother me? I don't care what they do. I just don't want you guys putting such disturbing visuals in my head."

Another glance was exchanged, and I decided it was up to me to change the subject.

"So, you guys are going to Disney World tomorrow, huh?"

Their faces instantly lit up. "Yep!" Chloe exclaimed. "Courtesy of my Aunt Jess, who is not only gracious enough to drive us there, but to pay for our tickets too."

I smiled. "You guys are so lucky."

"We'd be luckier if you were coming with us," Sophia said with a pout.

Chloe nodded. "We feel so bad we're going without you."

I waved my hand around dismissively. "Don't feel bad. I'm the one who made the decision not to go to Florida."

"We know that, but still..." Chloe said, giving me a sympathetic look.

"Don't worry about it," I said. "As long as you bring me back a souvenir, I don't care."

The girls both grinned and nodded.

"Well, we should probably go to bed soon," Sophia said, glancing down at her phone. "We have to get up super-early tomorrow."

"That's fine," I said. "I should go check on Abby anyway. Call me tomorrow and tell me about all the fun you two had, okay?"

"We will!" they said at the same time, before waving and saying their goodbyes.

I disconnected and shut my laptop. Placing it on the coffee table, I got off the couch and headed for the stairs. I was sure Abby was doing fine. Periodically, I could hear her lightly snoring through the baby monitor, but that was it. Apparently, her crying attack was enough to knock her out for the rest of the night.

As soon as I took the first step, I heard what sounded like a tapping sound coming from behind me. Freezing in place, I listened for a few seconds to see if I would hear it again, but I didn't. Nothing but silence. Figuring I was just hearing things, I jogged up the stairs and went straight to Abby's nursery.

"Hey, Abby," I whispered as I neared her crib. Peeking in, I could see she was still fast asleep. So far, this was the easiest babysitting job ever.

Reaching down, I brushed my hand against her chubby little one and smiled. I'd always secretly wished my parents would give me a little brother or sister. Sometimes it was lonely being an only child, and I often wondered why my parents never gave it another go. They claimed it was because they felt they'd hit the jackpot the first time around. I'm not sure I ever believed that, but I never questioned it.

"Let me know if you get hungry, okay?" I said softly. "Just start crying and I'll be right up—"

My words were halted by another sound. This time, it sounded like something falling against the pavement on the driveway. It was so sudden and loud, it made me gasp and jump.

Quietly, I made my way over to the window to look outside. Sure enough, the garbage can that had been standing in the driveway earlier was now on its side.

A nervous lump began to form in the base of my throat. *Don't freak out. It was probably just the wind or a raccoon that knocked it over.*

But had the wind or a raccoon made that tapping sound I'd heard before coming upstairs?

Unrelated instances, I assured myself.

Or so I thought...until I heard that same tapping sound again, only this time it was louder.

I stepped back from the window as my heart began to pound against my ribcage. *Calm down, Emma. You're doing it again. You're freaking yourself out over nothing.*

But what if it wasn't nothing? Right now, Abby and I were the only people at home on this entire street. My parents were with Mark and Rachel. Logan was out with Riley. Matt's house was completely dark across the street. The families that lived further down the road weren't going to be arriving for at least another couple of days. It was just me and a baby, all alone. If someone were to try and break in—

No. I was letting my overactive imagination get the best of

me, as usual. Nobody was trying to break in. It was windy out, and there were raccoons. Two very common things found in nature every day. Nothing to freak out over.

But then the tapping came again, only this time I swear it sounded like it was coming from *inside* the house.

A wave of chills ran down the length of my spine as I rushed over to close the door to the nursery. Unfortunately, there wasn't a lock on the inside of the room, but there was a chair I could jam under the doorknob if need be.

With shaky hands, I pulled my phone out of my pocket. I wanted to call someone. Anyone. Well, anyone but my parents. I didn't want to interrupt their important dinner. And anyone but Chloe and Sophia, because they were probably in bed now. And anyone but Logan, because he would make fun of me for being such a scaredy-cat.

But my fingers had a mind of their own. As soon as I turned on the phone, I found myself going straight to my contacts, tapping on Logan's name and calling him.

Before bringing the phone up to my ear, I noticed the battery symbol was filled with just a sliver of red and I silently cursed myself for forgetting to charge it earlier. Hopefully, it would at least make it through this phone call.

After the third ring, I was seriously regretting my decision to call him. He probably wasn't even going to answer. Maybe Sophia was right. Maybe he and Riley were...*doing it*...right now, and my phone call was interrupting them...

With that sickening thought, I was about to remove the phone from my ear to end the call when he suddenly answered.

"Emma?"

"Oh, hey, Logan," I said casually.

"Is everything okay?" he asked. In the background, I could hear music and people talking. So at least I probably wasn't interrupting anything too intimate between him and Riley.

"Um, yeah," I said, quickly losing my ability to sound calm.

"Are you sure?"

"Um…" I began chewing on one of my fingernails. "Well, I don't know. It's probably nothing, but I've just been…hearing some things."

"Hearing some things?" he echoed. "What kind of things?"

"I'm not sure. It's probably nothing. There was a crashing sound outside and I noticed something knocked the garbage can over, and I've been hearing this weird tapping sound."

There wasn't even a pause on his end before he said, "It's probably just an animal looking for food."

"I know. I thought that, too. But you know how I am."

"I do." I could hear the smile in his voice.

"Right," I continued. "But some of these noises sound like they're coming from *inside* the house."

He was silent for a moment. "I'm sure they're not."

"I know. I'm getting myself freaked out over nothing." I sighed as I left the nursery and started down the stairs. "I just needed to call you, so you could talk some sense into me."

Another crashing sound came from outside and it startled me so much I let out a shriek.

"Emma? Are you okay?"

I flipped on the porch light and glanced out the narrow window next to the front door to see what was going on outside. My heart was pounding so hard I thought it might burst through my chest.

But my anxiety was short-lived. As soon as the light was on, I could see what was most likely causing all the commotion: two cats having an epic brawl in the driveway.

With a relieved giggle, I finally answered Logan. "Yeah…yeah, I think I'm good. Just a couple of stray cats duking it out in the driveway." I opened the door and stepped out onto the porch and was immediately hit with a strong gust of wind…which also hit the tree right next to the house, causing one of its branches to tap against the side of the house.

"And the tapping was just a tree branch in the wind," I breathed, running a hand through my hair. "Oh my God, I'm such a dork. I'm sorry, Logan. I shouldn't have called you. Get back to your date and pretend this phone call never happened."

I expected to get some sort of smartass comment from him, but instead, I got nothing.

"Logan?"

The other end of the line was filled with silence. No Logan. No music. No sounds of people talking. I glanced at my phone. It was dead.

"Great," I muttered, going back inside the house and locking the door behind me.

I had just made an idiot of myself with Logan, and he was never going to let me hear the end of it.

Still, I was glad I'd been able to identify the source of the sounds, and now I could get back to sitting on the couch and watching TV.

I took a few minutes first to see if I could find a phone charger anywhere around the house but had no luck. What, did the Reynolds never have to charge their phones? Or did they just like to hide the cords after using them? Either way, I was now officially without a functioning phone, unless I woke up Abby to take her next door to my house so that I could grab my own. But then I ran the risk of Abby realizing her mommy wasn't back yet and I'd have to endure another crying fit for the next half hour.

No, thank you. Mark and Rachel would probably be home

soon, anyway.

With a sigh, I plopped onto the couch, grabbed the TV remote, and began flipping through the channels to see if there was anything good on. I settled on *The Texas Chainsaw Massacre*—probably not the wisest choice for someone who had nearly just given herself a heart attack over two cats and a tree branch, but I did love a good slasher flick once in a while.

Not that I was paying much attention to it, though. As I curled up on my side and rested my head against the arm of the couch, I found my train of thought beginning to steer toward Logan and his date with Riley.

What did he see in her, anyway? Sure, she was gorgeous. And she had an amazing figure. And was very flirtatious and—

Never mind. I answered my own question.

I frowned as the movie faded to a commercial. Girls like Riley had it so good. They never had to work to make a guy interested in them. They didn't need to change their appearance or their personalities. They just showed up and had their pick of whatever guy they wanted. They never had to take compatibility quizzes to find a soulmate. They were compatible with everyone.

And I, apparently, was compatible with no one.

I just hoped Logan realized he was nothing but a rebound for her. But of course, he knew, and he didn't care. He wasn't looking for a girlfriend. He wasn't looking for a serious relationship. That was the reason he and Grace broke up, after all. But maybe Riley would be the girl who made him feel differently about the whole girlfriend thing. Maybe she would be the one who could finally crack the code to his heart, and she'd go home at the end of the summer and they'd embark on a long-distance relationship, much like my parents did when they were teens, and someday they'd get married and have kids and…

…And why was I even giving this any thought? I sat up, hugged my knees to my chest and told myself to get a grip.

Once the movie was back on, I focused on that for a few minutes until I heard another sound coming from outside. This one sounded like a car door slamming. I glanced at the clock on the wall. It could have been Mark and Rachel arriving home, but I'd only heard one door shut.

The irrational part of my brain kicked in and alerted me that this could be an intruder. On the off chance it was, I quickly scanned the room looking for anything I could use as a weapon. It was my only option since I couldn't even call the cops if I had to.

I bolted into the kitchen and was grabbing the first object I could find when I heard the front door fly open and crash against the wall.

"Emma?" a frantic voice called out.

I recognized the voice immediately and breathed a sigh of relief.

"Logan?" I said, stepping out of the kitchen.

I saw him before he saw me. He was standing in the foyer, peering into the living room with wild eyes. When he heard my voice, he turned to look at me. His tight expression softened as he raked a hand through his hair, stalked over toward me…and threw his arms around me, pulling me close into a tight embrace.

For a moment, I stood there stunned. Five seconds ago, I thought somebody was going to break into the house, and now I was being bear-hugged by Logan. Not exactly the outcome I'd been expecting.

Without thinking, I wrapped my arms around him and returned the gesture.

"Logan," I said in a strained voice. He was holding me so

tight I could barely breathe. "Are you okay? What's wrong?"

He let go of me so quickly I nearly stumbled from the sudden lack of support. "What's wrong? *What's wrong?* You tell me!"

I stared at him in confusion. He sounded angry, like he was mad at me. "I don't—"

"You called me up and basically told me you thought someone was in the house," he said, waving his phone around above his head. "And then you screamed—"

"It was more of a shriek," I corrected him.

He didn't even bat an eye before continuing like I hadn't spoken. "And then nothing. Complete silence. I asked if you were okay, and you said nothing. I tried calling you back like three hundred times, but you didn't pick up. I thought you were..." He let out a heavy sigh as his shoulders slumped forward. "I thought you were in danger."

Oh...so apparently, my phone had cut out before he'd had a chance to hear me tell him about the cats. "I-I'm sorry," I stammered. "I thought you might have heard me tell you it was nothing before my phone died."

"Yeah, well, I didn't." He dragged a hand down his face and leaned against the wall behind him.

"And I couldn't find a charging cable, so I didn't even know you were trying to call," I added weakly. "I thought of going next door to get mine, but then I'd have to wake up Abby and—"

"It's fine," he said softly. "I'm just glad you guys are okay." His gaze flickered down to my hand. "Were you planning on baking something?"

"Huh?" I blinked and lifted my hand to reveal the object I'd randomly grabbed in the kitchen to use as a weapon.

A spatula.

"Oh," I said with a giggle. "Um, no. I thought maybe you were going to be an intruder, so I just blindly grabbed something I could use to beat someone with if necessary."

"That wouldn't have worked very well," he said with a small smile.

I returned his smile. "Yeah, probably not." I paused for a moment before saying, "So, after you point me in the direction of a charging cable for my phone, you can feel free to return to your date."

He pushed off the wall with a shrug. "Nah, it's okay. Matt's giving Riley a ride home later. And it wasn't an official date, really. I might as well just stay here."

"Oh, okay," I said, assuring myself that the giddy feeling that suddenly came over me had to do with the fact I was going to have a big, strong male around for the rest of the night to keep me safe.

Not because of the fact he wasn't going back to his date, which supposedly wasn't even a date at all.

"I'm going to go return this to the kitchen," I said, holding up the spatula.

"Please do, before somebody gets hurt," he teased.

I rolled my eyes as he disappeared into the living room. After returning the cooking utensil, I joined him on the couch.

"What are you watching?" he inquired, glancing at the TV. He must have recognized the movie right away because he turned to me with a judgmental look. "Seriously, Emma? This is not the type of stuff you should be watching while all alone and hearing strange noises. Especially considering how paranoid you are."

"I'm not paranoid," I grumbled, even though he was right. "Besides, I wasn't paying too much attention to it, anyway." *Because I was too busy wondering what you and Riley were doing on your date.*

I pushed that thought away and cleared my throat. "You can change the channel if you'd like."

Logan smirked. "No, I want to see how jumpy you are."

"I'm not jumpy," I lied.

"Riiiiight," he said, drawing out the word slowly to emphasize how much he didn't believe me.

I ignored him and focused on the movie instead. But thirty seconds later, a strong hand suddenly clamped down on my shoulder. Startled, I let out a yelp as the jackass sitting next to me burst out laughing.

"Not jumpy, huh?"

I turned to smack his chest, but his hand shot out and grabbed my wrist before I had a chance to make contact.

"That was too easy," he said with a grin.

"You're such a jerk," I mumbled as I tried to no avail to remove myself from his grasp.

"It's not my fault you're so easily frightened."

"Me? What about you? You're the one who abandoned his hot date to rush home because you thought I was in danger."

His grin faltered slightly. "I was worried."

I stopped struggling against him. "You didn't have to worry. No matter what, I would have made sure Abby was safe."

He sat up and leaned forward, closer to me. "I wasn't just worried about Abby."

"Right," I said, nodding slowly. "You were also worried about the TV and the Playstation. Don't worry, I would have protected them, too." I flashed him my own grin.

But he didn't seem amused by that. "Emma," he said, his eyes darkening as they locked onto mine. "I'm serious. You scared the hell out of me."

I stared down at my lap. "It wasn't intentional. I'm sorry."

"You don't need to be sorry," he said softly, letting go of my wrist and moving his hand to the side of my face, where his thumb lightly grazed my cheekbone, sending another set of chills cascading all over my body—only for a very different reason this time.

My breath hitched in my throat as I lifted my head to look at him.

Logan's gaze lowered to my mouth and my heart began to race inside my chest. "Emma," he said, his voice barely above a whisper as he leaned closer.

"Logan," I whispered back as I began to lean as well. Some sort of invisible force was pulling me toward him and I didn't fight it. I didn't even try.

I had no idea what was happening, but whatever it was, it ended as soon as it began, as the sound of the front door opening snapped us out of it and we quickly broke apart.

Mark and Rachel had arrived home.

Logan moved to the other side of the couch with impressive speed before they made it to the living room, making it look like we hadn't just been about to...

To what? Kiss? No, that's not what was going on. Was it? No, Logan would never kiss me. And I sure as heck would never kiss him. I was crushing on Matt, and Logan had girls like Riley throwing themselves at him everywhere he went. I'd be the last girl he'd ever want to kiss. And he'd be the last guy I'd ever want to kiss. We had mutual feelings of not wanting to kiss each other. It's what made our non-relationship so special.

"Logan," Mark said as he and Rachel entered the room. "I was surprised to see your car in the driveway. What are you doing home so early?"

"Uh..." For once, Logan seemed to be at a loss for words. The guy was usually the master of coming up with lies and excuses on the spot. "Um, I…"

Mark tilted his head and glanced at his son curiously. "Date didn't go so well, I take it?"

Logan shook his head. "The party was kind of lame, so I figured I would just come home and help Emma out with Abby."

"Well, that was nice of you." Rachel smiled and then glanced over at me. "Emma, sweetie, are you feeling okay? You look a little flushed."

Her inquiry made my face feel even hotter than it did before she'd asked. "Yeah, I'm fine," I replied, getting up from the couch.

Luckily, she didn't press me any further on the subject. "So, how was the little one for you? Not too much trouble, I hope."

"Not at all," I assured her. "She cried for a bit after you left, but she's been sleeping peacefully ever since."

"Oh, good. I'm going to go check on her. Thank you again, Emma." Rachel turned and left the room as Mark dug his wallet out of his pocket, presumably to pay me.

"Okay, let's see what we've got here," he said, opening it and instantly frowning. "Hmm. Looks like I've left some of my cash in my office. I'll go grab it."

"No," I said quickly. Mark leaving to go get money meant Logan and I would be left alone. "It's okay, you don't need to pay me."

Mark chuckled. "Emma, don't be ridiculous."

"No, really. I barely had to do anything. Keep your money. I have to…go."

Mark furrowed his brow as he put away his wallet. "Emma, are you sure you're okay?"

"Yeah, I'm sure. I just…" My gaze flickered over to Logan, who was watching me intently with a look on his face I'd never seen before. One I couldn't quite place.

Tearing my eyes away from his, I awkwardly mumbled, "Have a good night," before grabbing my laptop off the coffee table and practically running out of the house.

I wasn't sure if Logan and I had been about to kiss, but one thing I did know—but didn't want to admit to myself—was that in some small way…I wished we had.

Chapter 24

LOGAN

"Logan." Matt waved his hand in front of my face. "Are you even listening to me?"

No, I wasn't listening to him. I could see him. I could hear the words coming out of his mouth, but I wasn't listening. He could have been speaking Greek for all I knew, and it wouldn't have sounded any different to me. No, I wasn't listening to him.

Because I couldn't stop thinking about Emma.

When I'd gotten that phone call from her the other night, saying she was hearing things, I'd immediately brushed it off as just being her overactive imagination. Her paranoia. But, when I'd heard her shriek and the line went dead, something inside me snapped. Even though I knew there would be a logical explanation for what was going on, it didn't stop me from going into panic mode. I had to leave that party and make sure she was safe.

So, that's what I did. I informed Riley I had to leave. She offered to come with me, but I declined. I asked Matt to take her home and I bolted.

And then broke the law by driving about fifteen to twenty miles over the speed limit the whole way home.

For the entire ride, I tried convincing myself that the fear settling in the pit of my stomach had everything to do with the safety of my baby sister and nothing more. Not that I wanted anything bad to happen to Emma, but there was no way the blinding dread that had taken over me could have had anything to do with her. It had to just be Abby.

But when I burst into the house and heard Emma's voice…saw her…I couldn't breathe for a moment. Of course, everything was okay. In the back of my mind, I'd known it would be. But seeing for myself that she was safe and sound, it was too much for me to handle.

And without thinking, I'd walked over to her, wrapped my arms around her, and pulled her close. I held her so tight I was probably cutting off most of her oxygen, but it didn't matter. I didn't hold her for long. Because as relieved as I was that she was okay, I was also furious with her for scaring me. For making me think something had happened to her.

So, I scolded her and made fun of the fact she was prepared to protect herself with a spatula.

A *spatula*.

That was so typically Emma.

Then, on the couch, I'm not sure what had come over me. My mind was still cloudy from all the wild thoughts and scenarios that had been playing in my head the entire way home. I wasn't thinking straight. I wasn't thinking at all.

And I'd almost kissed her.

I'd almost kissed Emma.

Emma.

I'd never been so relieved in my life to see my dad and Rachel. I wanted to leap off the couch and give each of *them* a kiss when they walked into the living room, interrupting what would have probably been the biggest mistake of my life.

I couldn't kiss Emma. I didn't *want* to kiss Emma.

I didn't.

So why, after two days, couldn't I get her off my mind?

"Sorry," I muttered to Matt. I leaned forward and hid my face in my hands for a moment while I regained my composure and pushed all thoughts of Emma out of my brain. "What were you saying?"

It was the 4th of July and Matt and I were attending Justin's annual Independence Day pool party/cookout—an all-day event that ended right after sunset, when everyone would get in their cars and drive into town to watch the fireworks.

If the events of the other night hadn't taken place, I would have called Emma and forced her to go with me, but I was currently trying to avoid her. Much like Riley was trying to avoid me, apparently. She hadn't spoken a word to me since I'd arrived.

"I was saying that—"

As soon as Matt started talking again, my attention was immediately drawn to something—or some*one*—on the other side of the pool from us.

"What's that all about?" I interrupted him, motioning over to Grace. She was talking to a girl while holding up a video camera pointed at her face.

Matt followed my line of vision and smirked. "Oh, you don't know? Grace is trying to become an Internet star."

I blinked at him. "A what-now?"

Matt chuckled. "She's documenting her summer vacation and uploading the videos on some website that's looking to turn someone into the next big Internet reality sensation."

I groaned and facepalmed. Apparently, I'd gotten out of that relationship just in time.

"Are you kidding me?"

"Nah, man," Matt said with a grin. "I thought everyone knew."

"Well, I didn't," I said. And then I made the mistake of

glancing back over in her direction.

Her icy gaze met with mine and she immediately stopped talking to the girl in front of her and started making her way in my direction.

"Oh no," I moaned. "She's coming over here." I contemplated getting up and leaving the deck. Or, better yet, leaving the party altogether. But she was too fast, and in the blink of an eye, she appeared before me, looming over me, encasing me in her shadow.

"And here is Logan Reynolds, my ex-boyfriend," she explained bitterly to the camera. Her eyes flickered to me. "So, how have you been since you ripped my heart out of my chest and then stomped on it?"

I glowered at her and slouched back in my chair. "Grace, *you* broke up with *me*, remember?"

"I do remember. I broke up with you because you were cheating on me."

"I wasn't cheating on you," I said through clenched teeth, and then stared directly into the camera and said, "I wasn't cheating on her. She *thought* I had feelings for someone else, which I *didn't. She* ripped *my* heart out and stomped on it."

Grace forced a laugh and lowered the camera. "Nice try, Logan, but nobody's going to buy that. You couldn't have cared less that I dumped your sorry ass. If you had, you would have called. You would have tried to work things out with me. Instead, you moved on with your life like we'd never been together in the first place. Did you ever even love me?"

She pointed the camera at me again and I reached up and placed my hand over the lens. "Grace, if you want to talk about this, then you need to put the camera away. Otherwise, I have nothing more to say to you."

With a huff, she removed my hand from her camera.

"There's nothing to talk about. I just wanted all my followers to see the face of the jerk who tried to ruin my summer. But FYI, I'm doing just fine without you."

"Great, so glad to hear that," I said sarcastically as she began to walk away. When she was gone, I turned to Matt and asked, "How was I with her for so long?"

Matt shrugged. "I don't know, man, I always wondered that."

I shook my head. "Okay, sorry about that. You've been trying to talk to me about something. What's up?"

"Oh, it's nothing, really," Matt said, playing with the tab on the top of his Coke can. "I was just saying that I think I'm going to ask out Emma."

I'd been in the middle of taking a drink of my own Coke when he finished his sentence, and I almost spit it out. "Wait, what? Emma who?"

He glanced at me sideways. "The only Emma we know, you moron. Your Emma."

My Emma.

My Emma.

I stared at him, my mouth agape. "But why?"

He looked confused, like he wasn't sure why he had to explain himself. "She's cute. Actually, she's kind of *hot*. I enjoyed playing mini golf with her the other night and it was pretty obvious she's into me. I don't know, I think she might be fun to hang out with. If nothing else, she might be a decent hookup."

I felt a knot beginning to form in the pit of my stomach. My plan to get Matt and Emma together was working and I'd barely had to do anything other than having them hang out one time. It couldn't have possibly been that easy, could it?

I should have been elated at this news. I should have been pulling him into a hug and giving him a bro kiss on the top of his head. I should have been thanking him for saving me from a family trip to New York. I was free. Once he asked out Emma and they went on a date, I was free. Free from the trip. Free from spending all my time with Emma.

Free.

But I wasn't elated. That knot in my stomach was making me feel queasy. Swallowing hard, I spoke before I could stop myself.

"I'm not so sure that's a good idea."

"Why not?" Matt asked, looking confused.

"Because," I said, and I realized I suddenly had no control over what I was saying, "she's not exactly your type."

"Dude, my type is *female,* and she fits that description quite nicely." He flashed me a grin.

I gripped the can of Coke in my hand so hard I almost crushed it. "Come on, let's be real here. Dating her would be committing social suicide. Guys like you don't date girls like Emma."

Stop. Talking.

Matt shifted uncomfortably in his chair. "What do you mean, girls like Emma?"

"She's a nerd. She's boring and lame. She passed up a trip to Florida with her best friends so that she could stay behind and organize her *book collection.* Who does that?"

"Um, I don't—"

"She's never even had a boyfriend. That alone should be a red flag."

I'm serious. Shut. Up.

"She's a loser, Matt." The words felt wrong on my tongue. They tasted bitter. But by this point, it was like somebody else had taken over my body and was speaking for me, and I was powerless to stop it.

Matt looked skeptical. "If she's such a loser, why have you been spending all your time with her lately?"

I was really hoping he wouldn't ask that.

"Because Rachel's been forcing me to," I replied, the knot in my stomach beginning to harden and grow. "I did something kind of shitty, and Rachel told me if I didn't make it up to Emma, she'd convince my dad to make me go with them on their trip to New York in a couple weeks. So, that's why I've been hanging out with her. It's not because I've *wanted* to."

Matt studied me for a moment before nodding slowly. He opened his mouth to speak, but Justin interrupted by calling out his name from over at the grill.

"I'll be right back," he said to me before getting out of his chair.

I blinked as my head started to clear up. What was I doing? Matt just told me he wanted to ask out Emma—which was the goal I'd been trying to reach for the last couple of weeks—and now I was trying to talk him out of it? What the hell was wrong with me?

"Wait, Matt," I said before he had the chance to walk away.

"Yeah?"

"I'm just messing with you, man. I think you *should* ask Emma out. I actually think you two would be good together."

Funny. Those words felt wrong, too.

He looked like he didn't know what to think as he turned and headed over to Justin.

As soon as he was gone, I leaned forward and buried my face in my hands. I felt terrible. Horrible. I was such a jerk. I was ruining Emma's chances with Matt. On purpose. All the girl wanted was to find love, and here I was, taking that possibility away from her. Again.

And I had no idea why.

I had to fix this.

Or, at the very least, I had to make myself feel better.

Taking out my phone, I got up and walked around the side of the house where it was more private, and I dialed Emma's number.

She picked up on the second ring. "Hey, Logan."

For a split second, I was worried this conversation was going to be awkward, considering we hadn't spoken since…well, since I'd almost kissed her. But as soon as I heard her voice, my concerns flew out the window. Her voice sounded normal. Pleasant. Friendly.

I smiled. "Hey."

After a pause, she said, "What's up?"

I ran a hand through my hair. "Not much. I was just wondering what you were up to today."

"Oh," she said. "Nothing, really. My parents just left with your dad and Rachel to go to their friend's cookout. I'm just chilling here with all my book friends."

"All alone?"

"No, not all alone. What part of 'book friends' did you not understand?"

I couldn't help but chuckle. The girl had book friends. She was taking the definition of *nerd* to new heights.

"Emma, it's the 4th of July. You should be out having fun with your *real* friends."

"Yeah, well, my *real* friends are in Florida, so…"

"*I'm* not in Florida," I pointed out.

She was silent for a moment before saying, "You consider yourself my friend?"

I shrugged even though she couldn't see it. "Sure, I do. I mean, we hang out all the time. We talk. I don't hate you as much as I used to. So, yeah. I think I consider myself your friend." I paused and then added, "Whether you like it or not."

She giggled, and it was like music to my ears. "I never thought I'd live to see the day you and I would label each other as friends."

"Yet here we are." I grinned as I nudged a random rock with my foot. "So, I was wondering if you were going to the fireworks later?"

"I wasn't planning on it," she said with a sigh. "I usually go with Chloe and Sophia, and since they're not here, I figured I would sit this one out. I'm pretty sure going to watch fireworks by yourself makes you a loser."

I cringed at her choice of words. *Loser.* I'd just told Matt she was a loser. Shaking my head, I said, "You won't be by yourself. You can watch them with me."

"I don't know. I'm not really in the mood to hang out with your friends—"

"I meant we could watch them alone. Just the two of us." Actually, I hadn't known that's what I'd meant until I'd said it.

"Oh." She sounded relieved. "Well, in that case, sure. Yeah. I'd like that."

I ignored the sudden quickening of my pulse. "Great. Pick you up a little after eight?"

"Sounds good," she said. "I'll go break the news to all my book friends."

I rolled my eyes. "Dork," was all I said before hanging up.

So, I was going to go watch fireworks with Emma. Alone.

Perfect. It would give me plenty of time to tell her about how my plan had worked. How Matt was going to be asking her out. She'd be so happy. I couldn't wait to see the smile on her face.

The knot in my stomach twisted as I made my way back toward the party, but I paid no attention to it. It was nothing.

Probably something I ate. Maybe a stomach bug.

It was the only explanation.

Chapter 25

LOGAN

I knocked on Emma's front door at about eight-thirty. As I stood there waiting for her to open it, I found myself growing increasingly nervous. I couldn't decide whether to tell her that Matt was planning on asking her out—*if* he was still planning on asking her out. We never spoke of it again after we met back up. He didn't mention it, and I didn't dare to start the conversation again.

I was worried I'd really screwed things up, although Matt did have a mind of his own. If he wanted to date Emma, he would date her, regardless of how anyone else felt about it. I'm sure he dismissed everything I'd said and would be calling her or showing up at her door any moment now to ask her out.

My nerves instantly dissipated when she opened the door and greeted me with a warm smile.

"Hey," she said.

"Hey," I returned the greeting.

While everything was fine between us over the phone, now that we were standing face-to-face, things felt a little awkward.

"Ready to head out?" I asked her.

"Yeah," she said, stepping out onto the porch and shutting the door behind her. She stared ahead at the driveway in confusion. "Where's the Mustang?"

"Over there," I said, pointing to my own driveway. "We're taking the pickup truck tonight."

"Oh, fancy," she said with a smirk.

The truck was my dad's. It was about ten years old and had seen better days, but he was obsessed with it. So obsessed, I was surprised he let me take it out for the night. I just figured a truck would be nice for the fireworks because we could sit in the back and watch them, instead of standing in a crowd full of obnoxious people.

"I'm glad you agreed to this," I said as we climbed in. "I couldn't stand the thought of you sitting at home all alone."

She glanced at me curiously as she buckled up. "Why is that?"

I shrugged, putting on my own seatbelt. "You should be out enjoying stuff like this. You know Chloe and Sophia aren't going to skip fireworks in Florida just because you're not there with them. So why should you?"

"Good point," she said as I pulled out of the driveway.

We fell into an uncomfortable silence as I began to drive, so I turned on the radio. I didn't know what to talk about, and it appeared she didn't either, since she wasn't attempting to spark up any conversations herself.

It was about a ten-minute drive into town and I could tell before I even made it anywhere near the waterfront, where they were going to be setting off the fireworks, that this was a bad idea. There were large crowds of people everywhere and traffic was backed up nearly a half a mile.

"This should be fun," Emma muttered, staring out her window.

I couldn't help but agree with her sarcasm. I wasn't usually turned off by large crowds—I could take them or leave them—but I wasn't in the mood tonight to fight my way through hundreds of people, or to even try to find a parking space.

Glancing in the rearview mirror, I saw that nobody had pulled up behind me yet, so I put the truck in reverse, backed up a few yards to the nearest side street and turned down it.

"What are you doing?" Emma asked.

"I'm taking us somewhere a little more private." I turned my head to glance at her. "Unless you'd rather deal with that cluster of madness back there, in which case, I can turn back around."

"No, no," she said. "Private sounds nice. I like private."

She smiled, and I had to quickly avert my gaze back to the road. My grip tightened on the steering wheel as I struggled to push certain thoughts out of my head. Thoughts of being alone with Emma, in private. This was a bad idea. I should have just stayed in the line of traffic, circled around for a while looking for a parking space, and then walked down to the waterfront and enjoyed the fireworks with everyone else. Safety in numbers.

I could have still changed my mind and turned around, but I didn't.

Instead, I kept driving. Driving to somewhere more private.

"Where are we going?" she asked.

"You'll see." I turned down another street that moved us farther away from our destination. There was a hill nearby with a scenic turnout at the top with an impressive view of the town, and I figured it would be the perfect place to watch the fireworks from a distance. Chances were good nobody else would be up there; most people enjoyed being part of the crowd for things like this. Usually, I was one of those people.

But not tonight.

It only took a couple minutes to get there from where we were, and she seemed to figure out my plan right away as soon as I turned up the hill.

"You're taking me to Lover's Lookout?"

"Lover's Lookout" was what most of the kids at our school referred to this area as. For some reason, it was a popular spot for them to park their cars and make out with each other, even though it wasn't too far from the road. However, the road was not well-traveled, and there were no street lights nearby, so it was fairly private.

"As a matter of fact, I am," I said with a slight smirk. "It will be the perfect spot to watch the fireworks, far away from people. I can't guarantee we'll be the only ones there, but it'll be more tolerable, anyway."

"Sounds good to me." She paused for a moment. "I've never been to Lover's Lookout before. I certainly never thought I'd ever end up there with *you*."

"Well, lucky lady, you play your cards right and perhaps there will be fireworks *inside* the vehicle tonight, as well as outside. If you catch my drift." I gave her a dramatic wink, to which she responded with a giggle.

"Oh, Logan," she said in a breathy voice, fanning herself. "You're so *bad*."

I grinned as we made it to the top of the hill and I pulled into the turnout. So far so good—not another human being in sight.

"Looks like we have the place all to ourselves. For now, at least." I pulled right up to the guardrail and cut the engine. "They should be setting the fireworks off right over there, so we'll have a perfect view of them."

"This is nice," Emma said with a smile. "Usually Chloe and Sophia drag me right into the middle of the biggest crowd they can find and there's always somebody there who ruins the experience for us. Like last year, it was a group of older guys who continually kept brushing up against us, trying to cop a feel.

One of them managed to grab my butt and then tried to brush it off as an accident."

My jaw clenched at the thought of some disgusting pig laying his grubby hands on Emma. Whoever he was, he was damn lucky I hadn't been there to witness it.

"Well, you don't have to worry about me groping you," I said. "Unless you *want* me to." I wiggled my eyebrows.

I had no idea what had gotten into me tonight. I was *flirting* with her.

"We'll see how the night goes," she said suggestively.

And she was flirting right back.

Time to change the subject.

I cleared my throat. "Hey, your birthday is next week, isn't it?"

She blinked at me in surprise. "It is. I can't believe you remembered."

"How could I forget? Harassing you on your birthday every year was always one of my favorite pastimes."

That wasn't a lie. Growing up, I was forced to attend all of Emma's birthday parties up until I was eleven. The last one I attended—her eleventh—was when she tried to push me down the stairs. If I remembered correctly, that was the year I'd saved up as many spiders as I could find outside, placing them inside a jar with holes in the lid. I placed the jar inside a box right before going over to her house and wrapped it up in some pretty pink wrapping paper I'd found lying around inside a closet. When I presented her with the box, she actually seemed touched that I would get her a gift. I remembered feeling guilty at the last second and almost grabbed it back, but I wasn't quick enough.

She'd opened the box, saw what was in the jar, screamed, threw it to the ground where it shattered, and all the little critters came scurrying out, invading her bedroom. She freaked out, started hyperventilating, and then chased me out of the room and down the hallway, where she then attempted to kill me on the staircase before her mother intervened.

Rumor had it that she wasn't able to sleep in her bedroom for about a week after the incident. Not until her father had managed to find and kill every last spider.

Yeah, not one of my finer moments. Actually, none of my moments with Emma growing up could be considered fine. I was always a jerk to her. Always taunting her. Teasing her. Pranking her. I'd always enjoyed making her mad at me. I liked the way her nostrils would flare, the way her eyes got so wide they almost fell out of their sockets, the impressively high pitch her voice would reach as she screamed at me, all the different shades of red her face would turn…

Emma chuckled softly. "You did successfully ruin most of my childhood birthdays."

"I'm sorry," I said, and I meant it. Emma had never done anything to deserve the treatment I'd given her growing up. "I'll make it up to you this year. I promise."

A light bulb suddenly illuminated above my head. I *would* make it up to her this year. Matt was going to ask her out. I would tell him to ask her out for her birthday. I would plan the perfect, most romantic date for the two of them. It would be like something out of one of her romance novels. A night she would never forget.

With the love of her life.

My best friend.

I would be redeemed.

Awesome.

"Oh really?" she said, clearly intrigued. "What do you have planned?"

"You'll just have to wait and be surprised," I replied with a grin. A grin that felt too big for my face.

We fell into a silence then, and I racked my brain trying to come up with something to talk about. But I couldn't. All I kept thinking about was the bombshell Matt had dropped on me earlier. How he wanted to ask Emma on a date. I still hadn't decided if I should tell her about it. The angel on my right shoulder told me I should. The devil on my left shoulder told me to keep quiet and hope that what I'd said to Matt earlier was enough to keep him from asking her out.

But that's not what I wanted. I *wanted* Matt to ask her out. That was the whole point of all of this. Why *wouldn't* I want them to get together? It was what she wanted. It was apparently what *he* wanted now as well. The only other way this could have worked out this perfectly was if I had just paid him to ask her out and skipped all the stuff in between. Like getting to know Emma a little better and realizing she wasn't so bad after all...

"Can I ask you something?" I said. I figured if I spoke, I wouldn't think. Thinking wasn't something I wanted to do at the moment.

"Yeah, sure," she said, glancing at me curiously.

I stared ahead at the view in front of us. The sun was setting fast, casting a blanket of dusk over us. "If Matt were to ask you out, say tomorrow, do you think you'd be ready?"

"Ready?" she echoed. "What do you mean?"

"I mean, do you think you'd be ready to date him? Do you think you'd feel comfortable around him, talking to him, do-ing...other things with him?"

She considered it for a moment. "I think so. I'm not as shy and flustered around him as I used to be. I didn't have too much trouble talking to him the other night during mini golf. I think I've made some progress. Thanks to you."

"I've barely done anything," I mumbled, tracing the steering wheel with my finger.

"That's not true," she said, shaking her head. "You've definitely helped get me out of my shell. Because of you, I'm willing to try new things. Do new things. I think I'd be fine around him." She glanced down at her hands resting in her lap. "Although, I'll be perfectly honest with you: I'm still terrified at the thought of kissing him."

I swiveled my head in her direction. "Why is that?"

She glanced over at me with an expression that indicated she felt I should already know the answer.

"I've never kissed anyone, remember?" She looked away again. "What if I'm…you know…bad at it?"

I couldn't help but smile. "You won't be bad at it."

"How do you know that?"

"I don't. I'm just assuming. But even if you were terrible at it, Matt wouldn't hold it against you. He's not that kind of guy."

"It doesn't matter, I'm still going to embarrass myself." She sighed heavily and rested her head against the window next to her. "You even said it yourself, remember?"

I did remember. I'd teased her about this on a couple of occasions over the last two weeks. I'd put the idea into her head that she might be bad at kissing. I told her she'd want to get her first one out of the way. I'd even joked that I could help her practice.

I'd been a jerk and had given her a complex about the whole thing, and now she was convinced her first kiss was going to be a disaster. And there was nothing I could do to assure her that everything would be fine. That *she'd* be fine. That is, other than…

I swallowed hard. No. No way. I wasn't going to offer her my services. That would be weird. And…bad. Very bad, in every way.

Not that she would take me up on it, anyway. I was pretty sure I was the last guy in the world she wanted to kiss.

But it probably *would* help her to practice with somebody. No amount of reading how-to magazine articles or practicing on her hand or a pillow was going to prepare her for the real thing. I'd just be helping her out, nothing more. I'd be doing a good deed. A *selfless* deed.

"I'll kiss you," I blurted out before I had a chance to finish thinking the whole thing through.

She whipped her head in my direction and stared at me with wide eyes. "What?"

I silently berated myself for saying it. Why couldn't I just keep my mouth shut? It's like I had no control over what I said anymore. Words just fell out of my mouth with reckless abandon these days.

"I'll kiss you," I foolishly repeated. I had the perfect opportunity to backtrack, to pretend I hadn't said what she thought I'd said, but I didn't.

Why didn't I?

She narrowed her eyes at me. "Ha-ha, Logan, very funny."

"No, I'm serious." I unbuckled my seatbelt and turned toward her. "I could kiss you and tell you if you're bad at it. And if you are, I can help you."

She studied my face for a moment with an unreadable expression. "That wouldn't…I mean, that's not…w-we can't…what if—"

I'd broken her.

"Emma," I said softly, placing my hand along the side of her face and looking her straight in the eye. "It's no big deal.

271

It'll just be a kiss. An *educational* one. A learning experience. Nothing more."

"But," she said, lowering her gaze from mine, "I want my first kiss to be special."

And it wouldn't be special with me.

"I know, and your first *real* kiss—with Matt—*will* be special. This will just be a practice kiss. You don't have to count this one."

What was I doing? Why was I trying so hard to convince her to kiss me? Why did I care whether she embarrassed herself with Matt or not? None of this made any sense to me.

But she was considering it. I could tell by the way she nibbled nervously on her bottom lip, the way she was suddenly looking at everything around us but me. When she finally returned her eyes to mine, she said, "Just a simple, quick kiss?"

I didn't know how much she could learn from that, but I shrugged and said, "Sure. Whatever you want."

She slowly began to nod. "Okay, then. Let's do it."

My eyebrows shot up in surprise. "For real?"

"Yeah, for real." She unbuckled her seatbelt and moved closer to me. "Just promise me you'll be honest, okay? If I'm bad, I want to know."

My pulse quickened as I moved my hand from her face to the back of her neck. "Are you sure? I don't want to—"

"Logan," she interrupted, "just kiss me." Her voice was urgent, like she wanted to get this over with before she had a change of heart. Before she realized how stupid this was.

We couldn't kiss each other. That would be weird. Even if it was just for educational purposes. People shouldn't kiss other people they didn't have feelings for, unless they were actors and getting paid millions of dollars to do so. So why was I slowly leaning toward her? Why was she leaning toward me?

I had a sudden flashback to the other night. This wasn't the first time we were being drawn to one another, but the only difference now was that there'd be no interruption. No Dad or Rachel to unknowingly stop us from making a terrible mistake. Only we could stop ourselves now.

But we didn't.

At the very last second, when she closed her eyes and I closed mine, I almost pulled away. I almost put a stop to it. But she needed my help. I couldn't let her down. Not now.

So, I didn't stop it. Instead, I let my lips brush lightly against hers. At first, she stayed perfectly still, and I was afraid she might have changed her mind a little too late. But then she relaxed. We both did, and I took the opportunity to press my mouth firmly against hers in a simple, quick kiss.

But something was wrong. That simple, quick kiss felt strange. Foreign. I couldn't explain it, but it instantly sent me into panic mode.

I yanked myself away from her and returned to my side of the vehicle, letting my head fall against the headrest as I struggled to calm myself down.

I could feel her eyes on me, but I didn't dare to look at her. I was afraid if I did, I might…

No. I wouldn't kiss her again. Once was enough. *More* than enough. That wouldn't happen again.

"So…" Emma's shaky voice trailed off. She wanted to ask me how it was, I could tell. But she was either too shy to, or she just didn't want to hear my answer.

I didn't make her ask the question. "You were fine," I said, my voice strained. "It was fine."

"Oh." I could hear the disappointment in her voice, and from the corner of my eye, I could see her deflate beside me. "Fine" was probably not the term girls liked to hear describe their kissing ability, but I didn't know what else to say. The kiss was simple. It was quick.

It was fine.

"I want to try again," she said in a small but confident voice.

I turned to look at her. "What? No, you don't need to try again. Like I said, you were fine."

"That was barely a kiss," she said, sitting up straight. "Matt's not going to kiss me like that. That's how you would kiss a relative or a friend. I need to know how to *really* kiss."

A feeling of dread pooled in my stomach. "Emma—"

"You said if I was bad at it, you'd help me. So, help me!"

"You weren't bad at it. I said you were—"

"*Fine*', yeah, I know. I heard you." She took a deep breath and closed her eyes briefly. When she reopened them, they were wide and pleading.

"Logan." She reached over and placed a hand on the center of my chest. "Please."

I inhaled sharply at her touch…at the fact she was practically begging me to kiss her. Emma Dawson, the girl who'd always claimed she hated me more than anything else in the world, wanted me to kiss her. Again.

And I wanted to.

So. Bad.

But just to help her. To teach her. To guide her. To show her there was nothing to worry about.

"Okay, but—" I started to say, but I was interrupted by Emma leaning forward, grabbing my face with her hands, pulling me toward her and pressing her lips against mine.

It was a bold and unexpected move. I didn't know she had it in her. I was shocked—so shocked that I immediately froze, not knowing what was happening, or what I should do.

The kiss was already different this time. No hesitation. No reluctance. Her mouth was on mine, taking possession. Control.

And I came completely undone. It took only a few, brief seconds before my lips melted and molded to hers. It was a perfect fit, like our mouths were specifically designed for one another. For this very moment.

I moved closer to her, silently thanking myself for taking the truck instead of the Mustang; it had a bench seat, so there was no pesky console between us getting in the way. She moved closer too, and I wrapped my arms around her waist and pulled her as close to me as I possibly could.

But it still wasn't close enough.

My mind was afire with all sorts of thoughts. Thoughts like, I was stealing her first kiss. The one she'd waited for and dreamed about her whole life. The one reserved for Matt, my best friend.

My best friend.

Emma was just days—maybe *hours*—away from becoming my best friend's girl, and here I was, kissing her in the front seat of my dad's truck…at Lover's Lookout. What kind of best friend does that? And she didn't even know he was going to ask her out. If she'd known, if I'd told her, she probably wouldn't be kissing me. She would have saved this special moment for *him*. Not me.

I was a terrible person. A terrible friend. Because even those thoughts weren't enough to make me break away from this. Instead, I was grabbing a fistful of her hair, tilting her head and deepening the kiss. Putting everything I had into it. If I was going to steal her first kiss, I was at least going to make it worth it for her.

But the most disturbing thoughts rolling around in my head

had nothing to do with Matt, but with Emma herself. About how soft and warm her lips were, and how they tasted like strawberries. How smooth and silky her hair felt laced through my fingers. How this didn't feel at all like a first kiss for her, because she wasn't bad. She wasn't even just *fine*.

She was...

She was...

My mind went blank. I'd shut off all thoughts. They were too distracting, taking me out of the moment. I didn't want to think. I just wanted to feel.

For a moment, we broke apart. To catch our breath, or maybe to end whatever this had turned into. But as soon as our eyes flew open and met, I was hit with a revelation so earth shattering, it nearly knocked the wind out of me.

I didn't *want* it to end. Whatever this was, I wanted more of it. It had nothing to do with wanting to help her out. We'd gone way beyond that point.

I just wanted *her*.

She must have felt it too because our gaze lasted no more than a second or two before our lips connected again, this time with an urgency so intense I couldn't breathe. My heart pounded inside my ribcage, threatening to rip out of my chest at any moment. She was making me *nervous*. No girl had ever made me nervous before. Not Grace. Not Riley. No one.

Just Emma.

And that's when I knew this was wrong. This was no longer a practice kiss, it was something else. Something I didn't understand—because it didn't feel like it was being controlled by lust or hormones.

It was something I'd never felt before.

So, I ended it. I broke the kiss and shot back in my seat so forcefully my head almost hit the window.

As I struggled to catch my breath, I stared out the windshield in shock. The fireworks had already started, and I hadn't even noticed. Hadn't even heard the explosions until now.

I snuck a glance over at Emma—her eyes wide, lips swollen, hair tousled, chest heaving—and saw she was just as surprised about the fireworks as I was.

I knew I had to say something. One of us had to address what had just happened, and something told me it wasn't going to be her. She'd be waiting for feedback.

"That was, um…" I drummed my fingers against the steering wheel. "Better."

She turned to look at me with devastated eyes. Apparently "better" was no better than "fine", so I was going to have to elaborate.

"Sorry, what I meant to say was that you have nothing to worry about. Trust me. That was…you were…"

She watched me, waiting for me to finish the sentence, but I had no plans to. I couldn't tell her what I'd *truly* thought about the kiss. It would have sent her running and screaming from the truck.

Instead, I said the very next thing that popped into my head.

"He's going to ask you out." My words cut through the silence like a knife and I wished instantly that I could take them back.

She blinked and turned to me. "I'm sorry, what?"

"Matt," I said. I couldn't look at her, so I kept my eyes focused on the fireworks. "He's going to ask you out. He told me this afternoon."

I glanced back just in time to see her jaw drop. "W-what? Are you serious?"

I nodded slowly and lowered my gaze to my lap. "He thinks

you're cool and he wants to go on a date with you." I paused and glanced over at her. "How does that make you feel?"

Her mouth clamped shut for a moment as she stared ahead. "Confused," she said softly, but then shook her head and said, "I mean, I'm just surprised. I didn't think it would happen this fast. Or at all."

I forced a grin onto my face and reached over and nudged her shoulder with my hand. "What did I tell you, Dawson? I know what I'm doing."

But that was a lie. I *didn't* know what I was doing. I could still taste the lingering flavor of strawberry lip gloss on my tongue and it made me want to pull her against me and kiss her again, to pick up right where we'd just left off. To...

I placed my hands on the steering wheel and gripped it so tightly my knuckles turned white.

I needed some air.

Opening my door, I exited the vehicle as quickly as I could, walked around to the front and leaned against the bumper. Emma followed suit and joined me just a few seconds later.

"This is a really nice view," she said quietly.

"It is," I agreed with a nod.

"Logan..." she began to say but then stopped herself.

I glanced sideways at her. "What?"

She ran a hand through her hair and stared down at the ground, where she was kicking at the dirt with her shoe.

"Do you..." She took a deep breath and held it for a moment before letting it out. "Do you think Matt and I would be good together?"

No, I don't. "Yeah, I do."

"Really?" Her eyes searched my face, looking for any indication I might be lying.

But she didn't find any. I made sure of that.

"Matt's a great guy. He'll treat you right." I could feel a muscle in my jaw contract as I clenched my teeth. "You'll be perfect together."

She gave me a smile, but it didn't quite reach her eyes. "Thank you, Logan. For everything." She slid her arm around my back and leaned into me, resting her head on my shoulder.

I breathed in the intoxicating scent of her apple shampoo and my heart sank inside my chest.

Something didn't feel right. I should have been happy. Happy for Emma. Happy for Matt. Happy for myself. But I wasn't.

I was miserable.

And I knew why.

I was falling for Emma.

And I was about to lose her.

Chapter 26

EMMA

Oh my God, oh my God, oh my God.

As I paced the floor of my bedroom, I held my cell phone in one hand, and chewed nervously on the nails of my other one.

Where the heck were Chloe and Sophia? Why weren't they calling me back? I'd left them voicemails, telling them there was an emergency, and that they needed to call me immediately. It wasn't that late, so I was sure they weren't asleep yet—especially since it was the 4th of July. They were probably out celebrating, completely ignorant to the fact their best friend was about to have a total freak-out.

A sudden knock on my door stopped me in my tracks.

"Honey?" my mom's muffled voice said from the other side. "Is everything okay? I keep hearing footsteps downstairs. Are you pacing?"

I walked over to the door and opened it. "Everything's okay," I told her, trying to act nonchalant.

I wanted to tell her. Normally, I told my mom everything because she was one of my best friends. But I couldn't tell her about this. Not yet. Because I didn't even know what *this* was.

And besides, I didn't want to get her hopes up for nothing.

Mom glanced at me suspiciously, eyeing me up and down. "I'm not buying it. 'Fess up, or you're grounded."

I crossed my arms over my chest. "You can't ground me

for not telling you something."

"Uh, yes I can." She turned her head and yelled down the hallway, "Jake, I can ground Emma for not telling me something, right?"

"Absolutely," my dad yelled back from his office.

I rolled my eyes. "Seriously, Mom, there's nothing to tell you. Everything's fine. I'm just waiting for Chloe and Sophia to call me back."

"Oh, so you'll tell *them* something, but not your own mother?"

My phone rang in my hand. "Sorry, Mom, gotta take this," I said, adding, "Love you," before shutting the door in her face.

I didn't bother to look to see who was calling me back. It wouldn't matter because I'd be put on speaker phone anyway. "Oh my God, what took you guys so long to call me back?"

"Sorry," Chloe said on the other end of the line. "We were busy."

"But we called you back as soon as we got your messages," Sophia added.

"So, what's the emergency?" Chloe asked. "Are you hurt? Are you in the hospital? Did somebody die?"

Sophia gasped. "Oh no, who died?"

"Nobody died," I said, "and no, I'm not hurt or in the hospital. But something happened tonight. Something…bad. Or good. I-I don't actually know which."

"Okay…" Chloe paused. "And that something would be…?"

"Logan kissed me," I blurted out.

This time, both girls gasped and then followed it up with a "*WHAT?!*" so loud, it nearly punctured my eardrum.

"Logan kissed me," I repeated. "Or, I kissed him. Actually,

we kissed each other…"

The girls were silent for only a second before they started bombarding me with different questions at the same time. Somehow, I was able to understand a few of them. Such as, "How did that happen?" and "Is he a good kisser?" and "Did you like it?" and "Are you going to kiss him again?"

So many questions I didn't have answers to.

I sank down to the floor and leaned against the side of my bed. As Chloe and Sophia continued firing off question after question at me, my mind wandered off to earlier that evening.

I wasn't sure exactly what had happened, or *how* it had happened. At the time, it all seemed like a great idea: kiss Logan to find out if I sucked at it. In retrospect, it was a terrible idea. Kissing was supposed to be special. Intimate. It wasn't supposed to be educational. Especially a first kiss. I'd been dreaming about my first kiss for nearly four years. I always figured it would be with someone I was in love with. I always thought it would happen in a romantic setting. I always thought it would be organic, like I would look at him and he would look at me and we would just be drawn together by some invisible force until our lips touched and it would be…perfect.

I *didn't* ever think it would happen inside a pickup truck. At a popular make-out spot. With Logan Reynolds.

The first kiss was just whatever. It was the "simple, quick kiss" I'd requested, and it should have ended with that. But no, I couldn't stand the thought that I was just a "fine" kisser. Matt would never stay with a girl who was "fine".

So, I demanded that Logan kiss me again.

Why would I do that?

What was I thinking?

Was I even thinking?

"Emma? Are you still there?"

Chloe's voice broke me out of my fog. "Yeah, sorry. You guys were asking too many questions, I couldn't keep track."

"So? How did this happen?"

I explained everything. How the topic of Matt had come up—and the topic of how I'd never kissed anyone. How Logan had offered his assistance. How I agreed to it. How the first kiss was nothing. How the next two were...

"Is he a good kisser?" Sophia asked.

"I don't know," I said, playing with the hem of my shirt. "I don't have anyone to compare him to. I will say, though, I didn't hate it."

That was an understatement. While it was true I had nobody to compare him to, I didn't have to.

That kiss was amazing. Butterfly-inducing. Mind-numbing. Perfect.

I grazed the tip of my finger against my lips as they morphed into a smile. As a flash of warmth washed over my face. I was blushing.

"Emma, do you *like* Logan?" Chloe asked.

I forced the smile into a frown. What kind of a question was that? Chloe, more than anyone else in this world, knew how I felt about Logan. How I'd always felt about him. She'd always been the one I'd go to right after he did or said something hurtful to me. I'd either be yelling about him to her, or crying on her shoulder over him. She should have already known the answer to the question.

Problem was, *I* didn't even know the answer to that question anymore.

Truth was, over the last couple of weeks, I'd started to see a different side of him. Yeah, he was still infuriating. Insufferable. Arrogant. But at the same time, I couldn't help but notice he'd matured over the years. Just the simple fact he was helping me out with Matt to make up for lying on the compatibility test was proof of that. The old Logan from seven years ago wouldn't have tried to make it up to me. He would have laughed in my face, rubbed it in, and said something lame like, "Too bad, so sad."

But not this Logan.

Still, that didn't mean I liked him. That wasn't reason enough to like him. So what if he was also hot, sort of funny sometimes, and also kind of sweet when he wanted to be?

Guys like that were a dime a dozen. Like Matt, who was also hot, funny, and sweet.

My head fell back against my bed and I stared at the glow-in-the-dark stars I still had stuck to my ceiling from years ago.

"I'm honestly not sure," I finally answered. "But there's more to the story."

"More?" Sophia said and then gasped. "Oh my *God* Emma, did you two—"

I knew exactly where she was going with that question, so I stopped her as quickly as I could. "No, we *didn't*," I assured her. "What I was going to say was that he told me…he told me that Matt's planning on asking me out."

Both girls squealed with excitement.

"No frickin' way!" Chloe yelled into my ear. "Is he sure about that? How does he know?"

"He heard it from Matt himself, apparently."

"Oh my God, Emma," Sophia breathed. "So, you mean to tell us that over the course of one night, you were kissed by one of the hottest guys at our school *and* you were told you're about to be asked out by one of the *other* hottest guys at our school?"

"Yeah," I said with a chuckle. When she said it out loud, it sounded ludicrous.

The girls both sighed.

"Man, we chose the wrong summer to take this trip," Chloe said. "I wish we could be there to help guide you through all this."

"I don't really need guidance," I lied.

"Are you sure about that?" Sophia asked. "I mean, it seems like you're now faced with quite the predicament: Logan or Matt?"

"Obviously, she's going to choose Matt," Chloe said. "She's been in love with him forever. Him asking her out will literally be a dream come true for her."

"Yes, but," Sophia argued, "she and Logan have a history together—"

"Yeah, a history of him torturing her non-stop."

"Because he has *liked* her this whole time—"

"Whoa," I interjected. "Soph, what are you talking about? Logan has *never* liked me, just like I've never liked him."

"I disagree."

"Well, I disagree with your disagreement," I said. "And either way, this shouldn't even be a debate, because Logan doesn't like me *now*."

"But he kissed you," Sophia pointed out.

"It was a *practice* kiss."

"Practice *my butt*. It was *his* idea to 'practice' this kiss, was it not?"

"Yes, but—"

"That boy wanted to kiss you," Sophia said. "He's probably wanted to kiss you this whole time. The way you described it to us, sounds like he enjoyed it just as much as you did—if not *more*."

My heart skipped a beat at the possibility that what she was saying could be true.

"Okay," I said, shaking my head, "that's enough. Soph, Logan doesn't like me and never has. In fact, he was on a date with Riley the other night, remember? Why would he want *me* over *her*? You guys haven't seen her, but she's a total smoke show."

"And so are you, sweetie," Chloe said softly. "You know, I hate to admit it, because I'm mostly Team Matt all the way, but Sophia does make a compelling argument."

I groaned. They were creating teams now?

"Okay, that's enough," I said with a sigh. "Obviously, when Matt asks me out, I'm going to say yes. This is what I've always wanted. Yes, that kiss with Logan tonight was…nice…but it didn't mean anything."

I knew Sophia was pouting without even being able to see it. "For what it's worth," she said, "I'm Team Logan, and I hope that after a good night's sleep, you come to the realization that you are, too."

Nope. No way. Logan and I…that was never going to happen. Ever.

Glancing at my alarm clock, I said, "Speaking of a good night's sleep, I should probably let you guys go."

"Okay," Chloe said. "Well, good luck with whatever you decide."

"There's nothing to decide on," I said weakly, not wanting to get into another long debate. "But thank you. 'Night, girls. Love you both."

"Love you, too!" they said in unison and hung up.

I set my phone down on the floor next to me and buried my face in my hands.

Sophia's words swam back and forth inside my head. There was no way that Logan could like me, right? He'd been a jerk to me practically my whole life, and I'd returned in kind. Besides, I wasn't his type.

But that kiss…

That kiss kept replaying in my head, and every time it did, I got more and more confused. Because I wasn't just recalling the kiss. I was recalling the exact moment Logan told me about Matt's intentions of asking me out.

And how I should have been more excited about it.

But I wasn't.

Picking myself up off the floor, I walked over to the window that faced Logan's house. There was a light on in his bedroom, but the curtains were pulled so I couldn't see in. I sat down on the end of my bed and stared down at my phone. I had the sudden urge to text him.

And say what? *I had a nice time tonight, thanks for the kiss?* Yeah, right. I placed my phone on the nightstand and fell back on the bed. I would do what Chloe and Sophia suggested. I would get a good night's sleep, and in the morning, when my head was clear, everything would make more sense to me.

***

When I woke up the next morning, I was just as confused as I was before I went to bed. My "good night's sleep" turned out to be restless. All I could do was toss and turn and try to force myself to stop thinking about what happened in that stupid truck.

That stupid kiss.

With stupid Logan.

"So, do you and Logan have any big plans today?" Mom asked at breakfast.

I could feel heat rising to my cheeks as I replied, "Nope, not that I know of," and took a big gulp of orange juice, hoping she didn't notice I was blushing.

"You two have been spending an awful lot of time together this summer," Dad said, looking up from the newspaper. "Is there anything you'd like to tell us?" He ended his sentence with a wink.

"What? N-no," I said, shaking my head so hard I was afraid I'd given myself a concussion.

"Jake, stop teasing our daughter," Mom said, giving him a warning glance. She turned to me. "I think it's nice you and Logan are becoming so close. I never understood what that feud was between you two, anyway. Never made any sense to me."

I *so* didn't want to be talking about getting close with Logan right now, so I excused myself from the table. "I'm going for a jog."

Both of my parents stared up at me, mouths agape.

"Are you feeling okay, honey?" Mom asked. "You've never gone for a jog in your life."

I shrugged. "There's no time like the present to start exercising and eating healthy." I glanced down at my empty plate which, just a few minutes ago, had been piled high with bacon, eggs, pancakes and an entire bottle of maple syrup. "I'll start with the healthy eating tomorrow."

Mom smirked and took a bite of her own pancakes. "Okay, sweetie. Have fun on your jog."

I wasn't sure how to have fun on a jog, but I just nodded and went upstairs to my bedroom and threw on a pair of workout shorts, a tank top, and sneakers. Grabbing my earbuds, I plugged them into my phone, picked out some jog-appropriate music, and headed out of the house.

Just in time to see Matt heading out of his.

He saw me at the exact moment I saw him, and we smiled and waved at each other simultaneously.

"Hey," he called over to me from across the street.

"Hey," I called back, suddenly feeling very nervous.

In a bold move, I walked down my driveway and crossed the street over to him. On any other day, I would have run and hid after Matt said hello to me. But not today. Knowing what I knew now, that he was planning on asking me out, I had the confidence to strut right over to him and start a conversation.

I had Logan to thank for that.

"Going for a run?" he asked, sizing up my attire.

"I'm going to try," I said with a smile.

He chuckled softly. "I take it you're not normally a runner?"

"What gave you that impression?"

"Runner's intuition," he said with a lopsided grin. "I'm a runner myself, so I can easily spot other runners in a crowd."

"Really?" I said, impressed.

"No," he said, his grin widening. "It was just a lucky guess, actually."

"Oh," I said with a laugh, feeling stupid. "Well, either way, you were correct."

We smiled at each other and fell into an awkward silence. I didn't know how or when he was planning on asking me out, but I figured now was the perfect time for him to do so.

But it didn't feel like he was heading in that direction. Maybe he didn't want to keep me from my jog. Maybe he had a set plan of how he was going to go about doing it. Either way, I was impatient, so I figured I would help him along.

"So," I said, "I had a lot of fun the other night, at mini golf."

"Oh, yeah, me too," he said, his smile broadening.

"We'll have to do it again sometime," I suggested. If that wasn't handing him the opportunity to ask me out, I didn't know what was.

"Definitely," he agreed with a nod. "We'll have to find something else that Logan's bad at, so we can beat him and Riley again."

My shoulders slumped forward in disappointment. He thought I was suggesting just another friendly hangout. This was supposed to be when he said, *"Definitely, but we should go alone next time, just you and me. Like on a date."* But he didn't.

Instead, he started walking toward his Jeep and said, "I'll talk to Logan and Riley and set something up. See you later. Have fun on your jog."

Why did everyone keep telling me to have fun on my jog? It was a *jog*. And why didn't he ask me out?

And why would we have to hang out with Logan and Riley again? There was no way I could stomach another night of watching Riley touching Logan and flirting with him, and then watching him enjoying it, touching and flirting back.

It was disgusting.

I was too busy asking myself all these questions that I didn't even notice when Matt pulled his Jeep out of the driveway and drove off, leaving me standing alone on the curb.

At least now I had fuel for my jog.

Putting in my earbuds, I turned up the volume on my music as loud as my eardrums could handle, and started down the street.

I wasn't used to jogging or running, so it only took a couple of minutes before I started getting cramps. Slowing down to a walk, I continued towards the park that was about a half mile down the road.

I was disappointed that Matt hadn't asked me out yet, but somehow not as disappointed as I thought I was going to be. What was wrong with me? That kiss with Logan was still messing with my head.

Matt's the one you want, Emma, not Logan, my mind assured me.

But I wasn't sure if I could believe that. I didn't know what to believe anymore. My kiss with Logan had successfully turned my world upside down and had me questioning everything.

Like, for instance, my feelings for Logan.

Breaking back into a jog, I ran as quickly as I could the rest of the way to the park, trying to distract myself from that thought. By the time I got there, I was spent, so I plopped down on the first bench I could find to catch my breath.

As I sat there waiting for my heartbeat to calm down, I closed my eyes and reveled in the feeling of the early morning sun against my face. The park was quiet. There were no kids around yet, just a couple of people walking their dogs. Another couple of people were jogging, but doing a way better job at it than I was. It was the perfect time to sit and reflect.

Which was the last thing I wanted to do, so I started to turn up my music even louder when my phone chimed.

For a split second, I thought maybe I'd received a text, but when I lit up the screen, I saw it was a notification.

Emma Dawson, you've been tagged in a video.

I smiled. Chloe and Sophia were probably starting to upload some of their vacation videos. Maybe from their trip to Disney World the other day.

Excitedly, I clicked on the notification, expecting it to bring me to one of their pages, but it didn't. Instead, it brought me to *Grace's* page.

That was weird. I wasn't friends with Grace on *any* social media sites—let alone in real life, either—so why was she tagging *me* in a video? It must have been a mistake. But two other people were tagged as well, Logan and Matt, which made me think maybe…just maybe it hadn't been a mistake.

Turning off my music, I stared down at the video's thumbnail and read the title: *"#TruthHurts"*.

My heart started pounding again as my finger hovered over the little play arrow. Something in the back of my mind was warning me not to tap it. Not to watch whatever it was Grace felt I should see. Grace was not a nice person. I highly doubted she was tagging me in anything good.

But my curiosity got the best of me, and with one little tap of my finger, I hit play.

Chapter 27

LOGAN

"Logan, are you okay?"

"Mmhmm," I mumbled as I pushed scrambled eggs around my plate.

"Are you sure?"

I glanced over at my dad and shrugged. "Yeah, Dad, I'm fine. Why do you ask?"

"Well, for starters, you're never up this early in the morning unless it's a school day."

"Maybe I just wanted to have breakfast with my family for a change," I said.

Rachel, who was sitting across from me at the table, beamed. "That's really nice, Logan." She thrust a spoonful of applesauce toward Abby's mouth, but Abby pursed her lips and turned her head the other way in defiance.

"No," Dad said to her while eyeing me, "that's really *suspicious*." He took one final sip of his coffee and stood from the table. "But I'm not complaining. It's nice to see my son once in a while." He ruffled my hair as he walked by me.

"I'm heading out now," he said, leaning down to give Rachel a quick kiss.

"Okay. Have a good day at work, honey," she said.

"I will." He gave Abby a kiss on the top her head and then turned to me and said, "Have fun with Emma today." He gave me a wink and a grin before saying goodbye to everyone and walking out the door.

I could feel my face beginning to burn. Was I *blushing*? No. No way. Guys don't blush. At least, *this* guy doesn't.

I lowered my head and shoveled a forkful of eggs into my mouth.

"Okay, Logan," Rachel said as soon as my dad was gone. "Out with it."

"Out with what?" I asked with a mouth full of food.

"Whatever's bothering you. Something is bothering you, I can tell. What's up?"

I shook my head. "Nothing's 'up'. Nothing's bothering me."

Rachel shook her head. "You're lying. Come on, Logan, you know you can talk to me, right? About anything? With full stepmother-stepson confidentiality. Unless you're in trouble, in which case I may have to tell your father." She paused. "You're not in trouble, are you?"

Yes, but not the kind she was thinking of.

With a sigh, I sat back in my chair and drummed my fingers against the kitchen table. "No, I'm not in trouble."

"Does this have something to do with Emma?" She gave me a small smile. "I couldn't help but notice you blushing when your dad mentioned her name."

I groaned and leaned forward, burying my face in my hands. She'd caught me.

"It *does* have something to do with Emma!" she said, sounding mighty proud of herself. She placed a hand gently on my arm. "Logan, what's going on?"

I dropped my hands to the table and stared blankly down at my breakfast. As much as I didn't want to talk about it, I also *did* want to talk about it. But I had nobody to talk to. I couldn't talk to Matt, for obvious reasons. I didn't want to talk to my dad about it just yet, before I knew exactly what "it" was. I certainly couldn't talk to any of my boneheaded friends about it either, so that kind of left Rachel as my only option.

"Emma and I kissed last night," I confessed quietly.

Rachel gasped, bringing a hand up to her mouth. "Oh my God, are you serious? It's about time."

I narrowed my eyes at her. "What's that supposed to mean?"

Rachel rolled her eyes. "Oh, Logan. Dear, sweet, naive Logan. You do realize it was never a matter of *if* you and Emma would kiss, but *when*, right?"

I felt my breakfast food beginning to churn in my stomach. "I have no idea what you're talking about."

"Of course, you don't." Rachel chuckled as she made another attempt at feeding Abby. "So, this kiss. How did it happen?"

I suddenly felt very uncomfortable talking to her about this, but I answered anyway. "It was…we were just practicing. She'd never kissed anyone before and she was freaked out at the idea of Matt being her first. She didn't want to embarrass herself. So, I offered to help her and I…kissed her. And then she kissed me back."

"So, it wasn't a real kiss, then?"

"Not the first one, no."

Her eyebrows shot up. "The *first* one? There were more than one?"

I could feel my face burning again. "Yeah." I took a deep breath and then let it out slowly. "Rachel, I think I might have feelings for her."

I expected her mind to be blown by this revelation, but she didn't even bat an eye.

"You don't seem surprised by that," I said.

"Because I'm not. You two have been spending time together non-stop for the past couple of weeks, it was bound to happen." She smiled. "But I don't understand why you seem upset about it. This is a good thing! Right?"

"Wrong." I pushed my chair back and got up, grabbing my plate to take it over to the sink.

"Why isn't it a good thing?"

I leaned against the counter and crossed my arms over my chest. "Where do I begin? For starters, Emma is about as interested in me as Abby is in that applesauce you're trying to force-feed her right now."

Rachel smirked as Abby once again snubbed her offerings—this time by pushing away the spoon with her chubby little hand. "Abby just doesn't know what she wants. She thinks she wants the mashed bananas because that's what I've been feeding her lately and she knows she likes them. But I have a feeling once she tries the applesauce, she'll forget all about the bananas."

I stared at her in amusement. "I'm guessing Matt's the mashed bananas and I'm the applesauce in this scenario?"

She smiled. "All I'm saying is that just because Emma's always been in love with Matt, that doesn't mean she can't develop feelings for you too. It seems like you guys have gotten really close the last couple of weeks."

I sighed. "It doesn't matter either way. Matt told me yesterday that he likes her and is planning on asking her out. Which means even if she said no—which would *never* happen—she's off-limits. Once your best friend expresses interest in a girl, that's it. You can *never* pursue her. There are rules against that kind of thing."

Rachel frowned and shook her head. "Boys and their stupid rules. I mean, I get it. I do. But let me ask you this: is Matt in love with her?"

I shrugged. "I highly doubt it. He barely knows her."

"Are *you* in love with her?"

I opened my mouth to say "no", but no sound came out. *Dammit, where's my voice?*

"That's what I thought," she said with a grin.

I glared at her. "You didn't give me enough time to respond."

Rachel gave up on the applesauce, stood and walked over to me. "Logan, if you think you may have feelings for Emma, you need to tell her."

"*That's* not going to happen," I said, shaking my head. "Were you not listening like five seconds ago, when I explained that Matt likes her?"

"I was listening," she said, "but—"

"But nothing." I pushed off the counter and left the kitchen. Rachel grabbed Abby and followed me to the living room. "I'm sure these feelings don't mean anything, anyway. What I felt last night was just hormones. I'd be having these same thoughts no matter *who* I'd kissed. Emma's not my type. We have nothing in common. It would never work out between us. And…"

My voice trailed off as my eyes flickered over to the large bay window in the room that faced the street. Faced Matt's house. Where Matt was currently standing outside. With Emma. Talking to her. Laughing with her.

And, most likely, asking her out on a date.

How lovely.

Swallowing hard, I motioned out the window and said, "Besides. I'm too late."

Rachel followed my gaze. She opened her mouth like she was going to say something, but she didn't. Instead, she turned to me with a sympathetic smile and a comforting pat on the shoulder.

As much as I appreciated her trying to console me, I shrugged off her hand and said in a calm, cool voice, "Whatever. No big deal. I'm going to go take a shower. By the time I'm out, I will have forgotten all about this, anyway."

I knew she didn't believe me, and she shouldn't have. Because I was lying. But what else could I do? Run out the front door and yell, "I object!" in the middle of his date proposal?

That would go over well.

I just had to suck it up and accept the fact my best friend was getting the girl. But what did I care? Maybe I *did* have feelings for Emma, but they were probably fleeting. Besides, I didn't need her. I could go over to Matt's house right now and simply tell Riley she was my girlfriend, and she'd be my girlfriend. Or I could go ask out any waitress at Rodeo Roy's. Or call up any girl I went to school with. I could have any girl I wanted.

But I want Emma.

No, I didn't. I forced that thought out of my head as I made my way upstairs and went straight to the bathroom, where I was going to take a hot shower and scold myself for even *thinking* I had feelings for Emma Dawson.

Fifteen minutes later, I emerged from the steam-filled bathroom feeling no better than I had before. No matter how hard I tried, I just couldn't convince myself that I was fine with Matt asking Emma out.

Because I wasn't. Not at all.

As I threw on some clothes, my brain started concocting all these ideas of how to sabotage their relationship. How to convince Emma that *I* was the one she wanted, not *Matt*. But then my brain reminded me that sabotaging their relationship was wrong, and also the quickest way for me to lose my best friend, and destroy whatever sort of relationship Emma and I had started to form.

The devil and angel on my shoulders were so busy duking it out, I barely heard the whistling of my phone on my nightstand.

Great. Probably Emma texting me to tell me the great news. That Matt had asked her out. And that she'd accepted. And that now she and I didn't have to hang out anymore.

With a heavy sigh, I grabbed the phone and stared at the black screen, not wanting to turn it on and read the words for myself. But it had to be done. If I didn't read the text and respond, she'd probably come over and tell me in person. That was the last thing I wanted right now.

With my thumb, I hit the power button and swiped to unlock the screen, seeing right away that I was wrong. There was no text from Emma. Instead, the whistling had come from a notification.

Logan Reynolds, you've been tagged in a video.

Intrigued, I tapped on the notification and it brought me straight to…a video from Grace?

As soon as I saw the name of it, *#TruthHurts,* an uneasy feeling crept into the pit of my stomach. When I saw Emma and Matt had been tagged in it as well, my blood turned cold in my veins.

What the hell was this?

Turning up the volume on my phone, I dropped onto the end of my bed and hit play on the video.

And immediately wished I hadn't.

I saw right away the video was of me and Matt at Justin's party yesterday. We were being filmed from behind, without our knowledge, and the microphone was picking up everything we were saying.

Everything.

"I think I'm going to ask out Emma."

"Wait, what? Emma who?"

"The only Emma we know, you moron. Your Emma."

"But why?"

"She's cute. Actually, she's kind of hot. I enjoyed playing mini golf with her the other night and it was pretty obvious she's into me. I don't know, I think she might be fun to hang out with. If nothing else, she might be a decent hookup."

"I'm not so sure that's a good idea."

"Why not?"

"Because she's not exactly your type."

"Dude, my type is female, and she fits that description quite nicely."

"Come on, let's be real here. Dating her would be committing social suicide. Guys like you don't date girls like Emma."

No. No, no, no. This couldn't be happening.

"What do you mean, girls like Emma?"

"She's a nerd. She's boring and lame."

I stared down at my phone in horror, frozen. Unable to move. Unable to do anything but listen to myself...to my own voice, saying horrible things about Emma.

Things like, *"She's never even had a boyfriend. That alone should be a red flag."*

Or, *"She's a loser."*

And then the icing on the cake: my explanation to Matt about how I was only hanging out with Emma for selfish reasons, and because Rachel was forcing me to—not because I *wanted* to.

I felt sick to my stomach.

Emma was tagged in this video.

I had to get to her before she saw it.

I couldn't let her see this.

"*Fuck*," I hissed. I took off out of my room and bolted down the stairs.

"I'm heading out," I yelled to Rachel over my shoulder as I flung open the front door...to reveal Emma standing before me on the porch.

"Hey," I said casually, hiding my surprise. Not knowing if she'd seen the video yet, I didn't want to jump the gun and start apologizing and explaining myself.

Her skin was covered in a light sheen of sweat, her face was flushed, and some of her hair had fallen out of her loose ponytail. She looked like she had run here, but not just from next door. She was breathing too heavily for that, and judging from her attire, and the earbuds hanging from around her neck, it appeared maybe she had been out for a jog.

If she'd been out for a jog, there was a chance she hadn't seen the video yet.

But when our eyes met, I knew right away. She had seen it. All of it. Had listened to every last word I'd spoken about her. I could tell by the tears welled up in her eyes. The pained expression on her face.

My heart sank. My throat closed up. "Emma," I managed to croak.

"So, I'm not Matt's type, huh?" she said in a shaky voice. "Because I'm a 'nerd'? Because I'm 'boring and lame'? Because I'm a '*loser*'?"

I closed my eyes tightly, hoping when I opened them again, I'd be staring at my bedroom ceiling because this was all just a dream. A bad dream. It couldn't be real.

But it *was* real. When I reopened my eyes, she was still standing there, looking angry. Hurt. Betrayed.

Dammit.

"Emma," I tried again, keeping my voice as calm as possible. I took a step forward. She took a step back. "It's not what you—"

"What was this, Logan?" she asked. Her voice was more high-pitched now, which meant she was about to lose her cool. "Was this whole thing some sort of a sick joke? A prank?"

I blinked. "What? No, of course not—"

"What, did you want to get my hopes up, make me think I had a chance with Matt, just so you could take it all away and humiliate me?"

Oh, God. She thought Grace and I were in on this together. She thought I had something to do with the video being posted online.

"*No,* not at all," I said, taking another step toward her. "Emma, why would I do something like that?"

Her eyes widened. "Why? Because that's what you do, Logan! That's what you've *always* done!" She placed a hand on her forehead and stared down as she began to back up.

"Oh my God, how could I have been so *stupid?*" She was asking herself, not me. "How did I fall for this? How did I not realize right away what you were doing?"

"Emma, I wasn't doing *anything.* This wasn't a joke or a prank, I swear."

Her eyes returned to mine. They were bloodshot now from holding back tears. "Oh, that's right. You were *forced* to hang out with me. By Rachel. How could I forget that part?"

I swallowed, trying to dissolve the hard lump that had formed in my throat, but it was as solid as a brick and not going anywhere. "Emma," I said, reaching out to her, "if you'd just let me explain—"

She jerked away from me. "Don't touch me," she said in a low voice. "And don't explain anything, Logan. I can't…" She stopped and shook her head. "I can't do this right now."

Turning on her heel, she quickly descended the front steps and started speed-walking toward her house.

No. I wasn't going to let her walk away without hearing my defense. That wasn't fair.

"Emma," I said, following her across her front yard and up the porch steps. "What you heard in that video isn't—"

"Logan!" she bellowed, turning back around right in front of the door. "It's over, okay? You got exactly what you wanted: I'm angry, I'm upset, I'm...heartbroken." Her voice cracked. "You know, I actually thought we were becoming friends. I thought maybe..."

I watched her, eager to hear her next words. She thought maybe *what*? That we were becoming *more*?

But she didn't finish her sentence. Instead, she said, "I thought maybe you'd changed, but I'm such a fool. You're just the same old Logan you've always been—not caring about anyone but yourself. Not caring how your actions affect other people. Not caring if you hurt them."

I gaped at her. "That's not true."

She laughed, but there was no amusement to be found there. "Isn't it? Logan, you lied on that compatibility test for selfish reasons, not even giving a second thought to the fact you were robbing somebody—*me*—of a genuine match. And then, when you found out you'd been matched up with *me*, you stood me up, not caring how that would make me feel. I cried *all night*, thinking my date didn't show up because he saw me and wasn't interested." She paused for a moment. "Although, I guess I *was* right about that."

That familiar knot began to form in the pit of my stomach. I remembered the night I stood her up. How effortless it was for me to just walk away. I *hadn't* cared if it hurt her or not. It hadn't even been a thought in my head.

"Emma—"

"You took me on that Ferris wheel, knowing that I was afraid of heights. That must have been really amusing for you, watching me freak out and have a panic attack. Classic Emma, huh? I'm sure it made for a great story to tell your friends."

I furrowed my brow. "No, that's not—"

"You got my hopes up, making me think I could actually get Matt to like me, but when it appeared that maybe he was starting to, you talked him out of it by telling him how much of a loser I am. Why? So you could rub it in my face when I realized it was never going to happen? So you could tell me to my face that I'm a loser and that nobody will ever love me?"

Did she really believe that? Did she actually think I would stoop so low as to spend nearly two weeks of my summer with her to just *pretend* like I was helping her get Matt?

Of course, she did. Why wouldn't she?

"I wouldn't do that," I said, my voice defeated. At this point, I was wasting my breath.

She ignored my claim as she bit her lower lip. To stop it from quivering. "You stole my first kiss," she said, her voice barely above a whisper.

The lump in my throat began to dissolve. "I didn't…"

What I wanted to say was that I didn't steal it. She let me have it. And yes, I did take it, but we *shared* that kiss.

"Emma," I said softly. "You have to listen to me. What you heard on that video—"

"What I heard on that video," she interjected, her voice eerily calm, "was proof that you're a heartless jerk. You always have been, and you always will be." She paused for a moment before adding, "Your mother would be so disappointed in you."

It was like she had slapped me across the face. Punched me in the gut.

She might as well have.

I could tell she regretted the words as soon as they were out of her mouth, but by that point, it was too late. The damage had been done.

I stepped back and raked a hand through my hair. "Wow," I breathed. It was the single harshest thing anyone had ever said to me. Her words cut through my chest like a dagger and stabbed me directly in the heart.

She stared at me, wide-eyed and stone-faced. Her face was expressionless, but the tears that had begun flowing down her cheeks revealed her true feelings.

She didn't mean it, I tried to assure myself. *She's just speaking out of hurt and anger.* And maybe that was true, but that didn't stop it from completely and utterly destroying me.

Because she was probably right.

"I guess we know how we really feel about each other now," I said coolly, willing myself not to break down in front of her.

Emma's face crumpled as she nodded. As more tears began to flow. "Yeah," she managed to say, "I guess so."

Our eyes locked for a moment and despite everything, I wanted to pull her in and hold her close to me. I wanted to apologize profusely and whisper against her hair that nothing I said on that video was true; that I only said it because I had feelings for her at the time, but I just didn't know it yet. I wanted to hold her face in my hands, brush away her tears with my thumbs and then kiss her until we both ran out of breath.

I wanted to fix what I'd broken.

But I didn't get a chance to do any of that. Emma quickly turned, opened her front door, went inside the house, and

slammed the door in my face.
    I had ruined everything.

Chapter 28

LOGAN

I could feel my blood beginning to boil as I climbed behind the wheel of my Mustang and slammed the door shut.

I was mad.

Mad at myself for being so stupid. For not realizing or admitting to myself sooner that I had feelings for Emma. For saying horrible things about her to Matt that simply weren't true.

I was mad at Emma for not letting me explain my side of the story. For thinking my mother would be disappointed in me.

I was mad at Matt for being the guy Emma was in love with, and for deciding—out of all the girls he could choose to date—that Emma was the one he was interested in.

But mostly, I was mad at Grace. In fact, words could not describe how angry I was at her for posting that video, which was why I was currently putting my car into gear and burning rubber out of the driveway.

Grace and I needed to have a talk, and I figured now would be a great time to pay her a visit.

It felt weird pulling up in front of her house. It had only been a few weeks since the last time I was over there, but it seemed like a lifetime ago. I had a lot of good memories of this house—of Grace's bedroom in particular—but those memories were quickly fading.

I couldn't get rid of them fast enough.

I was afraid she might have gone out early with her friends, so I was relieved to see her car was in the driveway when I arrived. I tried to remain calm as I got out of the car and walked up to her front door, but my fury came through when I pounded on the door. I could have just rung the doorbell, but that wouldn't have allowed me to get some of my aggression out. The more I could get out of my system before I saw her, the better.

It took only a few seconds for the door to open, and suddenly Grace stood before me, looking like she was heading out for a photoshoot.

I studied her for a moment. Her makeup had been expertly applied. Her hair had been styled to perfection. Her curves filled out her halter top and short skirt as though the clothes had been tailored specifically for her.

But she couldn't have looked more hideous to me at the moment and I found myself wondering how I'd managed to stay with her for so long.

Her lips curled into a sinister smile when she saw me. "Hello, Logan. What brings you by?"

She knew damn well what brought me by. My hands balled into fists at my sides. "What the hell is wrong with you, Grace?"

Grace's smile only faltered slightly as she blinked innocently at me. "What are you talking about?"

"Cut the crap," I said through clenched teeth. "Why did you do it? Why did you post that video?"

"Oh," she said with a slight chuckle. "The video? That's why you're here? Logan, it's no big deal."

"No big deal?" I echoed. "You filmed a very private conversation without my consent and posted it for the entire world to see—tagging the one person you knew it would hurt the most."

She rolled her eyes. "My fans wanted drama, so I gave them drama. Besides," she said with a shrug, "you're lucky posting that video is *all* I did."

I narrowed my eyes at her. "What's that supposed to mean?"

Her smile disappeared as she stared at me with her cold, gray eyes. "Emma stole you from me. I could have—and *should have*—done a lot worse."

I inhaled sharply and took a step back. This. *This* was what I was talking about to Emma, when I told her about why I'd lied on the compatibility test. I always had a sneaking suspicion that Grace would turn into a psycho if I ever broke up with her. I had no doubt in my mind that posting that video was the kindest thing she'd thought of. I shuddered to think of what other ideas she had come up with.

And I feared that whatever they were, it was possible they were still on the table.

"Listen, Grace," I said, my voice low, "you leave Emma alone. Do you hear me? She had nothing to do with why we broke up, and I'd better not find out you've concocted some other scheme to get back at her, or—"

"Or what?" She flipped her hair over her shoulder and placed her hands on her hips. Her eyes danced around my face as her smile returned. "Why, Logan, if I didn't know any better, I would think you had real, genuine feelings for the nerd."

I took a deep breath and held it, trying to keep my anger to a minimum. "So, what if I do?"

She smirked. "Logan Reynolds? Having real, genuine feelings for *any* girl? Not possible." She stepped out onto the porch and slowly made her way over to me. "If you weren't capable of loving *me*, you're certainly not capable of loving some 'boring, lame loser' like Emma Dawson."

I winced at her insulting words, especially considering they were mine, but quickly recovered and gave her a smirk of my own. "Grace, I'm more than capable of loving someone…just not *you*. And this right here is exactly why. Emma didn't do anything to you. She didn't do *anything* wrong, but you posted that video anyway because you're a terrible person. You intentionally hurt someone who didn't deserve it."

Grace threw her head back and laughed. "Are you serious, Logan? You think *I* hurt Emma?"

"Yes, I do." What did she think was so funny about that?

Her laughter subsided, and her smirk returned. "Then may I suggest you go back and watch that video again. Because if I recall correctly, those were *your* words, coming out of *your* mouth, spoken in *your* voice." She took another step closer to me, invading my personal space. "*I* didn't hurt Emma, Logan. *You* did."

Lifting up her chin, she motioned past me and said, "We're done here. You may leave now."

She turned around, whipping her hair at me, and stalked back into her house, slamming the door behind her.

With a heavy, defeated sigh, I returned to my car. Grace was right. I *was* the one who'd hurt Emma. Sure, Grace should have never filmed and then posted that video online, but I never should have said any of those things to begin with. Why couldn't I have just been the supportive best friend? Why couldn't I have just told Matt I thought it was a great idea that he was planning on asking Emma out?

Oh, that's right. Because I was selfish. Because I wanted her all to myself, even though I wasn't the one she wanted.

Emma was right. My mother *would* be disappointed in me.

I drove home in a fog, paying only enough attention to keep myself from running stop signs or hitting pedestrians. I wasn't even aware I'd pulled into my driveway until I came to a complete stop and turned off the car.

My phone rang beside me on the passenger seat. Reaching over blindly, I picked it up and answered it.

"Hello?" I said. Deep down, I was hoping it was Emma, calling to say she was ready to hear my side of the story. But the voice that spoke back to me was not hers. It was Matt's.

"Dude, what's Grace's problem?" he asked into my ear. "I just saw that video she posted online. What a wench."

I closed my eyes and pinched the bridge of my nose. "I guess that's one way to describe her," I muttered.

"Please tell me Emma hasn't seen it yet."

"Oh, she's seen it alright." I leaned my head back against the headrest and stared up through the sunroof at the clear blue sky. "And now she hates me. More than usual, that is."

Matt sighed. "I'm sorry, man. That sucks."

"Yep. It does." I paused for a moment. "You're still planning on asking her out, right?"

It was Matt's turn to pause. He was silent for so long, I thought maybe we'd been disconnected. "Matt?"

"No," he said finally. "I'm not, actually."

"What? Why not?" I sat up straight in my seat. "Matt, you need to still ask her out."

"Sorry, man. Not going to happen."

"This doesn't have anything to do with what I said about her yesterday, does it?" I asked quietly, not wanting to know the answer.

He didn't even miss a beat. "Absolutely."

Dammit. This was all my fault. I'd successfully talked him out of wanting to date Emma. I was a terrible friend. Just a terrible person in general. "Look, Matt, I didn't mean anything I said, alright? You'd be lucky to date Emma. Seriously, she—"

"Whoa, let me stop you right there," Matt interrupted. "Logan, me not asking out Emma has nothing to do with *what* you said. It has to do with *why* you said it."

"What's that supposed to mean?"

Matt chuckled softly. "Dude, it doesn't take a rocket scientist to figure out you've got the hots for Emma."

I groaned and lowered my head onto the steering wheel. "What are you talking about?" I asked, feigning ignorance.

"You know what I'm talking about. The way you were talking about her yesterday, I could tell you *really* didn't like the idea of me dating her, and you were trying to turn me off to the idea. At first, I thought it was because you actually believed the things you were saying about her, but then it all started to make sense. You don't want me dating her because *you* want to date her. Logan, you're in love with Emma."

My jaw dropped as I sat back up. "I am not."

"You are, too. And once I realized that, she became off-limits to me. You're my best friend, Logan, I'm not going to pursue the girl you're in love with."

"I'm not in love with her," I denied through clenched teeth. Did I kind of like her? Sure. Did I enjoy hanging out with her? Definitely. Was she an amazing kisser? Undoubtedly. But was I in love with her?

No. No way. I'd never been in love with anyone before. I wouldn't even know *how* to be.

"You can deny it all you want," Matt said, "but that won't make it true."

I sighed and shook my head. "Even if I was in love with Emma—which I am *not*—she's not in love with me. She's in love with *you*, Matt. You're the one she wants. You're the one she's *always* wanted. She's had the biggest crush on you for years now. If you want to be with her, then you should be with her. I'll be fine with it. I swear."

"Bullshit," Matt said. "Look, Emma's cool. I like her, but not as much as you apparently do. I'm not willing to ruin our friendship over a girl."

Matt and I had agreed long ago that we would never let a girl come between us, and this was the first time that pledge was being put to the test.

It looked as though we had both kept our word.

And now, neither of us would end up with the girl.

"It doesn't matter, anyway," I mumbled. "Emma's not a possession, and she doesn't belong to either one of us. She hates me now more than ever, and she's probably mad at you too because I'm sure she thinks you're going to listen to what I said, and not ask her out because of it." I frowned. "I really screwed this up, didn't I?"

"Nah," Matt said. "I don't think so. Maybe she hates you right now, but she'll get over it once she cools down. After you get a chance to explain everything, and tell her how you feel about her, I'm sure everything will be fine."

I wished I could believe that, but I didn't.

I opened the door and got out of the car. "Listen, Matt, I'll talk to you later, okay?"

"Yeah, sure. Are you going to be okay?"

"I'll be fine," I lied and disconnected.

I shut the door and leaned my back against the car. I pointed my gaze toward the Dawson house and stared up at Emma's bedroom window.

Turning my phone back on, I dialed her number. I knew it was a waste of time, and that she would let it go to voicemail, but I didn't care. I had to at least try.

Sure enough, after a few rings, her pre-recorded voice spoke up, telling me she was unable to take my call and to leave a message.

I paused briefly after the beep as I contemplated hanging up. But I couldn't do that.

"Emma," I said, keeping my eyes on her window, hoping to see her appear at any moment. "I know you hate me right now, and I don't blame you, but please…we need to talk. There are things I want to say to you, but I don't want to say them over voicemail or a text. I need to tell you in person. So, *please*, call me back."

I ended the call, feeling defeated. She wasn't going to call me back. She didn't want to hear what I had to say. Even if I had the chance to tell her, she probably wouldn't believe me, anyway. I'd lost her trust and I was unlikely to ever get it back.

"Hey, Logan!" came a cheery voice from across the street.

I turned my head to see Riley making her way over to me. I hadn't seen her since I'd abandoned her at the party the other night to go home and check on Emma and she'd seemed pretty perturbed about that at the time.

Great, just what I needed—another confrontation with a girl who hated my guts.

"Hey," I said cautiously, forcing a smile onto my face.

Surprisingly, she returned the smile. Maybe this wasn't going to be as bad as I thought.

"What are you doing?" she asked as she approached. She leaned next to me against the car and followed my line of vision over to Emma's house. "Being a creepy stalker?" she teased.

I snickered and raked a hand through my hair. "What's up, Riley?"

She shrugged. "Nothing, really. I'm *so bored*. Matt's gone for the day, and all I'm left with over there is Jade and her weirdo friends, and I fear they may be preparing for some sort of satanic ritual or something. I had to get out of the house before I became their human sacrifice." She paused and then added, "Although, I'm probably safe, considering I'm not a virgin." She ended with a wink and grin.

I couldn't help but laugh at that. After the morning I'd had so far, it felt pretty good.

"If you're not doing anything today, would you like to hang out?" she asked.

I glanced down at my phone. It had only been a minute since I'd left that voicemail with Emma, and even though I knew she wouldn't call me back, I would probably spend the entire day checking my phone every few seconds on the off chance that she would.

That was no way to spend a beautiful, sunny, hot summer day.

"I'd love to," I said, stuffing the phone back into my pocket. "We could go to Funland Park. Have you been there yet?"

She threw her head back and laughed. "Not since I got up here, no, but I did go there a few times as a kid. Do they still have that sketchy metal roller coaster that feels like it's going to collapse every time you ride it?"

I nodded. "Not only do they still have it, but they've never upgraded it, so it feels even sketchier than it did when we were kids. You should hear the sounds it makes. I swear, one time I was standing near it, a screw came out of nowhere and landed right in front of me. It had to have come from the ride. Screws don't just fall out of the sky like that from nowhere."

Riley giggled and hit my arm. "You're making that up!"

"I'm not," I said with a grin.

"Yeah, right." When her giggling subsided, she said, "Well,

I can't wait to ride it. I like a good thrill."

My grin faltered as the connotation of what she'd said was not lost on me.

Don't do this, Logan. Tell Riley you don't want to hang out after all. Go to Emma instead. Knock down her front door if you have to. Barge into her house and demand she listen to you. Apologize for every terrible thing you've ever done to her. Tell her you love her. Kiss her. Kiss every last bit of breath out of her. Hold her close and never let her go again...

I pushed all those thoughts away. Emma didn't want me. She hated me. No amount of apologizing or groveling would change that. Even if she did forgive me, we were never going to be anything more than just neighbors. Acquaintances.

After one last glance at Emma's house, I turned back to Riley.

"I like a good thrill, too," I said, my lips forming into a smirk as I motioned toward the car. "Hop in."

Chapter 29

EMMA

"Emma? Honey? Is everything alright?"

At the sound of my mother's muffled voice through my bedroom door, I quickly wiped away the tears from my eyes as I sat up on my bed. "Yeah, Mom, everything's fine."

By the time I'd stormed into the house, my dad had already left for work, and my mom was just getting ready to leave. When she saw me rushing up the stairs, she'd called after me, asking if I was okay, but I didn't answer her. I just ran straight up to my room and slammed the door shut.

Being the concerned mother she was, there was no way she was going to leave for work when she knew something was wrong with her daughter. And even though I really didn't want to talk about what happened, I also didn't want to make her late for work. She would stay outside my room all day to find out what was going on if I let her.

"Can I come in?" she asked softly.

"Yeah, sure," I replied, smoothing out my hair.

The bedroom door slowly opened, and my mom poked her head in. "Emma, what's wrong? Did something happen on your jog?"

Yes, something happened. Somebody tore my heart out of my chest and broke it in two.

But I didn't tell her that. Instead, I just sniffled and lowered my head, staring blankly at my hands resting on my lap.

"Sweetie." Mom sat down next to me and put an arm around my shoulders. "What's going on?"

When I didn't answer, she continued.

"Does this have something to do with Logan?"

I blinked at her in surprise. "How did you know?"

Mom smiled. "Mother's intuition. Plus, I thought I heard the two of you talking on the porch." She sighed. "What has he done now?"

"I'll show you," I said, grabbing my phone. I brought up the video, hit play, and handed it to her.

I observed her face intently as she watched the video. I wanted to see the precise moment where finally, after eighteen years, my mom realized that Logan Reynolds was a good-for-nothing jerk.

The corners of her mouth twitched downward. "What is this?" she demanded.

"It's a video that Logan's ex-girlfriend took at a party yesterday. She posted it online this morning for everyone to see."

"I'm sorry, what?" Mom's voice hardened as her eyes narrowed in concern. "Honey, are you being bullied?"

I blinked and said, "What? No." But then I paused and thought about it for a second. I guess in a way, I sort of *was*.

Mom stood up. "What's Logan's ex-girlfriend's name? I'm going to call her mother right now—"

"No, Mom." I grabbed her arm and forced her back onto the bed next to me. "I don't need you to call Grace's mom, okay? That'll only make things worse. Besides," I said, glancing down at my lap, "the video being posted online is not really what I'm upset about right now."

"Did Logan have something to do with this video being uploaded?" Mom asked, her voice tight. I think she was afraid of what my answer might be.

"No," I said quietly. "At least, he's claiming he had nothing to do with it. He said he didn't know Grace was filming. And I guess I believe him. I wouldn't put it past Grace to do this to get back at him for their breakup, but…none of that excuses what he said about me."

Mom placed a hand on my knee. "Sweetie, is it at all possible that this video was taken out of context?"

I stared at her blankly. "What?"

"I just…" She took my phone back and began to play it again. "I just don't get the impression he means a word of what he's saying here."

"Mom," I scolded her. "Why would you say that?"

"Because…" She sighed heavily as she finished watching the video for the second time. "For starters, he doesn't sound like *he's* believing a word he's saying. And then the video ends abruptly, like maybe there was more to his conversation with Matt, but Grace didn't want you to see that part." She pursed her lips together. "I definitely think something is amiss here."

"*Amiss?* Mom, face it. This is what Logan thinks of me. It's what he's *always* thought of me. And what's worse, this video was taken *yesterday*. Just a few hours before we…" I clamped my mouth shut before I could finish the sentence.

My mom titled her head to the side. "Before you what?"

I played nervously with the hem of my shirt. "Before we kissed."

Mom's jaw dropped, and her eyes widened in surprise. "You *kissed?*"

I nodded. "It started out as just practicing, but then…I don't know, it seemed to become something more." I lowered my gaze. "At least, to me it did."

"Oh, Emma," she breathed. She brushed a strand of hair away from my face. "Do you like Logan?"

319

My vision blurred as a fresh wave of tears threatened to spill over. "I don't know. Maybe I do, but it doesn't matter. You heard what he said on the video."

"Well, did you confront him about it?"

"Yes, I did."

"And what was his explanation?"

I opened my mouth to respond, but then realized I couldn't. Because he hadn't given me an explanation.

Because I hadn't given him the opportunity to.

With a groan, I leaned forward and buried my face in my hands. What if my mom was right? What if there was a perfectly good explanation as to why he said what he did? What if his words *were* taken out of context? He had tried to talk to me about it, but I was so upset, I just kept interrupting him.

"I didn't let him explain," I admitted, letting my hands drop back onto my lap.

"Then maybe you should," Mom said softly. "Honey, I know Logan has done and said a lot to you over the years that has upset you, but I don't think this is like all the other times. I could be wrong, and if I am, I'm sorry and I will join you in hating his guts. But for now, talk to him. Let him explain himself."

I nodded solemnly and brushed away the tears from my eyes. "Okay, I will."

Mom smiled. "Good." She leaned forward and planted a kiss on the top of my head. "I wish we could talk more, but I have to get to work. But we can finish this conversation later, *after* you talk to Logan again." She stood up. "And who knows? Maybe we'll have something to celebrate."

"Mom," I said, rolling my eyes. I smiled back and told her to have a good day at work as she left my bedroom.

I was already feeling better. My mother's "intuition" usually didn't steer her wrong, so if she truly felt there was more to that video than met the eye, then maybe that was the case. And since she'd helped me calm down, maybe now I could let Logan tell me his side of the story without rudely interrupting him.

For a few minutes, I did nothing but stare at the blank screen of my phone, willing my thumb to hit the button to light it up, swipe the screen to unlock, and dial Logan's number. But something was preventing me from doing so. Maybe it was that horrible comment I'd made about his mother being disappointed in him. I was so ashamed of myself for saying that, especially because I didn't actually think it was true, but I was hurt, and the words just came out before my brain had a chance to approve of them.

It was very possible *he* didn't want to talk to *me* right now.

With a sigh, I stood from the bed and walked over to the window that faced Logan's house. Just as I approached, I saw his Mustang pull into his driveway. He must have gone somewhere after our fight.

I watched for a minute while he remained inside the car. He appeared to be talking on the phone and I couldn't help but be curious as to who he was talking to.

All I knew was that it wasn't me.

A short while later, he exited the vehicle, shut the door and leaned against it…and almost immediately glanced up at my window.

I quickly took a step back, far enough away that I could still see him, but he wouldn't be able to see me. Holding up his phone, it looked like he was starting to dial a number, and my heart fluttered in my chest. Was he trying to call *me*?

I got my answer when my own phone rang in my hands. Excitedly, I swiped to answer it. "Hello?"

"Hey. Is this Emma?"

The voice on the other end was a male's voice, but it didn't belong to Logan. Confused, I glanced back out the window and saw Logan was now talking into his phone...but not to me.

I narrowed my eyes. If this wasn't Logan, who was it?

"Yes, this is Emma," I replied cautiously. "Who is this?"

"This is Justin," the voice said.

My mind drew a blank. "Justin?"

He chuckled softly. "Yeah, Justin. Justin Daniels? You've been to a couple of my parties this summer?"

Ah, *that* Justin. Why was *that* Justin calling me?

"Oh, hey, Justin," I said, trying my best not to sound as disappointed as I felt. "How did you get my number?"

"I have connections," he said. "I know a guy who knew a guy."

Well, this was weird. "Okay...um...so, what's up?"

"I just wanted to say, I saw that video that Grace posted online this morning and I was appalled. I can't believe she would do something like that. And I can't believe Logan would say those things about you."

I returned my attention to the window and watched as Logan ended his phone call.

"Yeah, I couldn't believe it, either," I said distractedly.

"None of what Logan said was true, you know," he continued. "You're not a loser, or a nerd. From what I can tell, you seem pretty cool."

The corners of my mouth turned down as I saw Logan glance over towards Matt's house...and saw that Riley was making her way over to him.

"Thank you," I said to Justin, watching as Logan greeted Riley.

"No problem," he said. "Hey, I was wondering if maybe you'd like to go out with me sometime? Like, on a date?"

That drew my attention away from the window. "I'm sorry, what did you just say?" I couldn't possibly have heard correctly. There was no way Justin Daniels had just asked me out.

"I'm asking you on a date," he said, his voice laced with amusement.

Okay, so I *had* heard him correctly. Still, this made no sense. "Um…"

I didn't know how to respond to that. I barely knew Justin. I knew *of* him, and what I knew was not great. He had a terrible reputation when it came to girls. I'd heard all the stories. All the rumors. He was bad news. Logan had made sure I knew that.

It was a little more than suspicious that Justin would randomly call me after seeing that video and tell me he wanted to date me. So, I opened my mouth to reject his offer, but my words were halted by what I was witnessing outside my bedroom window.

Logan and Riley were talking now. Smiling and laughing. She was touching his arm. I would have given anything to know what they were talking about…what was putting that smile on his face, even though he'd seemed miserable just a short while ago when I'd slammed the front door in his face.

"Emma? You there?"

I blinked at the sound of Justin's voice. I'd forgotten for a second that I was still on the phone with him.

"Yeah, sorry," I mumbled.

"So, would you like to go out with me sometime?"

I stared at Logan and Riley. Watched as he said something to her and motioned to his car. Watched as she climbed in. Watched as he did the same, right after one more quick glance in my direction. Watched as the car pulled out of the driveway and disappeared down the street.

My heart sank in my chest. Of course, he and Riley would go off somewhere together. Why wouldn't they? They'd been flirting all summer. They'd gone to that party together the other night. He liked her. He thought she was fun and sexy. She was everything he was trying to get *me* to be…so that he could get his best friend to like me.

Logan didn't like me. He'd made that very clear in that video. Perhaps this was the one time in my mom's life that her intuition was wrong. There was no context. No misinterpretation.

He didn't like me. He liked Riley.

But why should I care? I didn't like *him* either. The feeling was mutual.

"Emma?" Justin's slightly annoyed voice broke through my thoughts.

"Sorry," I said, closing my eyes tightly and shaking my head. "Sorry, Justin, I was just a bit distracted."

"That's okay," he said. "Look, if you need some time to think about it—"

"Yes," I said, reopening my eyes and staring out at Logan's empty driveway. "I mean, yes, I'll go out with you."

What? Emma, what are you doing?

"Great!" he said. "How about tomorrow night? We can catch a movie or something."

"Sounds great," I said through clenched teeth. *No, it doesn't! Take it back! Tell him you were just kidding!*

"How about I pick you up around seven?"

"Perfect," I said, forcing a smile.

"Awesome. Just text me your address and I'll see you then."

"Will do." I ended the call and took a deep breath, holding

it in until I began to see stars.

When I finally let it out, I began to panic. I had just agreed to go on a date with Justin Daniels, the school's biggest player. The guy who obviously had some sort of ulterior motive for asking me out. What was wrong with me?

The answer was simple. Logan thought I was a loser. He didn't want me, and he had successfully talked Matt into not wanting me either. Perhaps Justin couldn't be trusted, but he was the only guy who maybe *did* want me, despite everything that was said in that video.

It wasn't the best decision I'd ever made, but I didn't care. Besides, if Logan found out I was going on a date with Justin, he would probably freak the hell out.

That was reason enough for me.

Chapter 30

LOGAN

"Well, that was fun!" Riley said as I pulled the Mustang into my driveway.

"It was," I agreed with a smile as I turned off the car.

I'd spent the entire afternoon with Riley. It was the first time since she'd arrived here that we'd gotten to spend some quality time together. It was the first time we'd had a chance to hang out alone somewhere other than a party, and it was nice. Like she said, it was fun. I got to know her a little better. She was witty. She was interesting. I found out we had a lot in common.

But it didn't matter. None of that was enough to distract me from what had happened earlier with Emma. In fact, being at Funland Park did nothing but remind me of her. Remind me of the Ferris wheel fiasco, or how she'd embarrassed me by beating my ass at the ring toss game.

I couldn't get her out of my head, no matter how hard I tried.

"You want to come in for a bit?" Riley asked, motioning towards Matt's house.

I took my phone out of my pocket and lit up the screen. No voicemail from Emma. No text. Nothing.

"Yeah, sure," I replied glumly, even though I really just wanted to go inside my own house and sulk.

"Cool." Riley grinned as we got out of the car and started

across the street. There were no vehicles in the driveway, meaning neither Matt, nor his or Riley's parents had made it home yet.

When we walked through the front door, Riley yelled upstairs, "Hey, Jade, I'm back!"

We were greeted with silence.

"Hmm," Riley said. "Either she's not here, or she's got her headphones on."

We headed for the kitchen and when we got there, we both immediately noticed a note stuck to the refrigerator, signed by Jade.

Riley took it down. "*Gone to Kara's. I'll be back for dinner,*" she read aloud. With a smirk, she said, "I think Kara is their leader."

I snorted. "You don't actually think Jade's a member of a satanic cult, do you?"

"Satanic? No. I'm leaning more towards Wiccan."

I laughed. "Man, I remember when she used to only wear pink and never went anywhere without her Barbie dolls."

"Sadly, those days are gone," Riley said with a sigh. She glanced around the kitchen. "I guess this means we're all alone, huh?"

"Yeah, I guess so…" I said slowly.

Her lips formed into a seductive smile. "Nice. What would you like to do?"

I would like to get a phone call from Emma, so I could explain everything to her.

I shrugged. "I don't know."

"Well, I have an idea." She grabbed my hand and said, "Come with me."

She led me out of the kitchen and up the stairs.

"Where are we going?" I asked, even though I was pretty

sure I already knew the answer.

"You'll see," she said with a wink as we made it to the top. We continued down the hallway to the very last door at the end. The guest bedroom. Most likely the one she'd been staying in.

"I'm lucky," she said, opening the door. "They've got two guest rooms here, so I don't have to share one with anyone. That would have been a nightmare."

"Yeah," I agreed with a nervous chuckle. There was only one reason Riley would be bringing me upstairs to the room she'd been staying in, and it wasn't to show me her stamp collection.

"Have a seat," she instructed, pointing to the bed.

"Um, no thanks," I said. "I don't mind standing."

Riley giggled and placed a hand on my chest, taking a step forward to make me take a step back. After a few more steps, I felt the edge of the bed hit the back of my legs, causing me to stumble backward and land exactly where she wanted me.

"There, that wasn't so hard, was it?" She wrapped her arms around my shoulders and placed her hands on the back of my neck. "Logan, I have a confession to make."

I had a feeling I knew what that confession was, and my heart started pounding in my chest. "Oh yeah? What's that?"

"I like you," she said, point-blank. She paused and smiled sheepishly. "But you probably already knew that, didn't you?"

I cleared my throat as I stared up at her. "Uh, well, maybe," I admitted.

Slowly, she straddled my legs and lowered herself onto my lap.

"Do you like *me*?" she asked, running a hand through my hair.

I swallowed hard and nodded. "I do." Instinctively, I placed my hands on her hips to hold her in place.

My answer seemed to please her. Biting her lower lip, her eyes held onto mine briefly before lowering to my mouth.

"Well then," she said, "what should we do about that?"

I didn't know what to say. If she had asked me that question a couple weeks ago, I wouldn't have said anything; I would have just thrown her on the bed and started kissing her, and then one thing would have led to another...

But I didn't want that. Not now. Not with Riley.

"Look, Riley..." How could I break this to her? How could I tell an incredibly hot girl that I just wasn't feeling this? That she wasn't the one I wanted?

"Shh, Logan," she whispered, placing her forefinger against my lips. She must have sensed my hesitation. "You don't need to worry, okay? I know you're not looking for a serious relationship. I'm not either. I'm just looking to have a little fun."

Normally, that would have been music to my ears. A girl like Riley not looking for a relationship, just to hook up? That was a dream come true for a guy like me. Or, it would have been. Two weeks ago.

"Riley," I tried again, but she leaned in and placed a gentle kiss on my forehead, one on my cheek, one on my jawline, and then finally moved to place one on my lips.

I quickly turned my head to avoid it, and she froze.

"What's wrong?" she asked, her voice laced with confusion. She most likely wasn't used to getting rejected.

"I'm sorry," I said, removing my hands from her hips. "I can't do this."

Her jaw dropped slightly as she slid off my lap and took a seat next to me on the bed. "Okay..."

"It's not you," I assured her, even though that was probably the last thing she wanted to hear. "I just...I think I like someone else…"

"It's Emma, isn't it?" she said softly. "You like Emma."

I gaped at her. "How did you know?"

"Honestly? I didn't," she mumbled. "I just suspected. I've seen the little looks you two give each other, and the jealousy coming from both of you. I just ignored it because I wanted to believe I was reading too much into things. But I guess I wasn't."

I leaned forward and buried my face in my hands. "Riley, I'm sorry—"

"Logan," she interjected, "you don't have anything to apologize for. Like I said, I wasn't looking for a relationship. I think you're hot and I wanted to forget about my ex-boyfriend for a while."

"I don't know what's wrong with me," I said, dropping my hands onto my lap and staring down at the floor.

"You're in love, dummy, that's what's wrong with you," she said, nudging my shoulder playfully. "So, why are you here with me right now, and not over at Emma's house declaring your love for her?"

"Because I screwed up and now she hates me. She won't even talk to me."

With a dismissive wave of her hand, Riley said, "I don't know what you did, but it can't be that bad. She won't hate you forever. That girl has got it bad for you."

I glanced at her with one eyebrow arched. "Oh yeah? What makes you think that?"

She shrugged. "Why *wouldn't* she? You're a great guy. You're smart, you're funny, you're hot. What's not to love?"

"I'm a jerk," I muttered. "That's how she's always seen me, and that's how she always *will* see me. Especially now."

Riley frowned. "What did you do that was so bad?"

With a sigh, I said, "Long story short, my ex-girlfriend recorded a private conversation between me and Matt yesterday, where I said some not-so-nice things about Emma, and then she posted the video online. And tagged Emma in it."

Riley inhaled sharply. "Oh, that sucks. What kind of things did you say about her?"

I grimaced, not wanting to repeat the words. "Things like how she's a lame nerd and a loser, how she's never had a boyfriend, how I was only hanging out with her because my stepmother was pretty much blackmailing me into it."

"Oh, Logan," Riley breathed, and then narrowed her eyes. "Wait...why would you say those things if you have feelings for her?"

"Because I'm an idiot," I muttered.

With a sympathetic smile, Riley placed a hand on my arm. It was the first time she'd done so without it being a flirtatious gesture. "So, what are you going to do to fix this?"

"I don't know. She won't talk to me. She won't listen to my side of the story. I'm not sure there's anything I *can* do."

Riley shook her head. "No, there's got to be something. You just need to think outside the box."

I turned to look at her. "Why are you being so cool about this?"

"Honestly?" she said. "Because I'm a hopeless romantic. Also, I'm just relieved that you rejected me because you have feelings for someone else and not because you're not attracted to me. I'm not sure my fragile, post-breakup ego could handle that."

I couldn't help but chuckle. "Riley, I doubt there's a guy alive right now who's not attracted to you. You're a catch."

She giggled and blushed as she lowered her gaze to the floor. "I'm 'a catch'? Oh my God, you sound like my *grandmoth-*

er."

We glanced at each other and laughed as my phone began to ring.

I quickly removed it from my pocket and glanced down, hoping to see Emma's name on the screen. Instead, I saw Matt's name. My shoulders slumped forward in disappointment as I swiped to answer.

"Hey, Matt."

"Dude, have you heard?" he asked, skipping the greeting.

"Heard what?"

He paused for a moment and an uneasy feeling came over me.

"Matt? What is it?"

"Emma," he said finally. "She agreed to go on a date with Justin tomorrow."

My breath caught in my throat as that uneasy feeling turned into dread. "Please tell me you're joking."

"Unfortunately, I'm not. Justin told me himself and then he bragged about it to some of the other guys. He bet them that he'd make it to at least second base with her by the end of the night."

I gritted my teeth so hard I was lucky they didn't all shatter. "If he does, I will kill him."

Riley, not privy to what our conversation was about, raised her eyebrows and gave me a quizzical look.

I stood from the bed and began pacing the floor in front of it.

"Matt," I said slowly, trying hard to control my rage, "now would be a really good time for you to go over to her house and ask her out. There is no way, if given the choice, that she would choose Justin over you."

Matt sighed, and I could tell he was annoyed. "Once again,

I'm not going to ask Emma out. Maybe now is a good time for *you* to tell her that you're in love with her."

I pinched the bridge of my nose as I felt a headache coming on. Ignoring his suggestion, I said, "Could you at least go over there and try to talk some sense into her?"

"No," he said sternly. "I'm staying out of this. I told you because I figured you would want to know, and I figured it would inspire you to stop being such a pansy and just tell the girl you love her already. You don't want her going on this date? You tell her yourself."

And with that, he ended the call.

Muttering a few choice swears, I raked a hand through my hair as I began to pace again.

"Okay," Riley said, "what was that all about?"

"Emma is apparently going on a date with Justin tomorrow," I replied through clenched teeth.

Riley blinked in surprise. "The guy she almost kissed at that party?"

Thanks for the reminder. "Yeah, that guy."

"How did that happen?"

"I have no idea!" I said, throwing my hands in the air. "And Matt is refusing to try talking her out of it."

"Why don't *you* talk to her?"

I stopped pacing. "Because there is no way she's going to listen to me. She won't even return my calls so I can apologize to her. I kind of doubt she'll open her front door to me so I can talk her out of going on a date with a douchebag."

Riley nodded in agreement. "What are you going to do, then?"

It was a good question. I could go straight to Justin and threaten him to stay away from Emma, but all that would do is make him want her even more. I could go to her dad and warn him about Justin, and tell him he should forbid her from going out tomorrow night, but she would find out and then she would hate me even more than she already did.

There was nothing I could do.

"I don't know, but I'm going to have to come up with something." My gaze flickered over to her. "I'm sorry, Riley, but I should probably go."

She nodded like she understood. "Good luck, Logan." She stood and walked over to me, giving me a soft kiss on the cheek. "She'll come around. Trust me."

I wished I could believe her, but I didn't.

I left Matt's house and as I crossed the street, I eyed Emma's bedroom window. Her car was in the driveway, so there was a good chance she was home. From the looks of it, both of her parents were home as well, and I considered walking up to her front door and knocking. Maybe either Olivia or Jake would listen to me. Maybe they would pass a message along to her for me. Or, maybe they would tell me to get lost and slam the door in my face, much like their daughter did earlier.

Stopping at the end of my driveway, I decided to try reaching out to Emma herself one last time. Pulling out my phone, I typed out a text.

Me: Emma can we talk?

I only waited a few seconds before sending another one.

Me: please? that video is not what u think it is

Nothing. She wasn't going to respond. So, I typed up another one.

Me: Emma i'm in love with u. pls forgive me so we can go back to lover's lookout and finish what we started last night.

I didn't send that one.

Maybe I should have.

At this point, I wanted to tell her how I felt about her, but I didn't want to do it through a text. I wanted to do it in person so that if she told me she felt the same way, I could immediately pull her to me and kiss her.

And if she *didn't* feel the same way?

I guess I would cross that bridge when I got to it.

Knowing she wasn't going to respond to my texts, I sighed and continued up the driveway.

As soon as I was inside the house, my dad, who was home from work earlier than usual, poked his head out of the kitchen.

"Logan? Can we talk?"

That was universal dad-language for "you've done something bad and now you're in trouble." Great. What now? Did Rachel actually go through with talking him into making me go on that New York trip? Or did I do something else I'd forgotten all about?

"Sure," I said warily as I made my way toward the kitchen. "What's up?"

Dad motioned for me to take a seat at the table. "I heard about the video."

My breath hitched in my throat. "Seriously? How did you find out about that?"

He sat down across from me. "Emma told Olivia, Olivia told Rachel, Rachel told me."

Of course. By now, it was probably the talk of the town.

"Okay, what about it? I swear, I had nothing to do with it being posted online. Grace did that all on her own. I didn't even know she was filming our conversation. If I had, I would have grabbed that camera, smashed it to the ground, and kicked it into the pool."

Dad furrowed his brow. "Logan, I know you had nothing to do with the video being posted. I'm more concerned about what's in it. I thought you and Emma were becoming friends?"

"We were," I said. "I mean, we were becoming…something. I don't know. But it doesn't matter. I didn't mean anything I said in that video, but Emma won't let me just explain that to her. And now she's going on a date tomorrow with a guy who is likely going to take advantage of her, and there's not a thing I can do about it."

He studied me for a moment before saying, "Rachel also told me about the kiss."

With a groan, I lowered my forehead to the smooth, hard surface of the table. "Why did she tell you about that?"

I could tell he was amused. "Rachel is a gossip. I thought you knew that? But I think she told me because she's worried about you."

I lifted my head. "Why is she worried about me?"

Dad sat back in his chair. "She thinks you're in love with Emma." His eyes searched my face. "Are you in love with Emma?"

I pushed my chair back and stood from the table. "I don't really feel like having this conversation right now."

"Logan." Dad reached out and grabbed my arm as I walked past him, stopping me in my tracks. "Can I give you some fatherly advice?"

"I would prefer it if you didn't."

"Well, too bad, I'm going to give it to you anyway." He

smiled. "Girls like Emma are hard to find. If you *do* have feelings for her, then you need to tell her."

I was getting sick of everyone telling me that. Yanking my arm out of his grasp, I snapped, "You're forgetting the fact that she currently hates my guts."

"Then you need to do whatever you can to change that," he said, as if it were the easiest thing in the world to do.

"Yeah, I'll get right on that," I said, turning to leave the kitchen. However, I only made it a few feet before I stopped, as a nagging question suddenly popped into my head. One that I needed an honest answer to.

"Dad?" I said, my back still to him.

"Yeah?"

I spun around. "Do you think Mom would be disappointed in me? With how I turned out?" I asked softly.

Dad's eyes widened, his jaw dropping slightly. "What? Of course, not. Why would you even ask that?"

I didn't tell him that Emma was the one who'd put the thought into my head. Instead, I shrugged. "I don't know," I mumbled, averting my gaze to the floor.

I heard the scraping of chair legs against tile as my father stood. "Logan, your mother would be proud of you and of how well you've turned out. She'd probably be *surprised*, considering I've been the one raising you, but I think she'd be mostly proud." The corners of his mouth turned up in a smile. "There's nothing to be disappointed in. You're smart, you're well-liked, you're good-looking. You've stayed out of trouble, for the most part. You're well-adjusted. You've got a good head on your shoulders. Do you need me to keep going?"

I shook my head as a lump began to form in my throat. "I don't want to feel this way about Emma," I said, the lump quickly beginning to dissolve. "I don't want to tell her how I feel because if I do, and she feels the same way, I'm just going to end up hurting her. I already have."

"Logan—" Dad reached out to place a hand on my shoulder, but I dodged him.

"I'm going up to my room," I muttered, turning around and leaving the kitchen.

I had so many thoughts swirling around my head that I didn't even realize I'd made it up the stairs until I was in my bedroom with the door shut behind me.

The words I had just spoken to my father began to sink in and I realized how true they were. What the hell was I doing? Wanting to confess my feelings to a girl who would be better off without me? Dad was right. A girl like Emma was hard to find and she deserved somebody a lot better than me. Better than Justin. Better than Matt, even.

If I truly loved her, I needed to make things right. I needed to undo my mistakes.

Starting with going back to the beginning. To what started this all.

I was going to find Emma her real Number 7.

Chapter 31

EMMA

Logan: Emma can we talk?

Logan: Please? That video is not what u think it is.

I had read and re-read Logan's last two texts about a hundred times since he'd sent them to me last night. And every time, my thumb lingered over the keyboard, itching to type out a reply.

But I couldn't bring myself to do it. Not yet, anyway. I kept replaying the video in my head—and on my phone—and every time, it just made me feel worse. Because hearing his words never hurt any less.

With a sigh, I tossed my phone onto my bed and turned back to the bookshelf in front of me. I'd been working on my book organizing project since nine o'clock this morning and two hours later, I was almost done with it. Which, while exciting, was also disheartening. After I was done with that project, what did I have left? Besides my debilitating fear of flying, there were two major reasons I chose to skip the Florida trip with Chloe and Sophia: I wanted to organize my book collection, and I wanted to meet, and fall in love with, my perfect match.

And now I was almost done with the former, while the latter…well…you know how that turned out.

I picked up the last book from the floor. This was it. After I placed this on the shelf, the project would be complete. It was so anti-climactic. I'd had nearly an entire year-long build-up for this and it was done in two hours. Now, I had nothing left to do with my time.

Unless I wanted to come up with *another* way to organize my collection. Like, I could go really wild and crazy and organize by the colors of the spines, in alphabetical order by color—

My thoughts were interrupted by a knocking on the front door downstairs and I was thankful for that. I was becoming dangerously close to spiraling out of control with this whole organizing thing. But I was desperate. I was bored.

Placing the last book on the shelf, I took one wistful glance around my room, and then headed downstairs.

I had no idea who would be knocking on the door at eleven o'clock in the morning, seeing as though both of my parents were at work, but I fully planned on peeking out the side window first to see who it was. If I didn't recognize the knocker, I would just pretend I wasn't home.

I didn't like to answer the door to strangers.

In the back of my mind, I wondered if maybe it were Logan standing on the porch, hoping I would answer the door so he could talk to me. I didn't know how I felt about that prospect. Part of me didn't want it to be him because I wasn't sure I was ready to talk to him just yet. The other part of me, however, *wanted* it to be him so I could hear his side of the story, forgive him, and then go back to the way things were before yesterday. You know, like hanging out together. Making out together…

I closed my eyes tightly as I shook my head, trying to get rid of that thought. *No, Emma, you do not want to make out with Logan again. Logan is a jerk who doesn't like you. And you don't like him, remember? Get over it. Move on.*

The person on the other side of the door knocked again, breaking me out of my fog and reminding me to look out the window to see who was out there. Pulling the curtain aside slightly, I saw right away it wasn't Logan.

It was Riley.

Confused, I swung open the door to reveal the last person, besides Logan, that I wanted to see at the moment.

"Riley," I said, my voice tight.

"Hi, Emma!" she said brightly, flashing me a grin. "Can I come in?"

Even though she asked, she didn't wait for a response. Instead, she brushed past me through the doorway and stepped into the foyer.

"Yeah, sure, come right in," I said dryly, shutting the door behind her.

Riley stopped and glanced around. "Nice house. It looks a lot like Logan's."

It irritated me that she knew what the inside of Logan's house looked like. Crossing my arms over my chest, I said, "That's because our dads had these houses built around the same time and they decided to go with a similar floor plan."

"Ah, I see."

I eyed her curiously. I was pretty sure she hadn't come over just to see what my house looked like. So why *had* she come over?

As if she could read my thoughts, she answered my question. "Look, Emma, I was wondering if maybe we could engage in some girl talk?"

Engage in girl talk? This was beyond weird. Riley and I had barely said anything to each other since she'd arrived up here; she'd been more focused on Logan than anyone else. So, why did she suddenly want to talk to me, girl-to-girl?

"Okay…" I said slowly.

"Great." Riley smiled briefly before it faded. "Okay, I'm just going to cut right to it. I heard you're going on a date tonight with Justin, and I'm here to strongly encourage you *not* to."

I blinked. "Excuse me?"

"Don't go out with Justin tonight."

I shook my head in confusion. "How do you even know about my date with Justin tonight?"

"Logan was in my bedroom last night when Matt called and told him."

It was like I'd been punched in the gut. Logan had been in Riley's bedroom last night? I suddenly felt sick to my stomach. There was only one reason why he would have been in her bedroom…

"That's it!" she exclaimed, pointing to my face. "That's the look!"

I narrowed my eyes at her. "Look? What look?"

"The look of jealousy I was telling Logan about." Her lips curled into a smug smile. "I knew I wasn't just imagining it."

"Riley, what are you talking about?" I swallowed as a wave of bile began rising to my throat.

Logan was in Riley's bedroom last night. Did they—

"Just so you know," she said, "nothing happened. *I* wanted something to happen, but he politely turned me down."

I let out a breath and the bile instantly dissipated. "Seriously?" How—or *why*—would Logan turn down a girl like Riley? It made no sense…

"Yes, seriously." Riley ran a hand through her perfectly straight hair. "Not one of my finer moments, but I'll survive. I didn't come here to talk about Logan rejecting me, though. I came here to talk you out of going out with Justin tonight."

"Why?" I asked. "Why do you care?"

"*I* don't," she said. "But Logan is beside himself with worry about you going on that date. He thinks Justin is bad news and just wants to use you for…well, you know."

That wasn't a surprise. I didn't need Logan to have Riley tell me that. I wasn't stupid. I knew all about Justin's reputation. The whole town knew about Justin's reputation. But I wasn't going out with him because I wanted to, or because I thought I could be the one to change his bad boy ways. I was going out with him to annoy Logan.

Mission accomplished, apparently.

"Tell Logan he doesn't need to worry," I said. "I'm a big girl and I can take care of myself."

"I'm sure you can, but Emma, do you even like Justin?"

I couldn't help but snort at that question. Did I like Justin? Of course not! I barely knew the guy. And sure, he was hot, but I was pretty sure that was where his good qualities ended.

"That's what I thought." Riley smirked. "You're just going on this date to get back at Logan, aren't you?"

What would make her think that? Unless she knew about everything. The kiss. The video. "N-no," I stammered.

"Oh, sweetie." Riley placed her hands on my shoulders and looked me straight in the eye. "Just *agreeing* to go on that date was enough to get back at Logan, if that's what you were going for. This is destroying him."

My breath hitched in my throat. "W-why do you say that?"

Riley sighed. "Sorry, I'm not going to spell it out for you. You're a smart girl. I'm sure you can figure it out on your own."

Letting go of me, she took a step back. "You should go talk to him. Give him a chance to explain himself." She paused and then added, "You may not think so right now, but Logan is a good guy."

She moved toward the front door and then turned around. "No matter what, just please reconsider your date with Justin tonight, alright?" And with that, she let herself out of the house.

Well, that was weird.

So, nothing happened between Logan and Riley yesterday? I couldn't help but feel overjoyed at the thought, but then I chastised myself for feeling that way.

Why did I even care?

I kept asking myself that question as I walked to the kitchen. After finishing my organization project, I deserved to take a break with a good book and an iced tea by the pool. The last thing I needed right now was to obsess over what Riley had just told me. Sure, nothing happened between her and Logan, but he'd still been in her bedroom. Why? Why had he spent the entire day with her instead of me?

Oh, that's right, I had shunned him. I'd slammed the door in his face. I'd told him…

I'd told him his mother would be disappointed in him.

That was, quite possibly, the bitchiest thing I had ever said to anyone in my life. And I hadn't even meant it; I just said it in the heat of the moment. No wonder he spent the day hanging out with Riley. She would never say something that terrible to him.

I was so distracted by my thoughts, I wasn't even aware I had poured myself a glass of iced tea and had placed the pitcher back in the refrigerator. With a shrug, I grabbed the glass and my worn-out copy of *Pride and Prejudice* and went out the back door to the deck.

As soon as I took a seat on the lounge chair next to the pool, I removed my phone from my pocket and stared at it.

Call him. Text him. Follow Riley's advice. Do something, *Emma!*

My pulse quickened as my thumb hovered over the power button, as I considered turning on my phone and calling him.

You can do this. Just find out why he said what he said, and if you don't like his answer, then you at least get to slam the door in his face again! You'll enjoy that!

I smiled at the thought. I *would* like that. A lot.

With my mind made up, I turned on my phone at the same time it chirped at me. I had received a text.

From Logan.

Logan: Can I come over? I have something 2 give u I think u will like.

That instantly intrigued me. What could he possibly have to give me that I would like? Biting my lip, I started to type back when another text came through.

Logan: Before u say no, I promise u won't b disappointed.

And then immediately after, another one:

Logan: Please? I'll b quick. I promise.

With a sigh, I began to move my thumbs across the screen, typing out a reply.

Me: Ok. Fine. Come on over. I'm out back, by the pool.

My pulse quickened as I tapped "send". What had I done? I wasn't ready to talk to Logan. Not yet. Or was I? I didn't know. But now, I was stuck talking to him no matter what, unless I quickly ran inside the house and locked all the doors and windows—

"Hey."

I jumped at the sudden sound of a voice behind me. Swiveling my head around, I saw that Logan had taken the shortcut to my backyard by jumping over the fence.

His signature move.

"God, Logan," I breathed, "you scared me."

"Sorry," he said, giving me a half-guilty, half-heart-melting smile.

Averting my gaze, I stood from the lounge chair and stared down at the ground. "I hate it when you jump the fence like that."

"I know," he said, strolling over to me. "But not to worry, that was probably the last time I'll ever be doing that."

Curiously, I glanced at him, trying to figure out what he meant by that.

When our eyes met, I had to fight to keep butterflies from taking flight inside my stomach. Dang it. Why did he always have to look so good? Even in a stupid t-shirt and khaki shorts, he was infuriatingly gorgeous. Almost to the point where it made me forget for one second why I was mad at him.

"What do you have for me?" I asked, point-blank. I figured I might as well cut to the chase. The quicker we got this over with, the quicker he would leave, and the quicker I would stop recalling what happened the other night, in the front of his dad's pickup truck…

"Can we sit and talk first?" he asked, motioning to the patio table.

I nodded as we both walked over to it and took a seat across from each other.

After a moment of uncomfortable silence, Logan cleared his throat and said, "Thank you for letting me come over. I know I'm probably the last person in the world you want to see right now."

I nodded again, but this time I could feel the corners of my mouth threatening to turn upward into a small smile. The thing that sucked, and one of the main reasons I had been actively ignoring all of Logan's texts and calls, was that Logan was nearly impossible to stay mad at. Sure, I'd spent the last seventeen years of my life being constantly mad at him, but after the last couple of weeks, I realized I was tired of hating him. Tired of being mad at him. Because at the end of the day, Riley was right.

Logan was a good guy.

But it still didn't excuse what he'd said about me in the video.

"What do you want to talk about?" I asked, running my hand nervously across the table's grainy surface.

He took a deep breath and let it out. "Everything. There's so much I want to say to you, Emma."

Once again, I had to look away.

"Starting with saying I'm sorry," he continued. "And assuring you that nothing I said in that video accurately describes what I actually think of you."

That was a start. "Why did you say it all, then?" I asked quietly.

Logan sighed again as he dragged a hand down his face. "Honestly? I have no idea. Or, at least, I had no idea at the time."

"And now?" I asked. "Do you know now?"

"Yes," he said without any hesitation.

I stared at him in anticipation, waiting for him to elaborate.

"And…?"

He lowered his gaze to the table. "I don't know, Emma. Those words…they just came out. When Matt told me he was planning on asking you out, it was a gut reaction."

I swallowed. "Why?"

"Why?" he repeated, returning his gaze to me. "Because I like you, Emma."

My jaw dropped as my heart practically leapt out of my chest. I was about to ask him to repeat himself, but I didn't have to.

"I like you…a *lot*. And I'm not talking about the you I tried to get you to be. Although, that you is pretty great, too." He paused to smile. "But I like the you you've always been: smart, stubborn, witty, annoying." He paused again. "Beautiful."

I couldn't breathe. What, exactly, was happening here? Was Logan…confessing feelings for me? Impossible. Logan didn't like me. He had never liked me, just like I had never liked him. Our lifelong relationship had been based on a mutual dislike of one another. It was what made our relationship so great—the fact that we had no relationship at all.

But that kiss the other night…that had changed things.

No, maybe it went even further back than that. Maybe—

"Emma," he continued, "these past couple of weeks have made me see you in a different light. They've made me realize that I *really* enjoy hanging out with you. Even when you're hyperventilating on a Ferris wheel or dragging me through an art museum. Ever since we started spending time together, I haven't wanted to hang out with anyone else. Not with my friends, not with Riley. Emma, I just want to be around *you*.

"I feel like I'm a better person around you. Or, at least, you make me feel like I *want* to be a better person. And that's…that's why I said what I said to Matt on that video. Because I was jealous that not only did *you* like *him*, but that he liked you back. As soon as he told me he was going to ask you out, I knew I would never stand a chance with you. So, I said those horrible things, hoping it would change Matt's mind. But what that video *didn't* show was that right after Grace stopped filming, I came to my senses and told Matt that I was just messing with him. That I thought you two would be good together."

I sat there, perfectly still, frozen by what he was telling me. I was hearing his words, but I was having a hard time processing them.

Logan likes me? Logan likes me...

"And as for what I said about Rachel blackmailing me to hang out with you," he went on to say, "it's true. She did, and that's why I came up with this idea to help you get Matt. But Emma, it's not why I continued spending time with you. I could have just bribed Matt to ask you out, but I didn't. Because I genuinely wanted to help you. I don't expect you to believe that, but it's true."

I could feel tears beginning to well up in my eyes. "Logan," I managed to croak, but he wasn't finished just yet.

"And this sort of leads me to why I really wanted to come over here; what I wanted to give to you." He reached around and pulled something out of his back pocket. An envelope.

He placed it on the table in front of him, keeping it under his hand. He stared at it and said, "I also want to apologize for lying on that compatibility test. That's how all of this started in the first place and I am truly sorry for that. You were right, what you said. It was selfish of me. I never once stopped and thought about how me lying on that test could impact somebody else. But it did impact somebody—*you*. I stole your opportunity for a summer romance with your perfect match, and

I don't blame you for hating me for that. But I'm here to make it all up to you. I'm here to give you what you deserve. What you should have gotten in the first place."

My eyes lowered to the envelope. "What is that?" I asked, my voice barely above a whisper.

Logan smiled. "My redemption, hopefully." He pushed it over to my side of the table. "I like you—hell, maybe I've liked you all along—but I know I'm not the right guy for you. I don't deserve you. I've been rotten to you our whole lives and for no reason other than I'm a jerk. But Emma…" His eyes searched my face, and I wondered what he was looking for. "Justin doesn't deserve you, either. And honestly, neither does Matt. I know you're in love with him, and he *is* a great guy, but you two aren't destined to be together. He's not the great love of your life." He tapped his finger on top of the envelope. "*He* is."

My eyes widened as I glanced back at the envelope. I was so confused, still reeling from everything Logan had just said to me. I didn't know what to say. What to do.

"What are you talking about?" I asked, finally finding my voice. "Who is *he*?"

"Your real Number 7."

I shook my head slowly back and forth. "I don't…I don't get it."

Logan sat back in his chair. "I decided last night there was only one way to make all this up to you: I had to go back to the beginning. To the test. So, I called a few people and got the contact information of one of the Computer Club geeks—Alex Porter. I went over to his house and explained everything to him and asked if he would run your test results against the algorithm again—without *my* test in there to screw everything up, of course. He was hesitant at first, but a few Andrew Jacksons later, and he was on board. He ran the tests again, and that envelope—" he pointed to it, "contains the name of the guy you *should* have been matched up with."

I could feel his eyes on me, as he waited for my reaction. I wasn't sure what he was expecting. Did he want me to jump up and down, cheering? Did he want me to thank him profusely? I wasn't even sure how I felt about all of this. One minute he was telling me he liked me and the next he was encouraging me to go be with someone else.

And boys thought *girls* were confusing?

"Logan," I began, but once again, he interjected.

"I don't know who it is," he said. "I told Alex I didn't want to know. But *he* saw the name, and good news: he happens to know for a fact that this guy's match didn't end up working out for him. But for now, he hasn't been notified of his true match. Alex figured he wouldn't let him know just yet, that way you could see the results first and if you weren't happy with them, this guy doesn't ever have to know. No harm, no foul. But if you *are* happy, then…" He sighed and ran a hand through his hair. "Then Alex will notify him and you two can spend the rest of the summer together. Fortunately, you'll still have plenty of time together before school starts back up in the fall."

He pushed his chair back and stood. "I know this doesn't make up for everything, but I hope it's at least a start." He took a step back. "Take care, Emma."

With a small, sad smile, he turned and walked away. I opened my mouth to call after him, to stop him, but no sound came out.

I didn't know what to do. I had never been so conflicted about anything before in my entire life. Part of me was elated to know that Logan liked me. He *liked* me. But another part of me really wanted to know whose name was in that envelope.

This was the main reason I skipped the Florida trip. To spend the summer with my soulmate. And Logan had just delivered that opportunity to me.

I frowned as I watched him turn the corner around the side of the house.

What are you waiting for? Go after him! He likes you! You like him, too!

I stood with the intent of following him, but my feet remained planted firmly on the ground, not allowing me to move. My eyes fell to the envelope. Inside of it was the name of my perfect match. The guy I was most likely destined to be with. At least, for the summer.

There was no way I could pass up this opportunity. Just because I'd spent some time with Logan and we were getting along now, that didn't mean *we* were meant to be together...right? If he had answered every question on that test honestly, he would have literally been the last person that algorithm would have ever matched me up with.

And then none of this would have happened.

Chewing on my bottom lip, I swiped the envelope off the table.

I knew what I had to do.

Chapter 32

LOGAN

I was an idiot.

What the hell was I thinking? Confessing to Emma that I liked her? And then handing her an envelope containing the name of another guy who was perfect for her?

Moron.

And then, I failed to plead with her not to go on her date with Justin, nor did I even attempt to grill her on where they were going.

Imbecile.

Oh, and then I just walked away, not even giving her a chance to respond to my confession. *"Oh, hey, Emma, I really like you. Okay, bye."*

Fool.

Not that I wanted to hear her response, anyway. The girl hated me. And rightfully so.

Jerk.

"Dude, are you okay?"

The sound of Matt's voice broke me out of my loop of internal self-hatred, and I was thankful for the interruption. Blinking over at him, I said, "Yeah, I'm fine. Why do you ask?"

"Because you keep getting killed," he replied, pointing to the TV screen. "In the same spot. Because you haven't moved from it in like two minutes."

"Oh, right," I grumbled. With my thumb, I pushed the left

stick on the controller to move forward in the game…and immediately got killed again by some punk to my right. "Whatever." I dropped the controller onto the couch beside me, crossed my arms over my chest, and scowled at the TV screen.

Matt and I had been playing video games in his living room for a couple of hours now. After I left Emma's house, I went straight to Matt's, hoping that spending some quality time with my best friend would take my mind off everything.

No such luck.

With a sigh, Matt paused the game and turned to me. "You did the right thing, Logan."

"I know. But it doesn't mean I have to like it."

"Hey, you had your chance to tell her how you feel—"

"I *did* tell her."

"Yeah, you told her, and then you handed her the name of her soulmate in an envelope. You should have just told her you loved her and then kissed her."

"Easier said than done," I mumbled. "Obviously, she doesn't like me back. If she did, she would have followed me when I left her house. She would have called me by now. She would have done *something*. She didn't do anything, and that's fine, but now I'm freaking out not knowing if she's still going on her date with Justin tonight."

"Why don't you call Justin and ask him?" Matt said with a shrug.

It was a great idea. Why hadn't I thought of that? Taking my phone out of my pocket, I dialed Justin's number.

He picked up on the second ring. "Logan, my man, what's up?"

I tapped my fingers nervously against the arm of the loveseat.

"Hey, Justin," I said casually. "I heard you're going out with

Emma tonight?"

He chuckled. "Yeah, I *was*, until she called up about an hour ago and cancelled on me."

My eyebrows shot up in surprise. "She did?"

"Yep. Girl sure knows how to bust a guy's ego. Brutal."

I couldn't help but smile. *That's my girl.*

Except, she wasn't.

"Why are you asking?"

"Um…" My voice trailed off as I realized I had no good excuse to be asking Justin about his dating life.

"Ah, I get it," he said with a chuckle. "I'm stepping on your toes, aren't I?"

I suppressed a groan. Even *Justin* knew how I felt about Emma?

"Dude, I thought you two were just friends," he continued, taking my silence as confirmation. "If I had known you liked her, I never would have asked her out."

We both knew that was a total lie. Justin didn't care who liked who, or who was dating who. If he wanted a girl, he did whatever he had to do to get her. I could count on more than two hands how many relationships he'd broken up since Freshman year.

I didn't know what to say, but that didn't matter. He wasn't done yet.

"Well, maybe you're in luck. She gave me the whole 'it's not you, it's me' spiel and then said there was someone else."

A tiny glimmer of hope ignited within me before I realized that someone else wasn't me.

It was whoever was in that envelope.

"She didn't happen to say who that someone else was, did she?"

"Sorry, man," Justin said, not sounding sorry at all. "Are we done talking about my rejection? I've got stuff to do."

I cleared my throat. "Yeah, sorry, I just—"

The line went dead.

I turned off my phone and sighed.

"So? Is their date still on?" Matt asked.

"Nope," I said, dropping my head back and staring up at the ceiling.

"That's a good thing, right?"

"Yep."

"But you don't seem happy about that."

"I am," I assured him. I leaned forward and buried my face in my hands. "But she told him there was someone else."

"Oh yeah? Maybe she was talking about you."

I removed my hands to look at him. "She wasn't. If she had been, she would have called me, or texted me."

Matt shrugged. "Not necessarily…"

"She knows how I feel about her," I said. "I laid it all out there for her. If I were that someone else, I would know by now."

She was probably meeting the guy right now. They were probably at Dream Bean, sipping on iced teas and discussing their favorite Jane Austen books. His was probably *Pride and Prejudice*, just like hers. Because, you know, they were perfect for each other. They had everything in common. That's why the stupid algorithm paired them up.

Matt gave me a sympathetic half-smile. "Hey, why don't we go somewhere and do something?"

I blinked over at him. "Like what?"

"I don't know. Like go on a road trip or something. Or go see a movie. Or anything, really. Whatever will get your mind off Emma."

At this point, nothing was going to get my mind off Emma.

I couldn't stop wondering who her Mr. Right might be. I hadn't lied to her; I really didn't look to see who he was, but now I was regretting that decision as I racked my brain, trying to think of what guy at our school could possibly be worthy enough to be with her.

I came up blank.

"I don't know…" I said finally, not convinced I wanted to do anything but go home and sulk.

"How about we go to the beach?" Matt suggested. "Might do you some good. There will be plenty of eye candy in bikinis there to distract you."

I held back a snort. Who cared about random girls in bikinis? I'd seen Emma in one and there was no way any girl at the beach would compare.

Still, Matt was right. It would probably do me some good to get out and try to clear my head of everything.

"Okay, let's do it," I said, jumping up from the couch.

Matt set down his controller and turned off the TV. "Great." He tossed me his keys. "Go get the AC running and I'll be out in a sec."

I nodded as I left the living room and headed for the front door.

The first thing I noticed upon exiting Matt's house was that Emma's car was missing from the driveway across the street. Presumably, she had taken it to go meet with her new Number 7. Taking a slow, deep breath, I walked over to Matt's Jeep, opened the door, turned the vehicle on, and cranked up the AC as requested. Since it felt like a sauna in there, I chose to shut the door and wait outside of it.

Where is Emma? I couldn't stop myself from thinking. *And who is she with? Why didn't I look in that envelope? Why didn't I tell that nerd to give me the guy's name?* I lightly banged the back of my head against the side of the jeep. *Stop it, Logan. It's over. It doesn't matter now. This is none of your business.*

But I had to know. Taking out my phone, I dialed Alex's number. Surely, he would tell me. He would have told me last night, if I'd wanted him to.

After a few rings, I was brought to his voicemail. Swearing under my breath, I ended the call without leaving a message. Okay. Who else would know this information? Besides Emma, that is.

Chloe and Sophia. Of course! There was no way she wouldn't have called her best friends and told them about this. Turning my phone back on, I scrolled through my contacts, hoping to see either of their names in the list. Sure enough, Chloe's number was in there. I couldn't remember ever asking for her number in the past, but I had half the school programmed into my phone, and couldn't remember how I'd gotten their numbers, either.

I tapped on her name and listened in anticipation for her to pick up. I only had to wait two rings.

"Logan?" she greeted me slowly. She sounded confused— and rightfully so. Even though her number was in my phone, this was the first time I'd ever called her.

"Hey, Chloe," I said casually, as if we were the best of friends who talked on the phone every day. "What's up?"

"Um...not much..." she replied. I heard her whisper something to someone in the background, but I couldn't hear what she said. "Why are you calling me?"

No sense beating around the bush. "Have either you or Sophia talked to Emma since yesterday?"

"Maybe. Why?"

My eyes flickered over to Matt, who had just walked out the front door. He glanced at me curiously as I held up a finger to indicate I'd only be a minute.

"Did she tell you I gave her the name of her real Number 7?"

"Maybe. Why?" she repeated.

I pinched the bridge of my nose as I tamped down a sudden, intense feeling of annoyance. "Did she happen to tell you who it was?"

"Maybe. Why?"

"Oh my God, Chloe," I muttered through clenched teeth. I took a deep breath and held it for a moment before letting it back out. "You're not going to give me any information, are you?"

There was a long pause on her end. "Honestly, Logan, why should I? You hurt my best friend."

"I *love* your best friend," I blurted out before I could stop myself.

Another pause on her end. "Wait, what?"

Interesting. Did Emma not tell her friends that part? The part where I told her I liked her? Why would she leave that out?

"I'm in love with Emma," I said, resting my head against the Jeep again and staring up at the blue sky above me.

"Whoa," Chloe breathed. I heard her whisper something to someone again before saying, "Okay, Logan, I'm putting you on speaker."

Great, just what I needed. With a sigh, I said, "Hello, Sophia."

"You're in love with our girl?" she said in response, cutting right to the chase.

I shut my eyes tightly and nodded. "Yeah, I am."

"And now you want us to tell you who her real Number 7 is?"

"Yes, I do." I rolled my eyes at Matt, who was still giving me a quizzical look.

"Logan, we don't know who it is," Chloe said.

I pushed off the side of the Jeep. "You just said a minute ago that she *did* tell you who it was."

"I lied. Emma called last night and told us you handed her an envelope with the name of her real match in it, but she wouldn't tell us who it was. I'm not even sure *she* knew who it was at the time she called us."

"But she didn't tell you anything else?"

Like how I'd confessed my feelings for her?

"No," Chloe replied. "Why? Is there more to the story?"

"Apparently not," I mumbled. "Thanks anyway, guys. Sorry to bother you."

"Logan—" Sophia began, but I hung up before she could continue.

"Dude." Matt stalked over to me and snatched my phone out of my hand.

"Hey," I protested, "what the hell?"

"I'm confiscating your phone for the rest of the day," he said, placing it in his pocket. He knew there was no way I'd reach in there to grab it back.

"Why?"

"Because if I don't, you're either just going to check it every three seconds to see if Emma has texted you, or you're going to call every single one of your contacts and ask them if they know who Emma's mystery man is. Neither one is healthy and neither one is going to get your mind off Emma."

He was right. "Okay, fine," I grumbled as I made my way to the passenger side of the Jeep.

"Oh, by the way, there's a party at Jackson's house later. We should go."

I groaned. Jackson—the jerk who pushed me and Emma into the lake at Justin's party. Why were there so many parties going on around town lately? Didn't these kids have anything better to do with their time? Like, couldn't they just read a book or something?

Oh, God. Emma had ruined me. I was now thinking that reading was a preferable activity to partying.

"That's fine," I found myself saying, even though the idea of attending yet another party was about as appealing as…well, the idea of reading a book.

"You'll get through this," Matt said as he opened the door and got into the vehicle. "There are plenty of other fish in the sea."

"Yeah," I agreed glumly as I climbed into the passenger seat.

Sure, there were a lot of other girls in the world. In our town, even. The problem was, though, I didn't want any of them. I wanted Emma.

She just didn't want me.

***

"Oh, man, you have got to try the punch." Matt held out a red plastic cup for me to take, but I politely pushed his hand away from me. An hour into the party, he was already buzzed, and now he was quickly working his way toward wasted.

Matt and I ended up having quite the Bro's Day Out. After spending a couple of hours at the beach, we went to Rodeo Roy's for a bite to eat. After that, we went bowling, went to see a movie, and now we were at Jackson Rowe's party. While it was great to spend the time with my best friend, who I'd barely seen since school let out, I was both mentally and physically exhausted from our day together.

"No thanks," I said. "I'm apparently the designated driver now."

Matt laughed. "Whoops, sorry about that. I wasn't thinking."

"It's okay." It really was. When it came to drinking, I could take it or leave it. I was often a casual drinker at parties. I never got drunk because I didn't like to let my guard down around Grace. I didn't trust her. Besides, she *did* like getting drunk at parties, so I was already used to being the designated driver.

I glanced down at my watch. It was a little after eleven. If Matt had it his way, we'd still be here for another two hours at least, and that thought made me want to go bang my head against the nearest wall.

"Hey, you thinking of leaving soon?" I asked him as he took a swig from the cup he'd just offered to me.

He shook his head. "We just got here."

"Yeah, like two hours ago."

"What's the rush?" He finished off the rest of the punch and tossed the empty cup onto the floor with all the others.

I ran a hand through my hair. "I'm just not feeling it."

He studied me for a second before saying, "Man, you've really got it bad, don't you?"

I nodded. He was referring to Emma, of course. "You've done a great job trying to distract me, but nothing's working. I just keep picturing her out with whoever was in that envelope and it's driving me crazy. What if he's not a nice guy? Like, sure, they have stuff in common, but what if he's also a creep? What if he tries putting the moves on her and won't take no for an answer. What if—"

"Logan." Matt put his hand out to stop me from talking. "Stop freaking out about this. Emma is a big girl, she can take care of herself. Besides, I'm sure the guy is nothing but a perfect gentleman, who will treat her with nothing but the utmost respect. She probably had the time of her life with him today..."

His voice trailed off as he saw the expression on my face, which I'm sure mimicked that of a kicked puppy.

"I want to go home," I muttered.

Matt gave me a sympathetic half-smile. "I was kind of planning on staying a couple more hours, but here—" He reached into his pocket and pulled out his keys. "Why don't you take my Jeep? I'll hitch a ride home with someone else."

I glanced around the room and had a hard time finding somebody I would deem sober enough to get behind the wheel. "How about this? I'll come back for you later. Just text me when you're ready to leave."

"That works," Matt said with a grin. "Oh, yeah, before I forget." He reached back into his pocket and pulled out my phone.

"Thanks," I said, taking it from him. "Have fun."

"Oh, I will," he said. He averted his gaze to a redhead who was standing on the other side of the living room, smiling seductively over at him. I vaguely recognized her as a sophomore who went to our school. A cheerleader, I think.

I briefly admired his ability to move on so fast from one girl to another, but then I remembered he was never in love with Emma. He just thought it would be fun to date her, nothing more. He had nothing to move on *from*. His heart wasn't broken like mine was.

I gave him a slap on the back before saying goodbye and making my way through the crowd, toward the front door.

After climbing into the Jeep, I decided to take the long way home. I always loved driving at night in the summertime. Windows down, radio blasting. I figured tonight would be a good night to just go for a drive, to clear my head. So, that's exactly what I did. I drove all over town. Past Funland Park. Past Lover's Lookout. Past the art museum. Past everywhere I'd spent any time with Emma this summer. And once I realized that's what I was doing, I immediately drove home.

I pulled up to my house at around quarter to midnight. I was pleased to note that not only was Emma's car parked safely in her driveway, but all the lights were off in her house.

She was probably fast asleep in her bed, already dreaming about her new boyfriend.

Scowling at the thought, I got out of the vehicle and locked it before heading inside the house.

As soon as I stepped into the foyer, I pulled out my phone to make sure the volume was turned up all the way. I didn't want to risk not getting Matt's text or call when he was ready to leave the party.

When the screen lit up, I froze immediately. I had received a text. Two hours ago.

From Emma.

Emma: Midnight. Meet me under the stars.

My heart began to pound against my ribcage. What was this cryptic message? Did she want to talk to me about something? And if so, what? Did she want to thank me in person for handing her soulmate to her?

I glanced at the time on my phone. It wasn't midnight yet, so that was good at least. But what if she had been expecting me to respond during the last two hours? And because I hadn't, due to the fact Matt had my phone, what if she had decided not to meet with me after all?

And where were we supposed to meet, anyway? *Under the stars* could have literally meant anywhere on the planet.

Except…

There was one particular place she could be referring to…

The place where we fell asleep together. Under the stars.

The abandoned lot at the end of our street.

I quickly ran back out of the house. For a moment, I contemplated taking my car to get there faster, but I didn't want to wake the neighborhood with the roaring of my Mustang. Besides, I didn't have to go very far.

So, I kept running. I ran as fast as I could toward the end of the street, being careful not to trip over any rocks or twigs along the way. Seeing as though there were no streetlights to help light my path, I was practically running blind. But I didn't care. I needed to get there, and I needed to get there fast.

I made it there in less than a minute, which meant I had about nine minutes left to spare. I stopped at the end of the driveway to catch my breath and calm my nerves. *Please be the right spot…*

Turning on my phone's flash, I slowly began my trek up the long driveway. When I got to the end of it a few seconds later, I knew immediately I was in the right place.

Emma was sitting cross-legged on a blanket in the middle of the empty lot. In her lap was an open book, and in one of her hands was a flashlight, shining down on the pages. I couldn't help but smile at how adorable she looked. I almost didn't want to disturb her.

Clearing my throat, I said, "I take it I'm in the right place?"

She jumped slightly at the sound of my voice as she pointed the flashlight at me. "You're early," she said, pushing herself up from the ground. "I wasn't sure you were going to make it. I never heard anything back from you."

"Yeah, sorry about that. Matt had my phone all day."

She arched an eyebrow. "Why?"

To keep me from obsessing over you. "It's a long story," I said with a smile. I glanced up at the sky. "You're lucky I knew where to go. There aren't any stars out tonight."

She followed my gaze. "I know. When I sent that text, I didn't realize how cloudy it was."

We fell into an awkward silence as our eyes met.

"So," I said slowly. "Why did you want to meet me here?"

She bit her lower lip as she started toward me. She stopped when she was only a few feet away and folded her arms tightly over her chest.

"You're a jerk," she said, "and I hate you."

I inhaled sharply as my heart sank in my chest. *This* was why she wanted to meet me here? To tell me how much she hated me? What, did her perfect match turn out to be a perfect loser, and now she was blaming me for that, too?

Unbelievable.

I instantly went into defensive mode and crossed my own arms over my chest. "Did you seriously ask me to come here just to tell me things I already knew?"

She narrowed her eyes into a glare. "I'm serious, Logan. You're the worst. You're selfish. You're immature. You're mean."

"Okay," I said, throwing my hands up in the air and backing away from her. "Look, you're entitled to feel this way about me, and you're even entitled to tell me all about it, but can this wait for another time? I'm just really not in the mood right now."

You've already destroyed me enough for one day.

She shook her head back and forth. "No, this can't wait. I need to get this off my chest. I let you speak your mind earlier, and now it's my turn."

Something in the tone of her voice made me think I really didn't want to hear what she had to say. But she was right. It *was* her turn, whether I liked it or not.

"Fine," I said, defeated. "Go ahead. Tell me all about why you hate me."

She seemed somewhat surprised that I would give in so easily, but I wasn't going to fight it. If she wanted to rip into me about how much I sucked and how much she hated me, I would let her. Maybe it would help me get over her.

If it didn't kill me first.

She slid off her glasses and set them to rest on the top of her head before continuing. "You know, you told me earlier that I make you want to be a better person. Well, you have the opposite effect on me."

I didn't know how to respond to that. "How so?"

"I snuck out of the house again," she said. "And now I'm also trespassing again. And this time, *you* didn't force me into doing either one. I did it all on my own volition. That's not like me, Logan. You've said it yourself in the past: I'm a goody-goody. I follow the rules. But now...I'm breaking the law *and* my parents' rules, and I don't care! In fact, I *like* the way it feels to go against what I'm *supposed* to be doing. It makes me feel..."

"Alive?" I finished for her.

Her eyes locked onto mine. "Yes. Alive."

I ran a hand through my hair and sighed. "Okay, I fail to see what's so wrong about that."

"Of course, you don't," she said, averting her gaze to the ground. "Logan, I've spent my entire life living in a shell, and I like it there. My shell has protected me from everything. It's safe. But somehow, you've managed to crack that shell, and now I feel so exposed, and it scares me. And I hate you for that."

I swallowed hard as a feeling of guilt started to form in the pit of my stomach. "Emma, I'm sorry. That was never my intention."

She poked at the ground with her sneaker before returning her gaze to mine. "Wasn't it? You were trying to change me so that Matt would be interested in me."

"I know, and that was stupid. I get that now." I paused and took a step closer to her. "You of all people shouldn't have to change yourself to get a guy to like you, Emma, because…you're perfect."

Despite the darkness that surrounded us, I could see tears welling up in her eyes, and I feared I had said something wrong.

With a sniffle, she reached into her back pocket and pulled out a piece of paper folded in half.

No, not a piece of paper. An envelope. The one I'd given her earlier.

"You said in the beginning of all this that you thought the compatibility test was stupid. Why did you think that?"

I shrugged. "I don't know. Computers are smart, but they can't possibly decide who truly belongs together. It's all based on an algorithm that just compares answers. Just because two people have a lot in common doesn't mean they're meant to be together. It's why a lot of the matches haven't worked out. Not everything is as black and white as a computer sees it."

"I actually agree," she said, holding out the envelope for me to take. "Here."

I eyed it curiously as I reached out to grab it. "What is

this?" I examined it as soon as it was in my hands, and my breath caught in my throat. "You haven't opened it."

She hasn't opened it…

Her bottom lip quivered slightly as she shook her head. "No, I haven't."

All day long, I'd been obsessing over who this guy might be, wondering if she was out on a date with him, and she still didn't know whose name was in there.

But why not? And why was she giving it back to me?

"I don't understand…" I stared down at it in disbelief.

"I don't want it," she said, her voice shaky. "There's only one name I want to be in that envelope and you had Alex remove it from the database."

My jaw dropped slightly at what she was implying.

She was talking about *me.*

"But," I said numbly, "you just told me you hate me."

"I do," she said, nodding emphatically. "I hate you because somehow…you made me *like* you." She bit her lip. "I like you, Logan. I don't want to, but I do. You may be selfish, immature, and mean, but you are also funny, sweet, and caring, and—"

"Emma," I interrupted, but she kept going like she hadn't even heard me.

"And we have nothing in common, so this makes no sense at all—"

"*Emma.*"

"But I can't stop thinking about you, and I—"

I didn't bother to say her name again. At this point, there was only one way to get her to stop talking.

I leaned forward and kissed her. It was quick. It was simple. It was everything.

Not knowing if this was what she wanted, I pulled away

369

almost immediately, giving her a quizzical look.

Her widened eyes searched my face before finally settling on my mouth. "Logan," she breathed…before throwing her arms around the back of my neck and pressing her lips against mine.

Yes. Instantly, my own arms shot out and wrapped around her waist, lifting her up off the ground slightly as I pulled her as close to me as I possibly could.

It had only been a couple of days since the last time we'd kissed, but it had been far too long. I realized immediately how much I'd missed the warmth of her lips, the taste of her strawberry lip gloss, the smell of her apple shampoo. I'd missed the way she felt in my embrace—soft, warm, *perfect.*

I didn't want to ever let her go.

She whimpered slightly as I deepened the kiss and I almost lost it. Why had I wasted my entire life making this girl miserable when I could have been doing *this* all along instead?

That thought alone was enough to make me hate *myself.*

I'm not sure how long we stood there in our embrace, but by the time we parted, neither of us could breathe.

I rested my forehead against hers while I struggled to regain my composure. My heart was beating a mile a minute, threatening to burst through my ribcage. This was worse than what I'd experienced after our first kiss. Maybe it was because this time, it wasn't practice. This time, it was real.

In an attempt to calm myself down, I did what I do best: I decided to make light of the situation.

"I knew it," I murmured, my lips forming a smirk.

She pulled away slightly, giving me a curious look. "You knew what?"

"I knew you were in love with me," I said.

Emma rolled her eyes. "You did not."

"I did." I flashed her a cocky grin. "You've *always* been in love with me, haven't you?"

She snorted. "Hardly."

"Admit it, Dawson. I saw the way you were looking at me in all those pictures in my mom's scrapbook."

"I was crying in most of those pictures!" she exclaimed.

"Yeah, crying because your love for me was unrequited."

She pushed on my shoulders to try escaping my grasp, but I held on tightly. Quickly realizing her attempt was futile, she gave up the fight and went limp in my arms.

"Maybe it was *you* who was always in love with *me*," she said with a smile.

"Maybe it was." I tucked a strand of hair behind her ear as her smile faltered slightly. "Emma, I'm sorry I lied on that compatibility test, but I would do it all over again in a heart-beat. And maybe that makes me selfish, but I don't care."

Her face fell, and I knew right away I'd said the wrong thing.

Because it *was* selfish of me.

Classic Logan. Selfish to the core.

Glancing down, Emma grabbed the envelope I'd forgotten was still in my hand and took it back.

No…don't change your mind. Not now. Not after that kiss…

"I don't care, either," she said. She held up the envelope and ripped it in half. Then ripped it into thirds. Fourths. Fifths. She kept ripping until it was nothing but a handful of confetti, which she let fall freely to the ground.

"Wow, I really have done a number on you, haven't I?" I asked. "The Emma I knew two weeks ago would have never littered."

With wide eyes, she glanced down at the mess, then back at me.

371

"But she's not completely gone, is she?" I asked with a grin.

"No, she's not." She returned the grin before kneeling onto the ground to pick up all the pieces.

I knelt beside her to help. "Good, because I like her most of all."

The blanket of night hid the blush on her cheeks I figured was probably there. But that was okay. I'd have plenty of opportunities in the future to make her blush.

And I'd make sure to take advantage of every single one.

"Now you'll never know who Number 7 is," I said, grabbing a handful of shredded paper pieces off the grass.

Emma turned her head and eyed me suspiciously. "You didn't put your own name in the envelope, did you?"

Man, I wish I had thought to do that. It would have been pretty funny. Although, I'm sure Emma wouldn't have thought so if she'd opened the envelope, hoping to find her true match, only to see my name in there instead.

"That would have been a brilliant idea," I said with a smirk, "but no. I didn't put my own name in there. I swear."

I couldn't tell if she believed me or not, but she didn't press the issue. Instead, after picking up the last piece, she placed a hand along the side of my face and leaned forward to kiss me lightly on the lips.

My heart fluttered inside my chest.

"I can't wait to tell all my book friends about this," she joked, a small, playful smile tugging at her lips.

I snorted. "Oh my God, Dawson, you are such a dork."

She made a face and gave my shoulder a gentle punch. "You love it, though."

She was right. I did.

More than she could ever know.

Chapter 33

EMMA

"Okay, make a wish!" my mother exclaimed, motioning to the ginormous slice of cake sitting on the table in front of me.

I glanced down at the one lit candle sticking out the top of it and closed my eyes. I had one wish. I had to make sure it something good.

But what was there left to really wish for? My book organization project was not only complete, it was a total success. I was now officially an adult. And I had a pretty awesome boyfriend.

A boyfriend who was currently leaning toward me and whispering in my ear, "If you make your wish about me, I'll make sure it comes true later."

I pushed him away as I felt blood rushing to my cheeks. How dare he make me blush in front of my parents!

I should have expected that, though. Classic Logan.

But they didn't appear to have heard him. If they had, my father probably would have been scowling at him instead of grinning at me.

I was at a loss of what to wish for, so I didn't wish for anything at all. I didn't really believe in that stuff, anyway. Instead, I just blew out the candle and said, "Okay, who's going to help me eat this?"

Even though it was just one slice of cake, it was large enough to feed our entire table of four. Rodeo Roy's was known for their large portions of everything.

When my parents told me they wanted to take me and Logan out for dinner for my birthday, and told me I could choose the restaurant, I didn't even have to think about it. As much as I disliked Rodeo Roy's, I think subconsciously I was sentimental about it. After all, it was the first place Logan and I had eaten at when we started hanging out this summer.

Maybe that made me a dork, but this restaurant now held a special place in my heart.

"What did you wish for, Pumpkin?" Dad asked, cutting off a piece of the cake with his fork and putting it onto his plate.

"She's not supposed to tell anyone, Jake, or it won't come true," Mom informed him, exchanging a glance with me and shaking her head.

I shrugged as I took my own forkful of the cake—chocolate with chocolate frosting, my favorite. "It doesn't matter, I didn't wish for anything." I turned to Logan. "I already have everything I want."

Logan's eyes held mine while he smiled and grabbed my hand under the table. My parents, sitting across from us, both erupted into a simultaneous, "Aww!"

And then out of the corner of my eye, I saw a flash.

"Dad!" I turned my head to glower at him. He was grinning at me from ear-to-ear while holding up his cell phone. "No flash photography, please. Or any photography at all."

"Sorry, couldn't help it," he said, not sounding sorry at all. "You two just looked so sweet there for a moment."

I rolled my eyes. Dad had become so annoying since Logan and I announced our relationship. Logan's dad, too. This was, after all, what they had always wanted—for their two kids to get together and fall in love. It was a dream come true for them. Logan and I often had to wonder if our dads were more excited for our relationship than *we* were.

Mom glanced down at her watch. "Okay, Dad and I have to leave in a few minutes, but first, we have one more present to give you." She reached into her purse, pulled out an envelope and handed it to me.

My eyes widened at the sight of it. Another envelope? What was going to be in this one? I snuck a glance at Logan to see if he maybe knew, but he was avoiding eye contact with me.

Hesitantly, I pulled the envelope closer and opened it.

When I pulled out its contents, I stared down at it in confusion. "It's…a travel brochure. For Florida." I returned my gaze to my parents. "Thanks…it's what I've always wanted?"

Mom and Dad both chuckled softly. "Sweetie, the gift isn't the brochure." She looked at my dad with an expectant look, as if waiting for him to explain it to me.

Clearing his throat, he said, "So, we haven't officially done anything yet, because we wanted to wait to see what your reaction would be first, but…your mother and I would like to buy two round-trip plane tickets to Florida for you and Logan for one week, so that you can visit Chloe and Sophia."

My breath hitched in my throat. Plane tickets? *Plane* tickets? As in, a ticket that I would use to get on a plane? That would then take off into the sky? *That* type of plane ticket?

"Um…" I didn't know what to say. I was suddenly paralyzed by the thought of setting foot onto an airplane.

"Now, we know how you feel about flying," Mom said. "Which is why we haven't purchased the tickets yet. But if you do decide to take us up on our offer, we have already checked with Chloe's aunt, who said she would be more than happy to let you two stay with her and the girls for the week you're there. We know how much you've missed your friends, and both your father and I think this would be a wonderful experience for you."

I opened my mouth to speak, but no words came out. I glanced back at Logan. "Did you know about this?"

A slight look of guilt passed over his face. "I may have been consulted at some point about it, yes."

I glanced back at the brochure. "This is a really nice gesture, but…I mean, plane tickets are so expensive. And, do you really feel comfortable letting your teenage daughter and her boyfriend go off to Florida alone?" I was looking for as many excuses I could find to justify turning down what was actually an amazing opportunity.

"The plane tickets aren't as expensive as you think," Mom said. "And yes, we *are* comfortable letting the two of you go to Florida alone. You're both eighteen now, and we trust you. Besides, I'm sure Chloe's aunt will make sure you behave."

"But what about…" My voice trailed off. I was failing to come up with any other excuses.

"You don't have to decide right now," Dad assured me. "Take a couple days and think about it. No pressure, alright?"

I nodded as Dad threw some cash onto the table for a tip. "Your mom and I are going to take off," he said. He slid out of the booth and placed a hand on my shoulder. "Since you're an adult now, I think we can extend your curfew a bit." He glanced at Logan. "Have her back by midnight, please."

Logan nodded. "I will, sir. And not a second later, I promise."

Dad groaned. "Logan, I've told you not to call me 'sir'." He paused for a moment before adding, "You can just call me *'Dad'* from now on."

"DAD!" I cried out, mortified, as he burst out laughing.

"Sorry, Pumpkin, I couldn't help myself." As his laughter subsided, he held out a hand to help my mom out of the booth.

"Have fun, you two," Mom said. Even though she smacked my father's arm for his little joke, she was suppressing a grin.

"We will, thanks," I mumbled as I waved them goodbye.

As soon as they were gone, I turned to Logan. "Sorry for my dad. He's got a terrible sense of humor."

"It's okay," he said with a smile.

"So," I said, glancing back at the brochure. "You knew about this?"

"I did," he said with a slow nod. "They asked me my opinion, and I told them I didn't think you'd go for it, but suggested they try, anyway. I did it for mostly selfish reasons, because I would love to take this trip with you. You know, I've never been on a plane, either?"

"No?" My eyebrows shot up in surprise.

"Nope. And to be honest, the thought of flying makes me a little nervous, too. But just think: we could take a selfie on the plane, and add the photo to the *Logan and Emma's Book of Firsts*."

He was, of course, referring to his mother's scrapbook which, while wasn't an official book of "firsts", did seem to heavily lean toward that theme.

"I don't know…"

"Well, hey," he said, snatching the brochure out of my hands, "like your dad said, you don't need to decide right now. So, let's get out of here and take advantage of the fact we still have about four hours left before I have to get you home. What do you say?"

As another country song began to loudly play over the speakers and everyone around us started cheering, I said, "Yes, please."

"Great." Logan slid out of the booth. "Where would the

birthday girl like to go next?"

Hmm. That was a good question. I normally didn't do much on my birthday. After I stopped having parties as a kid, most of my birthdays were spent just having a nice dinner at home with my parents, and then a sleepover with Chloe and Sophia. I'd never had a boyfriend on my birthday to take me out on a nice date anywhere.

Where did girls like to go on their birthday dates?

I thought about it for a moment. I wanted to go somewhere special. Somewhere romantic. Somewhere that held an even more special place in my heart than Rodeo Roy's.

And then it came to me. With a smile, I stood from the booth and took Logan's hand in mine.

"You'll see."

***

"I can't believe out of all the places you could have chosen to go for your birthday, you wanted to come *here.*"

I looped my arm through Logan's as we walked through the entrance of Funland Park. "Why not? The name suggests we're going to have fun. Why wouldn't I want to have fun on my birthday?"

Logan shook his head. "I thought you hated this place?"

"I do." I removed my arm from his and instead slid it around his waist. He returned in kind, draping his arm across my shoulders and pulling me close. "But I wanted to give you another chance to win me a stuffed animal."

Logan groaned. "That game is rigged, Emma."

"Then how did *I* win so easily?" I said with a giggle.

"You're just that good, I guess." He sighed in defeat. "Okay, fine. I'll try to win you something."

"Yay!" I threw my other arm around him in a sideways hug. "You're the best boyfriend ever!"

Boyfriend. That word still felt very weird to say, like it wasn't part of the English language. But I liked it. A lot.

He chuckled softly. "I haven't even won you anything yet."

I placed a soft kiss on his cheek. "You will. I have faith in you."

"Okay," he said with a grin. "I'll try the ring toss again. Maybe I'll win you a blue monkey to go with your fuchsia one."

"That would be nice. She gets kind of lonely sometimes."

With a smirk, Logan said, "I'm going to pretend you didn't just say that, weirdo." He reached into his back pocket and pulled out his wallet as we approached the ring toss booth. Handing the boy behind the counter a couple of bills, he turned to me and said, "Wish me luck."

"Good luck," I said, giving him a thumbs-up.

My phone rang in my pocket, and I had a sudden feeling of déjà vu—especially when I saw who was calling.

"Hey, Chloe," I said into the phone. "What's up?"

She and Sophia had already called me first thing in the morning to wish me a happy birthday, and to assure me that they'd gotten me a "kick-ass" birthday gift that I would get immediately upon their return.

"Hey, Em! Sophia and I were just wondering if your parents had given you their gift yet…?"

Even *they* knew about the potential Florida trip?

My gaze flickered over to Logan, who was, as expected, failing at every toss of the rings. Suppressing a smirk, I turned around and walked away to give him some privacy. Maybe he'd have better luck if I wasn't watching.

"You mean the Florida brochure?" I asked.

"Um, I guess?" Chloe sounded confused.

"That's how my parents presented it to me," I explained to her. "They haven't bought the tickets yet because they didn't know if I would want to go or not."

"Why wouldn't you want to go?" Sophia asked. As usual, I was on speaker. "Emma, your parents are paying for you and your *boyfriend* to spend a week alone in *Florida*. How awesome is that?"

"It's pretty awesome, but…" I took a deep breath and held it for a moment. I'd never really had a conversation with the girls about my fear of flying. I'd always been embarrassed by it. After all, I was afraid of something I'd never even done. How did that make any sense?

"But what?" Chloe asked.

Maybe it was time to come clean and tell them. They would understand and they wouldn't pressure me about going anymore. But I *did* want to see them. And like my mom had said, it *could* be a wonderful experience…

"Hey, check this out."

Logan's voice behind me pulled me out of my thoughts. Spinning around, my jaw dropped as I saw he was holding out a blue stuffed monkey for me to take.

"Oh my God, you actually did it?" I said with a laugh.

"Did what?" Chloe asked.

"Oh, sorry, guys," I said to her and Sophia. "I have to go. Logan just won me a monkey."

"A what-now?" Sophia asked.

"I'll call you guys tomorrow, okay? And I promise I'll consider my parents' offer."

"Please do!" Chloe exclaimed. "We miss you so much!"

"And we miss seeing Logan shirtless!" Sophia added.

"Soph!" Chloe scolded her. "He's our girl's boyfriend now! You can't say things like that anymore!"

"It's okay," I said with a giggle. "Talk to you tomorrow. Love you both!"

"We love you, too, Em!" they said in unison before I hung up.

"So?" Logan said, still holding out the monkey. "Are you impressed?"

I eyed him suspiciously as I took the monkey from him. "I'm not sure. I didn't see you actually get one of the rings over one of the bottles."

"It happened," he said, but something in his voice made me think otherwise.

"Logan," I said, locking eyes with him, "don't lie to me."

We engaged in an intense staring contest for a moment before he finally ended it with the rolling of his eyes. "Okay, I didn't actually win it. I just convinced the guy to let me buy it. Happy now?"

I broke out into a grin. "Very." I hugged the monkey close to me. "I love him and will cherish him forever."

Logan threw his arm around me. "I'm glad. What are you going to name him?"

I blinked up at him. I was eighteen now. I didn't need to still be naming stuffed animals.

Even though I kind of wanted to.

"Mr. Darcy," I replied without even thinking about it.

Clearly amused, Logan said, "*Pride and Prejudice*?"

"Yep. I named the fuchsia monkey Elizabeth, so it only makes sense to stick with the theme."

"How cute." Logan chuckled. "Okay, what's next?"

I glanced around the park. There wasn't much for me to do

there, since I hated most of the rides. However, as soon as my gaze landed on the tall, round structure in the distance, I knew what I wanted to do.

"I want to go on that," I said, pointing.

His eyebrows shot up in surprise. "You want to go on the Ferris wheel again?"

I nodded. "I do."

Logan looked doubtful. "Are you sure?"

"Yes, I'm sure." I grabbed his arm and started pulling him in the direction of the ride. "And it looks like Beck is working it tonight. Maybe we can get him to stop it at the top again."

Logan looked at me like I was crazy. "What has gotten into you?"

We stopped at the end of the short line of people waiting to get on.

"Nothing has gotten into me," I said. "I just...I don't know. I'm not as scared of it as I used to be. Besides, I'm sure the sunset would look amazing from up there."

He nodded in agreement. "It would." The line began to move and he turned to me. "Are you sure you're going to be okay with this?"

"I promise."

I smiled at Logan's cousin as we approached him.

"Hey, you two," Beck said with a wave. "Back for more, huh? Want another couple of minutes at the top?"

Logan glanced at me. "That's up to you."

"Yes, please," I replied.

Logan reached for his wallet, but Beck waved his hand and said, "This one's on the house. Go ahead and get in."

He motioned to the empty car that had just stopped at the bottom and Logan took my hand and led the way. Once we were settled in, the wheel began to move.

Instantly, my pulse began to race, and I stopped breathing. *It's okay, Emma. You've got this! You've done it once before and you can do it again!*

Logan placed his hand over mine. "You doing okay?"

"Mmhmm," I said, nodding my head. I wrapped an arm tightly around Mr. Darcy and squeezed him hard as we approached the top.

Breathe…

I didn't realize until we came to a stop that I had closed my eyes, and now I didn't know how to reopen them.

"Wow, you were right," Logan said. "The sunset *is* amazing from up here."

Oh, yeah, the sunset. I wanted to see the sunset. That was the whole point of riding this thing.

Forcing my eyes open, I inhaled sharply at the view that immediately greeted me. The sun was just starting to slowly disappear below the horizon, illuminating the sky with the most gorgeous hues of red, orange and purple I'd ever seen.

"This is so beautiful," I breathed.

I expected Logan to agree with me, but he said nothing. Curiously, my eyes flickered over to him and I found him staring at me; a small smile tugging at his lips.

"What?" I asked, suddenly feeling all paranoid.

"Nothing," he said. "I was just wondering how I got to be so lucky." He reached out and caressed the side of my face, gently running his thumb across my cheekbone.

Leaning in, I brushed my lips against his in a quick, soft kiss before resting my head against his shoulder. I felt so safe and secure in his arms, just like the last time we were here. Only this time I didn't *need* him to hold me. I just *wanted* him to.

It was hard to believe I was currently 60 or so feet above the ground, but I didn't even feel nervous anymore. I had Logan to thank for that. He hadn't cured me of my fear of heights or anything, but he had helped to make it all a little more manageable. He'd shown me that it wasn't all as bad as I thought it was. Maybe he'd be able to do that with some of my other fears as well.

Such as flying.

"I want to do it, Logan," I said suddenly.

He stiffened beside me. "Um, what?"

I giggled when I realized what he probably thought I'd meant. "The Florida trip. I want to do it."

He gaped at me in awe. "Are you serious?"

"Yes," I said, nodding. "I'm serious. I want to take a plane ride with you to Florida. And then I want to do all the other things I've always been too afraid to do, and I want to do them with you."

Logan's sparkling hazel eyes danced around my face, searching for any indication I might be lying.

"Those are some heavy claims, Dawson. Do you really think you're up for the challenge?"

I pretended to think about it for a moment. "I'm pretty sure I can handle it."

"Well, I'm on board, then," he said with a smirk. "And maybe—just *maybe*—I'll let you continue to drag me around to boring places to do boring things. After all, that was part of the original deal, wasn't it?"

"It was," I said with an enthusiastic nod. I immediately started thinking of what types of activities I could torture him with for the next month and a half.

The wheel started moving again, and we slowly began our descent toward the ground. Taking his hand in mine, I nuzzled up against him, closed my eyes, and took a deep breath—not out of fear this time, but out of pure contentment.

"This is going to be a great summer," Logan whispered into my hair before planting a kiss on the top of my head. "And I can't wait to spend every second of it together."

I couldn't help but smile at that. Apparently, we had more in common than we thought.

ABOUT THE AUTHOR

Amanda Abram is an amateur author with dreams of making it big in the world of writing. She has dreamed of being an author since she was a little girl writing weird short stories that she would read aloud at Author's Teas (most likely to the embarrassment of her parents) and penning *Full House* fan fictions in her composition notebooks. In her early twenties, she graduated to writing novel-length *Harry Potter* fan fictions before taking the plunge and embarking on the journey of original fiction.

Challenge Accepted is her second published novel.

77148817R00231

Made in the USA
Middletown, DE
18 June 2018